PRAISE FOR *SOMEONE ELSE'S SECRET*

"Suspenseful and dishy, *Someone Else's Secret* exposes the dark underbelly of a moneyed summer town and the lengths one outsider will go to belong. Spiro brings Martha's Vineyard to life with delicious precision; I felt like I was there with my toes in the sand, a glass of rosé in my hand, and plenty of reasons to look over my shoulder. If the walls in these summer estates could talk, they would say, 'Trust no one.'"

—Jessica Knoll, *New York Times* bestselling author of *Luckiest Girl Alive*

"*Someone Else's Secret* is a sandy, sun-soaked, character-driven exploration of what happens when there are no good options, when the truth turns out not to be enough, when following your heart proves impossible. It is a novel about being young and very young and then not so young after all and about finding the strength to fight for all those former selves."

—Laurie Frankel, *New York Times* bestselling author of *This Is How It Always Is*

"*Someone Else's Secret* explores the realities of young love, coming-of-age, and the traumatic events women often face. Julia Spiro handles these difficult issues gracefully by pulling us into her fictional journey but also elevating the voices of women everywhere who are sure to recognize a part of themselves along the way."

—Wendy Walker, national bestselling author of *The Night Before*

"In *Someone Else's Secret*, debut author Julia Spiro has crafted a timely exploration of the weight of secrets and what it takes to tell the truth. When an ambitious recent college graduate lands a 'cushy' job among the elite of Martha's Vineyard, she gets an unwelcome lesson on the dark side of power and privilege. A compelling and cautionary tale that pulses with authenticity."

—Karen Dukess, author of *The Last Book Party*

"*Someone Else's Secret* is a gorgeous debut that, from page one, sets itself apart from the rest . . . Julia Spiro has written a story that is truly a breath of fresh air. The layered plot and rich cast of characters plunge the reader into a masterful story of secrets, ambition, and the fragile bonds of friendship. *Someone Else's Secret* is perfect for book clubs and should be on everyone's summer 2020 list."

—Liz Fenton & Lisa Steinke, bestselling authors of
The Two Lila Bennetts

"In *Someone Else's Secret*, Julia Spiro weaves a relatable, heart-wrenching tale full of secrets, lies, denial, and redemption. A dizzying dance with the truth for fans of Kristin Hannah and for women everywhere."

—Rea Frey, author of *Not Her Daughter* and *Because You're Mine*

"*Someone Else's Secret* is at once an arresting work of storytelling and a page-turning exploration of the violent power dynamics that weave throughout Martha's Vineyard and other glamorous summertime retreats. I was left haunted, moved, and in awe of Julia Spiro's taut prose. A propulsive riptide of a book."

—John Glynn, author of *Out East: Memoir of a Montauk Summer*

"Engaging and perceptive, *Someone Else's Secret* uses the sunny idyll of Martha's Vineyard as the backdrop for a coming-of-age story about two women navigating class, desire, and the things that go unspoken."

—Sam Lansky, author of *The Gilded Razor*

SOMEONE ELSE'S SECRET

SOMEONE ELSE'S SECRET

JULIA SPIRO

LAKE UNION
PUBLISHING

Text copyright © 2020 by Julia Spiro
All rights reserved.

Published by Lake Union Publishing, Seattle

www.apub.com

Amazon, the Amazon logo, and Lake Union Publishing are trademarks of Amazon.com, Inc., or its affiliates.

ISBN-13: 9781542022354 (hardcover)
ISBN-10: 1542022355 (hardcover)

ISBN-13: 9781542022361 (paperback)
ISBN-10: 1542022363 (paperback)

Cover design by Faceout Studio, Spencer Fuller

Printed in the United States of America

First Edition

For my parents.

Prologue

2019

Years later, it was the image of the lighthouse—its bowed face rising up from the dunes like a tree with roots stretching to the center of the earth and its unassuming flicker of light against the night—that burned brightest in her memory. She remembered other things, too, but they had become blurrier. The tickle of the beach grass against her legs. The way the fog had wrapped around her body. Feeling cold, damp. The roar of the ocean, so loud that she couldn't even hear her own thoughts. Most of these details she remembered, but only through a milky lens that she couldn't seem to wipe clean, even after all this time.

She dreamed of the lighthouse many times, possibly hundreds. And it was always the same dream: she saw the lighthouse down the hill. It called to her. She went to it, descending a dark path of sand and stone. She needed to get there. There was something on the other side. She could hear noises. She started to walk along the curved perimeter of the lighthouse, inching toward whatever was there. And just as she rounded the bend, her eyes shot open and the dream ended.

That morning, she was already half-awake when her alarm went off. She rubbed her eyes, feeling achy and sticky with sweat. She looked up at the ceiling, wondering how she would be able to peel herself from her mattress and pretend to be normal until it was nighttime again. *Ten more minutes,* she told herself, remaining in bed and hitting the snooze button on her phone, unable to face the effort required to go about her day, to be someone who wasn't carrying around this memory like a lead weight. She drifted into a hazy delirium, somewhere close to sleep but not quite there. And she returned to the dream once more, as usual, right where she had left it the night before. Once again, she was there on the beach. The ocean roar grew louder as she approached, and the rushing of the waves and their crashing against the shore made it seem like the entire beach was shaking. The wind whistled through the beach grass and sand, teasing her with whispered secrets. She could feel the mist from the water on her face. She could smell the salt. The lighthouse stood before her, a passive lump of material yet somehow alive at the same time, beckoning her, calling her, pulling her closer. She waited. And then she heard something. But this time, it wasn't the familiar noise that she usually heard. It wasn't just the wind and the sounds of the water at night. It was a voice, calling to her. A tiny, little voice, tucked away in the corner of the lighthouse's dark shadows. She kept moving forward, and the little voice grew louder, more desperate. Over and over, the voice called to her. She moved closer to it, still unable to see the source. Darkness, and more darkness, but the voice continued to escalate. She needed to see it; she needed to keep going. Stepping closer, she approached the voice, until it became a scream, a wrenching, metallic scream that was suddenly right before her, echoing through her ears, piercing her heart. And she saw, at last, who the voice belonged to. She stared back.

Her eyes opened, and she gasped for air. She felt weak. She looked down at her hands, as though to make sure she was awake, that this was real. Her hands were shaking. She felt afraid. She'd finally seen what was on the other side of the lighthouse that night. Except how was it possible? It didn't make sense. What she'd seen couldn't be true, she told herself. Because the screams, the little voice, the desperate cry for help that had been haunting her for so long now hadn't come from someone else. They had come from *her*. What she'd seen on the other side of the lighthouse, finally, was herself. There she was, terrified, lost, hurting. And she was calling out, begging, screaming with all her might: *Stop, stop, stop!*

Chapter 1

LINDSEY

2009

Lindsey Davis took the job out of desperation. She was in denial that summer would actually come. She was hoping that, instead, a great, global natural disaster would rocket humanity into panic, and her small problems would just disappear in the chaos. But summer did come, and on a crisp morning in late June, she found herself on board the ferry from Woods Hole, Massachusetts, to the island of Martha's Vineyard. She rode a Peter Pan bus for two hours from South Station in Boston to the ferry port and sat next to a middle-aged man wearing pink khaki shorts and a yellow button-down shirt.

"First time on the island?" he asked her as he settled in to his seat, tossing a canvas bag into the storage space above.

"Yes," she said. "I mean, I went to the Cape once when I was a kid, but that was a while ago."

He laughed as he sat down. "You still *are* a kid, kid. Enjoy it while it lasts." He put earphones in and shut his eyes.

They didn't speak again for the remainder of the ninety-minute drive. Lindsey dozed off, and when she woke, the bus was approaching a bridge that stretched across a grass-banked canal. On the other side, a rotary was decorated with thick hedges carved out to say CAPE COD.

Lindsey knew that the man next to her was right; she was basically still a kid. She had just graduated from college two weeks ago. The graduation festivities at Bowdoin had lasted for three entire days. There was a decadent barbecue, an arts fair, and a carnival set up on the main quad. Lindsey was relieved to have the days packed with distracting events and activities. She didn't have anything to say whenever someone asked her what she was doing next.

Bowdoin had been Lindsey's first-choice college because of its arts program. The school had an unparalleled arts department within a small, intimate, picturesque Maine campus. Lindsey had combed through a Bowdoin brochure she found in her college counselor's office and had known that it was where she wanted to go. Bowdoin felt far away from her world, a place where she could start over and become whoever she wanted to be, a place where she could learn about art without everyone around her wondering why she was bothering. It seemed elite and intellectual yet somehow informal and welcoming. She dreamed of one day being a curator or director at a major museum or gallery. Bowdoin, she thought, could help her get there. She loved that art was, in her opinion, the only truly universal language among humans. There were no wrong answers about art, she thought; what you saw, how you saw it, how it made you feel—it was all dependent on the person, the light, the setting, the experience. Art had the power to equalize and bring people together. The art world, however, she had come to learn, did not equalize people; it judged and scrutinized those who wished to enter.

Lindsey had applied, assuming that she wouldn't get in. A long shot, she'd thought. No one from her public high school had gone there, at least not in recent years. So when a fat envelope from Bowdoin arrived in her parents' mailbox, offering her a partial scholarship for field hockey, she was shocked. Even with the scholarship, the price tag would leave her with a mountain of student debt. She told her parents that she'd be happy going to the University of Maryland instead. It was close to her parents' home in Rockville, and she could graduate nearly debt-free. But they insisted that she go to Bowdoin. "This is what you want. You've got to go for it, Linds," her mother had said. "We'll make it work," her father had agreed, nodding. Part of her had wished that they'd just said no. In a way, it would have made things a lot easier. Later in her life, Lindsey would struggle with this more: the conflicting feelings of gratitude toward her parents for the sacrifices they'd made for her and the subsequent feelings of pressure she put on herself to never let them down.

She went, and she spent four years learning about art, making art, volunteering at the school's art museum, and working at a local gallery in Brunswick on weekends. She made friends, mostly girls from the field hockey team, many of whom were also there on a scholarship. Her closest friend was a tiny girl named Rose. "I'm probably the only Mexican on the planet who even knows what field hockey *is*," she had said to Lindsey during their preseason training when they first met. Rose was from the Bronx but had attended a private boarding school in New Hampshire on a full scholarship for high school, and she'd proved herself to be one of the best players in the country. She was much better adjusted to northeastern customs than Lindsey was. She had the same Adidas bag for her gear that everyone else at Bowdoin seemed to have, and she knew how to braid her hair into two french pigtails and tie the ends with ribbons on game days. Lindsey carried her gear in a shiny duffel bag she'd won at a raffle once at her local gym back home. She didn't know how to french braid. She learned what she could from Rose.

Bowdoin, Lindsey realized quickly during her freshman year, only had the illusion of being as open-minded and as welcoming as she'd thought it was. She loved her professors, and she did like many of her teammates. The education she received and the access to art were outstanding. But underneath the facade of the J.Crew and Patagonia–cloaked student body was actually a highbrow exclusivity that she had never seen before. At Bowdoin, it wasn't cool to be *showy*. Instead, it was cool to use your old L.L.Bean backpack from middle school, the one with the big reflective stripe across the front pocket. It was cool to drive your mom's old Volvo station wagon that made a funny noise whenever it started and smelled of stale graham crackers. It was even cool to have holes in the faded cable-knit sweater that you stole from your dad. Lindsey had insisted on going shopping at the outlets with her mom before school started. She got a new black backpack, new l.e.i. boot-cut jeans, new black leather boots, and new slim-fitting V-neck sweaters on sale from Bebe. But after a few weeks on campus, she realized that she'd gotten it all wrong. Everything she owned was too new, too desperate, too revealing. In between classes one day, she walked to downtown Brunswick alone and went to the local thrift store, where she bought a ratty, oversize Lands' End men's sweater in navy blue and a hunter-green fleece jacket that wasn't Patagonia but looked similar. She wore those items more than anything else throughout her freshman year, pretending that she'd had them forever.

By sophomore year, Lindsey understood how to fit in at Bowdoin. She and Rose became roommates. They mostly hung out with their teammates, at least the ones who were there on scholarships like they were. In their off-season, they partied together, drinking cheap white wine or White Russians in their dorm rooms, listening to music, letting loose and enjoying the few months when they didn't have to worry about the pressures of a looming championship. Lindsey didn't date anyone seriously, but she had a few flings that lasted a semester or two each. She'd already lost her virginity at fifteen, to her high school boyfriend at the time. Sex wasn't a big deal to her, but emotional intimacy was. Though she'd figured out how to socially fit in at Bowdoin, the thought of seriously dating one of the white-bread, Waspy guys there didn't seem like a real possibility for her. Once they realized where she came from, she thought to herself—once they realized that she was poor, uncultured, had never even been out of the country—they wouldn't want to date her. It would just never happen. But guys pursued her. She was smart, friendly, and pretty, with wavy brown hair, pouty lips, and a toned body. Though she resented them most of the time, she also had large breasts, no matter how much she worked out. This, she knew, was also one of the reasons she was perpetually pursued. But she just acted like she wasn't interested, even if she was. "I don't want anything serious," she would tell guys the next morning. Dating casually was better for her anyway; she needed to stay focused on her long-term plan.

She had wanted to move to Boston after graduation and land a spot in one of the top Newbury Street galleries, eventually getting a job at the Museum of Fine Arts in the hopes of becoming a curator there. Boston had become a familiar city to Lindsey during her time in college, and though it was expensive, it was more manageable than Manhattan, which she had ruled out long ago. She was confident that with her résumé and with the connections that Bowdoin had to offer, her plan would work.

But when the recession hit in 2008, Lindsey panicked, feeling like she suddenly had no practical skills whatsoever. She'd spent the last few years learning about the meaning of brushstrokes and the use of light on canvas. What good was that going to do her now? What had she been thinking majoring in art history? It couldn't have been a worse time to go into the arts. As her graduation date approached, she aggressively interviewed at galleries all over Boston. The most established galleries that actually payed decent salaries were never hiring. The other ones seemed to offer only part-time jobs or unpaid internships, even for college graduates. This wasn't a problem for many of her classmates, who took the unpaid internships without hesitation. They didn't need the money. Lindsey could take an unpaid internship, too, she knew, as long as she worked a paying job most of the time and just did the internship part-time. She could waitress at night, work in a store during the day, and maybe two or three days a week do the unpaid internship. She was more than willing to do whatever it took to get her foot in the door.

But somehow, even these part-time, unpaid internships were elusive to her. The galleries seemed entirely impenetrable. It was as though anyone who got hired at one of them had a connection, and a job was just magically created *for* them.

The problem was, as Lindsey saw it, that she had no one to call on her behalf. No one who mattered, anyway. She was smart and presented well—she was pretty, put-together, articulate, passionate, and she had a great résumé. But none of that mattered if she didn't have someone to vouch for her. Particularly in the art world, all that seemed to matter during that year was maintaining the support of wealthy patrons. They were the lifeboats that kept the arts afloat. And Lindsey was a charity case, a sinking weight. Who would want to take her on board?

Rose was moving back to New York to work in finance. She'd already spent the summer before her senior year at Goldman Sachs, and they'd asked her to return after graduation. Lindsey was envious of her friend and annoyed by the sense of security that she'd had all throughout senior year, knowing exactly where she was going next. She felt embarrassed to have chosen such an impractical professional field that appeared to be promising her nothing.

"Yeah, but at least you have the balls to do something you *love*," Rose had told her when Lindsey heard back from another gallery letting her know that they weren't hiring. "It's not like I *want* to work in finance."

"Thanks, Rose," she had said, suddenly feeling significantly younger than her friend, like she was a child being consoled by a babysitter. What she couldn't express to Rose, or anyone, was that it wasn't just about her love of art. It was more than that. She wanted to be part of a different world. She wanted to have a job that would give her an identity she was proud of. She wanted to be interesting.

She kept checking in with galleries during the rest of her senior spring, hoping that a job would surface, but nothing ever did. And so, on graduation day, she stared out at the podium ahead of her, waiting to be called onstage to receive her diploma. She held back tears. She was going to move back home to Rockville, into her childhood bedroom, and maybe get a job as an assistant in the insurance office where her dad worked. It would take her decades to pay off her student loans. The fact that she'd have to do it while working at a job she never wanted made her heart sink, and she felt foolish and indulgent for choosing to go to Bowdoin in the first place.

Graduation fell on a broiling hot day when the air was stagnant and ripe. Hungover students fanned themselves with the graduation program. "2008 was a tough year on our country," one of the student speakers sermonized to the impatient, sweating seniors. "Our class is facing the most brutal job economy in recent history. But we're facing it *head-on*." Lindsey rolled her eyes. The only people facing it head-on, she thought, were the ones who had been born into a dynasty of privileged ignorance, where true wealth was already designated to them and life's options had no bounds. Or the smart ones, like Rose, who had the foresight to pursue a career that would actually make money. Everyone else, like Lindsey, wasn't facing the future head-on. They were facing it with an empty checking account and a stack of debt.

After the graduation ceremony, there was a traditional Maine lobster and clambake served under a gleaming white tent. "Wow," Lindsey's dad had said as they stood in the buffet line, eyeing the fresh, whole lobsters; the heaps of steamers; the raw oysters; and the pyramids of glistening corn on the cob. "I hope you didn't get too used to this kind of fancy food." Lindsey didn't respond. Since her time at Bowdoin, she actually *had* gotten used to it. The food there was fresh, local, and abundant, and the students were spoiled by it. *Farm to table* was how the school described its cafeteria offerings.

She sat with her parents at one of the picnic tables on the edge of the tent. Her mother struggled with the lobster crackers and finally gave up, focusing on her corn instead. Even though Lindsey had grown up in Maryland, an East Coast hub of seafood and agriculture, her parents hadn't exposed her to much of it.

Lindsey barely spoke during the meal. She felt ashamed that, as her parents' only child, she was graduating jobless. Her parents, out of kindness, hadn't really acknowledged it, instead acting thrilled that they got to have their little girl back home with them. Their kindness somehow made it worse. They'd gone to so much effort to send her to Bowdoin because it had been what she'd wanted. And all she'd had to do in return was prove to them that it was worth it, that it would pay off in the end, that it would lead to something *great*. But here she was, with nothing to show for it. They sat with Rose and her parents, who had driven up from New York that morning. Lindsey felt embarrassed throughout the meal. Without their families, Lindsey and Rose had been able to form and project their own identities at school, at least somewhat, and had blended in with their classmates. But now, flanked by their fast-talking parents, who didn't know how to crack their lobsters, who hadn't even gone to college themselves, their true identities were revealed. They returned to being outsiders once again, and Lindsey kept looking around at her classmates at other tables, searching for judgmental glances. Rose didn't seem bothered by any of it. She seemed relaxed, happy, proud of her parents. Lindsey envied her for this. Not only did she feel guilty for disappointing her parents but she felt even worse for being ashamed of them. They'd done nothing wrong, and yet they embarrassed her. Maybe if she were moving on to an impressive job, like Rose, she would have more confidence, she thought. But she was moving on to nothing. She'd never felt lower.

As they ate, Lindsey looked up to see Professor Graver, her adviser, walking toward them. Professor Graver was an art historian with long gray hair and an eclectic dress collection. She tapped Lindsey on the shoulder as she approached.

"There's someone you need to meet," Professor Graver said to Lindsey. "An alum I once taught. I might have found the perfect job for you." Professor Graver apologized to Lindsey's parents for stealing their daughter for a few moments, but they looked proud to see her monopolized by a professor. "Go on." Lindsey's dad nodded to her, as though he knew that Lindsey had something more important to do than sit with them—the kind of acknowledgment that was a compliment but also made her feel sad.

"Thank you, Karen," Lindsey said. Professor Graver had always insisted on being called by her first name. "That's great. What kind of job?" Lindsey asked as they walked from her class tent to an alumni tent pitched a field over. Karen had told Lindsey the day before that she was determined to help her find a job, but Lindsey had just assumed that her good intentions wouldn't result in anything real.

"Well, the job itself is temporary and, to be honest, not what you want." She was blunt. "*But* this family has a lot of connections in the art world, and it might lead to something fantastic for you. They're one of the school's most prominent donors."

Karen marched toward a tent with a sign that read **30TH REUNION**. The fields smelled of fresh-cut grass and beer, a sour combination that tickled Lindsey's nose and reminded her of her first day on campus four years ago, when she had been just as nervous for what was to come next. "Ah," she said, pointing across a sea of tables, "there's Jonathan Decker."

Lindsey looked across the tent to where Karen signaled. Jonathan Decker looked younger than his former classmates, all in their early fifties. Next to him sat a thin, petite woman with red hair blown into a pristine shoulder-length bob. The woman couldn't have been more than forty years old, at least a decade younger than her husband, and yet there was something about her that felt older—or perhaps just more disenchanted—than the man by her side. She was beautiful, and even from a distance, Lindsey felt intimidated by her wintry elegance. Lindsey hunched her shoulders forward slightly as they walked toward the pair; maybe if she scrunched her body inward enough, she thought, her breasts wouldn't look so large and Jonathan's wife wouldn't hate her.

Lindsey was wearing a sundress with a scoop neck, though, and there wasn't much she could do at this point to cover up. It didn't matter, anyway: wives always hated her. They hated how Lindsey's body was at once voluptuous and toned and how her somewhat unruly hair gave her the appearance of being wild, someone who might convince their husbands to do something shocking. She wished she could tell the wives that she hated the effect her body had on men, too, that she wished it had no effect at all. She could already feel the inevitable head-to-toe scan and ensuing eyebrow raise as they approached.

"Jonathan," Karen said, waving, "this is the remarkable young woman I told you about."

Jonathan had been laughing as they neared their table; Lindsey wondered about what, as no one else was laughing. His laugh was boisterous, like a child's. He rose from his seat and extended his hand, a residual wheeze escaping his lungs in the wake of his comedic fit. "Good to meet you," he said. He was tall and thin, with a handsome face and big blue eyes. "I'm Jonathan Decker, and this is my wife, Carol." His wife held out her hand as well, but she didn't get up from her seat.

Lindsey smiled with her mouth closed, trying to look serious. "Nice to meet you," she said. "I'm Lindsey Davis."

There was a pause. Jonathan smiled at her and then put his hands in his pockets. Lindsey felt his eyes hover around her chest—just for a second but long enough that she started to shift her feet in her sandals and dart her own eyes off into the distance, unsure of a comfortable place to land her gaze. She quickly glanced at his wife, not realizing that she was staring at her. They locked eyes for a moment until Lindsey looked down. She felt as though she were on display, for sale. She could feel her cheeks flush.

"Well," Jonathan started, "I'm not sure how much Karen told you, but we need some help. We leave next week for the Vineyard, and our nanny just had to go back to her family in Florida. So we're in a bit of a bind." The way he said this made it seem like Lindsey, a stranger, was somehow responsible for whatever bind the family was in. How did this all relate to her? She waited for him to elaborate with some explanation. "So, do you like kids?" he finally asked.

Only then did Lindsey realize that the grand job prospect was this: they wanted her to be a nanny for the summer. And her professor apparently thought this was a great idea too. Lindsey's throat started to fill with panic, and her eyes stung with the threat of tears. She felt embarrassed, like she'd suddenly realized that she had her underwear on over her clothes. Everyone could see her failure; she was wearing it on her sleeve. She dreaded having to return to her parents' table with nothing to show but an offer for a summer gig fit for a teenager.

"In fact," Jonathan said before Lindsey could respond, "our little devils are around here somewhere." He craned his neck toward the lawn outside the tent where children, fueled by glasses of sugary lemonade, ran amok. "We've got two. Berty is five and Georgie is fourteen. There they are." Jonathan pointed outside the tent toward a great oak tree, around which the younger child ran. The older child, a girl, leaned against the tree trunk, sullen and alone. Lindsey nodded in that direction and smiled, as if to answer Jonathan's silent question: *Aren't our kids great?* The boy picked up a twig and threw it at his older sister leaning against the tree. Just the act of watching them from a distance was exhausting, Lindsey thought.

"Now, listen," Jonathan said, as if he could feel that he was losing Lindsey's interest by the second, "we know that this probably isn't what you had planned. Karen was once my teacher, too, so I know firsthand that she doesn't pick favorite students unless they're really exceptional, and she told me that you're one of her favorites. You're obviously an incredibly bright young woman. And we can help you get a job after the summer. I'm sure Karen mentioned to you that I'm a great supporter of the arts, always have been." Rich people liked to use that word— *supporter*—Lindsey had noticed, as though the fact that they bought expensive art somehow meant that they were doing community service.

"There are a couple of galleries in Boston that we're particularly fond of. And I'm on the board of the MFA."

The conversation felt like it was turning into some odd negotiation. The Deckers were desperate for Lindsey's help, but at the same time, Lindsey didn't have any bargaining chips of her own. She felt hot and could feel beads of sweat beginning to form under her bra and in her armpits.

"The job is easy, really," he continued. "You'll have your own room and bathroom, of course, total privacy, and basically we just need some help getting Berty to his daily activities and taking care of them both during the evenings that we go out."

"And of course," Carol chimed in, "you *can't* beat the Vineyard in the summer. We're right in Edgartown. Have you been?" It was the kind of question to which, Lindsey suspected, Carol already knew the answer.

"No," Lindsey replied. "Never."

"Well, then, you must come," Carol said, in a way that felt like a command. Lindsey wondered why this woman didn't want to know more about her; she was asking her to take care of her *children* for the whole summer. For all she knew, Lindsey could be a psychopath.

"So," Jonathan said, his eyes searching Lindsey's face for an answer, his brows raised and his smile earnest, "what do you think?" Before she could answer, he reached over to her and placed his hand on her shoulder. "I can *help* you, Lindsey." Lindsey felt the warm weight of his hand pushing into her until he released it a moment later. It was such an odd act, she thought, so invasive and personal yet out in the open, in front of his wife, in front of Karen. Something about the way he said it—he could *help* her—made Lindsey feel like she didn't have a choice.

She looked out at the two kids on the lawn. She didn't have siblings of her own, and she'd babysat only a handful of times in high school for the family next door when they occasionally needed an extra set of hands to help with their two toddlers. She wasn't even sure if she liked kids at all. Being a full-time nanny was simultaneously something that she felt too good to do and also underqualified to do. She looked back toward her class's tent, knowing that her parents were in there somewhere, telling some other parents how they'd driven all the way from Maryland and that their daughter was going to work in the art world. Maybe this job *would* lead to something better. Maybe Jonathan really *would* set her up with a top gallery job after this. And anyway, what other options did she have?

"Okay," Lindsey said, hearing the word come out of her mouth before she even decided to say it. "I'll do it." She regretted it the second she said it but felt like she was being pulled by a force out of her control.

Jonathan and Carol both smiled at her response, giving each other a quick look of relief. *Thank God.* Carol pulled out a datebook from her purse and asked Lindsey to write down her email address and phone number. "My office will get you all the information right away," Jonathan said as Lindsey walked away, waving goodbye. His office? Lindsey just nodded. She had to return to her parents. As she walked away with Karen, she realized that she hadn't even met the children. The Deckers didn't even know her. What if the kids hated her? Or worse, what if she hated them?

As they walked, Lindsey thanked Karen, who was beaming, as though she had just secured funding for Lindsey to start her own gallery instead of what was really going to be a dressed-up summer of indentured servitude. It occurred to Lindsey that she hadn't even asked about salary, and no one had mentioned it. But she had a feeling that whatever she'd be getting paid that summer would be more than she'd make at home.

She sulked toward her parents, forcing a smile on her face and deciding that she would lie to them. Not a real lie, she told herself, just an exaggeration of the possibilities of the job. She told them that she'd landed a job with a famed art collector. It was true, sort of, even if the job itself had nothing to do with art. Karen had told Lindsey on the walk back that Jonathan worked for his family's office in Boston.

"You know, they're the kind of family who's so rich that they have their own *family office*," Karen explained in a hushed voice. Lindsey nodded, though she wasn't sure what that really meant. "The Deckers have been huge champions of the arts—for *generations*. You must have been to the Decker Gallery in the Museum of Fine Arts, no?" Lindsey nodded again, this time remembering that she *had*, in fact, been there. Karen even told Lindsey, confidentially, that Jonathan had donated the funds for Bowdoin's new art building, though he didn't want to have his name on the building. "Sometimes the real *big-time* donors want anonymity," she had said.

So maybe this job might lead to something good, Lindsey thought. Her parents were supportive of her ambitions within the art world, but they didn't understand that the pathway there often involved unpaid internships and low-level receptionist gigs and now, adding to the list of shitty jobs, *nanny*. Her father was an insurance agent at a small shop in downtown Bethesda, and her mother was an elementary school nurse. They'd both held these jobs for most of their adult lives. Lindsey never knew what kept them motivated. The jobs were practical, laborious, humble. In comparison, Lindsey's professional desires seemed frivolous, and she often felt guilty admitting to her parents what she wanted to pursue. Especially because, she knew, she'd barely be making ends meet with whatever job she got next.

But her parents responded by telling her that they were proud. "Sounds promising," her father said with a smile. "And wow," he added. "The *Vineyard*. Fancy!" He elbowed her with a grin.

"How much will you be making? What about health insurance?" Her mother wanted to know more about the practical concerns, which angered Lindsey because she herself hadn't even thought to ask these questions and now she needed to know.

"It'll be fine," Lindsey said, swatting away the questions and suddenly feeling overwhelmed and strangely homesick. The more questions her mother raised, the more Lindsey wanted to burst into tears.

But Jonathan's office, in the form of a woman named Marcia, emailed her the very next day and answered those concerns. No health insurance, but a salary that would not only make for an incredibly comfortable summer but would also give her a plush cushion for whatever happened next. Free rent, free food, and days spent at the beach. Maybe it would be okay. Fun, even.

Two weeks later, Lindsey sat on the ferry, the wind whipping around her. She curled her knees up to her chest, hugging them toward her. Her fleece jacket was dusted with specks of ocean water, and she was cold, but she didn't want to go inside. The ride was only forty-five minutes long, and the inside of the boat smelled of hot dogs and stale coffee; she preferred to be out in the fresh air, despite the chill. A young boy stood by the railing and dropped a red plastic cup overboard. His mother snapped at him. Lindsey saw the cup bob in the waves below, and she watched as it grew smaller and smaller behind them.

The boat rounded the north tip of the island, and Lindsey could see, in the distance, the harbor of Vineyard Haven, a bucolic inlet peppered with white houses and wooden docks. As the ferry came into the port, passengers returned to their cars below or shuffled with their bags to the exit ramp. Lindsey remained seated; she wondered what would happen if she just stayed on the boat and let it carry her back to Woods Hole. Maybe she'd ride the ferry back and forth all day.

She strapped on her backpack and took her rolling suitcase, stacked with a duffel on top, and headed toward the exit. The wind had subsided, and the afternoon sun warmed her; she felt a brief sense of calm as she rolled herself and her belongings down the winding ramp toward the parking lot. Her body still felt like it was swaying with the waves even though her feet were now firmly planted on the ground. It was a strange feeling that made her slightly nauseous. Off the ferry, families were waiting to greet passengers. She spotted the man wearing the pink shorts; he was flagged down by a group of similarly dressed middle-aged men, one of whom squealed "Aloha!" before embracing him in a hug.

Lindsey saw the bus stop and checked the sign; ten minutes until the next bus to Edgartown, where the Deckers lived. She took a seat on the bench. The journey to the island, though without any real incident, had fatigued her, and she felt anxious. She suddenly realized that she was going to be living with total strangers for a summer, and an onslaught of questions and concerns bubbled up inside her. She tried to remind herself that she needed the job, and that's all that this was—a job. Not everything had to be something so important, she told herself. Maybe she'd even enjoy it. Rose had already started at Goldman and was miserable just two weeks into it: long hours, disgusting frat boys who ogled her whenever she walked by, dizzying spreadsheets, a culture of deep misogyny. At least Lindsey wouldn't have to deal with any of that, she thought. You're lucky, Rose had texted her the day before. Think of this as a vacation!

But now that she was actually on the island, waiting for the bus, Lindsey wished that she was anywhere else, doing anything that made her feel remotely important and in control of her own life. At Bowdoin, she had felt a sense of belonging and an identity that made her feel like she mattered. Now, she felt anchorless, like the little red cup jettisoned by the child, lost at sea.

Chapter 2

GEORGIE

_2009_

Georgie Decker begged her parents to let her stay at home on the Vineyard for the summer instead of going to sleepaway camp. For the last four summers, since she was ten, she'd gone to an arts camp in rural northern Maine for six weeks, and she hated it. She was fourteen now, almost fifteen, and far too old to be singing around campfires and being told when to eat her meals. She hated the noisy bunks that were always damp and stank of sweaty sheets and teenage hormones. She hated the total lack of privacy. She hated that you had to buy your shampoo and conditioner and, last year, maxi pads and then tampons, at the fly-infested canteen, in front of the senior campers who ran it. It was so humiliating. She also hated that, if she returned to camp, she'd be forced to see Leo, the boy she'd kissed in the rec hall last summer. After camp had ended, she'd sent him nine emails about their relationship. What did the kiss mean to him? How did he feel about her? If she and Leo weren't a couple, then what _were_ they? He'd responded to the first two emails but then stopped completely. Georgie continued to email him anyway. In the last one, she'd warned him that he'd never see her again and that he'd regret it for the rest of his life. You _blew_ it, she wrote. He still hadn't responded.

There was just no way that Georgie was going to return to camp. "The stress is giving me an ulcer," she'd said to her parents that spring when her mother was about to call the camp to sign her up. "Please don't make me go," she had whined, clutching her stomach for dramatic effect. She wasn't sure what an ulcer was, but she thought it was a convincing argument.

Her parents had relented, on the condition that she had to get a summer job. "No free passes this summer, Gigi," her father had said on the drive down from Boston, where they lived for the rest of the year. "I can't be the only one in this household with an income," he had said with a wink. Georgie wasn't confident that anyone was going to hire a fourteen-year-old with no work experience, but she'd do anything to avoid going back to camp. She'd find a job, no matter what.

Her mother suggested helping Mrs. Grakowski next door with her garden or helping keep the tennis courts clean at the yacht club. But Georgie didn't consider those *real* jobs. What she wanted was the kind of job that girls who drove cars and had second ear piercings had. She wanted to work around grown-ups. She wanted to be taken seriously.

But mostly, she wanted friends. Or, more specifically, she wanted her old friends back. She wanted them to accept her again. Getting a real job would help with that, she thought. It would make her look cool, independent. She needed to impress them.

She wasn't sure what had happened. She had grown up with these girls. They'd all spent countless summers together in tennis and sailing camp. Their favorite thing to do together was to go off the waterslide at the end of the dock at the beach club, over and over again until their lips were blue. All their parents knew one another. The summer families of Edgartown shared a closeness borne from a common understanding of the particularities of the island and, even more specifically, from the particularities of being wealthy and living in that old whaling town for just two months out of the year. Many of the children were like cousins to one another, having grown up together over the summers. But last year, when Georgie had come down to the Vineyard in August after camp, things had changed. Most of the other girls had been on island all summer already and had arrived in June with new bikinis, platform sandals, heavy coats of waterproof mascara layered onto their lashes, and long, flat-ironed hair. They were no longer interested in the water-slide. Instead, they wanted to sneak off behind the cabanas to take sips of warm Diet Coke with vodka, from a bottle one of them took from their parents' liquor cabinet. They'd break off in groups of two or three and then return to the beach, sauntering down onto their towels with snide grins. Georgie didn't really get what was so fun about it, but she went along with it the first few times. "Anyone want to swim out to the raft?" she'd ask. They all looked at her with disdain, like she'd suggested they shave their heads. "I'm good," her friend Catherine, the leader of the group, had replied, returning to her *Cosmopolitan* magazine. The other girls didn't say anything.

Georgie's uneasiness must have been obvious, because before the summer was over, she was cut out from the group completely. It had been a rainy afternoon, and everyone was hanging out in Catherine's pool house, painting their nails. Catherine wanted everyone to get dressed up and go to teen night at the Atlantic Connection, a nightclub in Oak Bluffs. "Everyone will be there," Catherine had said, waving her hands to dry her nails.

It didn't sound appealing to Georgie. She didn't own any strappy tank tops or short denim skirts like the other girls. She wanted to go see the latest *Harry Potter* film at the Edgartown Cinemas. "Why not go see a movie instead?" she asked.

Catherine sighed, pushing herself up from the sofa on which she'd been lying on her stomach. "Georgie, don't you think we're a little *old* to be spending our Saturday night seeing movies? I mean, we used to do that when we were, like, twelve." She snorted. Georgie didn't respond. "Maybe you should just go home. I mean, we don't want to make *you* feel uncomfortable," Catherine said, looking away. "You know what I *mean?*"

Georgie had nodded, scanning the room for a sympathetic look from anyone else, but the group remained silent. Catherine was their leader—that's how it worked. Except Georgie *didn't* know. She didn't understand. What had she done wrong? She and Catherine had been the closest out of all the girls, at least at one point. She had even confided in Georgie, the summer before, that she felt like an outsider in Edgartown. "People at the club look at us like we don't belong here," she had said. "We're black, but come on, we're the *whitest* black family I know!" Georgie wasn't sure at the time what Catherine had meant by that. Catherine's family had belonged to the beach club as long as the Deckers had. It was true, though, that Catherine's family was one of only a handful of African American families at the club. Georgie just hadn't ever thought about it before. Years later, she realized that that was the problem: she'd never *thought* about how Catherine had felt. She had assumed that Catherine didn't have any problems, that she was perfect, that her world was perfect.

But at the time, Georgie felt like she was the outsider. She continued to try to fit in, using her allowance money to buy makeup and magazines at the drugstore, making conversation with them all at the beach club about the latest celebrity breakup. But it was clear: they didn't like her anymore. It didn't matter what she wore, or what she did, or where she went. It was like there was something ingrained in her, something that she couldn't change, that made her permanently deficient and unable to fit in. She felt that she was just inherently uncool.

Things weren't that different for her at school either. She had a close group of girlfriends there, too, but Georgie secretly hated them. Not actually. She didn't hate *them*, but she hated the fact that they were dorks. She hated the fact that she knew she was no better than they were and yet felt that she somehow belonged in a higher social rank.

Her mother, Carol, had seemed most disappointed at the end of last summer when Georgie had stopped hanging out with Catherine completely. "Georgie, what did you *do*?" Carol had asked when she saw Georgie sitting alone on the beach at the club, away from Catherine and the other girls.

"I don't know, Mom," she'd said, tearing up. "They just don't like me anymore."

"Well, I hope you can find a way to make it right." She had patted Georgie on the head and returned to her own lunch table with the other women in their tennis whites. Georgie had decided, then and there, that the next summer would be different. She'd reinvent herself, start over, be who she wanted to be.

Now summer had arrived. Carol had driven down with Georgie and Berty that morning from Boston. Georgie's dad, Jonathan, would be coming the next day, straight from work. Georgie sat in the kitchen with Carol, who was making a list of weekly tasks for the cleaners, who, to her frustration, had cleaned the house the day before but had forgotten which duvet covers went on which beds. "Everything's all backward now," Carol huffed as she jotted down instructions.

"I want to work at the Picnic Basket," Georgie declared to her mother.

"Mm-hmm." Carol didn't look up.

The Picnic Basket was the best gourmet café in town. It looked like a Nancy Meyers movie come to life—perfectly curated, warm, pristine, and shiny. It sold mostly organic takeout, foamy chai lattes, and a lavish selection of hand-dipped candles, ceramics, and other small home goods and gifts. But what made it special to Georgie was that it seemed to employ only beautiful, young girls. *Cool* girls. Every summer, she had always seen gaggles of them—slim, bronzed, and sparkly eyed—working behind the counter, as though they were ripe pieces of fruit just as delicious as the pastries they sold. To Georgie, those girls had it all figured out. They were the ones who always looked beautiful and were confident and fun and had no shortage of boys asking them out on dates. They were part of a club, and Georgie wanted in. Maybe that could be her, too, she thought. Maybe she could *belong* there. If she could pull it off, she thought to herself, Catherine might be impressed enough to allow her back into the group. Everything would change.

"Well, I don't know why you'd want to work around food all day long," her mother had replied, glancing up and giving Georgie a sympathetic gaze. "But *okay*, if that's what you want, why don't you see if they're hiring?"

Georgie didn't respond. Her mother had a way of making even the smallest victory feel like the biggest failure. Georgie didn't bother trying to explain to her mother why she wanted to work there; she wouldn't understand. Her mother wouldn't relate to the concept of wanting to be *like* someone, wanting to be *part* of something else. Her mother was too sensible, too straightforward, too practical to understand that kind of longing.

Georgie went to the Picnic Basket later that afternoon anyway and asked to speak to the manager, just as her father had advised her to do when she'd called him to ask for his advice. The manager was an African American woman in her fifties named Lucy who wore a long, colorful linen tunic and had chubby legs that poked out from underneath and sank into a pair of worn Birkenstocks. She had striking green eyes that seemed to look into your soul when she stared at you. Lucy was somewhat famous on the island. Her father was a prolific novelist who wrote thrillers set on the Vineyard, all with Vineyard-related titles: *Murder at Inkwell Beach*, *The Flying Horses Mystery*, *Illumination Night of Death*. Their family owned one of the large, ornate houses in Oak Bluffs that overlooked Ocean Park. They'd had it forever, and they were always throwing boisterous fund-raisers and events that spilled onto the house's grand patio, complete with live bands and Lucy's decadent catering.

There were actually two Picnic Basket locations. Lucy had opened the first one in Oak Bluffs years ago in a dark, cramped spot off Circuit

Avenue. It was still there but really just served as a to-go spot for sandwiches. The Edgartown location had become the flagship one. It was five times the size and more of a destination where you could hang out, shop for little gifts, and meet friends. And Edgartown was really the ideal location for a café that sold a single slice of avocado toast for twelve dollars. The customers barely even blinked at the prices. Anything for an organic breakfast.

"I was like you when I was your age," Lucy said when Georgie finished her pitch. "*Just* like you, in fact," she continued, gesticulating like a conductor as she walked Georgie through the café, showing her around. "Wanted to do things my own way." Georgie smiled but wasn't sure what Lucy meant. She respected Lucy, but she had no intention of living a quiet life on the island forever like Lucy had. By Lucy's age, she would be living in a penthouse apartment in New York, eating at fabulous restaurants, working as the editor of a magazine or maybe as a movie producer. She wondered if Lucy was married. She didn't think she had kids.

"Any questions?" Lucy asked when they finished a lap of the café. Georgie was confused. Did this mean that she had the job? She wanted to ask about salary but was too embarrassed. It felt too forward, too pushy.

"No questions," Georgie said. "I just want to add that if you hire me, I won't let you down. I'm very trustworthy, detail oriented, and hardworking." Her father had told her to say that, and she'd been trying to weave it into the conversation for the past ten minutes but hadn't had a chance. The words felt unnatural coming out of her mouth, like she was selling herself at auction.

Lucy smiled, folding her arms and leaning back slightly. "That's what I like to hear!" she said with a laugh. "You're hired. And you know what," Lucy added, "it's great to hear a young woman speak with such confidence. The boys, you know, they've got a never-ending supply of confidence. But girls . . ." She drifted off. "It's just refreshing." They walked toward the exit.

"So can you start tomorrow, at eight?"

Georgie nodded. Lucy told her that she'd pay her nine dollars an hour, in cash. It suddenly seemed like a lot of money. She imagined what she could do with it all. She could buy whatever clothes she wanted, whatever makeup, all the things her mother refused to buy for her. She'd finally have some *freedom*. She didn't want Lucy to think she was too eager, so she disguised her smile until she'd left the café and raced the seven blocks home. She couldn't believe that she'd gotten a job so quickly. She felt proud. And even though she had rehearsed those lines that she'd said to Lucy, she did actually feel, now, *confident*.

At home, she found her mother still in the kitchen, sitting at the center island, her laptop and leather datebook both open.

"How did it go?" Carol asked, still looking at her screen. Georgie reached across her mother at a bowl of fruit, picking up an apple.

"Really good," she replied, biting into the apple. "The Picnic Basket hired me!" Her mouth squirted some apple juice out onto the counter.

"That's great," Carol said, shutting her laptop. "And you're sure you don't want to do something outdoors? Something more . . . active? Or maybe those nice brothers and that blonde girl would hire you at Shirt Tales. You could get some retail experience. It's not too late to change your mind, you know."

Georgie rolled her eyes. She wanted to throw the apple in her mother's face. Ever since Georgie hit puberty last year, Carol had been constantly probing her about her body. Not so much about her weight but more about how she presented herself to the world. It was as if the second she sprouted anything resembling breasts, her mother wanted her to disguise them. Starting last year, every morning before Georgie left for school, her mother would almost always question her outfit—*Is that skirt too short? Isn't that top cut a little too low?*—as if Georgie needed a reminder that nothing seemed to fit her the way it used to. She hated the way her body was constantly changing now, totally out of her control. It seemed like every single day, something new happened to her body or appeared on it. Her thighs rubbed together ever so slightly now when she walked. She noticed a little bump of fat right below her belly button. Last year, she was able to wear cotton bras with elastic bands, or none at all. This year, she had to wear the real kind with stiff underwire that made her feel like she was in a straitjacket. Carol had taken her to Bloomingdale's to get fitted by an old woman named Mary, who had papery, cold hands and a thick Boston accent. Mary had told her she was a 32-B, and Georgie wasn't sure why, but this information made her want to cry. She didn't think it was fair that her body could change all on its own without any input from her. Carol bought her two Calvin Klein bras that Georgie picked out herself, one with pink polka dots and the other with blue stars. The rest of the bras Carol bought her were nude colored and reminded Georgie of the pounded chicken breast cutlets they served at camp. She hated the underwire of the bras and didn't know how women got used to them for the rest of their lives; it seemed torturous to tolerate it for so many years.

"Mom, it's *fine*," she said. Her eyes suddenly felt hot and on the verge of overflowing with salty tears, the same feeling she'd had in that dressing room with Mary. She looked down at her feet. "I thought you'd be proud of me for getting a job." Her feelings were hurt, but not so much that she couldn't manipulate her mom's feelings in return. "*Dad* will be proud of me. You wouldn't understand because you don't even work."

Georgie marched out of the kitchen as she said it. She was good at throwing zingers at her mom but only if she removed herself from the conversation immediately afterward. She was too much of a coward to stand by her insults. Her signature move was to say something hurtful and then run. Not that her mother was really bothered by anything she said anyway. If she was, she certainly didn't show it.

"The new nanny starts tomorrow," Carol yelled after her. It infuriated Georgie that her mother didn't even acknowledge what Georgie had just said. It was like nothing ever got to her. She was unflappable. "Her name is Lindsey," Carol said. "Remember?"

Georgie stopped and turned back toward the kitchen. It was obvious to her that her mom was mentioning the nanny to remind Georgie of what she was: a kid. She had to give her mom credit: she knew how to come right back at Georgie with a subtle but piercing jab. And this was the perfect example. Georgie and her mother had spoken about how the nanny wasn't there to take care of *her*; she was there to take care of Berty. The mention of the nanny was clearly a ploy to put Georgie back in her juvenile place.

"I really don't know why you're telling me this," Georgie said, cocking her hip, her words now fueled by an angry breathlessness. "It's not like I need a nanny. I can take care of myself. I'm going to be making my own money, and I don't need anyone watching me. I'm not the same as Berty." Carol didn't respond. Her head was tucked back down into her datebook, into which she was scribbling some notes. For once, she wished her mother would show her some glimmer of softness. But she was all bones and ice.

She'd seen her mother cry only once, a few years ago, and she wasn't supposed to have seen it. Her mother was hosting the Children's Hospital annual fund-raising gala that night. Jonathan's father, Georgie's grandfather, had been a revered surgeon there, and Carol had been on the board for as long as she and Jonathan had been married. An hour before Carol and Jonathan were supposed to leave, Georgie heard them arguing in their bedroom.

"You know how important this night is to me, Jonathan," her mother said. "How you can do this to me, on tonight of all nights, is just beyond me. It's deplorable."

"I'm sorry," her father said. "I didn't know she was going to be there. But I can't exactly tell Mark that he can't bring whomever the hell he wants as his date when he's giving twenty-five grand to your charity. Unless you'd like me to. I can make that donation go away, if that's what you want." His voice became louder.

"Forget it. It's just so *indecent*. The fact that you don't understand that . . ." Georgie heard Carol emit a sharp noise with the release of her breath. "You disgust me."

Georgie, at this point, was standing in the hallway, just outside her parents' door, listening. She'd never heard her mother say something like that to her father—something so pointed, so full of rage, so unraveled. It was like she was listening to other people she didn't know. Strangers.

"Just don't expect me to acknowledge her. I won't do it, Jonathan. I won't."

"Fine, fine." There was a pause. "You know she means nothing to me."

Her parents began speaking in hushed tones, and Georgie couldn't make out what they were saying anymore. She returned to her room. A few minutes later, her father went downstairs. "Ten minutes!" he bellowed to Carol, who was still getting dressed in their room. Georgie crept back into the hallway and peered into her parents' room. Her mother was sitting at her vanity, looking at herself in the mirror. She looked like an advertisement from the 1950s for the perfect wife—slim, not a hair out of place, skin like satin, sparkling jewels hanging from her ears. But Georgie could see that her mother was crying. She wasn't making any noise, but her face was striped with tears, like icicles clinging to the edge of a roof. Georgie stayed for another minute, watching her mother dab her face with a cotton ball and apply new makeup. She went back to her room without saying anything. Her mother never saw her. Georgie never knew who this other woman was or why her mother was so upset about it. But now that she was older, Georgie suspected that her father must have had an affair and gotten caught. Even though she suspected it, the reality of that situation wasn't something Georgie could fully accept. Her parents were married, they loved one another, they loved their children, their life, she thought. Imagining her father with someone else was like imagining the ocean filled with air instead of water. It just didn't make sense. After that, Georgie tried to find more clues about this woman and what had happened between her and her father, but nothing came of it. Georgie never heard her parents fight about it again.

Now Georgie went to her room, slamming the door behind her. The hardwood floor was littered with clothing, half-unpacked and spilling out from several suitcases. She didn't feel like unpacking yet, but she wanted to pick out her outfit for tomorrow, so she started to riffle through her bags for pieces of clothing.

Georgie opened her window to let in some air. The window looked right out over Lighthouse Beach, a narrow strip of sand with a gleaming white lighthouse at the end. From her room, she could just make out the people on the beach, the lighthouse planted amid them all like a giant, sleeping guard dog. It was a beautiful, sunny day, warm but not too hot. Blankets and towels were laid out, and children ran through the sand, kicking it up into the faces of sluggish sunbathers. A group of tanned teenagers played volleyball. She could see that one of the girls wore a bright-pink bikini. The color popped against the beach, like an electric neon sign: OPEN FOR BUSINESS.

She continued combing through her bags until she found a pair of cutoff jean shorts that she had made herself earlier that year, in anticipation of the summer. Her mother would never let her buy ratty cutoffs, so she'd taken a pair of scissors to an old pair of Abercrombie jeans and made them herself in an act of defiance. Lucy had gone over the dress code with her earlier that day: a Picnic Basket T-shirt that she couldn't find at the moment but that she promised she'd give to Georgie the next morning, shoes of some kind, and that was basically it. Georgie decided on the cutoff shorts, her Nike sneakers, and a Dave Matthews Band concert T-shirt, even though she'd be changing out of that once she got there. It was a fantastic outfit, she thought, the kind that her mother would describe as *slovenly*. Georgie wasn't allowed to wear any of it at the clubs they frequented all summer. She wasn't even really allowed to wear stuff like that in their own house. That's why she liked it so much; the outfit itself was a rebellion. She especially liked the T-shirt. She hadn't actually gone to a Dave Matthews Band concert—she'd never been to *any* concert—but she'd found the shirt left behind in the upperclassmen girls' locker room at school once, and she'd taken it. She hadn't considered it stealing, since she'd seen the shirt sitting there abandoned for an entire week. Georgie had been waiting until the summer to wear it; she didn't want to wear it at home in Boston in case the real owner happened to see her, even though she didn't know who the owner was. She imagined that the shirt belonged to a pretty girl, probably a senior, who had gone to the concert with her boyfriend. He'd probably bought her the shirt as a gift so that she'd remember that night forever. *Maybe people will think that my boyfriend bought me this shirt,* Georgie thought.

Her mom was wrong, Georgie told herself. This was the perfect job for her. She would get her old friends back, make some new friends at work, and have a real social life here. Maybe she'd get a boyfriend. Maybe she'd fall in love. She assessed the outfit one last time and smiled to herself. *Not only will this be the best summer yet,* she thought, *but this will be the summer when I grow up. Maybe this summer, a guy will actually buy me my own concert T-shirt.*

Chapter 3

LINDSEY

The Decker house was smaller than Lindsey had imagined. Their street, which ran parallel to the harbor, was packed with narrow houses covered in gray, weathered shingles and clean, white trim paint. Some had shutters and window boxes brimming with vibrant flowers, which made the neighborhood look like a cluster of delicate dollhouses. The Deckers' house had budding hydrangea bushes all around it and a bright-red front door.

The bus had dropped her off at the station in Edgartown, and she'd walked from there, down Main Street, and then over five blocks to the house. Though it was only a ten-minute walk, Lindsey felt exhausted when she arrived. The sidewalks weren't meant for rolling suitcases, and she felt like she was incredibly loud as she clamored through town with her luggage, mouthing *Sorry* to everyone she passed, trying to wedge herself between them and the curb.

She wanted to take off her fleece jacket once she got to the house but was worried that she'd have visible sweat stains on her T-shirt underneath, and she decided that it would be better to keep it on and suffer a little. There was no doorbell, just a brass knob in the shape of a fish on the door, which she lifted and knocked twice, being careful not to bang too hard. She heard some shuffling inside, and seconds later, Carol swung open the door. Carol stood there in silence for a few seconds, and Lindsey wondered if maybe she'd made some mistake by coming there. Had she arrived on the wrong day?

"Lindsey," Carol finally said, as though searching for her name in the back of her mind. "Come on in." Her iciness was the same as what Lindsey had observed at the Bowdoin graduation.

Lindsey turned sideways to get her suitcase and duffel bag through the door without knocking anything. She already felt too big for the space. Inside, the house was cool and clean, though somewhat cluttered with oriental rugs, oil paintings with ornate gold frames, and cumbersome dark-wood furniture. When she'd met the Deckers at Bowdoin, Jonathan had described their home to her as "our little beach cottage," and she had imagined an airy house with translucent curtains blowing in with the sea breeze. But this house was stately, muscular, and masculine, and it felt layered with tight rooms and hallways, the floors and walls covered in rich fabrics and patterns. It felt more wintry than summery.

The house smelled of old porcelain, polished mahogany, white lilies, and bacon, a fact that would remain a mystery to Lindsey for years after that, as she learned that the Deckers rarely ate bacon or cooked it in the house. Standing in the foyer, Lindsey could feel the house's creakiness in the wide wooden floorboards and the staircase with sunken steps.

"Berty won't be home until the afternoon," Carol said. She didn't ask about Lindsey's trip. "A temporary babysitter is bringing him home from tennis camp in a little while. And Jonathan's back in Boston until later. So *thank God* you're here." She didn't mention where the older child, the teenager, was. Lindsey wondered what Carol was so busy doing that she had to hire another sitter to bring the younger child home from tennis that day. It was hard to understand how someone could seem so tense and full of stress in such a beautiful setting.

Carol wore tennis whites herself, consisting of a short skirt and long-sleeve top embossed with a tiny red, white, and blue triangular flag on the left breast. Her red hair was styled the same way it was when

Lindsey had first seen her at Bowdoin: tightly groomed into a clean bob. Lindsey wondered if she had already played tennis or was going to play later. She imagined that Carol's hair would somehow look the same before and after.

Lindsey placed her bags on the floor at the base of the stairs and then followed Carol on a tour of the house. In back was the kitchen, with a large island covered in wood at its center, the kind that served as a giant cutting board. A bowl of red apples sat in the middle. The kitchen was connected to an informal living room with a couch covered in a pattern of bright-green and purple flowers. An old television was nestled into the built-in bookshelf, which was otherwise filled with books and sterling silver sailing trophies in the form of cups, vases, and platters.

The entire back wall of the informal living room was a sliding glass door, which opened onto a brick patio atop a rolling lawn that sloped down to the water. There wasn't an expansive white beach, like Lindsey had imagined, but instead an old stone wall separated the water from the lawn. A wooden dock jutted out from the wall into the water. To the left of the dock, only about a block away, was Lighthouse Beach, which marked the divide between the inner and outer harbors. The beauty of the view was overwhelming to Lindsey. She couldn't believe that this was what she would wake up and see every day.

The tour continued. There was a formal living room, a library, and Jonathan's office on the other side of the house, as well as a formal dining room. Carol had only waved her hands toward those rooms; Lindsey wouldn't be spending much time there, she explained. Lindsey had to stop herself from chuckling out loud as Carol showed her around; to think that this was their *summer* house.

Carol guided Lindsey to her room on the second floor, which faced the street, not the ocean. The bed had a metal frame and a yellow-and-white quilt. It was a simple room with one wooden dresser; a small, empty closet; and an adjacent bathroom that looked as though it had been remodeled recently. Though more minimal than the rest of the house with its patterns and cushions, the room was beautiful and inviting.

"So Berty will be back in a few hours, at which point I'll get dinner ready. Just for tonight," Carol said, making it clear that it would be the last time she prepared dinner all summer. "You should feel free to use this afternoon how you'd like. Get settled in. I've got to run out to my barre class with Kim, but I'll be back before Berty's home." Lindsey nodded and eased her bags onto the floor, trying to do so without making too much noise. Carol lifted her wrist to look at her watch and pushed her mouth sideways as though she were late. When she raised her head to look at Lindsey again, her face had returned to a steely expression. "Now," Carol said, standing in the doorway, "no guests up here, understand?" Carol glanced over at the bed when she said this.

Lindsey was caught off guard by the question. What did she mean, no *guests*? Did she think that she was going to bring guys back to the house? Or did she mean friends? Carol hadn't mentioned a single house rule until now. Lindsey remembered the way Carol had looked at her on graduation day at Bowdoin. And the way Jonathan had as well. She felt misunderstood, misidentified. She wanted to blurt out to Carol that she wasn't that type of person, that she didn't even want all the male attention she received, that she was here to work, that she was ambitious and cared about her career and that she'd never mess that up by bringing some *guy* back to the house.

"Of course not" was all she said. "I understand."

"Wonderful," Carol said. "Okay, then. I'm off. Enjoy your afternoon."

Lindsey waited to move until she heard Carol go all the way down the stairs. She was relieved that Jonathan wasn't home yet. She didn't want to be alone in the house with him, at least not on her first day. She'd gotten an uneasy feeling around him when they'd first met, but perhaps even more unsettling was the fear that Carol would judge her for simply being in the presence of Jonathan without her. Lindsey knew that she had to be careful.

She unpacked, placing her clothes in the dresser and hanging a few dresses and sweaters in the closet. She needed to go to a pharmacy to buy tampons, shampoo and conditioner, and a few other staples that she hadn't wanted to fly with. She also needed sunblock, something she'd never really worn until last summer, when she began forming freckles along her shoulder tops and collarbone. The sun always turned her a golden bronze, and she never burned. But she'd reached the age where she had to start thinking about her own health and beauty. She didn't want to look older than she was.

After she unpacked, she changed into a floral sundress that she'd just bought from the Gap, on sale—white with small pink flowers—and flip-flops. She twisted her long, thick brown hair into a bun on top of her head. Her hair wasn't curly, but it wasn't really straight either. She felt that it was a frizzy nuisance, always making her hot and forming unruly wisps around her face.

She looked up the nearest pharmacy on her phone and found that it was about a mile walk outside of town, on Upper Main Street. She figured this would be a good way to explore the area. She had started to feel the anxiety of being in the home of complete strangers, and she couldn't quite relax even in the solitude of her own room. She eyed the paintings and antique furniture as she left the house, wondering how much it all cost and where they'd bought it.

She walked back up Main Street the same way she'd first come. But this time she looked around more. She noticed that Edgartown was distinctly *white*: the houses, the fences, the people. In Rockville, Lindsey had grown up with Indian neighbors on one side and Korean neighbors on the other. Her neighborhood felt like somewhat of a melting pot, even though all the residences on her parents' cul-de-sac street consisted of nearly identical prefab houses in shades of faded red and brown, with tiny bright-green lawns out front. During her twenty-minute walk, she saw only a handful of people who weren't white. Edgartown was a weird place, she thought.

It became obvious right away to Lindsey who was a tourist and who wasn't. The tourists tried too hard, with bright lipstick, outfits that were too perfectly matching in pastel patterns, and wedge heels— or the opposite, wearing fanny packs, graphic T-shirts, sneakers, and thick white socks, the occasional windbreaker tied around a waist. The summer regulars, she noticed, seemed more at ease. Faded polo shirts, relaxed khaki pants, linen dresses, flip-flops, sunglasses hanging on a salty string of Croakies. And then there were the actual locals, she observed, the ones driving rusted-out cars, honking their horns at tourists glued to their cell phones while crossing the street. There was a hierarchy to this place, she saw. And despite her effort to dress casually that afternoon, Lindsey felt like an obvious tourist, an outsider, just as she had her freshman year at Bowdoin. Her dress was too low-cut, her bun too high on her head, her curves too pronounced.

Main Street in downtown Edgartown was lined with boutiques offering lightweight cashmere shawls in pastel pinks, bow ties dotted with sailboats, pearl earrings, and bracelets with charms in the shape of Martha's Vineyard. Store windows displayed colorful leather sandals and shift dresses in fuchsia and turquoise, straw purses with ornate scrimshaw on top, and swim trunks decorated with martini glasses and nautical flags. It was so flamboyant, Lindsey thought, all these colorful things for sale that no one actually needed.

After a few blocks, Main Street turned into Upper Main Street, where the shops were replaced by boutique inns and some restaurants. Lindsey had to do a double take when she passed by a beautiful white-picket-fenced house surrounded by rosebushes, with a sign in front that read **DUKES COUNTY JAIL**. When she looked closer, she saw that the windows had iron bars inside. Edgartown was like an alternate universe in which even criminals seemed to be living the white-picket-fence dream.

She found the pharmacy a few blocks up the street and bought what she needed. The box of tampons was visible through the pharmacy's plastic bag, and Lindsey felt self-conscious about it as it swung off her arm on her walk back into town. She put in her headphones and listened to Fleetwood Mac as she walked. She began to think that this summer might be all right after all. It was an opportunity, she decided, to refocus and prioritize. She'd make some money, develop a great tan, and have evenings free to work on her résumé and to research potential jobs. By fall, she'd be refreshed and ready to figure out her next steps. She smiled to herself as she approached downtown Edgartown, getting lost in the beat of the music. Then she almost got hit by a pickup truck pulling out of the gas station.

"Jesus Christ!" the driver yelled out the window, craning his head toward her. "Don't you look up when you walk?"

Lindsey hadn't been paying attention at all and had walked straight past the gas station parking lot without pausing to check for cars. She had been one of *those* people. She was mortified, her outfit and giant bun now feeling like a ridiculous costume. She ripped her earbuds out. "I'm sorry!" she said, though her voice came out only as a whisper. She had to yell it again. "I'm sorry—I just didn't see you."

The driver, she noticed, looked about twenty-five. His truck was red, and the bed was piled with fishing rods that poked out the back. He was handsome, and Lindsey felt her face flush. He had a strong and defined jaw covered in scruff, and his nose was dotted with faded freckles. He had soft eyes, which were wet, as though he had just been laughing or crying. She could tell that his shoulders were broad from the way he leaned out the window, his arm folding over the car door. He didn't seem like a tourist or a summer person. *A real local,* Lindsey thought.

They locked eyes, and Lindsey stood there, silent, for a few seconds before realizing that she was blocking him. "Idiot," she muttered to herself. She shuffled forward and gave him a stiff wave, regretting it immediately. He probably saw her box of tampons. She kept her head down as she walked, trying to make herself as small as possible, and only looking back moments later when she was certain he had sped off, which he had. *Good thing the Deckers' world only includes summer people,* she thought.

Chapter 4

GEORGIE

At any time of day, the Picnic Basket smelled of hot biscuits and brewing coffee. The café sold salads and sandwiches made with ordinary ingredients but given whimsical names (*The Mermaid's Kiss: tuna salad with sprouts on wheat bread*) as well as an array of oversize baked goods. It also sold various overpriced knickknacks: hand-glazed ceramic bowls, wooden cutting boards, ocean-scented candles, and seven-dollar birthday cards. It was always filled with glowing mothers and beautiful nannies wearing caftans over their damp bathing suits, their children clinging to their legs and begging for one of the massive chocolate chip cookies in the glass case. But the Picnic Basket was unique in that it was open year-round. Most of the other restaurants and shops in Edgartown were open only during the busy summer months.

"What, am I just going to abandon my people? Us locals need to eat in the winter too," Lucy said when she explained to Georgie why she stayed open all year. As a result, the café became a true representation of the island: the Greenwich, Connecticut, mothers with their monogrammed Goyard beach bags waited in line for their coffees right behind the local construction workers in their paint-splattered Carhartts.

Georgie had imagined that she'd be working behind the counter, taking orders and managing the cash register. That's where all the beautiful girls worked, decked in slim-fitting T-shirts that said WHAT'S A PICNIC WITHOUT THE PICNIC BASKET? and wearing baseball caps, their hair often pulled into long braids cascading down their backs or thrown into messy buns that perfectly stuck out from underneath their hats.

On her first day, she arrived fifteen minutes earlier than Lucy had told her to come in, only to find Lucy and the staff already gathered around the big communal table in some kind of meeting. Georgie froze when she walked in, certain that she had messed up the time of her arrival and now positive that she would be fired before she even started.

"Georgie!" Lucy exclaimed. "That's *right*. You're *here*. I totally forgot that today's your first day." Lucy lightly hit her forehead with her palm and rose from her seat on the table's long bench. "Everyone, this is Georgie," she said, craning her arm toward Georgie and then back toward the table. "Georgie, this is everyone."

Georgie waved and looked at the staff. Most seemed to be college age, maybe a few high school seniors, she couldn't quite tell. There were about ten people, mostly girls and just a few boys, all of whom were scrawny and gangly. One of the boys had his hair pulled back into a messy bun, and Georgie swore he was wearing eyeliner. A few of the girls gave her a smile. One of them moved over on the bench, silently offering her a seat. Georgie sat, trying to squeeze her legs tightly together so as not to take up so much room. She tried to pay attention to what Lucy was saying—there was a new kind of scone, maple something, and they were getting a new shipment of kombucha in later that day—but she was too distracted by the satisfaction she was feeling from being in her present reality. She'd done it. She *belonged* here. With *these* people. In *this* place. She looked across the table toward a beautiful girl with long black hair braided in two pigtails. The girl's face was perfect—round and smooth and clear, like porcelain. Georgie wondered what her life was like and if they might become friends.

"Now let's all fill Georgie in on Lucy's three house rules," Lucy said, waking Georgie from her trance. The staff sat upright in their seats; they had been zoning out too.

"Kindness, honesty, hard work," the crew mumbled, some louder than others.

"That's right," Lucy said, rising from her seat, declaring the meeting over. "You all do that and we'll have a great summer, no matter what hits us."

The staff rose from the table, dispersing throughout the café to their various posts. Georgie hung around, waiting for instructions from Lucy, who was busy scribbling into a notebook. She felt out of place as she waited. After a minute, Lucy looked up.

"Okay, let's get you started, Georgie. Follow me."

They walked toward the back of the café, down the hallway where the bathrooms were, and into an office room at the end. Inside, there was a desk piled high with paperwork. The floor was littered with excess boxes of merchandise. Georgie hoped that Lucy had only brought her there to get something.

"We'll start you in here," Lucy said, looking around with her arms crossed. "This is where I really need your help." Georgie surveyed the room. It was so crowded with junk that she could barely walk to the desk. The Picnic Basket had been around as long as she could remember, but the front room had been remodeled about ten years ago, and everything seemed to always be so organized and clean. The office was a disaster.

"Basically," Lucy said, "this is all the paperwork from the past decade, since the remodel. Bills, invoices, contracts, blueprints, even some old recipes. I wanted to make a cookbook at one point, you know." She sighed and pointed down at the boxes. "And all this . . . ," she said. "Well, this I just don't know what to do with. It's all the shit we couldn't sell."

Georgie panicked. This wasn't a quick project—it could take her all summer to go through it. If she wasn't going to be working up front, making friends, seeing customers, then what was the point of working there at all? But it was too late. She had asked for the job, and this was it. She stoically listened to Lucy's instructions, trying not to cry. Georgie was to sort and file everything by category and date and then digitize it all on Lucy's giant desktop Mac and create a digital database for all the excess merchandise. But there was so much stuff that it would take Georgie a few weeks to even begin sorting it all out on the computer. No matter how fast she worked, it was Georgie's sad fate to spend the entire summer alone in that dusty office.

"Oh, and you should take an hour lunch break whenever you want," Lucy said as she began to walk out of the office. Before Lucy left, she pointed down at a box of T-shirts. "And here are the T-shirts. Take one. When you're part of the team, you've got to represent!" Georgie looked down at the box of shirts, which previously had looked like such prized possessions to her, trophies signifying independence and glamour. Now they just depressed her.

Lucy shut the door behind her when she left, and the office became silent. Dust particles floated in the air, illuminated by the sunshine streaming through the window facing the back alley. Georgie's stomach tightened and she felt nauseous. She picked up a limp manila folder on the desk, her arm straining as though the folder weighed a hundred pounds. It was labeled RENTAL CONTRACT, 2002–2004. Georgie opened the folder, and inside was just a grease-stained takeout menu from Lattanzi's Restaurant and Pizzeria, along with receipts from a boat trailer. It was all a mess. She felt overwhelmed, and she hadn't even started yet.

Georgie returned to the box of T-shirts and picked out a size small. She held it up in front of her. The cotton felt stiff, and the shape looked boxy. Even though she was alone in the room, she put it on over her T-shirt and then wiggled her arms inside in order to peel her T-shirt out from underneath the new one. It fell across her body like a square pillowcase—tight around her stomach, looser around her breasts. Maybe inside the store, she wouldn't get the recognition she wanted, but at least she could wear the shirt outside, on her way to and from work, and people might see her and know she had a real job at the Picnic Basket. It was better than nothing, she thought.

She took out her phone and thought about sending a text to Catherine, telling her to stop by and say hi. But she decided not to. She should wait, she thought, let a few days go by, maybe run into Catherine naturally at the beach club. She didn't want to come on too strong, seem too desperate. But how was she going to let people know that she was here, that she had a *real* job at one of the coolest places in town, if she was sequestered in a closet in the back where she'd have no interaction with anyone? She resolved to just get to work and push through it.

She spent the next four hours going through paperwork and sorting it all into piles by categories. The work actually began to feel therapeutic, and she fell into a rhythm. When she took a break to use the bathroom, though, she wandered back into the main area of the café and immediately felt a pang of jealousy toward the other employees. She desperately wanted to be working up front, greeting people, being part of the action. She wondered, with resentment, if Lucy thought that having someone as young as Georgie working up front would make the store look bad somehow. Or maybe Lucy didn't trust her to work the cash register. Maybe she didn't think she was pretty enough.

Even though it was only June, and the true summer season didn't really pick up until July, the store was crowded as lunchtime approached. It was a little past noon now, and it was unusually warm out—a perfect beach day. Days of the week never seemed to apply on the Vineyard. It was a Wednesday, but it could have been a Saturday, considering how many people were coming in and out.

Georgie didn't rush back to the office. She noticed that the table with the coffee creamers and sugar was messy, so she started to straighten it out, wiping down the tabletop with a napkin and reorganizing the basket of coffee-cup lids, just so she could stay out of the office for a minute longer. She didn't see the man who came up beside her, not at first.

"Hey, can you pass me four packets of sugar?" she heard someone ask her. Georgie turned and looked and then froze. It was Brian Fitzgerald, her former sailing instructor. Georgie's parents were friends with Brian's, but she and Brian really only knew one another through sailing. Or, at least, *she* knew *him* through sailing. She had taken sailing classes every summer for years, and Brian had been one of her instructors up until a few years ago, when he started spending his summers on Wall Street during college. He must be about twenty-three or twenty-four now, she thought.

Georgie couldn't tell if Brian recognized her as well, but she scanned his face quickly for a sign. It had been a few years since she'd seen him. But he was just as handsome now as she remembered him being before. He had a sunburned nose and sandy-blond hair that fell into his hazel eyes. He was tall, and his frame seemed to tower over her. Georgie wondered if he was home for the whole summer or just visiting for the week.

She realized that she had just been standing there silently, and she quickly grabbed four sugar packets, her fingers fumbling. She handed them to Brian, and his hand brushed hers slightly as he took them, sending a little jolt up through her wrist. He looked her in the eyes. She was close enough to smell him. He smelled like ocean salt, laundry detergent, and sweat. It wasn't even a particularly good smell, but it somehow made Georgie feel weak and anxious, restless. She turned her head downward, feeling her heartbeat quicken.

"Thanks," he said and smiled, before ripping several packets open and dumping the sugar into his iced coffee.

"Babe, you need to cool it with the sugar!" Georgie turned to see a tanned, long-limbed girl with straight brown hair come up behind Brian and squeeze his shoulders. "You have an addiction!"

"A man has his vices. What can I say?" Brian said, and he turned and kissed the girl on the lips. The kiss was swift, just a peck, but the moment felt intensely intimate to Georgie, who was close enough to see the way their lips touched and parted. The girl ran her hand down Brian's back, leaving it to rest in the slight arch above his tailbone.

Georgie just stood there, her own mouth slightly open. She realized she wasn't moving again, so she grabbed a pile of straw wrappers and threw them out, just to look busy. She wiped down the rest of the table and straightened out a basket of napkins. As she returned to the office, she saw Brian and the girl walk out of the shop and down the brick sidewalk before getting into Brian's Land Rover parked outside. They looked as though they were headed to the beach, Georgie thought. She wondered what beach they were going to and how the girl might stretch out on her towel while Brian ran into the surf. She wondered if they had already had sex together.

Back in the solitude of the office, Georgie remembered her experiences sailing with Brian. She had started out in small bathtub-shaped boats called Optimists and later graduated to sleek racing boats called 420s. Georgie had loved sailing the Optis best, because she could do it alone and they never went too fast. They allowed her to feel connected to the water, the wind, to feel weightless. The 420s required more focus. If there was a strong wind, the 420s would cut through the water like sharks heading for their prey, swift and smooth.

One afternoon a few summers ago, Georgie's sailing partner had been home sick, so she sailed the 420 alone. It wasn't something she normally did, but the winds were calm that day, and she'd spent enough time skippering herself that she knew she'd be fine. But by the time she was halfway through the course, the winds had picked up, and she began to grow afraid. She could barely keep the boat upright; she was pulling the tiller hard, turning into the wind, and trying to release the sail all at the same time, but the wind kept crashing toward her in gusts, and water continued to splash up and into the boat, blinding her. She had to dig her feet into the shoulder of the boat and fall backward so that her body weight could right the vessel. The sea swells frothed angrily around her like burning mountains.

"Georgie!" Brian had yelled to her from the Boston Whaler he was driving nearby. The instructors always stayed close to the sailors, circling them in motorboats, barking instructions and advice. But Georgie had never really needed their help until now. Her arms started to shake with the weight of the wind.

"Let out your sail and take it down! I'll tow you back into the harbor!" Brian shouted. Georgie was scared, but she followed his instructions. She knew that whatever he told her was the right thing to do. Brian waited and watched while Georgie released her jib and mainsail. The sails flapped loudly, and the noise made Georgie's head hurt. The hull of the boat rocked with the waves, and her hair whipped against her face. Ocean spray beat against her skin, making her shiver and soaking her life jacket. She wobbled toward the bow of the boat. Brian had pulled up next to her, and he tossed her a rope from his boat. "Cleat this up here," he said, and Georgie frantically looped the rope a few times around the cleat on the bow. She was still shaking, but less so now.

"Just stay in my wake," Brian yelled, "and you'll be safe."

Georgie did what Brian said. She moved the tiller so that she stayed exactly in the wake of Brian's boat, like it was an invisible tunnel in which she couldn't get hurt. Every few seconds he would look back behind him, locking eyes with her and smiling, making sure she was okay. Though she was alone in her boat, Georgie felt as if she were right beside Brian, tucked under the canopy of his arm, sheltered from the wind. He was carrying her away from danger; she was with him; she was safe. She noticed the way he turned the wheel of the boat. His movements were smooth but also physical and sharp, as though he wasn't just turning the boat but also the entire ocean with just the bend of his wrist.

Now, Georgie looked down at the stack of dust-veiled papers and boxes before her. Somehow, the task seemed more manageable than it had an hour ago. She raised her fingers and ran them along the grooves of her lips and wondered what it might feel like to have them pressed against Brian's.

Chapter 5

LINDSEY

Although she really couldn't afford it, Lindsey decided she'd treat herself to a new pair of sunglasses from Summer Shades, the sunglasses boutique she'd seen on Main Street earlier that day. She knew the kind she wanted: classic Ray-Ban aviators, with gold frames and green lenses. She'd tried them on at Nordstrom when she'd gone there with her mom last week to buy a few new things before she left town. When she showed her mother the aviators and then the price, her mother said that she'd just break them or lose them and that it would be insane to spend over a hundred dollars on something she'd probably have for only a few weeks. "But I'll have them forever," Lindsey said.

Her mother had just rolled her eyes. "What about these?" she'd suggested, holding up an imitation pair that was half the price. Lindsey decided against it altogether, feeling guilty for asking her mom to spend money on something that she knew she didn't actually need. She never wanted to fight with her parents for this reason: they worked so hard to give her a good life, a college education, the support to pursue whatever she wanted, that Lindsey never felt entitled to disagree with them on anything. As a result, she didn't ever want to be confrontational. Not just with them, but with anyone. It didn't feel good to her to fight, even if it was just a friendly debate. There was something that frightened her in those first sparking moments of an argument, something that made her feel like she might lose her grip on whatever it was she wanted to keep. She found that it was easier to just let people win.

The store was empty when she entered, until Lindsey heard a high-pitched voice from the back yell out, "Be right with you!" Lindsey bent down to look into the lower shelves in the glass cases. It was quiet in the store, despite the street being crowded with tourists just a few steps outside.

"Lindsey? Is that you?" Lindsey stood and saw Joanna O'Callahan, one of her classmates from Bowdoin, standing behind the counter. Joanna had been on the field hockey team with Lindsey, but they weren't really friends. Joanna was part of a group of wealthy girls who all seemed to know one another through private New England prep schools. She wasn't on any kind of scholarship, like Lindsey and Rose. She was the kind of girl who went to places like St. Barts and St. Thomas over Thanksgiving break, who invited a dozen friends to her parents' ski house in Vermont for winter weekends, who always spent her summers here, on Martha's Vineyard. Lindsey thought that Joanna was beautiful, but in a way that seemed effortless, and she envied her for that. Her light-brown hair was infused with streaks of golden blonde, framing her round face, which was sun-kissed into a peachy-pink color. She even had a way of making the dead skin peeling off her nose look pretty, like it was marking the days spent in the sun and the sea. To Lindsey, Joanna looked like summer itself, like she had pure sunshine running through her veins.

Lindsey had to work hard on her appearance, watching her diet, wearing foundation on her face in the right spots, blow-drying her hair whenever she had time. But Joanna made it all seem easy. She made *everything* look easy. She seemed to glide through life like she was on ice skates—one smooth line with no bumps or cracks. Lindsey remembered a goal that Joanna had scored during their big game against Bates their junior year. Joanna had hit a clean, hard tomahawk shot in the last three seconds of the game, from a tough angle to the left of the goal. Bowdoin won the game, breaking a losing streak against Bates. Joanna had been the college hero that weekend, though she didn't really seem to care.

"It was no big deal," Lindsey remembered Joanna saying to her teammates after the game. "I just hit the ball." Lindsey had been practicing her tomahawk shot for months but never got the chance to do it in a game. She'd never even seen Joanna try it during practice.

"Hi!" Lindsey said now. "How are you?" She didn't know what to say. She felt like an intruder in the store, not a customer. She fidgeted with her hands and tried to casually swing her shopping bag full of tampons around her hips to hide it.

Joanna didn't answer the question, instead launching into her own set of questions for Lindsey. "So, what are you doing here? Are you just visiting? Are you here all summer?" Her pace was rapid, and Lindsey sensed a hint of judgment with the first question: What was *she* doing *here*?

"Yeah, actually, I just got here this morning. I'll be here until, like, early August," Lindsey said, hoping that her response was sufficient.

"That's amazing!" Joanna leaned her elbows on the glass case. "Do your parents have a place here?"

For a moment, Lindsey considered making something up about having cousins on the island, or a best family friend, maybe godparents. But she told the truth.

"No, I'm actually the nanny for a family here. In Edgartown."

"No way! Which family? Oh my God, you're going to have the *best* summer." Lindsey couldn't tell if Joanna's enthusiasm was sincere or contrived, but she was inclined to believe that it was sincere somehow.

"Yeah, I think it will be good," Lindsey said. "It's, um, the Decker family." Lindsey paused. It felt strange talking about them, like some kind of a betrayal. "Do you know them? Mr. Decker went to Bowdoin."

"Of course I know the Deckers! My parents are pretty good friends with them, actually. We've known them forever!"

"Cool," Lindsey said. She started to worry that her summer in Edgartown would feel like Bowdoin but without a Rose, without her other teammates. She wondered if Joanna's connection to the Deckers meant that she'd be seeing a lot more of her, and if Joanna would be embarrassed to know their nanny.

"Actually, our house is just around the corner from theirs, on Starbuck Neck."

"Nice," Lindsey said, not knowing where Starbuck Neck was. It sounded expensive.

Joanna leaned forward on the counter. "Mr. Decker is pretty cute, don't you think? I mean, like, for a dad, you know."

Lindsey wasn't sure how to respond. Yes, she had noticed that Jonathan Decker was handsome. He definitely had some Robert Redford qualities to him, with a boyish face and symmetrical features.

"He's a big flirt," Joanna added before Lindsey could respond. "And he likes to go out. I mean, I've seen him at the bars at night. *Without* Mrs. Decker." This surprised Lindsey. Sure, Mr. Decker had looked at her for a second too long when they met at Bowdoin, but otherwise the family had seemed so traditional to her, so *by the book*. She tried to imagine Jonathan out at a bar, flirting with young women. "But I think he's harmless," Joanna continued.

"I hope so," Lindsey said. "So you're here all summer?" She wanted to change the subject.

"Oh yeah, all summer. I have a job lined up at Hill Holliday, but I told them I won't be starting until September. I just needed *one last summer*, you know?"

"Totally." Lindsey had heard of that marketing firm—it was one of the biggest and best in Boston. She wondered why Joanna had a summer job at all. It wasn't like she needed to be making money.

"So I work here a few days a week just to get out and have some of my own cash, you know?" Joanna explained, as though she had read Lindsey's mind. "It's like, I love going to the beach, but I don't want to go *every* day, all day. I'd probably go crazy! So I'm here three days a week."

Lindsey nodded. "Totally," she said again. Though the absurdity of having a job just for fun almost made Lindsey laugh. This was exactly how she remembered Joanna from college: naive, sweet, genuine, but totally out of touch with reality. *Must be nice to be her,* Lindsey thought to herself.

"Give me your number," Joanna said. "Let's hang out."

Lindsey recited her number, trying to act nonchalant. During their four years at Bowdoin together, Joanna had never asked Lindsey to hang out. She'd never asked her anything. Joanna texted her: It's Jo.

"So, like, are you allowed to go out? Are the Deckers cool with that?" Joanna asked.

"Yeah, for sure," Lindsey said, though it hadn't actually occurred to her until then whether or not it would be awkward for her to go out in the evenings. Considering Carol's strict no-guest policy, Lindsey wasn't sure that she'd approve of Lindsey having her own social life either. But she was an adult, and Carol wasn't her mother. She'd just have to slip out on her nights off and pray that the creaking of the old wooden staircase wouldn't wake the family when she came home.

"Cool, I'll text you. I think there will be a bonfire tonight, actually. At Left Fork. Should be fun."

"Sounds good. Talk to you later." A couple walked into the store then, and Joanna shifted into shopgirl mode while Lindsey slipped out the door. She texted Rose immediately: You'll never guess who I just ran into. Joanna O'Callahan?! She wants to hang out with me. She stopped typing and then added: Weird. Whatever.

Joanna had never shown an interest in Lindsey during college, and she wondered why she was showing one now. Maybe Joanna was different outside school. Maybe they'd become friends. Part of her felt like Rose was going to be mad at her, like she'd gone behind her back with the enemy. Lindsey's initial instinct was to be suspicious, to assume that

Joanna was judging her, being condescending to her, except that, as she left the store, she got the feeling that she was wrong. Joanna seemed to actually be as nice as she presented herself to be. Perhaps, Lindsey thought, she was a genuinely friendly person. It just confused Lindsey as to why Joanna might want to be friends with *her*.

She decided to wait and see if Joanna would text her later about this party. It felt like more than a party; it felt like a chance to enter Joanna's world, to make connections that she would otherwise never make. She hadn't pursued it, but she wasn't about to turn that opportunity down. She glanced at her phone. Rose had responded: Is she as much of a snob on the Vineyard as she was at Bowdoin? Lindsey typed: She actually seems really nice. She paused, considering the text before deleting it. To be determined . . . , she wrote, then hit "Send."

A rumble in her stomach reminded her that she hadn't eaten anything since early that morning when she'd had a granola bar on the ferry. She had been too busy to notice, and now she felt starved. She didn't know how meals worked at the Deckers' house and whether or not she could eat what she wanted from their fridge or if she'd even want to. As a guest in someone else's home, eating felt incredibly private to Lindsey. The idea of Carol catching Lindsey eating alone in the kitchen felt more potentially mortifying than Carol catching her having sex with someone.

Lindsey had seen a café up the street that looked good, so she walked toward it. The possibility of there being a lack of food made her panic. Food was an important thing in Lindsey's family household. Some families liked skiing, or puzzles, or board games. The Davises like food. They *ate*; that's what they did. Her mother would usually know on Monday what the family was going to have for dinner every night that week. Even on busy mornings when Lindsey was rushing to school and her father was leaving early for work, her mother would make them all sit down for breakfast. She made eggs, usually, but sometimes french toast or, on a special day, chocolate chip pancakes. When Lindsey was in high school, she began to resent the importance of food that her mother had pushed on her. She hated that she was conditioned now to think of every meal as an event, a way of structuring her days, of planning. She wanted to think of food as an afterthought, like necessary fuel, and perhaps sometimes pleasure, but never an obsession.

Thankfully, Lindsey had a high metabolism and burned most everything off through sports that she kept up through college. Weight wasn't an issue for her, but the curves of her body were. That was a different thing, she'd come to realize after trying crash diets and juice cleanses, which left her ten pounds lighter but no less voluptuous. She wasn't overweight, but her body, since high school, was shapely in a way that always made her feel older than she was and out of place, noticeable. During her freshman year of high school, Lindsey went from wearing a C cup to a double-D cup. Sometimes she had to wear two sports bras when she played field hockey. The pressure of the two bras often hurt her ribs, but she liked the way it flattened her out. She felt like it was armor against being perceived as slutty or ridiculous or obscene. She hated the way her body made her feel vulgar, no matter what she wore. She grew tired of constantly feeling men's eyes bulge and hover around her chest.

Even though she knew that her body was always going to be robust, no matter how much weight she lost, Lindsey had built up anger toward her mother for making it difficult to stay thin. She was always cooking creamy pasta dinners or steak enchiladas or other recipes she'd seen in the food magazines that she refused to get subscriptions to but ended up buying each month anyway at the supermarket checkout line.

Lindsey rounded the corner toward the entrance to the café, above which swung a faded red sign with gold lettering—**THE PICNIC BASKET**. Outside, on a brick-laid patio, were wooden picnic tables, bike stands, and overgrown planters with flowers and vines spilling out. The line of customers waiting to order extended to the door of the café. It was crowded and loud. Amy Winehouse's lonely voice blasted through the speakers. Lindsey got in line and craned her neck to see the menu up on the wall above the cashier. She decided she'd get "The Garden Nymph," an all-veggie-and-cheese sandwich on wheat bread. In front of her in line was a young couple, about her age. The guy had his hand tucked into the back pocket of the girl's jean skirt. Lindsey made sure not to step too close to them in line. They were whispering into one another's ears. The girl was thin, with long hair—the kind that air-dried straight and glossy. Even from behind, Lindsey could tell that this was the kind of girl who looked pretty when she woke up in the morning or when she cried. The boyfriend, in his pastel, patterned swim trunks and white polo shirt, looked like many of the guys she had gone to Bowdoin with: preppy, privileged, and pretentious. Lindsey rolled her eyes at his back. *Another elitist asshole with a skinny girlfriend,* she thought. The guy slapped his girlfriend's butt when it was their turn to move up in line. Lindsey's face scrunched in disgust.

"Ouch!" the girl shrieked with a smile, swatting his hand away.

He responded by cupping her butt cheek in his hand and giving it a squeeze. "Cut it out!" the girlfriend yelled again. This time, Lindsey thought the girl might have actually meant it.

The couple ordered. An Arnold Palmer for the girl, an iced coffee for the guy. As they turned around after ordering, Lindsey caught a look at the guy's face. His lips were wet and coiled into a smirk, like he'd just won a bet. There was something about him that made Lindsey cringe. He radiated entitlement.

Lindsey took her time scanning the menu even though she'd already decided what she wanted. She waited for the couple to be out of earshot before she ordered. She wasn't quite sure why, but she didn't want them to hear her, as though the judgment of these strangers mattered to her. After she paid—a price her parents would *never* pay for a sandwich and drink—she turned to wait at the end of the counter. She looked for the couple, but they had gone. She found a free table by a window overlooking the street, and she put her things down and then went to find the bathroom. She figured that this was a place where she could leave her things out on the table and they'd be safe. Who, in Edgartown, would want to steal anything that Lindsey had?

The bathroom was on the other side of the café, past an area that sold housewares and candles. Lindsey walked through the area slowly, dragging her fingers across several glossy platters and bowls and picking up some candles to smell them. The bathroom was small and clean, and when she shut the door, Lindsey relished the semi-silence and calm. She glanced only briefly at herself in the mirror. Her hair had expanded into a frizzy halo from the island humidity. She shrugged.

On her way out, a pretty girl skated past her into a back room. The girl wore one of the employee shirts, but Lindsey thought she looked young, maybe thirteen or fourteen. She had that kind of awkward, pubescent build that Lindsey had had at that age. She was baby faced but with the newly emerging body of a young woman, that uncomfortable in-between stage.

There was something else about the girl that reminded Lindsey of herself at that age. Lindsey had convinced her aunt to let her work on the weekends at her photo-development store when she was thirteen. She wanted to make her own money so she could buy the Abercrombie shirts and platform shoes from Delia's that her mom thought were overpriced and tacky. Her job at the photo store was to sort through all the envelopes of developed prints and organize them by last name. Sometimes, though it wasn't really allowed, she would look through the photos. Most photos were of family events—children's birthday parties, sports games, weddings. The photos often made Lindsey sad, even the ones that at first seemed to feature happy people: fat couples smiling at expensive steakhouses, greasy teenagers dressed up for prom in blue tuxes and pink gowns, scared puppies cradled in the slippery hands of excited children, proud homeowners beaming toward their newly purchased mustard-colored house. As a teenager, she didn't know why seeing these private snapshots made her feel like someone had put a plastic bag over her head and left her gasping for air. She realized later that it was because she was scared that her own life would amount to the same thing: a few smiles caught on camera on a grassy knoll in a middle-class suburb, where she'd be wearing an old dress, hoping for something more but grateful to not have less.

As Lindsey ate her sandwich, she looked around at the other customers. Everyone looked like they were on vacation. Or like their whole lives were one big vacation. Lindsey realized that, so far, the only person in Edgartown she could remotely relate to was that teenage girl.

Her phone buzzed as she was finishing up her lunch. Beach bonfire tonight is on. South Beach, Left Fork. LMK if you're in. It was from Joanna. Lindsey smiled. Her mind started racing with possibilities and questions. She pictured tiki torches and cocktails with mini straws in them and imagined herself dancing barefoot on the beach. What would she wear? Who would be there? Did this mean that she and Joanna were going to be friends this summer? She didn't know where Left Fork was or how she would get there. But one way or another, she was going to this party. She wrote back: I'm in.

Chapter 6

GEORGIE

Lucy had told Georgie that her hours would be "loose. Come in the morning, leave in the afternoon." This bothered Georgie at first. It was as if she didn't have a real schedule because she didn't have a real job, like she couldn't be trusted, like she wasn't being taken seriously. But by four o'clock, Georgie was grateful for the flexible hours. Her body felt achy from working in a crouched position most of the day, and her skin craved the sun. She was thirsty. She went to the kitchen to tell Lucy she was heading out. Lucy was cracking eggs into a large metal bowl. Other kitchen staff members were running around her, cleaning and chopping, preparing for tomorrow.

"Hey, Lucy," Georgie said, suddenly worried that she might be leaving too early, "I think I'm done for today."

"All right. Great work, kiddo," she responded, only barely glancing up from the bowl to give a quick smile. It occurred to Georgie that Lucy hadn't even seen any of the work she'd done. As far as she knew, Georgie hadn't done *anything* all day. She had, in fact, made great progress on the piles of paperwork and cluttered boxes, but Lucy hadn't come to check on her even once. She realized then that her mother hadn't come by the café either. Not that she had said she would, but since it was Georgie's first real day of work, she had thought that just maybe—*maybe*—her mom would pop in to say hi.

Her disappointment lifted as she stepped outside, though. Somehow, the street and the town felt newer, like the pixilation of it all had been slightly turned up while she was at work. Or maybe it was just that *she* felt newer, different. The summer-afternoon air was potent with the smell of freshly cut grass and had an energy fueled by all the beachgoers returning to town after a day by the sea. In her Picnic Basket shirt, Georgie felt proud as she walked home. She felt older and more accomplished. She calculated that she had earned seventy-two dollars that day, before all the tax stuff her dad had tried to explain to her was taken out. She thought of the things she could buy with that money, all the things her mother wouldn't buy for her: one of the Tibetan-inspired cross-body purses that she'd seen older girls wearing, a big silver-and-turquoise ring, a pair of leather Rainbow flip-flops that her mom thought were tacky but that she thought were cool.

She decided to text Catherine. She'd waited all day. Hey! Just got to the island. Am working at the Picnic Basket. Beach day soon? She hit "Send," feeling proud, and stuck her phone in her back pocket. A few minutes passed without a response. *Give it time,* she thought.

As she rounded the corner off Main Street toward home, her pride was interrupted by remembering that today the new nanny was coming. She was annoyed with her parents for getting one, even though she knew that Berty needed help. Having a nanny meant that on the days that she would go to the beach club with her brother, it would look like the nanny was there for *her* too. It was so humiliating. Her mother had told her that the nanny had just graduated from Bowdoin. That's where they'd found her, at her dad's reunion. Georgie had sulked through that entire weekend, barely speaking to anyone. She didn't understand why she had to be there in the first place. Most of the reunion staff consisted of actual students who stayed for the weekend to make some money. Anytime a waiter or tour guide was in their vicinity, her dad would try to get Georgie to talk to them.

"Georgie here wants to go to Bowdoin in a few years," he'd tell them, patting Georgie's shoulder. But she didn't. At least she didn't think she did. She wanted to go to school in a city, where there was excitement—different people, cool restaurants and bars and shops. She didn't know if her father felt the need to push her in certain directions because he was being selfish or because he actually thought that's what she would want. Either way, he didn't get it.

She'd caught a glimpse of the nanny from afar, while her parents were meeting her. But she couldn't quite tell what she looked like. She wondered if she was pretty up close, if she was skinny, and what her voice sounded like. She just hoped she wasn't chatty. She'd had nannies in the past who loved to talk, who wanted to gently interrogate her, as though they hoped that she might reveal to them a way to get the family's approval.

Even though Berty required constant attention, Georgie didn't really understand why her mother and father couldn't be the ones to take care of him themselves. Her father spent most of the workweek in Boston, but he flew to the island every weekend. During the week, her mother always seemed to be too busy to take the kids anywhere, though Georgie wasn't quite sure how she spent all her time. One game of tennis seemed to take up the entire day. When she was home, her mother would often be on the phone with someone or hovering over her laptop, wearing her thick tortoiseshell glasses, which always indicated that she was busy working. Not really working, not like a real job, but doing charity work, mostly for the Children's Hospital and sometimes for the Conservation Society. Her dad's thing was the Museum of Fine Arts. Between the two of them, her parents gave a lot of money and time to various Boston institutions, Georgie knew, though she didn't know how much exactly. All their philanthropy seemed to blend together, like one big party.

Georgie let the screen door slam behind her as she walked into the house. She had decided, on the rest of her walk home, that she would carry herself with an air of indifference around the new nanny. If Georgie showed no interest, then maybe the nanny wouldn't bother her. She would be *cordial*, as her mother often reminded her to be.

The house was quiet when she entered. Berty was still at tennis, she guessed, but he'd be home soon. She stood still, waiting for a noise, until she decided that she was safely home alone. She went to the kitchen, opened the fridge, and took out a bowl of leftover macaroni and cheese. She began eating it with a spoon, not bothering to heat it up. If her mother saw her eating like this before dinner, she would give Georgie a look of severe disappointment. Or, worse, a look of total bewilderment. Her mother never seemed to get hungry. Georgie had never seen her eat anything straight out of the fridge, and she knew that she probably never would.

Georgie was shoveling in another spoonful when she heard footsteps coming down the stairs. She started to put the food away hastily so as not to get caught, but it was too late. A springy girl with a huge, messy bun on top of her head rounded the corner into the kitchen. The girl wore a short sundress, the kind that Georgie's mother would probably let her wear only as a bathing suit cover-up. She had slim legs and arms and a flat stomach but large breasts that popped from the top of her dress like loaves of rising bread. Her skin was olive toned and, as far as Georgie could tell, perfect. She didn't have any pimples or redness like the kind Georgie had on her cheeks, which always seemed flushed even when she wasn't blushing. So this was the nanny, Georgie thought. She hated her immediately.

"You must be Georgie," the girl said to her, raising her hand in a wave. "I'm Lindsey. The nanny. It feels so weird saying that, but I guess that's what I am." Was the nanny trying to be funny? Georgie noticed that she smelled like vanilla, warm and sweet.

Before Georgie could respond, Lindsey said, "Wait, I think I saw you at the Picnic Basket today. Do you work there?"

"Yes," Georgie said. "I do." Georgie sat up a little bit straighter, drawing her shoulders back and projecting her chest. She was still holding a spoonful of the macaroni and cheese, and now the spoon dangled in midair. She wanted to take another bite but felt too self-conscious, so she slowly moved it down into the bowl.

"That's *so* cool," Lindsey chirped. "I got a sandwich there today. Seems like a fun place to work. You know, I worked when I was your age too. It's pretty great to be able to make your own money when you're so young."

Georgie was annoyed that Lindsey had interrupted her and had condescended to her by pointing out her age, how *young* she was. She was obviously highlighting the differences between them. They weren't even that far apart in age, not really, anyway. She examined the nanny with a closer eye. She hadn't expected her to smell good and have perfect skin. She wondered what Lindsey had looked like at fourteen. She was probably perfect then, too, she thought.

"It's cool, I guess," Georgie responded, trying to sound aloof.

"Well, I just got home from walking around town. It's my first time here, you know."

"That's cool" was all Georgie could muster in response. She was embarrassed to still be holding the bowl of macaroni and cheese.

"I like it here," Lindsey continued. "I mean, I only walked around Edgartown today. There's a lot I still want to see."

"Yeah, the island's bigger than people realize." Georgie wanted to say more but wasn't quite sure how or where to start. She wanted to know what it was like to be her. "So do you know any people here?" she asked. Part of her was hoping that Lindsey would say no, that she didn't know anyone here, that she, Georgie, was her only friend on the whole island so far.

"Well, I actually just ran into a friend from Bowdoin at the sunglasses store. So we'll probably start hanging out. Small world, huh?"

Georgie felt a throb of jealousy and hurt. Lindsey already had friends and a whole life on the island, more than she had.

"That's cool. Do you have a boyfriend?" She felt her face redden with the question, as if she was accidentally flirting.

"No, not right now," Lindsey said casually. She didn't seem taken aback by the question. "I'm kind of looking forward to just doing my own thing this summer, you know?"

"Totally," Georgie said, and on impulse, she continued. "I had a boyfriend at camp last year." She paused. "But I'm over it." She hadn't expected to share anything with Lindsey, but she felt that the conversation might have the potential of making her feel important, connected, normal. She wanted to see how Lindsey would respond and if she was going to take Georgie seriously or not. It was a test of sorts, to see if they could actually be friends. To see if Lindsey would actually care.

"What happened, if you don't mind my asking?" Lindsey asked, leaning her body farther across the island counter, angling her face at Georgie.

"Oh, you know," Georgie said, deciding in that moment to lie. It was too embarrassing to tell the truth, at least at this point. "I just stopped liking him." She looked down, trying not to reveal anything more.

Lindsey paused for a few seconds. "Well, it sounds like he was a total loser," she responded, like she knew the real story.

Georgie smiled a little bit, grateful for hearing what she hadn't realized she needed to hear. It felt good.

"Okay, well, I'm going to take a shower and finish unpacking before your family gets home. It's so great to meet you, Georgie."

"You too," Georgie said.

Before Lindsey left the kitchen, she turned around. "I gotta tell you, I'm really happy that I have a friend here in the house."

"Yeah. See you 'round." Georgie smiled.

Georgie returned to her bowl of cold macaroni and cheese. The nanny was okay, she thought. Yes, she was really pretty, and Georgie was envious of the way her waist curved in but her breasts seemed to pop out and up. She was envious of the ease with which she spoke, how she seemed so naturally happy and comfortable—someone you'd want to be around. Georgie felt like even on her good days, she was always slightly sour, bitter, or, at her best, just awkward. But she liked the nanny more than she thought she would. She seemed to care.

She checked her phone, seeing that she still hadn't heard back from Catherine. But she'd seen on Facebook that she'd been to the beach club that day. Georgie knew that she was *here*, on island, and now she wished that she had never texted her. She'd probably run into her tomorrow at the beach club and it would be weird.

Georgie and her family went to the beach club on nice days. It's where she'd spent most of her time as a kid during the summers. The Deckers almost never went to any of the public beaches on the island. The club was on Chappaquiddick, a smaller island connected to the mainland by a narrow strip of beach and accessible by a small three-car ferry that ran back and forth all day between Edgartown and Chappy, as it was called. Tourists liked to go to Chappy for the untouched beaches and to see where Ted Kennedy had driven off the bridge and killed Mary Jo Kopechne. The ferry itself was somewhat of a novelty destination as well, because of its provincial charm. Two of the ferry captains had fallen in love and gotten married on the boat the summer before.

The beach club sat on a calm stretch of sand where the only waves were the ones from boats that passed by beyond the swim-barrier rope. It was perfect for children and their parents or nannies who could keep up with them but who wanted a buffer in the form of lifeguards and helpful staff. In addition to several lifeguards patrolling the water at all times, the club had a playground, a snack bar where children could order whatever they wanted and charge it to their parents' accounts, and an actual bar for grown-ups. That bar was tucked in back of the club, behind the grill, nestled in a dark, damp shed with a faded, carpeted floor and wood paneling. The bartender was always some scrawny college kid who the dads would tip well at the end of the summer if they made the drinks the way they preferred: strong. Whenever Jonathan would order a Planter's Punch, he'd give Georgie the maraschino cherry that was thrown on top.

"Careful," he'd tell her with a wink, "you might get drunk."

The routine was always the same, or at least it used to be. Before, she would spend long afternoons there with Catherine and their other friends, swimming and playing games under the dock. She wasn't sure what it would be like now. She'd have to sit alone, farther down the beach from them. On weekends, Georgie's parents would usually come to the club for lunch and maybe a quick swim. In the late afternoon, her father would order his Planter's Punch, and her mother would have some white wine. Her parents rarely spent the whole day there. There was always somewhere else they wanted to be or something else they wanted to do, though Georgie didn't know what.

She finished the bowl of macaroni and cheese and put the dishes in the sink. Her phone vibrated on the counter, and she saw that she had a message from Catherine: Definitely! See you at the club! Georgie deflated. She had hoped that Catherine would reply with a more definitive plan. She knew what this text meant. It was the kind you sent to someone you didn't actually want to hang out with. There was nothing for her write back now. Maybe tomorrow, she thought as she went up to her room, if Catherine saw her with Lindsey, she might think that Lindsey was her friend, not her nanny. It might make her look cooler, older. Maybe Lindsey would buy her cigarettes and beer or vodka, like the kind she'd once sipped with Catherine behind the club bathrooms. She had a plan now, but she needed Lindsey in order for it to work.

Chapter 7

LINDSEY

"If the teenager doesn't like you, you're *fucked*," Rose warned Lindsey on the phone. Lindsey was upstairs in her room, about to take a shower. She let the water run so that her voice wouldn't be so conspicuous. "Seriously, you need to win her over."

"I know, I know," Lindsey said, hugging the phone between her ear and chin while pulling clothes out of her suitcase and dumping them on her bed. She still hadn't finished unpacking. "I will. We just need some bonding time." Lindsey paused. "You know, I still haven't even *met* the younger kid. How weird is that?"

"Very weird. What about the parents? Are they creeps, or do they seem normal?"

"Well, the mom is super cold. She doesn't like me, that's clear. But that might just be how she is. Not sure yet. And the dad, I mean, I haven't even seen him since Bowdoin. But he definitely gave me a *vibe*. And, I mean . . ." Lindsey paused for a few seconds, considering telling Rose what Joanna had told her. "I don't know. He seems a little sleazy, but he's probably harmless."

"Well, if he gave you a vibe, he's probably a creep. Most of them are."

"Yeah. It'll be fine. I'll get through it."

"That's right," Rose declared. "You *will*. This is just a job—remember that. You're there to work. And listen, they're probably decent people. They're just WASPs. I mean, come on, you've only been out of Bowdoin for a few weeks and you've already forgotten what those people are like? That blue blood runs *cold*."

Lindsey laughed, and it felt good to laugh, but part of her wanted to cry.

"You're right. Thanks."

"No problem. As long as you don't get swept up in the world of *Joanna O'Callahan*, you'll be fine."

Lindsey's stomach twisted. She had been about to tell Rose about the party Joanna had invited her to, but she couldn't bring herself to. Rose had reminded her of what an ice queen Joanna had been at Bowdoin, socializing only with those she deemed worthy of her presence. Lindsey didn't want to admit to her that maybe they were wrong about her. Or that maybe there was part of her that wanted to be accepted as one of those people.

"Now, I gotta go. I was hiding in the basement to take your call, but my boss keeps pinging me to come back upstairs. Literally, *kill me*."

"Hang in there, Rose. Thank you. Love you." Lindsey felt a pang of guilt for droning on to her friend when her own life seemed pretty easy in comparison.

"Love you too."

Lindsey hung up and stepped into the shower. Rose was usually right. She was practical, no nonsense. She called things how she saw them. The Deckers were probably a lovely family, Lindsey told herself, and it would just take some time to adjust to them. She did need to work on Georgie, though, she knew. She had overdone it with her downstairs. She'd been too talkative. But she had been thrown off by the fact that she had recognized her from the café earlier. She laughed a little bit to herself, acknowledging the fact that she had thought that she and this stranger shared something in common when actually, she and Georgie couldn't have more dissimilar circumstances. The truth was, Lindsey felt somewhat jealous of Georgie.

Georgie's life looked easy, luxurious, coddled. And Georgie was a beautiful girl, Lindsey thought. She was definitely going through that awkward phase where certain physical features needed to catch up to others, but Georgie had a graceful and delicate face with soft, round eyes. The girl had nothing to complain about, as far as Lindsey could see.

But she'd do what she needed to do in order to win Georgie over. Lindsey had accepted the sad reality that the kids were basically her bosses. They could complain to their mom or dad and get her fired. That would be it. And she wanted this job to work out. She wanted it to lead to something more. It *had* to. After this, what were her options?

Out of the shower, Lindsey changed into white jeans and a loose, lightweight gray sweater. She brushed her wet hair back, letting it air-dry. She wanted to look presentable and clean for the rest of the family when they came home. She wanted to look *wholesome*. She didn't even know if Jonathan would be home tonight, but if he was, she wanted to be a little bit covered up. It was still slightly too warm for the sweater, but it was the only thing that would disguise her breasts, so she put it on.

It was almost six o'clock when Lindsey came downstairs. Descending the staircase, she realized how steep it was. She gripped the banister as she walked. She could hear Carol talking to a child—Berty, she guessed. She took a deep breath.

In the kitchen, Carol was cutting a store-bought rotisserie chicken, its black plastic package out on the counter next to it. On the stove, a pot of broccoli emanated an earthy steam. Berty sat on a stool at the kitchen island, banging his silverware on the counter, watching his mother as she stabbed a few slices of the chicken and unloaded them onto plates. Her movements were clunky, as though the act was entirely foreign to her.

Carol turned from the stove, holding the pot of broccoli in one hand and ladling it onto a plate with the other. "Lindsey," she said, looking up, "how was the rest of your day? Are you all settled in? Anything you need?" Lindsey got the sense that the last question was rhetorical. It didn't seem like Carol would help Lindsey with anything she might need.

"My day was wonderful," Lindsey said, the adjective feeling odd coming out of her mouth. It was one of those words that she wouldn't normally say, but she felt like she had to elevate her speech around Carol. "Edgartown is so beautiful," she added. "I think I've got everything I need. And my room is perfect. Thank you."

Lindsey wasn't sure where to stand in the kitchen. Berty gave her a quizzical look, like she was already doing something wrong or unusual. Lindsey waited for Carol to say something, to introduce her.

"Great," Carol said instead, placing the pot in the sink. "So glad to hear it."

Lindsey nodded. The air felt tense, like Carol was scolding Lindsey for something she'd unknowingly done. Berty started to eat his food, ignoring Lindsey. He seemed used to a revolving door of nannies and household help. She decided to introduce herself to him rather than wait for Carol to say something.

"Hi," she finally said. "I'm Lindsey."

"Hello," said Berty, who looked up from his food briefly. He seemed small for his age, with a delicate frame, his bony arms covered in light peach fuzz.

"You must be Berty," she said. He nodded.

"Yes," he said. "Why yes, indeed!" Berty held his silverware up in the air now, waving it triumphantly, and he burst into laughter. Lindsey wasn't sure what was so funny, but she smiled.

Carol began cleaning up the rest of dinner. "So," she said, "Berty usually eats dinner around this time. Something easy, you know, chicken, whole wheat pasta." She briskly wiped down the countertops as she spoke. "And some vegetables. He likes vegetables. We get most of our things from Morning Glory."

"Do not," said Berty. "I do not like vegetables, indeed!" He burst into laughter again.

Carol continued, ignoring him. "He likes fish, too, once in a while. And always a glass of skim milk with dinner."

Lindsey nodded. "Got it," she said. "No problem." Without actually saying it, Carol had made it clear that Lindsey would be cooking Berty his dinner every night. Thankfully, Lindsey did know how to cook because of her own mother. But what if she hadn't known how?

While Berty ate, Carol explained the nightly routine. It seemed as though she had recited the instructions many times before, from the way she rattled off timelines and systems without pausing to remember anything. Dinner around six, free time for a couple of hours, and then a bath, putting on pajamas, brushing teeth, and bed.

"Sometimes his free time can include watching a movie, but only if it's one of the DVDs on the bottom shelf," Carol added. "And he likes being read to until he falls asleep. I don't always have time for that, but he'll be up all night if you don't do it." Lindsey glanced at Berty, relieved to see that he was engrossed in the bubbles in his milk. "And once in a while you can take him to the Dock Street Coffee Shop or to see Henry at the Edgartown Inn for breakfast—those are his favorites."

Tomorrow's schedule was typical, Carol said, and began at seven thirty in the morning, with breakfast for Berty, then his tennis camp, then playtime at the beach and sailing two days a week in the afternoon. Georgie couldn't believe how busy Berty was. He was *five*! She wondered if he actually liked all the activities or if anyone had ever even asked him.

"Oh, and *about Georgie*," Carol said. "She's at that age where, you understand, she doesn't want to be told what to do. But she should really be in bed by ten, if possible. She will tell you that she's allowed to be up later than that, and if you try to insist on it, she will fight you, but she's only fourteen, for God's sake." Lindsey nodded, already knowing that she wasn't going to force a bedtime on Georgie. It didn't benefit her to make an enemy out of the girl, and she knew better than to try to discipline a teenager with a bedtime. "Oh, and save her some of whatever you make for dinner. She'll also tell you that she won't want to eat dinner with Berty, but she will want dinner at some point." Carol sighed when she said this, like she had exhausted herself.

"Will do. I understand," Lindsey said, unsure of how else to respond.

"All the important numbers are on the fridge. And you can always text or call me if anything comes up." Carol paused. "If it's an emergency, I mean."

Lindsey nodded, hoping she'd never have to call her with an emergency.

"Tonight, I'll be just a few blocks away at the Victors' house for dinner," Carol added. "They live just over on South Summer." Lindsey was surprised; she had met Berty only a few minutes ago, and she barely knew Carol. Now she was being left alone with her kids on the very first night?

"Great," Lindsey said. "Thank you." She wasn't sure why she felt the need to thank her. All she was doing was taking instructions.

Carol went upstairs, and Lindsey sat with Berty as he ate.

"I have a pet butterfly," he whispered as soon as Carol left. "His name is Ocean. I guess maybe I will show you later. He lives in my room."

"Wow," Lindsey said. She wasn't sure why Berty was whispering. It was as though he felt the need to hide anything that brought him joy. "I'd love to see him."

"Maybe, maybe!" Berty kept laughing. He had a lot of energy, and for a brief moment, Lindsey understood Carol's exhaustion.

She made herself a small plate and picked at it while Berty finished his dinner. When he was done, he pushed his plate away and sprang off his stool. "*Cinderella!*" he screamed, pointing to the television. "I want to watch *Cinderella!*"

"Sure," Lindsey said, smiling. "We can do that." She found the DVD on the bottom shelf and started the film. Berty splayed himself on the floor and glued his eyes to the screen.

Lindsey cleared the dishes and put them in the dishwasher. She wrapped up the leftovers for Georgie and put them in the fridge. She wondered where Georgie was; she hadn't seen her since that afternoon. She thought about calling her down for dinner but chose against it. That would only annoy her, she decided.

She sat on the sofa. Berty was still on the floor, immersed in the film. Cinderella's evil stepsisters were ripping apart the dress that she and her mouse friends had sewn. Cinderella was crying in a heap of torn ruffles in the garden. Berty howled when the fairy godmother appeared.

"Not that movie again. Turn it *off.*" Lindsey heard a loud male voice bellow from the kitchen. Jonathan was standing there, holding a briefcase, a blazer hanging off his arm.

Berty froze and then turned to Lindsey. She reached for the remote control and frantically hit the "Stop" button. The screen paused on an image of Cinderella looking up at the fairy godmother as her old gown started to transform into a new one. She turned the television off completely.

"Berty, we've talked about this," Jonathan said, moving closer. He hadn't acknowledged Lindsey yet. She felt like one of his children, too, caught in the middle of a terrible act, and she braced herself for a scolding. "*Cinderella* isn't for you. Pick another film."

"Okay," Berty said, still on the floor but now sitting up, cross-legged.

Lindsey stood. "Hi," she said. "It's Lindsey." She wasn't sure if she should extend her hand to reintroduce herself. "Nice to see you again."

"Lindsey," Jonathan echoed. He stood a few feet away from her now. He was so tall and towering that it felt like his eyes cast spotlights down her entire body. "Glad you're here. All settled in?"

"Yes, everything is great. Really happy to be here."

"Good, good." Jonathan stood there for a minute, looking at her. She hoped that Carol wouldn't come downstairs in that moment. The air felt tense, uncomfortable, and she wasn't exactly sure why. Jonathan was still wearing a tie, but he'd loosened the top button. She could see that his neck was slightly sunburned. She wondered if he flirted with women at work. She wondered what his type was, and then she pushed the thought from her mind, ashamed.

"I'm going to go upstairs, then. I decided to come down to the island a few days early. Usually I fly down on Fridays." Lindsey realized that Jonathan hadn't hugged his son. Neither one of them had approached the other for any kind of embrace.

"By the way," he said as he left the kitchen and headed for the stairs, "some good friends of ours are having a Fourth of July party in a few weeks. The Fitzgeralds. We'll all go; we always do. You'll come with us."

"Great," Lindsey said. "Sounds fun."

"Well, the point is, these friends own one of the best galleries in Boston. It's called The Dempsey. Contemporary art. Just spectacular. If we play our cards right, they might land you a job there this fall."

Lindsey was surprised. Perhaps she had totally misjudged him. He was a busy man, and he had thought of a potential job for her, just as he'd promised he would back at Bowdoin.

"Thank you—that sounds amazing. I really appreciate this." She wasn't sure what else to say.

"This is all assuming, of course, that this summer goes well." He smiled, giving her the quickest spark of a wink, and then turned and went upstairs.

"New movie," Berty whispered. He was now rolling on the carpet in front of the television, waiting for her, or perhaps he had been waiting for his father to leave. He seemed upset, but Lindsey got the feeling that he'd had similar interactions with his father many times before. Jonathan might not have been as progressive as her adviser at Bowdoin made him out to be, she thought as she smiled at Berty and shoved a copy of *Milo and Otis* into the DVD player. It seemed like a safe choice.

She sank back into the sofa. Had Jonathan really just *winked* at her? She hugged her arms into her chest. And what did he mean, if the summer *goes well?* Lindsey felt sick. She wondered if coming to the Vineyard was a huge mistake. But it was too late now. She started to feel trapped in the Deckers' house. And for a moment, she desperately missed her parents and her childhood home.

A moment later, her phone buzzed with a text from Joanna: Party starting around 10. See you then!

Sounds good, she wrote back, pleased that Joanna had reached out to her to follow up. Now she just had to wait. It was still early. She made herself a cup of tea and scrolled through her phone while Berty watched the movie. *What is everyone* doing *upstairs?* she wondered. Georgie still hadn't emerged.

A few minutes later, Carol came downstairs. "I'll probably be home around ten or so," she said as she wrapped a shawl around her shoulders in the foyer. "Good night, Berty. Mommy loves you." Her voice trailed off as she left the house. Lindsey just sat there, confused; Jonathan hadn't left with her. Was he not joining her?

The sun had just set, and Lindsey looked outside. The sky was a bright burnt orange, and the ocean water looked black like oil. The moon was already visible in the sky—just a sliver, like a stray peel of onion cast aside.

"Be good, Berty," she heard Jonathan say a few minutes later. He was standing in the kitchen doorway. He had changed out of his suit into khakis and a light-blue sweater. "I'll be back later," he said to Lindsey. "I'm sure Carol will beat me home."

He left the house. Lindsey took out her phone and texted Rose: Okay, verdict is in. They are weird. The dad is really creeping me out. They might even be separated but living together? Really can't tell. No one in this family TALKS. Miss you.

Weird, Rose wrote back seconds later. Just keep your head down, do your job, don't get involved.

When the movie ended, she took Berty upstairs and helped him brush his teeth. In his room, he showed her his butterfly, which was wrapped up in a hanging cocoon in a glass terrarium. Berty smooshed his nose against the glass.

"Almost time!" he yelled. "Ocean is in the *lava* phase." Lindsey felt a funny feeling of sympathy for the unborn butterfly, being trapped in a cage within the Deckers' house.

Carol hadn't told her where Berty's pajamas were, and she felt strange going through his drawers to find them and then helping him put them on before bed. She'd just met him. But he seemed comfortable with her, easily letting her pull his pajama shirt down over his head and then picking out a book for her to read to him. She wondered when he had last been hugged by his parents, or by anyone.

Chapter 8

GEORGIE

Georgie stayed in her room while Berty ate dinner. She was hungry, but she refused to eat with her little brother. It was too embarrassing to do that in front of Lindsey. If she wanted to be actual friends with her, then she couldn't risk putting herself in situations that would make her look like a little kid. She sat on her bed and stared out the window, down toward the lighthouse. It was just before sunset. People were still scattered across the sand, huddled together in sweatshirts, sitting on blankets, having fun. She felt lonely.

She got up from her bed and stood before the mirror on the inside of her closet door, examining the way her thighs touched. She lifted her shirt to examine the little roll of fat around her belly button. She stood to the side and inhaled deeply, sucking in her stomach, trying to make it concave. After a few seconds, she released her breath and pulled her shirt back down. Georgie hated that her body was caught between how it used to be and how it was going to be someday. She wanted it to just go one way or the other. But that's how she felt about her life: locked between two things, not really existing in the middle. She retreated back onto her bed.

Curling her body over toward her bedside table, she reached out and grabbed her journal, a basic spiral notebook from CVS. She used to call it a diary but last year started calling it a journal instead. That felt more serious. She uncapped a pen.

Thin, Georgie wrote. She was making a list of things she wanted to be when she was older. She'd once read in *Seventeen* that if you wrote things down that you wanted in the future, they would happen, so she had started doing that once in a while. It was all about trying to create your destiny instead of living out your fate or something like that. *Successful,* she scribbled. *Owns a house in California,* she added. Then she crossed that out and replaced it with *Owns an apartment in New York City. Drives a convertible,* she wrote. *Married to,* she started to write, biting the end of her pen in consideration—*Brian Fitzgerald.* She pulled a small rose quartz gemstone out of her bag, something she'd bought at an airport gift store in Hawaii two years ago on a family vacation. It was supposed to promote self-love and friendship. She rubbed the stone in her fingers and assessed her future on the page, trying to wish it all into existence.

She decided that twenty-two was the age when she might actually be able to have these things, at least some of them. In Georgie's mind, twenty-two was the year when everything would come together. Weight would evaporate off her bones, her lips would slightly inflate, her jawline would sharpen, her legs might even elongate. And best of all, she'd be done with school. She'd be done with being told what to do, how to be, where to go, how to get there. She would no longer have to be clustered with her classmates or forced to do mundane homework assignments. She'd find the most amazing friends in the city, or she'd reconcile with Catherine and their other friends, and they'd all live fabulous lives together. Twenty-two was the age when she could *be.* Twenty-two was *freedom.* She just had to hold on until then.

She sometimes wondered what her own parents had wanted to be when they grew up and if they had ever wanted to live somewhere besides Boston, where they were both from. Her dad was from Boston, anyway. Her mom was from the south shore of Massachusetts, but she didn't talk much about her childhood. Georgie couldn't remember much about her grandmother, Carol's mom. She'd died when Georgie was six. But Georgie remembered the way her grandmother smelled like menthol cigarettes and how it sounded funny when she said *Carol*, putting a strong emphasis on the first syllable of the name, exhaling it in a nasal huff. She seemed to be a different species altogether from Carol. Georgie could tell, even as a child, that Carol never wanted to take her and Berty to the nursing home for their twice-yearly visits. The visits were quiet. No one had anything to say. Carol's father had died before Georgie was born. Georgie had never seen her mother's childhood home, never known what kind of school her mother went to, who she was as a teenager, what her hopes were, what she wanted her life to be. Georgie sensed that her mother was relieved when her grandmother finally died.

Georgie's father's parents had both died, too, but Georgie and Berty got to spend a lot of time with them before they passed. They had lived just around the corner from the Deckers, on Beacon Hill, and then they spent their last few years in a nursing home in Belmont. They had been very involved in Georgie's and Berty's early years, coming to school plays, recitals, family dinners. Sometimes Georgie's dad still talked about his parents like they were alive. Right after they died, he'd talk about them as if they were watching over, approving or disapproving of the family's behavior. "Mother wouldn't approve of this," he would say when Berty would act out.

Last year, Berty had started speaking in his version of a British accent. At first, the family thought it was funny, but it quickly began to drive everyone crazy. Eventually, Jonathan scolded Berty at dinner one night. "It's time to stop acting like someone else," he had snapped. "Enough is enough, Robert. Your grandparents would be ashamed." The family ate in silence for the rest of the meal.

As instructed, Berty stopped using the accent after that. But he couldn't help himself from saying "indeed" after almost everything.

Jonathan and Carol ignored it, considering it a trade-off that they'd tolerate. Georgie rejected Berty's odd behavior. She was embarrassed by him and didn't like not knowing whether he would erupt into a comedic fit in public at any moment. After one of his hysterics, Georgie narrowed her eyes at him. "You're so *weird*," she said. "What's wrong with you?" At first she thought he might cry, and she opened her mouth to apologize. But then his face quickly turned into a smile. "I guess I *am* weird," he responded, and went about his day.

She envied Berty for this. She wished that she was as sure of who she was, as proud of it. Her little brother defied all the norms by which Georgie felt stifled. Whereas Berty inherently knew who he was, Georgie was constantly looking around her for sources of inspiration simply on how to *be*. She watched television shows about twentysomethings living in Los Angeles, and she studied the way they spoke and flipped their hair, the way they bit their nails when they were stressed out or the way they sucked on the straws of their drinks when they were on dates. Georgie would try these things out, but she never felt natural doing it. Conversations were the thing that gave her the most anxiety. The truth was, sometimes she just had nothing to say that she considered worth saying. Sometimes her mind was just blank. Her parents and the other adults she knew seemed to have an ability to just talk and talk and talk. Was that a skill they learned over time? Or was there something wrong with her? What was there even to say at a certain point? she wondered.

One of the results of her social uneasiness was that Georgie often said nothing at all in conversations until she exploded with a comment or question that she knew wasn't really appropriate. It was actually all part of an effort to turn the attention away from herself and back onto others. She relished the brief moment of comfort it provided her while it made others squirm. But she knew that it wasn't always kind.

"You can't just put people in the hot seat like that, Georgina," her mother had said last Thanksgiving when Georgie had asked her aunt Barbara, her father's sister, whether she and her husband, who hadn't come to dinner that year, were getting a divorce. Georgie had heard her parents talking about it before Barbara arrived, and it seemed like everyone wanted to know, so she decided to ask Barbara in the middle of dinner.

"But it's not like I'm asking something out of the blue," Georgie responded to her mother. "I mean, you guys were talking about it behind her back! At least I asked it to her face."

"There are certain things that are simply not *yours* to discuss," her mother said. "Things that should only be discussed in private. And there are certain things that should never be discussed at all. Certain things that are meant to remain secret."

Georgie was confused by this. Obviously she knew better than to blurt out someone's secret. But it seemed to her that all the adults in her life kept everything trapped inside, even the things that everyone else knew to be true. They talked about things only in stunted whispers, in corners, under covers. Georgie thought it felt more honest and decent to talk about things in the open. She had things on her mind, and if she wasn't supposed to talk about these things, was she just meant to keep them stored away, festering and rotting and spiraling in the back of her brain?

After that Thanksgiving dinner, Barbara had pulled Georgie aside when everyone was in the living room digesting pie and doing puzzles. Barbara had seen the angry look that Carol had shot Georgie at dinner.

"Sweetie," Barbara said, "I don't mind that you asked me about the divorce."

Georgie was relieved. While she didn't totally understand her mother's scolding, it had still made her feel deeply guilty, and she had spent the hours after dinner sulking, unsure of how to apologize to her aunt.

"And," Barbara continued, "to answer your question, we *are* getting a divorce. But I'm happy about it. The truth is," she said, her mouth turning into a slight smile as she leaned closer to Georgie, "I just don't want to upset your mom. I'm totally fine talking about it, but you know how she can get about these things. Better to just keep it between us."

This confused Georgie even more. Turns out, it wasn't Barbara who was offended by the question but rather her own mother, and Georgie would have had no idea had Barbara not told her. Georgie didn't understand why conversations had to be such a minefield, like a game of emotional hopscotch with endless rules: careful not to offend this person by saying that, careful not to ask about this topic, only talk about those things with those people, and on and on. It made no sense to her that information about one person's life sometimes had to be kept secret just to protect someone else who wasn't even involved. With all these rules, Georgie felt that it was safer for her to say nothing at all going forward, for fear that she'd let something slip.

Down the hall, Georgie heard her parents talking. Her father must be home, she realized. She put her journal away and went into the hallway. Their bedroom door was slightly ajar, and she could make out their conversation clearly now.

"Why don't you just come to the Victors' with me? What am I going to tell them, that you're still in Boston?"

"I don't care what you tell them. I'm not going." Sometimes Georgie thought her parents sounded a lot like Berty when he was tired or hungry.

Georgie knocked on their door.

"Hi, Dad," she said. He turned around to face her.

"Hi, kiddo," he said, giving her a quick squeeze. Carol was sitting at her vanity, putting on earrings. "Your mom tells me you got the job? That's my girl."

Georgie nodded. "My first day was today!" She looked over toward her mother, who was focusing on the contents of her jewelry box.

"Well, then, we have to celebrate. What time do you finish work tomorrow? Why don't we all meet at the beach club for a late lunch?"

"Great!" Georgie said. "I think I can finish around two."

"All right, then." Her dad smiled at her. "Carol?"

"Fine," she said, still sitting. "Perfect." She rose and retreated into the bathroom.

"It's a plan. I'm going to finish some work downstairs. Great work, Gigi." Jonathan patted Georgie's head as he left the room. Georgie was alone, for a minute, in her parents' bedroom. The bathroom door was shut. She heard water running. She considered, briefly, ducking her head into the bathroom to see if her mom was okay. But she felt like she didn't know how to. What would she say? She went back to her own room.

A little while later, she heard her mom leave. By now, Lindsey had tucked Berty into bed, she figured, and it was safe for her to go downstairs and eat dinner. Her dad was probably working in his study. Just as she opened her door, Lindsey poked her head out of her own room down the hall.

"Oh, hey," she said. "I left you some dinner."

"Thanks," Georgie said. It was like the nanny knew what she was thinking. It bothered her.

"You know your dad's home, right? Or he *was* home. But he just went out."

"I know," Georgie said and went downstairs. She wasn't surprised, but she actually *hadn't* known that he had left for the evening. He wasn't going to meet Carol at the Victors'. He was going out alone, to the Reading Room, his men's-only club, or maybe even to a bar, wherever. He did that sometimes. Georgie knew. Everyone knew. They just didn't talk about it.

Chapter 9

LINDSEY

Berty asked her to read *One Morning in Maine*. It was a story about a young girl in a small coastal town in Maine who wakes up with a loose tooth, which almost derails her big plans for the day to go out in the boat with her dad. Berty ran his finger over each page of illustrations, his eyes wide, savoring every word as Lindsey read. "My dad took us to get clams once," he said when Lindsey read a scene in which the father takes the young girl and her sister digging for clams on the beach. "I know how to do it." Lindsey smiled at him. Berty asked her to read it a second time, but he fell asleep before she was halfway through. She turned the light out and shut his door.

Lindsey changed her clothes. She'd been planning her outfit in her mind all throughout the evening: a short denim skirt, a black cotton tank top, her blue hoodie, and flip-flops. The outfit flattered her because it showed off her legs, which were always tan and toned from running outside. Her shoulders and face had darkened just from the ferry ride that morning, and she thought she looked pretty, summery. She always tanned easily, unlike everyone else in her family, and no one knew where she got it from.

When she was a kid, Lindsey would tell her parents that she was sure she was adopted. It was the only way to explain her deeply bronzed skin and her parents' own pale complexions. She stopped saying that when she got a little bit older, though she always secretly wished that it might be true somehow. It wasn't about the color of her skin. She felt like she was different from her parents, more ambitious, more *something*. She loved them and was grateful for the life they had given her, but she always wished that she might someday discover something else about herself that proved her differences, like she'd been destined for a different path or that she'd had some secret, exotic heritage all along. But these wishes were fleeting, and for the most part, Lindsey accepted the reality that she was inherently ordinary. She knew that if she wanted to change herself, she'd have to change her circumstances. She would never be able to alter her DNA.

After getting dressed, she went down to the living room and cleaned up the kitchen. She noticed that Georgie had come down for dinner while she had been reading to Berty. She'd left her dirty plates out on the counter. Lindsey cleared them and wiped down the counters, somewhat resentful.

She sat on the floral couch in the living room and scrolled through her Facebook feed in the silence of the house. Many of her Bowdoin classmates who had landed cushy jobs on Wall Street or came from trust-fund families had posted photos of themselves drinking on rooftop bars and meeting after work for sushi or tapas in dark restaurants with beautiful waiters. Even though no one could see her alone in the Deckers' living room, she felt ashamed. Her desire to go to the party only intensified as she waited for Carol.

Around ten o'clock, Carol returned home, just as she said she would. Lindsey rose to greet her.

"How did the evening go?" Carol asked, placing her purse down on the front hall table and heading toward the stairs. Lindsey opened her mouth to respond, but Carol just kept walking up the stairs. "Thank you," Carol chirped from the second floor now. "Good night."

Lindsey stood there, hearing Carol's footsteps to the master bedroom. She heard the door close. She waited a few seconds. Maybe

Jonathan would be right behind Carol. But there was only silence. He was somewhere else entirely, she suspected.

Lindsey took out her phone and texted Joanna. I'll be there in about 30. Earlier that day, Carol had mentioned to Lindsey that the family had several bikes out front and that Lindsey should feel free to use one whenever she wanted. She had looked up the location of the party on her phone. *Left Fork,* as Joanna had told her. It was hard to find, because Left Fork was an unofficial nickname for part of one of the public beaches, named for its location down the left fork of the main road. *Go right and you'll find crickets, but go left and you'll find action,* Lindsey learned from the internet. It was just a fifteen-minute bike ride away. Lindsey waited a few minutes until the house fell asleep and the silence felt heavy and dense, like the air was made of wet cement. Then she slipped out the front door, being careful not to let it slam behind her.

Outside, the night air was warm and the stars were bright. She took one of the bikes and began to pedal away from the house. The bike had a wicker basket hanging off the front handlebars. She pushed on the pedals and cruised down the street, feeling the wind against her skin and through her hair. For a few seconds, the ride was exhilarating, and she felt far away from everything.

The neighborhood was still and dark, but a few blocks away, downtown Edgartown was alive with people coming in and out of bars and restaurants. Lindsey felt like she was going somewhere secret that none of these people knew about, and it made her feel special, like she belonged there.

She wove through the downtown streets toward Katama Road, standing on her pedals and leaning forward occasionally. She made sure to stay to the left when the road forked about a quarter mile up. The road had a well-maintained bike path, but there were no streetlamps to guide her. The houses were set too far back from the road to provide any light, so she had to bike slowly and carefully, staring straight ahead at the path with a steadfast gaze, the pavement rolling underneath her like a black ocean.

The path ended where the beach began, in a sudden way that caught Lindsey off guard and made her feel a wave of nerves, like she had somehow expected the road to go on forever. A few SUVs were parked in a small dirt lot, at the center of which was a narrow path leading to the beach. Lindsey propped her bike up against a bike rack, readjusted her tank top and the waistband of her jean skirt, and smoothed down her hair. She fixed a wedgie that she'd formed on the ride, glancing around first to make sure no one was there. She took off her flip-flops and decided to carry them with her, hooked between two of her fingers.

The path sloped upward and then dropped down to the beach and ocean so that she couldn't see the party as she ascended, but she could hear it: the crackling of a fire, laughter, the clinking of beer bottles, soft music. When she reached the top, she could see it, a few yards down the beach. About a dozen people were gathered around a small bonfire. She couldn't distinguish anyone's features in the dark; they were silhouettes against the flames. She kept walking, but her movements slowed, and she grew nervous. What if this wasn't the right party? It was too hard to tell from this distance in the dark. What if Joanna wasn't there for some reason? Part of her wanted to turn back, but she continued on. Her body stiffened as she walked toward the group, the people around the fire coming into focus.

She was relieved when Joanna saw her approaching and yelled to her.

"Lindsey!" Joanna rose and trotted toward her, embracing her in a hug. Lindsey could smell alcohol and something fruity, like strawberry. "I'm so glad you came!" she exclaimed. It was odd to hear her own name yelled out by Joanna with such exuberance. Joanna grabbed Lindsey's hand and pulled her toward everyone. "Guys, this is Lindsey!" Lindsey held her hand up in a robotic wave, uncomfortable with the introduction. A few people looked up and muttered "Hey" and "'sup."

"Here," Joanna said, thrusting her a Smirnoff Ice. Lindsey took a sip, inhaling the distinct scent of lemon and sugar. It felt sticky on her tongue.

Joanna tumbled down onto the sand, landing with her legs crossed like a pretzel. She was wearing white shorts and a blue cashmere sweater. Lindsey carefully sat down next to her. On Lindsey's other side was a skinny boy with pronounced cheekbones. He was wearing a backward hat and a Patagonia fleece jacket. He introduced himself as Whitney.

"Cheers," he said, clinking his beer can against her bottle. "Where are you visiting from?"

Lindsey wasn't sure why it was so obvious to him that she was a visitor. "Maryland," she replied.

"Nice," Whitney said, looking into the fire. "Bethesda? Chevy Chase?"

Lindsey hesitated before replying. "Rockville," she said, adding quickly, "basically Bethesda." Whitney nodded but didn't say anything else. The confidence that Lindsey had felt on her bike ride started to slip away.

Lindsey's eyes were still adjusting to the darkness after a few minutes. She looked across the fire, not knowing anyone but Joanna. Everyone looked about her age. Most of the girls were beautiful, with skinny bodies and long hair that blew across their faces. It was like they were all different versions of Joanna in pastel tops.

Across the fire, Lindsey saw a face she recognized. It was the same guy she had seen earlier that day at the Picnic Basket, the one with the big lips and the pink nose. Except the pretty girl whom he had spanked wasn't with him now.

The guy caught Lindsey's gaze across the fire. Between them, bright-yellow sparks spiraled upward before disappearing into the sky. He smiled at her and nodded, like he recognized her. Lindsey instinctively smiled back but quickly looked away. She could still feel his eyes on her. She tried to talk to Whitney, but he had turned his attention toward a cluster of people on his other side who were talking about boats, a conversation to which Lindsey could add nothing. And Joanna was in a deep flirtation with an arrestingly handsome, chiseled guy who leaned back on his elbows, though she kept glancing over at the guy from the Picnic Basket, as though trying to get his attention. Lindsey had nowhere to go and no one to talk to, and her face burned, knowing that the guy was still staring at her.

She decided to go get another drink from the cooler. She had finished her first one quickly, needing something to do with her hands and mouth while she sat there. She stepped away from the fire and walked a few paces toward a large cooler, which she discovered was filled with melted ice, cans of beer, and a few remaining Smirnoffs. She took a beer, opening it slowly, dreading her inevitable return to the bonfire where she'd have no one to talk to. The beer tasted sour and frothy.

"Hand me a Natty Ice, would you?" She heard a voice from behind her and knew it was the guy from earlier.

She picked up another beer from the cooler and handed it to him, her body only partly swiveling around to face him. She said nothing.

"I'm Brian Fitzgerald," he said, extending his hand. *Fitzgerald*. It was the same name that Jonathan had mentioned earlier, the friends who were big art collectors. She hoped it wasn't the same family. She looked at his hand before extending her own to shake it. He felt warm, almost hot, and he closed his hand around hers.

"I'm Lindsey," she said, tipping her beer toward him, and walked back toward the fire. "See you."

"Hey, that's it?" he called out as she turned away. "You're not very friendly." Lindsey stopped. She glanced over at Joanna, who was watching them.

She shrugged. "I'm just cold," she said. "I want to get back to the fire."

His eyes skimmed her body. "Okay," he said, nodding with a smile, like he knew that she wasn't actually cold at all. "See you around, Lindsey."

Back at the fire, Joanna turned to her immediately. "What were you guys talking about?" Joanna searched Lindsey's face for an explanation, like she'd done something wrong.

"Nothing," Lindsey responded, straightening her posture, suddenly feeling interrogated. "We just introduced ourselves, that was it. I saw him earlier today at the Picnic Basket, actually." There was an intensity to Joanna's question that made Lindsey feel like she was lying, even though she wasn't.

"Wait, when did you see him?" Joanna leaned in.

"At lunchtime. I went there to get a sandwich. I saw him there with some girl. I only remember because they were really touchy and flirty. It was noticeable."

Joanna didn't say anything, and Lindsey regretted her description of Brian and the girl. Joanna looked hurt.

"The girl's not here, though," Lindsey continued, trying to heal whatever wound she had just unknowingly opened. "So maybe I'm confusing him with someone else."

"No, you're not," Joanna said. She fiddled with her Smirnoff bottle, picking off the label. "You saw him with Jennifer. Fucking whore. She doesn't even *go* here. Her parents *rent* for a week every year. She and Brian used to have a *thing* or whatever. She's leaving the island tomorrow, thank God." Joanna stuck her finger in the sand and drew a circle. "Asshole," she muttered, looking up briefly at Brian, who was still standing by the cooler, talking to someone else now. "We were supposed to go to the beach today, Brian and I," she said, lowering her voice. "We actually dated all last summer. And this year I just thought that things were going to, you know, pick up where they left off." She paused. "Was the girl he was with tall and skinny? Brunette? Really pretty?"

"I guess," Lindsey said. "I mean, she wasn't *that* pretty," she added, to be kind. The truth was, the girl had been stunning.

Joanna sighed and looked forlornly into the fire. "Yeah. *Jennifer.*" She exhaled. "Also, that girl is literally *nineteen*—did you know that? She's not even old enough to drink."

Lindsey felt bad for Joanna, but she also didn't understand why she was so hung up on Brian. Joanna was beautiful in an effortless way, and as far as Lindsey could tell, Joanna had everything going for her: in addition to being beautiful, she was rich, confident, well educated, and popular. Lindsey didn't understand Joanna's desperation, especially not for a guy like Brian. What was so great about him?

"What is it about him?" Lindsey started to ask. "What is it that you like about him?"

Joanna looked away for a few seconds. "He's smart. So smart. He has an answer for everything. A solution for everything. That's why he left Wall Street, you know." Joanna's tone started to veer into one of justification, like she didn't believe her own words, like she had to prove something to herself. "He's got to do things his own way. That's how his mind works. So now he's working on this start-up thing. I'm telling you, he's going to be a billionaire." Lindsey nodded but didn't say anything. It seemed like there was more Joanna wanted to say.

"And when I'm with him," she continued, "I guess I just feel like I'm not *missing out* on anything else. Like there's nowhere else in the world that could be more exciting." She paused. "He makes me feel *chosen*, I guess. That probably sounds stupid."

"It doesn't, actually," Lindsey said. "I get it." She did get it. She understood better than Joanna knew just how powerful it was to feel special, to feel included. Maybe Brian was one of those guys who radiates that kind of dangerous energy, the kind that makes you feel like when you were with him, any moment was about to be the best moment of your life. "Mr. Decker mentioned being friends with the Fitzgeralds. Said they have some big Fourth of July party every year. Is Brian the same Fitzgerald?"

"Oh yeah." Joanna sighed. "That's him. Everyone knows the Fitzgeralds. They practically *own* Edgartown, and most of Boston. You'll see what I mean at the party. Everyone goes. His parents are actually really nice." Joanna paused. "I'm really glad you're here this summer, Lindsey. I know so many people down here, but none of them are real friends. If they were, they would have told me about Brian and Jennifer. You're a real friend."

"Of course," Lindsey said, taken aback. "Me too."

Joanna took another sip of her drink. "Fuck it," she said, then straightened up her back, exhaling. "I have an idea. Come with me." She grabbed Lindsey's hand again and pulled her away from the group, back down the path to the parking lot.

Chapter 10

GEORGIE

It was around ten o'clock when Georgie heard her mother come home. She knew it was her by her footsteps. She recognized the way her mother stepped with the entire flat of her foot and the familiar clang that her Tod's loafers or Jack Rogers shoes made against the wooden stairs. Georgie was in bed, but she couldn't sleep. She'd tried shutting her eyes and counting backward from one hundred. She'd tried reading a book. But she just couldn't sleep. Her leg kept twitching, and she tossed and turned, trying to find a comfortable position. She was nervous about returning to work. She wasn't anxious about the job itself anymore, now that she knew what to expect. Rather, she was nervous about potentially not having the job. The job was the one thing she felt like she had to identify herself now, to belong to, and she worried about it slipping away from her if she did something wrong. It had become important to her, so her first instinct was to panic about losing it.

Finally, she gave in to her insomnia and turned on her light. She took out her notebook again. She wanted to calculate her earnings for the entire summer so that tomorrow she could show her father what she'd be making.

When her parents had told her a few weeks ago that she had to get a job this summer if she didn't want to return to sleepaway camp, she'd gotten the feeling that neither of them actually thought she'd do it, even her dad, who usually showed more positivity and confidence in her. She knew they had assumed that she'd end up with one of those fake jobs that kids her age got, like babysitting for families who already have full-time nannies. When she'd actually landed the job at the Picnic Basket and returned home, triumphant, her mother's response had been disappointing and hurtful. Georgie had earned this job, completely on her own, and all her mother had to say about it was that being around so much food all day might not be a good idea. Once she showed her father, in meticulous detail, just how real her job was and what she'd be earning from it, maybe they'd both see that she was capable of more than they realized.

When she was done, she turned the lights off and got back under the covers. She was tired now, and it was getting late. She wondered where her dad was and when he'd be home. She wondered if her mom was asleep or if she was staying up, waiting for him. Georgie would never know. As she started to drift off, she heard the front door open and close. She waited, expecting her father's even, swift footsteps coming up the stairs. But instead, she heard silence. Someone had *left* the house, not entered it. But who would be *leaving* at this time of night? And then she remembered: Lindsey.

Georgie glanced at her phone. It was almost eleven. She remembered that Lindsey had told her about running into a friend from college. She was probably going to meet her, Georgie thought. One night on island and Lindsey already had a social life. She felt jealous as she imagined what kind of night they were having. Maybe they were going to one of the bars on Main Street. Maybe they were drinking beers out of bottles and listening to some guy tell jokes and laughing. Sometimes, when Georgie went out to dinner with her family, they'd walk home and pass some of the bars, where tan girls in strapless tops would hang on the shoulders of boys. Everyone always seemed loud and warm, spilling in and out of those bars, happy.

Or, Georgie wondered, maybe Lindsey went to meet a guy. Maybe she was on a date. Though it seemed late in the evening to be on a date.

Maybe she was just going to hook up with someone. At camp, when Georgie had kissed Leo, it had all been arranged through their friends, who had coordinated a time and meeting place for them. A boy named Ben had passed her a note during dinner one night, muttering under his breath that it was "from Leo." *Rec hall. Back bleachers. Eight p.m. Keep it secret.* Georgie snuck away from the nightly campfire and ran to the rec hall, in the dark, behind the tennis courts. Leo was there when she arrived. She sat next to him, and he leaned in and began to kiss her, sticking his tongue in her mouth and putting the palm of his hand against her breasts, which were just beginning to form like sore little mounds of dough. She had been worried, on the run over there, that her mouth was dry and that she wouldn't have anything to talk to him about. But once she got there, she realized that there wouldn't be any talking anyway, and that if her mouth was dry, he certainly didn't notice. This, she thought, was how adults did it: they just hooked up.

At school, Georgie's classmates acted like it was uncool to treat sex like a big deal, even her own friends who she knew had never even so much as held hands with a boy. But some girls she knew had already given blow jobs, or at least those were the rumors. Georgie needed to kiss Leo last summer because she was desperate to catch up to everyone else. And now, she still had a long way to go. She wondered how many times Lindsey had had sex. She wondered if she was going to have sex tonight. Georgie felt helpless, alone in her bedroom with all these unanswered questions. There was a whole world out there, and Lindsey got to go live in it, while Georgie was stuck here.

She sat still for another minute and then rose from her bed and walked to her door, opening it gingerly. The house was quiet except for the distant ding of the old grandfather clock in the formal living room. The light in her parents' bedroom was off; her mother wasn't waiting up. She looked down the hall toward Lindsey's room and noticed that the door was open just an inch or two.

She stood on the balls of her feet and inched toward Lindsey's room. She moved closer to the door, listening for any noise behind it. If she'd been wrong somehow, if she'd misheard the door opening and closing earlier, and if Lindsey *hadn't* actually gone out, then she'd just tell Lindsey that she thought she'd heard something and was checking on her. Her heart started to race as she stuck out her index finger and gave the door a gentle push. She watched as it swung open, almost on its own, as though inviting her in. The room was empty.

The room itself wasn't one that Georgie frequented. The Deckers' house had two guest rooms, both rarely used. It was disorienting, for a moment, being in her own house but in a room with which she wasn't really familiar. She thought about what it must be like for Lindsey to stay in this room and whether or not she liked it. She didn't know what Lindsey's room at her own house was like. Georgie looked around at Lindsey's belongings. A book called *Franny and Zooey* rested on the table, along with a crumpled bus ticket and a folded-up map of Martha's Vineyard. A suitcase on the floor was opened up and piled with colorful clothing, half-unpacked. A pair of running sneakers and what looked like a workout outfit were laid out on a chair. The bed was made perfectly, which seemed odd. But then Georgie realized that it was because Lindsey hadn't yet spent a night there.

Georgie looked into the bathroom. The counter was strewn with products: lotions, makeup, brushes, and a flat iron. There were makeup products Georgie hadn't seen before: a shimmery palette of eye shadows, a brown eyebrow pencil, a bright-red lipstick, an electric-blue eyeliner, a pink sponge that had been dipped in foundation. This was confusing to Georgie, because Lindsey had seemed, to her, to be so natural in her style and look. She'd never have guessed that Lindsey used all this stuff. Maybe, Georgie thought as she examined an eyelash curler, girls like Lindsey secretly used products and tools and tricks just to make them look like they didn't use anything at all. She felt like she'd been missing out. Her mother didn't let her use makeup, besides cover-up for pimples and the occasional swipe of mascara. *Tacky,* her mother would say about excessive makeup.

She ran her fingers along the shiny tops of various face and eye creams, opening up some of them to take a sniff. One was an herbal essential oil that poured out of a tiny rubber dropper. She released a drop into her palm and inhaled. It smelled like lavender and juniper berries. She rubbed it between her hands and on the sides of her neck. The scent felt luxurious and grown-up, almost androgynous, not like the lilac-scented body mist she used from Bath and Body Works. She put the product back where it was, being careful not to leave evidence that she had been there. She exhaled, relieved that she hadn't dropped or broken anything.

Before she left, she looked in Lindsey's closet. She ran her hands over the few items of hanging clothing, pausing on a white dress with sunflowers on it. Georgie took the dress out of the closet, off the hanger, and walked back into the bathroom. She held the dress up against her body, swiveling a little to each side, admiring her appearance.

She heard a noise from downstairs and froze. It was just the old house creaking, but it scared her enough that she quickly put the dress back, gave the room one last look to make sure nothing was out of place, and then darted back to her room, shutting the door behind her.

In bed, Georgie pulled the covers up to her chin. She wanted to stay awake until Lindsey got home. She wanted to know where she'd been, what she'd been wearing, what she had done and with whom. But soon, Georgie felt her eyelids grow heavy and her body start to sink into the sheets. She fell asleep, wondering what it would be like to have all the possibilities that Lindsey got to have: to go out, to have beautiful friends to share secrets with, to be free, to be independent, to be pretty, to feel the wind against your face, to drive, to drink, to wear lavender-scented oils that made boys want to smell you and touch you, and to not even care about any of it at all.

Chapter 11

LINDSEY

The way Joanna walked toward the parking lot made Lindsey uneasy. She was walking with a sense of determined purpose, her gait angry. Lindsey looked back at the bonfire as they slipped away down the beach, but no one seemed to notice that they were leaving. Away from the fire, the night sky felt darker and colder. The distant sound of the ocean rang heavy in Lindsey's ears, like someone yelling for them to come back.

"There. That's his car." Joanna pointed toward the end of the lot, toward a navy-blue Land Rover. "That's Brian's."

Joanna started toward it, and Lindsey followed. She assumed that Joanna must have left something in his car and she was just going to grab it.

When they approached the car, Joanna looked around. "What are—" Lindsey started to say.

"Shh," Joanna snapped, waving her hand behind her in Lindsey's face. *"Quiet."*

Lindsey wanted to know what they were doing, but she was too afraid to ask, as though if she did, Joanna might whip around and tell her to get lost. Walking a few paces behind Joanna, Lindsey realized how little she knew about her. She wondered if the rest of the people at the bonfire were Joanna's actual friends.

Then Joanna pulled a set of keys from her pocket, and Lindsey was sure that they were going to drive off with Brian's car, blasting the radio and laughing with their heads back. Lindsey started to walk around to the other side of the car, instinctively, to get in the passenger seat. Joanna grabbed her arm, holding her back. She held the keys out in her hand, one of them pointed forward, like it was a carving knife with which she was about to butcher a turkey. She held it still for a second and then stabbed it into the side of the Land Rover and dragged it all along the side of the car in a sudden and violent movement. Lindsey didn't realize she had gasped out loud until she found herself with her hand over her mouth, her shoulders hunched up at the sound of Joanna's key dragging through the gnarled layers of metal, breaking through and pushing inward. The key was like a snail, leaving behind a prickly road of destruction.

Before she had traced the entire car, she turned to Lindsey.

"Here," she said. "Try it." Lindsey stared at her without responding.

"Come on," Joanna goaded. "Just do it." Lindsey didn't want to; she didn't want to get involved. What if someone saw her and Joanna blamed her for the whole thing? She could feel Joanna's excitement, and she wanted to experience the same feeling. More than that, she didn't want to disappoint Joanna. So she took the key from her. It felt cold in her hand, and delicate, incapable of doing damage. She stepped closer to the car. "It's such a rush," Joanna said as she watched Lindsey push the tip of the key against the car, gently at first and then with more pressure, dragging it in a line. Joanna was right: it was a rush. She dragged a line through the car and then handed the key back to Joanna, almost tossing it, like a piece of dynamite. Joanna stepped back to assess their work.

"That'll teach him," she huffed. *"Cheater."* She exhaled. "Come on." She turned back toward the beach and started walking. Lindsey followed. Her hands were shaking. She'd never done anything in her entire life that was so blatantly *wrong*. But she justified it by reminding herself that Brian had wronged Joanna. He had lied to her. He wasn't a good guy. It didn't make it okay, and she started to become fearful of what might happen if anyone found out. But for now, she told herself, he had *asked* for it.

Joanna said nothing as she walked back to the party, Lindsey trailing behind her. As they ascended the dunes, Joanna turned back to her.

"We were peeing. *Got it?*"

Lindsey nodded, her head heavy as though she were locked in a trance. She felt fear start to set in as they approached the bonfire.

Nobody even looked up when they returned, first getting beers out of the cooler and then plopping back down around the fire as though nothing had happened. Joanna resumed her conversation with the handsome guy. Lindsey tried to join in, but Joanna turned her body away. Within minutes, Joanna and the guy were whispering in each other's ears, and Lindsey was blocked off. There was no one left for Lindsey to talk to. Whitney had disappeared, and everyone else seemed to be coupled up. She finished her beer over the next few minutes and then decided that it was time for her to leave. She felt out of place. She felt guilty. She rose, brushing the sand off her legs.

"Hey, I'm gonna head home," she said to Joanna.

"Wait," Joanna said. She got up and walked with Lindsey a few feet away from the crowd. "Thank you." She put her hand on Lindsey's wrist. Her hand felt cold. "I know what we did was a little bit crazy. But Brian really hurt me," she said, almost whispering. "He told me that he loves me, just last week. And then he acts like this . . . like, like he doesn't even care." She removed her hand, crossing her arms. "Don't worry," she said, as though she could tell that Lindsey was scared that someone would find out. "We're going to be fine. No one will know that it was us." She gave Lindsey a hug and then smiled and ran back toward the fire.

As she walked down the path toward her bike, Lindsey wondered if Joanna felt the same feelings of guilt that she was feeling. Revenge was a novel concept to her, one that she thought only characters in television shows pursued. Of course, there had been moments in her own life in which she'd wanted to cause harm to someone because of something they'd done, but she'd never actually acted on it. Her parents had taught her to forgive, to let go, to not stoop to someone else's level even if you wanted to. *An eye for an eye* was not how she was raised. She thought about the cycle of revenge. If Brian ever found out what Joanna had done, would he do something bad to her in response?

Lindsey didn't look back as she left the beach, putting her flip-flops back on in the parking lot and zipping up her hoodie. She saw a pair of headlights shining in the distance, coming toward her. The car seemed to be coming from the beach, not the road. *Shit,* she thought. Maybe someone saw them and called the cops. She mounted her bike, trying not to look at the car as it grew closer. But the pedals plummeted beneath her feet, and she nearly fell off. Somehow, the bike chain had come unhinged.

"Fuck," she muttered to herself, leaning herself on one leg. She got off the bike and kneeled down to examine the situation. She lifted the grease-covered chain and tried to put it back in its proper place, but the grease made the chain slippery in her fingers, and she struggled to set it right.

The lights from the car got closer, their beams expanding. Lindsey expected the car to keep driving on the beach past her. She remained kneeled, waiting. She was embarrassed to be alone, at night, trying to fix a broken bike just so that she could get home. But the car didn't continue on; it turned off the beach, into the parking lot, and rumbled right toward Lindsey. She looked up and was blinded by the lights but could just make out the shape of a pickup truck.

"You need a ride?" She heard a male voice from the car. Lindsey stood. She recognized the driver. It was the guy who had yelled at her outside the gas station. He was alone and wore a baseball cap and hooded sweatshirt. "That bike looks like it's giving you problems," he added.

It didn't seem like he recognized her, or if he did, he wasn't letting on. He pulled the truck up next to her so that she was standing just outside his window. She could have reached out and touched his face.

"Sure," she responded. "That would be great, actually. Thanks." Even though she knew that the Vineyard was a safe place, Lindsey would normally never get in a car with a stranger. No one would be waiting for her at home, and she didn't know her way around. Anything could happen. This was the second supremely dumb decision she'd made tonight, she thought. But she wasn't nervous, somehow. She had been nervous the entire time she'd been at the bonfire, and it was only upon this stranger's arrival that she felt her shoulders ease downward and her face relax. She felt that she could trust him.

He stepped out of the car, leaving the engine running. "I'm Dylan." He didn't extend his hand when he said that. Instead, he reached down and picked up Lindsey's bike, and as though it lacked both its cumbersome frame and heavy weight, he swooped it around to the back of the truck, placing it in the bed, under a line of fishing rods sticking out of a rack.

"I'm Lindsey," she said, watching him. She climbed into the passenger seat.

The inside of the truck smelled like freshly caught fish and stale coffee, a combination that somehow Lindsey found comforting. She noticed an open metal thermos in the cupholder, still sloshing some coffee around the bottom. The seats and floor were strewn with various things—a tackle box, a crumpled-up paper bag, a pocketknife, a wool hat, old mail. His radio was tuned to 88.7. The Grateful Dead played "Scarlet Begonias."

"Sorry for the mess," he said, as he put the vehicle into drive, as though he knew she was surveying the space. "My truck gets pretty dirty this time of year. I guess it's always dirty, though."

As they peeled out of the parking lot, Lindsey looked at the car's side mirror, and she could see Whitney standing there smoking, watching them drive away. She wondered if he had been watching her the entire time, and she felt as though she'd just been caught doing something wrong by getting in the car with Dylan. Had Whitney seen what she and Joanna had done? She felt a wave of dread wash over her, pulling her stomach into a ball. She could get fired. She wasn't sure why, but her instinct was to blurt it all out to Dylan and tell him what happened. But she didn't say anything. Even if Whitney had seen her, there was nothing to be done now.

"So where you headin'?" Dylan asked her, and Lindsey realized how quiet she'd been and how nervous she must have seemed.

"Just right into town," she said. "North Water Street."

"Oh," Dylan said, glancing sideways at her.

"I don't live there," Lindsey responded. "I mean, I'm nannying for a family for the summer. They live there. It's actually my first night on the island."

"First night here and already out at the beach parties? Seems like you know your way around pretty well." He glanced over and smiled at her for a second.

"I really don't know the Vineyard at all, actually. I just happened to run into a friend from college today, and she invited me to this party." She paused. "It was okay." She felt the need to explain to him: *That's not who I am.*

Their windows were down, and the night air rushed in and blew Lindsey's hair back. It made her cold but felt good against her skin. She imagined what it would be like to be in Dylan's truck every night—to be picked up by him and taken somewhere beautiful, somewhere under the stars, somewhere close to the ocean.

"Yeah, that's not really my scene." He turned his face toward her again, and his gaze disarmed her. "I was out fishing. No keepers tonight, though."

"Yeah, I kind of figured that from all the rods you have in back."
She laughed, but she cringed, embarrassed at her conversational medi-
ocrity. "So is that what you do? Are you a fisherman?"

"No, I'm a carpenter. Construction. But I fish whenever I can."

"That's really cool," she said, kicking herself again for sounding so
generic. Couldn't she come up with a better response?

They turned onto North Water Street. The lanterns on the street
glowed a fuzzy light, diffused by the sea mist. They looked like giant
balls of fluorescent cotton candy, bursting with tiny sugary beams. It
reminded Lindsey of a magnificent stage set. Her mother had once
taken her to see *The Nutcracker* in DC. Lindsey had stared in awe at the
glittering snow falling on the sugarplum fairy, the lights illuminating
her as she twirled among white-capped tree branches and sugar-crusted
snowflakes. The street tonight reminded her of that—a world so beautiful that it didn't seem real but rather frozen, trapped in a jewel box.
Lindsey didn't want the car ride to end. She felt safe.

Lindsey reluctantly pointed to the Deckers' house, and Dylan
pulled up in front. The house was dark except for a light above the red
front door.

"Thanks again for the ride," Lindsey said, opening the car door and
beginning to get out. Dylan got out, too, and then Lindsey realized that
he was going to get the bike for her from out of the truck.

"Right there is perfect," she said to him, whispering, as he held the
bike in his hands and walked it to the side of the house. Dylan put the
bike down and turned toward her. Standing together, Lindsey realized
how tall he was and how broad chested. She waited, not sure what to
expect but feeling like she couldn't just turn and leave. Something was
radiating between them. Was he going to kiss her?

"We better exchange numbers in case you break another bike or,
you know," he said, pausing, "get hit by a car outside the gas station."
So he did remember her too. Lindsey's face broke into a wide grin. She
couldn't help it. All this time, he had noticed her and remembered

her. She bit her lower lip, trying to stifle the intensity of it all. "Or," he added, before she could respond, "so I can take you out on a date."

Lindsey tried to come up with a witty response to counter her beaming smile, but all she could say was "Okay." She wasn't sure what to do with her hands, so she fidgeted them together and then stuck them in her back pockets. "Give me your number and I'll text you," she said, trying to regain her cool. Dylan recited his number, and Lindsey texted him: It's Lindsey, just as Joanna had done to her earlier that day. His phone chimed.

"Sorry, my date must be waiting for me." They both laughed, standing there beside the house, illuminated by the comforting glow of the streetlamps. They could hear the ocean waves gently lapping on the shore just a few yards down the hill.

"Well, I should get inside. But thanks again, Dylan."

This time, Dylan extended his hand to her. "Nice to meet you, Lindsey," he said.

His hand was warm, and his skin was rough and calloused. His fingers encased her hand easily. Her hand felt different in his than it had in Brian's. She didn't want to let go.

"See you 'round." Dylan turned and walked back to his truck, got in, and drove off.

Lindsey waited until he had turned the corner, his red taillights disappearing into the night, and then she walked quietly back into the house. Her smile was so big that she worried it might wake everyone up. She shut the door behind her carefully, trying not to make a noise. She rested her forehead on the door, just for a moment, relishing the silence and the feeling of excitement inside her.

"Did you have a good time?" She jumped at the sound. Jonathan was sitting behind her, on the stairs. How long had he been there? she wondered. Had he been watching her? Had he been watching Dylan?

She clasped her hands together, her arms creating a barricade across her body.

"Yes, thanks," she whispered.

Jonathan had a drink in his hand, something brown in a glass tumbler. He took a sip.

"Good." He nodded at her. He was blocking Lindsey's pathway to her room. She just stood there. He didn't seem to be in a rush. He sat in the silence as though there was something else he wanted to say. "Good night," he finally said. He walked toward her, and for a moment she thought he was going to lean in, try something, but instead he turned and went to his office, shutting the door behind him.

Lindsey practically ran up the stairs, trying to bounce off each step. In her room, she twisted the door's old-fashioned lock, trying the handle a few times to make sure it was really secure.

In the solitude and darkness of her room, Lindsey sat on her bed, trying to assess what had just happened. What had Jonathan wanted from her? Was he drunk? She picked up her phone and considered calling her mom or Rose. She considered booking a flight home tomorrow, forgetting it all and leaving this behind. But then she thought about how bad it had felt on graduation day when she had no options, no path forward. No, she decided, she wasn't going to leave. Nothing had actually happened. She could get through this. She had to.

Chapter 12

Georgie

Georgie left the house the next morning without saying goodbye to anyone. She was eager to get to work, but she also didn't want to see Lindsey. She was worried that Lindsey somehow might know that she'd snooped through all her things last night, that she'd held up one of her dresses in front of the mirror and imagined what she would look like in it. She took a quick shower, shaving her legs, and then put on her jean shorts again, one of her nude-colored bras that she'd die if anyone saw her wearing, the Picnic Basket T-shirt, and flip-flops. She threw her beach clothes into a bag so that she could go straight to the club after work. Her hair was still wet and dripping down her back when she ran out of the house, letting the front screen door slam behind her.

Walking into the café that day felt different. This time, Georgie knew the routine. Even though it had been only one day, she was no longer the new kid. She didn't feel self-conscious taking a blueberry muffin from behind the counter and pouring herself an iced tea. She couldn't remember feeling so confident before. This was where she belonged.

Georgie nodded hello to her colleagues, most of whom, though she didn't totally realize it, were severely hungover or maybe even still drunk from the night before and moved like slugs through the kitchen, and she took her breakfast with her into the back office. Lucy hadn't arrived yet.

Georgie's work was exactly as she'd left it the day before, so she picked up where she left off, sifting through the moldy piles of rental contracts and maintenance bills. She wasted no time, determined to make a dent in the paperwork that morning.

A few hours later, there was a knock on the door.

"Hey. Georgie, right?" The beautiful girl whom Georgie had noticed in their staff meeting yesterday had opened the door and was leaning in so that her long hair fell straight down, perpendicular to her head. Georgie just stared at her for a second, noticing her almond-shaped eyes and high cheekbones.

"Yeah. Hey."

"I'm Emma." She stepped farther into the office. "Listen, someone went home sick, so we're short-staffed. Lucy asked me to see if you could take a break from this and maybe clean up the main café area? You know, sweep, wipe the tables down, restock napkins, keep an eye on everything. Cool?"

Georgie sprang to her feet. Finally, she thought, this was what she'd been hoping for: a chance to be seen, to be part of it all.

"Of course, yeah, totally," she said, wiping her hands on her shorts. "Whatever you need."

"Great, come with me." Emma showed Georgie where the cleaning supplies were kept in a closet beside the kitchen. "Let me know if you need anything. I'm just right here behind the counter."

"Thanks, Emma," Georgie said as the girl twirled away behind the counter, smiling at a waiting customer and ringing up their order.

It was a busy time of day, the late breakfast rush and the early lunch wave, when people either wanted the last bagel or the first sandwich to take to the beach. Georgie started to sweep the floors. She'd never felt more pride in herself as she poked the broom underneath table legs, making sure to reach every corner, every slab of wood. When she finished that, she wiped the tables down and then moved to the coffee bar to restock it with sugars, napkins, and straws.

As she cleaned, she heard the jingle of the front door behind her and two male voices echo out in a way that felt too loud for the space, even on a busy day.

Georgie turned and saw that one of the voices belonged to Brian. He was with a friend, and they both sported printed swim trunks and polo shirts. Brian's face looked soft and puffy, like he had just woken up. His eyes were slightly swollen, and his hair stuck out in different directions. Georgie was tempted to reach out and touch his head, to run her hand through his hair and ruffle it like he was a dog. She watched out of the corner of her eye as they ordered breakfast sandwiches and coffees. She stayed off to the side at the coffee bar, hoping that Brian would need some milk and have to see her. He paid for his breakfast, and she could feel him moving toward her. Then, suddenly, he was right there, standing next to her. She tried to remain calm.

"I remember you," he said. He was now turning toward her, looking at her. And he *remembered* her. She had to tell herself to inhale. Exhale.

"Yeah, sailing," she said, her voice coming out as too confident, unfamiliar. Brian's friend stood to the side and stared at her, clearly annoyed. He shot Brian a glance that seemed to ask, *What are you doing, bro?* His presence made Georgie feel like she was doing something wrong.

"You were really good. Talented," Brian said as he peeled off the paper wrapping from a plastic straw. "Still racing?" He was close enough now that she could smell the muskiness of his sweat. He started to chew his straw, letting it dangle out of the corner of his mouth.

"Oh, no, not anymore," Georgie said. "I'm actually working here this summer." She felt a thrill rush through her body as she said the words.

Brian's expression seemed to change suddenly, as though Georgie had just taken off a mask and he was looking at someone else. This was it, she thought: she could finally describe herself in a way that reflected who she wanted to be. She had a job, she was independent, she would never be seen as a kid again. She hoped that her voice sounded steady. She could feel it shaking.

"Really," he said. "How old are you now, anyway?" His friend was still standing there but was looking down at his phone, impatient. Brian didn't seem to care. He was leaning against the counter, chewing his straw, and looking at Georgie.

"Sixteen," Georgie lied. She had said the word before she had processed it. She didn't even think about it. But she quickly rationalized it internally: she was just a month away from being fifteen. All she said was that she was one year older—barely any difference at all. It was hardly a lie. But it might make enough of a difference to Brian, she thought.

"Sixteen," he repeated as he jammed his straw into his iced coffee through the plastic lid. He turned the corners of his mouth up. Georgie could feel her cheeks bursting into rosy flames. "What's your name again?"

"Georgie," she said, suddenly feeling short of breath. She wasn't offended that he had forgotten her name. What mattered was that he wanted to know it. "I'm Georgie."

"That's right. Georgie." Her name sounded different coming out of his mouth, like a name she hadn't heard before, one that belonged to someone else. "Well, see you later, Georgie."

He smiled as he turned and walked with his friend to a table in back, just outside the door to the office Georgie was working in. They sat down, both of them stretching their legs out beneath them and draping their arms across the backs of the wooden chairs. The furniture looked too small for Brian's long limbs, like he was sitting in a doll's house.

Beneath her T-shirt, Georgie's chest had grown hot, and she could feel that she'd developed red splotches along her collarbone. That happened to her sometimes when she had high levels of anxiety or something embarrassing happened. She was now grateful to be wearing the Picnic Basket T-shirt, which covered it up. He had *smiled* at her. He had asked her what her *name* was. She looked around, wondering if anyone had just noticed what had happened. How could they not? It felt like fireworks had just erupted. From the cash register, Emma glanced up at her quickly. Georgie wondered if Emma had seen it all unfold and if she thought that Brian had been flirting with her. He *must* have been.

She finished cleaning up the counter and then swiftly walked back to the office, past Brian, pretending not to see him there for fear that she might explode if she made eye contact with him again. Inside the office, she shut the door and was comforted by the solitude of the space. She realized then that even though Brian had asked her name, he hadn't reminded her of *his* name, as though he already knew that he didn't have to.

Back in the office, Georgie could hear him and his friend talking, but she couldn't quite discern what they were saying. She put down a stack of papers she was sorting and moved toward the wall, slowly leaning and pressing her ear against it. The wall was cold against her skin. She felt some shame in the act of eavesdropping, even though no one could see her. But she couldn't peel herself away. She focused, trying to tune out other noises so she could hear Brian.

"Yeah, I told the cops about it . . . they say without any proof it'll be tough," she heard Brian say. Georgie pushed her ear harder against the wall. "Will cost me five grand, easy, maybe ten." A baby in the café began wailing. *Shut up, shut up, shut up,* Georgie muttered to herself. The baby's cry moved to the far side of the café, and Brian's voice somewhat came back into focus. She listened. "That townie is going to *get* it. I thought we'd moved on from the derby thing . . . I had. But if he wants to play ball, fine . . . Don't know what I'm going to do . . . He won't fuck with me again."

Georgie's eyes widened, and she found herself pushing her face even harder against the wall, trying to hear more. But the front door jingled, and the background noise increased again. She stepped away from the wall, unable to hear Brian over what had now become the lunchtime rush.

On the wall beside Lucy's desk was a small framed mirror. Georgie stood in front of it and examined her face. She could pass for sixteen, she thought. She turned her head to the side, examining her jawline and the ridge of her nose. Her hair was in a loose ponytail, and several hairs had fallen in front of her face—the really blonde ones that felt like a baby's hair. She looked pretty, Georgie thought, or at least, she told herself, like an actual teenager.

"Hey," she whispered into the mirror, "I'm sixteen. I work here." She picked up her iced tea and lifted the straw to her lips, tilting her head downward and looking up in the mirror, batting her eyelids. "No worries." She softly laughed to her reflection. "I'm around if you want to hang out." She liked the way the words came out of her mouth. It was as if, for a moment, she was someone else. She put her drink down and returned to her work. She wished that she had someone to talk to about Brian, someone to confide in, someone to nod supportively and tell her that yes, Brian was *totally* into her.

She returned to the pile of papers she was still organizing, and she tried to concentrate, but her body was still humming from it all. She could no longer hear Brian and his friend through the wall. She peered out from the office door and saw that they were gone. She felt restless and needed to get outside. The encounter had woken up her entire body.

She went over everything he had said to her, the way he'd smiled at her, the way he'd made his friend wait while they talked. That wasn't something guys did unless they liked you, she thought to herself. And why had he asked her how *old* she was? That must mean something, she decided. She thought about his smell and how the material of his shirt was thin enough to show his shoulder blades and arm muscles rising up like waves. But he was almost ten years older than she was, she reminded herself. He could have anyone he wanted. He was out of her league. Except that he'd given her just enough interest for her to latch on, and now she had started spiraling down that road of thought: *Maybe, maybe, maybe.*

The rest of the day went by slowly, each minute feeling longer than the next. She couldn't wait to see him again. Next time, she'd say something else. She'd be ready. She'd smile, or laugh, or maybe even reach out and touch his arm.

Just before two o'clock, she tidied up the stack of folders she was organizing and started to head out. As she walked toward the door to the café, she waved goodbye to the staff behind the counter and in the kitchen.

"Wait!" she heard from the back. "Georgie, hold on." Emma trotted out from behind the counter to meet her by the door. Georgie's stomach dropped. Maybe she was in trouble.

"Hey," Emma said, wiping her hands on her shorts, "some of us are hanging out tomorrow after work, probably just going to have some drinks on the patio out back. Lucy lets us chill there sometimes. So if you're interested, stick around after work tomorrow. It'll be fun." Georgie's mouth fell open. She had to rub her lips together to keep them closed.

"Sure, that sounds good," she said. "Cool."

"See ya tomorrow, then," Emma said, waving and returning to the register.

Georgie stepped outside and smiled to herself, biting her lip. She couldn't believe the day she'd had. It had possibly been the best day of her entire life. It was as if everything was falling into place. She was making friends, she was finding her own independence, maybe she was even falling in love. She felt, for the first time, like she was *in* it. She was where she was supposed to be.

Her steps felt lighter as she walked toward the Chappy ferry to go over to the beach club. She wondered if Brian was going to be there that afternoon, hanging out with his friends. She used to see him there after sailing camp, swimming or boating with his friends, though she only saw him from a distance. He never saw her. He and his friends would cruise over on his family's Regulator and tie up at the dock. She once saw him do a running somersault off the end of the dock, an act that everyone knew wasn't allowed. The lifeguard, a kid half Brian's size, threw up his hands and yelled out, "Come on, man, you know that's not allowed!" But Georgie could tell even then that the lifeguard didn't want to scold Brian. No one did. Brian emerged from the water and raised both his hands up as if to say *I'm innocent*, and the lifeguard had just smiled. There were no consequences for Brian. His type of charm worked on everyone, even other guys. He could get away with anything.

Chapter 13

LINDSEY

When her alarm went off at seven thirty, Lindsey was already awake. She had woken up a few minutes earlier and stayed still in bed, staring at the warm sunlight streaming in through the shutter slats, painting the room in bright stripes.

She'd decided not to tell her mom, or Rose, or anyone, about her strange encounter with Jonathan the night before. He was probably just an awkward guy, she told herself. Not everything has to *mean* something, she resolved. And what was he going to do, really? Hit on her in his own house with his wife and kids there? This was real life, she told herself, not a bad movie.

She thought about Dylan as she rose from bed: the ease of his walk, the way he had gently picked up her bike, the way he had looked at her directly in her eyes when he said goodbye, the way his hand felt on hers, the way her feet seemed to float off the ground when they were together. But in the light of day, she was angry with herself for thinking about him. It was obvious that Dylan wasn't part of Joanna's crowd. He was a local, a townie, and even though Lindsey had been on the island for only one night, she knew already that someone like him wasn't part of her future plans. Where could it possibly go?

She brought her phone with her into the bathroom, skimming through emails as she brushed her teeth. Her phone buzzed with a text from a number she didn't recognize. *Dylan,* she thought. She opened the text. Hey, it's Brian. Nice meeting you last night. Hope to see you around.

Lindsey let the brush hang out the side of her mouth, foam frothing at the corner of her lips. *Brian?* She had to reread the text again. She had barely spoken to him last night. She hadn't given him her number. There was no way he would have gotten it from Joanna, she thought. She decided not to respond. And then it occurred to her: Did Brian suspect that she had done something to his car? Was this his way of telling her that he *knew?*

She remembered then that Brian was a Fitzgerald, that he was part of the family who Jonathan had told her owned the art gallery. She'd been on island one night, and she'd already jeopardized her entire future. She rubbed her eyes with her palms. She knew that she had to walk a tightrope with Brian. She didn't want to lead him on, but she couldn't be rude either. She would respond to him later.

For now, she had to focus on her job. It was time to get breakfast ready for Berty. It was a beautiful, clear, sunny day, and she could feel the heated sunshine through her window, even in the early hours. Berty had tennis after breakfast, and then Lindsey was taking him over to the beach club. She was looking forward to that. She could see the club from the Deckers' living room, just across the outer harbor. The club's shoreline was dotted with red, white, and blue wooden cabanas that made the beach look like a traveling circus. From what Carol and Georgie had told her about the club, it seemed like Berty would have plenty of things to do there to keep him busy. She might even get to relax a little bit.

She got dressed, deciding on her one-piece swimsuit with navy-blue and pink stripes. It dipped low in the back, showing off the curve of her spine, but it gave her enough coverage in front to feel comfortable. On top of the suit, Lindsey put on her only bathing suit cover-up—white, loose, and with a fringed hemline. She pulled her hair back in a bun and packed a bag for the day.

Downstairs, she heard voices as she rounded the bend into the kitchen. Carol and Jonathan sat at the island, each sipping a mug of coffee. They both looked up as she walked in, and for a moment, Lindsey thought they seemed surprised to see her, like she had accidentally interrupted some intimate moment. She had started to feel that way a lot in the Deckers' house, like she was always in the wrong place at the wrong time.

"Lindsey," Jonathan said after a second. "Good morning." He smiled at her, a wholesome, friendly smile that belonged to a father, a doting husband, someone reliable and loyal. He seemed to be an entirely different person than the one she had seen last night. Had he mentioned to Carol that he'd seen her come in? she wondered. For a moment, she considered whether she had been drunker than she'd thought. Maybe she had exaggerated the interaction in her mind as being something more menacing than it actually had been.

"Good morning." She fidgeted, wishing that she'd worn real clothes over her suit instead of a somewhat translucent cover-up.

"Sleep okay?" he asked. Carol still hadn't said anything.

"Yes, great." She felt her voice raise up an octave, sounding too enthusiastic, too eager. "Everything is great." She felt her stomach rumble.

"Good, good," Jonathan said, rising. "I've got to do a little bit of work, and then I've got tennis at ten."

"What time did we all decide to meet for lunch? Two?" Carol asked him, seeming to ignore Lindsey.

"Yes, two." Jonathan gave her a kiss on the forehead, quick but gentle; then he turned and left the kitchen.

Lindsey was left alone with Carol, and despite her terrible encounter with Jonathan the night before, she somehow still felt more awkward with Carol. She smiled and exhaled. "Beautiful day, huh?"

Carol nodded. "It is a beautiful day, yes." She shut her laptop. "Berty is outside, as you can see," she said. Lindsey looked out onto the lawn. Berty was playing with what looked like a doll. "Georgie is already at work. But she'll meet us all at the club later for lunch."

"Great. Sounds good."

Carol went over some of the logistics with Lindsey again—directions to the tennis club, their account number at the beach club, what kind of sunscreen to use on Berty's sensitive skin—though Lindsey could tell it bothered Carol to do so. Her words were curt and quick, and she seemed distracted.

"I've already registered your name with the beach club. All you have to do is sign in when you get there. You can just put whatever you want on our tab. But Berty only gets one ice cream or treat a day." Carol stood and carried her coffee mug to the sink. "See you around two, then," she said and went upstairs. Lindsey felt as though Carol had given her a once-over with her eyes before leaving the room, and she wasn't sure if her expression implied that she approved of her outfit or not.

She called Berty inside for breakfast and made him a bowl of yogurt with granola and honey. He stirred it repeatedly but didn't seem interested in eating. After a few bites, he pushed the bowl away.

"I hate tennis," he whined.

"Well, think about it this way," Lindsey said, leaning on the counter so that she was level with him. "If you go to tennis this morning, then we can have the *entire* rest of the day to play at the beach. Doesn't that sound awesome?"

"I guess so," he whispered. "Okay."

She helped Berty get dressed in his tennis whites—tiny white shorts and a tiny white polo shirt with the same red, white, and blue triangular flag on it that she'd seen on Carol's shirt the day before. He even had special white sneakers just for tennis, he told her.

The walk to the tennis club was only a few minutes. It was part of the yacht club, which was located on the harbor, Carol had told Lindsey, but there was a separate area just for tennis. The club had clay courts, which smelled slightly of sulfur and created a kind of crunching noise when someone dragged a sneaker across them. Berty was in a tennis clinic with other kids his age. When they got to the club, he ran to his group immediately. They were gathered on one of the courts in back. There was a middle-aged instructor on one side of the net with a basket of balls. The kids lined up on the other side; they knew what to do.

Next to the court was a shaded area with some chairs and a watercooler. Five other nannies were already sitting there. One had a magazine open. They glanced up at Lindsey when she arrived, assessing her, the new girl. Some smiled; others didn't. Lindsey sat. She knew that none of them was the mother of any of these kids; it wasn't just that they were slightly too young to be mothers; it was that they looked different from the actual mothers. They weren't as polished; they all seemed a little bit exhausted. It was clear that they weren't there to socialize. They were working. They were outsiders. And she was one of them, a fact that she hated.

Lindsey was grateful to have a moment of peace while Berty was in his clinic. She watched as he and his friends took turns whacking their rackets against the ball, sometimes missing completely and just fanning the air. When the instructor's basket was empty, all the kids scrambled to pick up the balls and then stacked them on the faces of their rackets.

Lindsey's phone rang. It was Rose.

"Hi!" she said. "How are you?"

One of the nannies jolted from her chair and stood in front of Lindsey.

"No phones allowed," she yapped, pointing to a sign next to the watercooler with a picture of a cell phone and a red *X* over it. Rose was talking into Lindsey's ear. She nodded at the nanny in front of her.

"Rose," she whispered, "I have to go. Sorry. Call you later." When she hung up, the air was more silent than it had been before, and the other nannies stared at her.

"*Sorry,*" said the one who had scolded her. The girl had auburn hair and freckles all over her face, even on her lips. "They're just *really* strict here. No phones." The girl paused. "I mean," she said, her voice lower, "you can use them, to text or whatever, but just be discreet. Don't actually *talk* on them." Lindsey nodded. She noticed that her heart was racing. She hadn't even heard what Rose was saying. Something about her boss being an asshole.

She texted Rose: Sorry, I'm at this club where phones aren't allowed. Are you okay? She waited a few minutes, but Rose didn't respond. She'd call her later.

Looking around at the other women, she noticed that some of them wore outfits that seemed to be emulations of what Carol and other women in Edgartown wore—the flat, Navajo-style leather sandals, seersucker striped skirts, simple shift dresses—yet something about these girls seemed inauthentic to Lindsey, like they were trying too hard. She gazed down at her own clothing, at the silver Tiffany's charm bracelet that her parents had given her for her sixteenth birthday, and she knew that it was actually her own insecurity, her own feelings of inauthenticity, that bothered her, not theirs. She remembered how out of place she had felt her first week at Bowdoin.

Rose responded a few minutes later: No problem. She could tell that Rose was annoyed, even with just one text. But Rose didn't understand what this place was like, how different it was.

She looked at the text from Brian again, deciding to respond. She started typing something and then deleted it. You too, she finally wrote, hitting "Send" and putting her phone away, deciding that Brian was probably just being friendly.

When the clinic was over, the kids all high-fived one another and then ran to find their respective nannies. There was one mother who came to get her daughter, but she had been in an adult tennis clinic herself on another court.

"That wasn't so bad, was it?" Lindsey asked Berty as they left, walking down to the Chappy ferry to go to the beach club. She smelled the scent of bacon coming from the Daggett House Inn at the top of the street, and her stomach growled.

"I guess not," he said. He ran ahead of her when they got to the ferry.

"Hi, Ryan!" Berty high-fived a teenage deckhand as they walked on board. Lindsey handed him two passenger tickets that Carol had given her that morning.

They sat down on the passenger benches. Berty seemed jaded about the ferry ride; he'd taken it hundreds of times before already. But Lindsey was thrilled. The boat started to move, and it glided through the harbor, making its way to the other side just a few hundred feet over.

The club was just up the road on the Chappy side. **MEMBERS ONLY** read a sign on a white picket fence in front of the entrance. Berty swung the gate door open and barreled in. Lindsey stopped at the reception desk briefly. A young girl in a red swimsuit was manning the desk.

"Hi," Lindsey said, keeping an eye on Berty, who had gone ahead but was now waiting and looking back at her, annoyed. "I'm with the Decker family; I think Mrs. Decker called in. I'm Lindsey?"

"You're all set," the girl said knowingly.

Lindsey followed Berty forward, where the club opened up to a sweeping private beach. It was paradise. There was a long dock, at the end of which was a waterslide and a diving board. In the water was a giant inflatable doughnut and a wooden raft big enough to fit ten sunbathers. "Wow," Lindsey said to no one. The air smelled of burgers and saltwater, and there was an army of tan teenage lifeguards in red bathing suits parading around the club.

"Come on," Berty said, tugging her. "I need to get changed."

"Hi, Berty," a sun-kissed woman called out from inside the club office as they walked past it.

"Hi, Sydney!" Berty gave the woman a wave. Lindsey noticed that Berty was so much more animated outside his own home. He seemed to know everyone; he was embraced by everyone. At home, he was quiet, reserved.

In the women's bathroom, she got Berty changed into his swim trunks. "Let's *go*," he demanded impatiently once they were on. She made him wait another minute while she slathered him in sunblock.

Lindsey found a free spot on the beach, and she put her things down and then took off her cover-up. She was glad that she had worn her one-piece. Everyone at the club—parents, nannies, and kids—were all walking around in their bathing suits, but it was somehow still entirely conservative. A couple of young mothers wore skimpy bikinis and straw hats, but they were so flat-chested and thin that nothing about it was sexual. *Thank God,* Lindsey thought to herself, imagining the reactions she would have gotten if she'd worn a string bikini.

Berty liked to go off the waterslide at the end of the dock again and again. A couple of his friends from tennis were there, too, and they all took turns going off the slide, climbing up the ladder, and then waiting for their next turn. A bored lifeguard blew his whistle when one of the kids started to get on the slide before the previous kid had swum out of the way.

After a while, Berty was thirsty, so Lindsey took him to the snack bar. He wanted a lemonade. She got herself an iced tea. *Decker* was all she had to say. She wondered what the final bill was at the end of every summer. There were no prices on the menu. None of that seemed to matter to anyone there.

She and Berty went to their spot on the beach and sipped their drinks. When he was finished, he went and sat on the shoreline and started building a sandcastle. The club really was the perfect setup, Lindsey thought to herself. She could relax and suntan while Berty was just a few feet away, playing. Lindsey sank into her elbows and let the sun blanket her skin. She could get used to this, if this was what her summer was going to look like.

"Boo!" she heard, and she felt someone's cold fingers on her shoulders. She turned. It was Joanna. She was wearing a Shoshanna bikini with a pink gingham pattern and structured cups. Lindsey had seen it just yesterday in the store window of Nell. Joanna practically threw herself down onto the beach, stretching out on one of the towels that Lindsey had laid out, and released a dramatic sigh. Lindsey noticed that she was also wearing the exact Ray-Ban aviator glasses that she had wanted for herself. Now she couldn't get them.

"God, what a night, huh?" Joanna said.

"Yeah," Lindsey responded. It had been a night, though she wasn't sure which part had unnerved her the most: keying Brian's car, meeting Dylan, or the weird conversation with Jonathan. It had all become a surreal blur. "I'm kind of in shock about what"—she paused—"about what we did last night. To Brian's car." She wondered if Joanna knew that Brian had texted her. She opened her mouth to tell her but stayed silent. How would she explain it?

Joanna flipped over onto her belly, propping herself on her forearms.

"Don't *worry*," she said, swatting at Lindsey's thigh. "It's fine. In fact," she whispered, pushing her glasses down on her nose and peering out over them, looking around, "nobody will ever know that it was us. Brian totally thinks it was someone else." She smiled and raised her eyebrows.

Lindsey was relieved. She didn't like how Joanna had said *us*. She knew that she had participated in it, but Joanna was the one who'd really *done* it, in her mind. She just went along with it. Didn't that make her more innocent? she thought to herself.

"Well, that's good, I guess," she mumbled. "Who does he think did it?"

"Some townie guy," Joanna said, shifting her hips to get more comfortable on the towel. "There's this guy who has a rivalry with Brian.

Something that happened in the fishing derby a few years ago. I don't know; it's so stupid. But I guess Whitney saw the guy driving by the party last night on his way back from the beach, so obviously now everyone thinks that guy did it. Makes total sense." Lindsey's stomach tightened. *Dylan,* she thought to herself. As if Joanna knew that Lindsey felt guilty, she continued. "I mean, the townie guy *would* have done it anyway. I mean, probably." She paused. "Like, they're *enemies.* But whatever, who cares? The point is, Brian got what he deserved, and no one knows that it was us."

"Joanna," Lindsey said with caution. "That guy . . ." She paused. She wasn't sure how much she wanted to tell Joanna. She could sense already that she'd be judged if she revealed that Dylan had asked for her number and she was excited about it. "He gave me a ride home last night. My bike broke, and he saw me and drove me home. He seems really . . . nice."

Joanna rolled her eyes. "Lindsey!" She pushed her sunglasses down. "You *like* this guy. It's so obvious!"

"I don't even know him . . ." But Lindsey could feel herself smiling. "He does seem like a good guy, though." She looked around. "You don't think Brian's going to, like, retaliate, do you? I mean, Dylan had nothing to do with it."

Joanna didn't respond for a few seconds. "Listen," she said, "Brian and this guy—Dylan, right?" Lindsey nodded. "They already had a beef together. It's not like we created this. They already had it out for one another. This is just one more thing added to the list. It doesn't even *matter.*" Lindsey didn't agree with that logic. It wasn't right. Dylan was innocent. They were the guilty ones. How could Joanna just be okay with the fact that they were blaming someone else? "What's done is done," Joanna added.

Lindsey's only hope was that the whole thing might just go away. Maybe Brian wouldn't even care that much; maybe he'd just forget about it. Though she knew that wasn't going to happen. Her stomach churned.

"So has Mr. Decker flirted with you yet or what?" Joanna asked with a laugh, changing the subject. "I told you, didn't I? He's a little creepy, right?"

"I mean . . ." Lindsey chose her words carefully. She wanted to confide in Joanna, but she also didn't want to talk badly about her boss, especially when he knew Joanna's parents. "He does seem a little weird. I saw him last night when I got home. It was just . . . strange."

"Ew," Joanna huffed. "I mean, Mr. Decker is kind of hot, but he's, like, a hard *fifty*."

Lindsey shook her head and shrugged.

"Well, whatever. Next week is Brian's family's big party," Joanna said. "It's going to be so fun."

"Cool" was all Lindsey could respond. She was too distracted.

Joanna left an hour later. "I'm going home to my pool," she said, waving the sand off her towel. "It's so boring here now. All my girl-friends are gone this year. They're off in the *real* world, I guess."

Lindsey smiled, wondering if she should be somewhat offended.

"But thank God *you're* here," Joanna added.

Lindsey watched her as she left the club, her wet hair clinging to her back.

A few hours later, Carol and Jonathan showed up for lunch. Lindsey was playing in the water with Berty. They'd made up a game where he would hold on to her shoulders and she would swim like a sea creature, under and above the surface of the water. She got tired of the game after ten minutes, but Berty wanted to keep playing forever.

They heard Jonathan call from the beach. "Berty, can't you swim on your own now?"

Lindsey felt Berty's hands grip her shoulders tighter, and then he released them in one swift motion, plummeting himself into the water. He began kicking his arms and legs vigorously and swam to shore. When he could stand, he planted his feet and looked up at his father. Both his parents were standing on the beach, watching them.

"Of course I can!" Berty yelled back, yearning for approval. He ran to his towel. Lindsey followed him in, feeling uncomfortable in front of the Deckers in her swimsuit. She grabbed her towel as fast as she could and wrapped it around herself.

"We'll get a table," Carol said. She and Jonathan turned back toward the snack bar. Berty ran behind them. Lindsey tried to towel off as best she could and then threw on her cover-up. Immediately, big wet spots formed around her breasts. She pressed the cover-up over the rest of her stomach, trying to get the whole thing wet so that the spots would blend in.

Jonathan and Carol had put some of their things on a table and were standing in line to order. The menu was up above the ordering counter, so Lindsey had to crane her neck up to look. There was nothing healthy—a cheeseburger, BLT, grilled cheese, chicken salad sandwich. Lindsey wanted to order after Carol. She was curious what she was going to get.

"Hi," Carol said to the young girl at the counter. "Decker, 7625. Can we please have a cheeseburger, medium, a grilled cheese with tomato, and a garden salad with grilled chicken? Please put the dressing on the side. Jonathan?"

"A BLT, please. Thanks." It was Lindsey's turn. She had heard Carol order but didn't know what was for her or the kids.

"I'll have the turkey wrap, please. Thank you." She didn't really want that. She didn't want anything. She wasn't hungry all of a sudden. It felt too uncomfortable to eat lunch with them in the first place. They ordered a few iced teas and went to sit down.

"Georgie should be here soon," Carol said at the table. "Or at least that's what she told me."

Berty told Jonathan that he'd been off the slide a hundred times that morning. Lindsey was grateful that Berty talked so much. She didn't have anything to say.

A few minutes later, Georgie arrived. She was wearing her work clothes—jean cutoff shorts and a Picnic Basket shirt. She dumped her bag on the ground and sat down, looking around her as if she was trying to avoid someone or trying to find someone.

"Are you going to change?" Carol asked her before saying anything else. "Did you bring a suit?"

"Of course I brought a suit," Georgie said, annoyed. "I'll go change now." Lindsey shifted in her seat. She didn't see what was wrong with Georgie's outfit or why she needed her swimsuit on to eat lunch. It was as if Carol was ashamed of her in those clothes. *Work* clothes.

Georgie emerged from the bathroom in a white eyelet print dress. Lindsey couldn't tell what kind of bathing suit she had on underneath, but she had transformed from a normal teenager into a younger version of Carol—elegant, well groomed, and sophisticated. It didn't seem like her.

"So how was work today?" Jonathan asked.

"Good," Georgie responded, sipping an iced tea. "I saw Brian Fitzgerald."

Lindsey nearly choked. Did Georgie know something about what she'd done last night? Did she know that Brian had texted her? Had *Georgie* given Brian her number?

"How is he doing these days? I just saw his father at the club last week. Said Brian was working on some start-up idea. He always was a smart kid."

"Yeah" was all Georgie said. "He's really smart." Over the loud-speaker, their name was called, and Jonathan got up to go get their lunch. He came back with the food on two shiny red trays. Berty dove toward the grilled cheese.

"I took the liberty of ordering you a salad, Gigi," Carol said.

"Thanks." Georgie was pissed, that was obvious, but she didn't say anything else. Lindsey watched Carol dissect her cheeseburger. She ate the patty with a fork, ignoring the bun.

The rest of lunch went by quickly, and Carol and Jonathan left when they were finished. They gave Georgie and Berty pecks on the head and then walked out. Lindsey sensed a common feeling of relief between her and the kids when they were gone.

"We got a pretty great spot down the beach," she said to Georgie as they cleared the table.

"Cool. It's still pretty hot out. I need to get a tan."

Berty returned to his sandcastle on the shore. Georgie rolled out her towel next to Lindsey's and then took off her white dress. She was wearing a string bikini underneath, to Lindsey's surprise. Georgie looked around again, and this time, her eyes lingered on a group of girls down the beach. She dropped to her towel, lying on her stomach, and turned her head the other way.

"Cute suit," Lindsey said to her.

"Thanks." Georgie didn't lift her head. It was clear she didn't want to talk. Lindsey watched Berty for a few minutes, not saying anything.

Georgie released a sigh and flipped over, leaning back on her elbows. She turned her head toward the group of girls down the beach, her gaze settling on them. Maybe those girls had been Georgie's friends, and something had happened, Lindsey thought. Georgie hadn't mentioned any friends since Lindsey arrived.

"Everything okay?" Lindsey finally asked.

"Yeah, it's fine," Georgie said, turning to stare straight ahead at the water. "There's just, well, there's this *guy*."

Lindsey was surprised; she had assumed that Georgie was having issues with friends, not with guys. "Oh," she said, "guy stuff. What's going on?"

Georgie turned toward Lindsey so that she was on her side, as though to welcome the conversation and to keep it contained between the two of them.

"I mean," she whispered, "he's too old for me. I guess. Maybe not in a few years. I don't know. I just really like him."

"Well, how old is he?" Lindsey asked. She was thinking about how Georgie had mentioned Brian at lunch.

"I think he's, like, twenty-four?" she said. "Basically your age, I guess," she added.

Before Lindsey could even respond and tell her that twenty-four was too old for her, that she should find a nice guy her own age, Georgie interjected.

"*He* was flirting with *me*," she said defensively. "Anyway, it's dumb," she continued. "He used to teach me sailing when I was younger, and I think I've always liked him."

So maybe it wasn't Brian, Lindsey thought to herself, remembering that Joanna had said something about Brian being on Wall Street. *Must be some local kid,* she thought.

"I understand," she said, "but I think you're right. He's probably a little bit too old. At least for now. But you never know where life will take you. Maybe in a few years, when you're older, when you're eighteen, you'll be in similar places in life." Lindsey didn't really mean it; she was lying to Georgie, somewhat, but it felt like a kind lie and the right thing to do.

Georgie nodded. "You're right," she said. "Maybe it's just not the right time."

"Exactly." Lindsey couldn't believe how fast Georgie had come around.

"I mean," Georgie continued, "I've known Brian my whole life, basically, since I was a kid. Our parents are friends. I'm sure I'll still know him in a few years. Maybe later on it will be the right time."

Lindsey's ears pricked at the sound of Brian's name. What was it about this guy that everyone was so drawn to? He was charming, sure, and cute, in a way, but he seemed *ordinary* to her and somewhat arrogant. She didn't understand the magnetic pull he seemed to have on women.

"Well," she said, trying to figure out what to tell Georgie. She knew that there was nothing anyone could tell a teenage girl to convince her that a guy wasn't right for her. Georgie had a crush, and there was no going back. But she had to try. "Sometimes you think a guy is right for you, and he ends up being wrong for you." She started rambling then, telling Georgie about her own high school crush that had ended in heartbreak. Georgie nodded but didn't say anything. She took out a copy of *Glamour* from her bag and started reading.

In front of them on the beach, Berty knocked his sandcastle down with his feet, running through it with a slight scream. Lindsey looked at her cell phone but had no new messages. The phone itself felt like a duplicitous piece of evidence that she needed to bury deep down in her bag, like a forbidden weapon. She hadn't meant to, but already she had basically lied to Joanna, Georgie, and, in a way, to Dylan, and all the lies were somehow connected to Brian. She hadn't asked Brian to reach out to her, but he had. And now, not telling Joanna and Georgie that information somehow felt like she was actively lying to both of them. She hated the feeling of carrying secrets that she'd never wanted in the first place. She wished that she could extricate herself from the web she'd crawled into last night. But it was too late.

Chapter 14

GEORGIE

Georgie had wanted a string bikini for the summer more than anything. She had begged her mother to let her get one when they were out shopping on Newbury Street that spring, but Carol had refused.

"String bikinis are for *tarts*," she had said. "What's wrong with this one?" Carol had asked, holding up a tankini with a square neckline and wide shoulder straps. It was from the women's department and was one of those suits that was meant to suck everything in. "Or what about a simple, sleek one-piece? No *fussing*."

Sometimes, it was as if her mother wanted Georgie to hide her body, to make it as unattractive as possible. And Georgie noticed that even when it came to Carol's own body, she never wore anything that wasn't conservative. Carol was thin—always—and perpetually well groomed and styled, but her clothing exuded sophistication and seriousness, never sexuality. Georgie didn't argue with her about the string bikini; there was no point.

Instead, she had just waited until they were home, and then she covertly asked her father to use his credit card. He was in his office reading a book. She told him what she wanted to buy; she didn't have to lie with him.

"Mom won't let me buy one," she pleaded. "But it's what everyone wears now."

"You know I won't say no to you, Gigi," he had said, handing her his card with a smile but then quickly returning to his reading. Sometimes she wondered if he only said yes to piss off her mother, or if he said yes because he wasn't really listening to her in the first place. He often listened, but he rarely *heard* her.

In this case, as long as she got the bikini, she didn't care. She had tried to hide it from her mother when it arrived in the mail, but Carol had seen the package and opened it. She'd snatched the bikini in one hand and paraded into Jonathan's office that night.

"You want your daughter wearing *this*?" she had hissed at him. "You always get to be the nice one. And I have to be mean. Thank you for that. Thank you, Jonathan."

Georgie had hovered in the doorway, watching the exchange. Carol had stormed past her, dropping the bikini at Georgie's feet. Jonathan had looked up from his work with a smile. It was true: Her father did get to play the role of the nice parent. Carol was the only one who ever got stuck with the reprimanding, at least when it came to Georgie.

"Wear whatever you want, Georgina," Carol had called from the kitchen. "I don't care."

Georgie felt bad that she'd caused a fight between her parents, but she justified it by reminding herself that they were already always in conflict with one another. If they weren't fighting about this, they'd be fighting about something else. She just happened to be in the middle this time.

She had tried on the suit in her room. It fit her well, though she didn't quite have the confidence to wear it around the beach club, at least not without a towel tied around her waist. Still, wearing the suit made her feel older, cooler, prettier. And today was the first day that she got to wear it.

Georgie knew that it would piss off her mother if she came to the club dressed in her work clothes, which was why she did exactly that. As predicted, when she sat down at the table to join her family and Lindsey for lunch, her mother immediately snapped at her in a whispered tone. "Aren't you going to *change*, Georgina?"

"Yes, I'll be right back," Georgie said. She'd brought her bathing suit and a cover-up in her bag, but she'd purposely worn her work clothes not only to annoy her mother but also in the hopes that Brian or Catherine might see her and be reminded of how much she'd grown up this summer, how much older she was. But she didn't see either one of them, at least not until hours later, when she spotted Catherine and their other girlfriends down the beach, huddled in a circle, spraying tanning oil on one another. There was an intimacy in the way they did so, rubbing the oil on their shoulder blades and on the smalls of their backs, an intimacy that Georgie felt she'd never have with anyone. She waited for them to glance over and see her with Lindsey and maybe think that Lindsey was her friend, not the nanny. But they never looked over.

Her parents left quickly after lunch, and Georgie spent a few hours with Lindsey and Berty on the beach. By the time they got up to go home, Georgie's skin had turned a bubblegum-pink color, and she felt sweaty and sticky, like a glazed doughnut. Lindsey's skin hadn't burned but had developed an even deeper glow. As they walked home, Georgie felt a sense of relief that she *hadn't* seen Brian. Because if she had, then he would have seen Lindsey too. And next to Lindsey, she knew that she didn't stand a chance.

Back at home, she showered and then took out her journal once again, opening it up and sitting cross-legged on her bed with her hair in a towel atop her head. *Just because Brian is older than me doesn't mean we aren't right for one another,* she wrote. She'd tried to open up to Lindsey earlier about him, without actually telling Lindsey who he was, but Lindsey had been dismissive, as though the age difference made their relationship impossible. But she was wrong. If two people were meant to be together, then they would be, Georgie knew. That's what all the magazines said. How was this any different?

Chapter 15

LINDSEY

She tried not to think about Dylan that night. But she couldn't stop herself. Partially because of how she felt with him, how brown his eyes were, how strong his shoulders looked, but also because she felt the need to tell him the truth: that Brian thought that *he* had keyed his car when really, it had been Joanna and her. But she wouldn't tell him. She couldn't. It was too late now. And anyway, she hadn't heard from him. Maybe he wasn't interested in her.

Joanna had invited her over. I'm bored, she had texted Lindsey around dinnertime. Come over and drink champagne with me. Lindsey had just given Berty dinner and was putting him to bed. Carol and Jonathan were both at home that night. When Berty was asleep, she went back downstairs. Carol was in the kitchen, typing away on her laptop.

"Hi, Carol," she said with trepidation. She always felt like she was bothering her. "Sorry to interrupt. I was just wondering, would it be okay if I went to a friend's house for a few hours?"

"Lindsey," Carol said, lowering her head and lifting her eyes, "you're not a *prisoner* here, for God's sake. Of course. Go."

"Thank you," Lindsey said. She felt silly for asking now. It was like she was always *off* with Carol, like they spoke different languages and nothing translated exactly right.

"A new friend?" Carol asked as Lindsey was turning to leave.

"Actually, a friend from college. Joanna O'Callahan? I guess her family lives right around the corner."

"Of course." Carol seemed to animate suddenly. "The O'Callahans are wonderful. They're good friends of ours." She paused. "How nice of Joanna." Something in the way she said this made Lindsey feel like a charity case, someone Joanna was taking pity on.

"Yeah." Lindsey felt hot. She needed air. "Well, have a good night." Carol smiled at her as she left the kitchen and walked to the front door.

Joanna's house was just down the street and around the corner, she had told Lindsey. The walk felt nice. Lindsey realized it was the first time since that morning that she'd been alone. Her phone buzzed as she walked. **Hey, how about that date?** It was from Dylan. *Finally,* she thought to herself. She stopped in her tracks, smiling. She started to type and then put her phone away. She needed to wait a few minutes. Her heart raced a little.

She found Joanna's house and inhaled as she approached. The house was huge, with sleek white columns flanking the front door, large hydrangea bushes bordering the entire house, and a tidy cobblestone driveway winding toward a four-car garage off to the side.

"Welcome, welcome," Joanna said to Lindsey as she opened the front door. The house was also on the water, like the Deckers', except Joanna's house was open, airy, with high ceilings and white furniture, and the early-evening sunlight flooded the foyer. Inside, to the right of the front door, was a large-scale black-and-white photograph of a man in a bathtub.

"Is that a Mapplethorpe?" Lindsey asked, her mouth open. She'd studied Mapplethorpe at Bowdoin and remembered hearing about Christie's selling one of his self-portraits for almost half a million dollars.

"Yeah," Joanna said, unfazed. "My parents are into art. That's how they're such good friends with the Deckers, I think. And Brian's parents." She walked toward the back of the house, toward the water. "But

I kind of think it's bullshit. My parents aren't really *arty*, if you know what I mean. I think they just like the status." Lindsey nodded.

"Are your parents here?" Lindsey asked. Joanna raised her eyebrows and turned back to face her.

"No, I think they're out somewhere. I don't know." Joanna led her outside to the patio. "My little brother, Robbie, is around here somewhere." Lindsey didn't even know, until then, that Joanna had a little brother. She never spoke about her family.

The view outside Joanna's house was expansive, endless, spilling out to the horizon. A pool surrounded by bluestone was lit up by several underwater lights, casting a tranquility upon the backyard. There was a ten-foot-tall sculpture in the dramatic shape of a teardrop, made from shiny, mirrored metal, resting on a stone pedestal at one end of the pool. Joanna led Lindsey to a pair of chaise lounges, where there was a frosty bottle of champagne open. She poured Lindsey a glass. "Cheers," she said, taking a big gulp and refilling her glass.

Lindsey took a sip and stared out at the ocean. She listened to the sound of the waves, their soothing, cyclical crashing. She'd never been in a house this nice before. This place was magical, she thought. Why would anyone ever leave? She looked over at Joanna, who was texting someone. She wanted to tell Joanna about Dylan, and she searched for the right words. She didn't want Joanna to judge her.

"Hey," Lindsey began. "So that guy, you know, Dylan?"

"Um, *yeah*," Joanna said, drawing out the words. "What about him?"

"He asked me out." Lindsey took a sip. "I'm going to say yes."

"You should," Joanna said, to Lindsey's surprise. "I don't really know him, but I've seen him around. He's totally cute." Lindsey wondered, for a moment, if maybe Joanna was encouraging her to go out with him so that she wouldn't be in her way with Brian.

"Do you think that Brian's going to do something to him? I mean, does he still think he's the one who keyed his car?"

"Honestly, who knows," Joanna said, looking off toward the water. "I hope not." She paused. "Anyway, he's being nice to me again. I think everything will be fine."

"What do you mean, he's being nice again?"

"I mean, I think we're back on. Like, things are good between us. He apologized about that Jennifer girl. And he said he wanted to, like, *be* with me or whatever. He's even taking me to Alchemy for dinner this weekend. And that's a big deal for someone who pretty much only eats at Dock Street and Quarterdeck!"

"That's great," Lindsey said. She felt her throat tighten up. She couldn't tell Joanna now that Brian had texted her or that Georgie had a crush on him. She'd waited too long, and now it all had to be kept a secret.

"Beach club tomorrow?" Joanna asked as they finished the bottle.

"Yeah, I'll be there after Berty's tennis class," she said. "What days do you work at the sunglasses store?"

"Oh." Joanna waved her hand, laughing. "I'm gonna quit. I'm over it. I don't know what I was thinking bothering to get a job this summer, you know?" If Joanna wasn't so naive in her delivery, Lindsey would be offended. But she couldn't be offended by Joanna in this case; she had just been raised in a complete bubble. It wasn't really her fault that she was so clueless.

Lindsey got up to leave around ten. She had another early morning with Berty tomorrow. "Thanks," she said to Joanna as they walked to the door. "This was fun." And she meant it. She'd enjoyed hanging out with Joanna, listening to her talk about her summers on the Vineyard, all the fun bars they were going to go to and the things they were going to do. She felt like a different person with Joanna, someone who belonged on the island. She felt like less of an outsider.

On the walk home, she texted Dylan back. She knew that she had tomorrow night off. She always got one or two days or nights a week free, Carol had told her. How about tomorrow? she wrote back.

Tomorrow it is, he replied right away. There was something liberating about going out with Dylan and not knowing where he was going to take her. This was his island. She was new. And she had a feeling that she was going to love his version of this place. She thought about texting Joanna but texted Rose instead. She decided not to mention what had happened with Joanna and Brian, though. Where would she even begin?

The next day flew by—tennis, beach club, Berty's dinner. She didn't see Georgie at all that day. Dylan had said that he would pick her up at eight. She said okay but that she'd meet him outside. She didn't want Carol or Jonathan to see Dylan. She didn't even want them to see her getting into his truck.

She decided on wearing her favorite American Eagle jeans and a tight scoop-neck T-shirt, one that fit snugly around her waist and dipped just low enough in front. She had bought some new gold sandals from Petunia's Shoes on Main Street, and they complemented the pink toenails she had painted earlier that afternoon. She was already a deep bronze, and the whites of her eyes popped against her summer skin. Her hair had developed flecks of blonde throughout, and she let it dry naturally that night. The waves around her face made her look younger, she thought.

At exactly eight, Lindsey received a text from Dylan: I'm outside whenever ur ready. Take ur time. Lindsey peered outside the window on the second-floor landing. She didn't see Dylan's truck. She craned her neck down and saw that Dylan was standing there outside the front door, without a car. *Fuck,* she thought, *he's going to ring the bell.* She grabbed her phone, took one last look in the mirror, and ran downstairs and out the door. She exhaled and shut the door behind her, relieved that he hadn't knocked.

"Hi," she said and instinctively leaned in and hugged him, pressing her chest against his. She backed away after a second, embarrassed by her enthusiasm.

"Hi. Good to see you," Dylan said. He was wearing jeans, a white T-shirt, and the same baseball cap he'd worn the last time Lindsey saw him.

"You too," she said.

"I hope it's okay if we walk into town," he said as they turned down the street. "My truck's in the shop right now, so this was our only option. But hey, it's beautiful out, right?"

"Of course," she said. "It's such a nice night."

"I was thinking we'd just grab some food and then maybe walk to the beach, check out the stars?" He paused and looked over at her again, waiting for her approval.

"That sounds great," Lindsey said, again trying hard not to reveal her eagerness. She felt like she knew Dylan already, and it was a good feeling but a strange one. She couldn't tell if it was because she felt comfortable around him or because she already knew things about him that she shouldn't know, like his rivalry with Brian. Maybe it was both.

As they walked, Lindsey could sense that he was nervous. His hands were stuffed in his pockets, and his shoulders were slightly raised.

"I actually had a whole different plan," he said. "I was gonna take you up island. That's where the best sunset is. But we'll save it for another time when my truck is back."

"What's wrong with your car?" she asked.

"It's really dumb." Dylan sighed. "There's this summer kid who's had it out for me ever since I turned him in to the Derby committee for cheating, and now he thinks that I trashed his car, so he destroyed mine as payback. The thing is, though, I *didn't do it*. I really didn't." He was almost laughing as he explained it. "And what's even crazier is that when I turned him in last year, he never even got punished. He got to stay in the Derby, and they didn't even disqualify the fish that he got by cheating. I don't know why he has it out for me so bad." He paused. "The Derby is a big fishing competition here, by the way. It gets . . . intense."

Lindsey felt her cheeks grow hot. Brian had already gotten his revenge on Dylan. She started to open her mouth to tell him the truth, to explain everything, but she couldn't bring herself to do it. She didn't want him to hate her. And she didn't want to ruin things for Joanna either. Maybe Joanna was right: what's done was done. What was the point in trying to change things now?

"What an asshole," Lindsey found herself saying. She couldn't look him in the eyes.

"Yeah," Dylan said. "The guy didn't even try to hide it either. He just came to my house with his friends, and they started whacking my truck with baseball bats like they were in some fucking movie. I came out of the house screaming at them, and they ran off." Lindsey peered over at Dylan as he spoke. He was smiling and shaking his head, as though this was all actually pretty funny. Like he had expected it.

"And then to make it worse," Dylan continued, "my boss somehow got wind of it all and told me that if I was stirring shit up with guys like him—guys from *those* kinds of families, you know, *rich* families—he'd have to reconsider my position." He shook his head and grunted. "It's so predictable. I mean, those guys always win here. Always. So now I'm gonna have to come up with the money to repair my truck, and I might lose my job at the same time. But it is what it is."

Lindsey wasn't sure what else to say. She wished that she could turn and run into the woods, disappear.

"Well, are you going to press charges?" she asked. "You should," she said, not sure where she was going with the suggestion. Dylan chuckled.

"No. I know it wouldn't swing in my favor. Why bother?" They both paused. "Look, it doesn't matter," he said. "I don't know why I even brought it up. I'm happy we're doing this tonight. The rest isn't important." Lindsey looked at him and noticed that his eyelashes were blond at the tips.

She didn't ask anything else about the truck. Lindsey was shocked at how calm Dylan was about all of it. It was as if he had grown used to being mistreated, to life being unfair, to guys like Brian always getting what they wanted with no consequences or sacrifice.

The conversation shifted, eventually, to their families. Lindsey told him about her parents and how they didn't understand why she wanted to work in art. "I mean, unless you're the artist, what are you actually doing in art?" her mother had asked her at graduation earlier that summer. "But if that's what you want to do, then you should do it." Lindsey knew that her mother didn't intend to disparage her desire to be a curator. She was always supportive in the end. She just didn't understand the life Lindsey wanted.

Dylan told Lindsey about his parents. "Divorced when I was five," he said. "Dad moved off island. Don't see him much." Neither Dylan nor Lindsey had any siblings, a fact that, when discovered, caused them both to look up from the brick sidewalks and smile at one another.

Dylan took Lindsey to a restaurant called the Seafood Shanty, right on the water. They went upstairs, where there was a patio overlooking the entire harbor. Lindsey could see the lighthouse and the Deckers' house up the slope. It all looked impossibly far away from where she sat. The harbor glowed with lights from the houses along the Katama shoreline. All the boats bobbed like bathtub toys in the gentle water.

They sat at the outside bar. Lindsey ordered a margarita. Dylan got a beer. After their first drink, their knees started touching under the counter. She worried that her face looked greasy. She and Dylan were so close together. They picked a few things from the menu to share— fried calamari, shrimp cocktail, fish tacos—and by the time their food arrived, Lindsey wasn't self-conscious about digging in. She felt relaxed from her cocktail and started to let herself enjoy it all. The restaurant had started to fill up, and there was a joyful, unpretentious, and light-hearted atmosphere around her, a nice break from everything else she'd experienced on the island so far.

"This is so good," she said to Dylan as she ate, and he seemed pleased and relieved that she was happy with his choice for dinner.

After they ate, they ordered one more round of drinks—now their third—and they had reached the point where conversation just happened on its own. Dylan was funny and quick, not as brooding as Lindsey had first thought upon meeting him. He made her laugh. She felt at ease with him. She wanted to kiss him.

As Lindsey sipped her drink, she looked up and saw Brian and his friend Whitney walking out to the deck, both of them with a beer in hand. Lindsey didn't know how long they had been there. Even though she could see the entrance from where she sat, she hadn't noticed them come in. She had been too absorbed in her conversation with Dylan and too enchanted by the water view. She and Brian locked eyes, and he nodded at her. Dylan craned his neck slightly to see what she was looking at, then looked at Lindsey. Brian and Whitney were leaning against the railing of the deck, across the way from them but out of earshot.

"You know him?" Dylan asked in a somewhat accusatory tone. "That's the guy," he said.

"Not really," she said, feeling unsettled and on edge for the first time that night. She wasn't sure what her story was going to be. "I met him once last week. Actually, the same night I met you." She realized, as she said it, that she was inching closer to consolidating all the facts about that night, and she wanted, more than anything, for the subject to change. She worried that a fight could erupt at any moment.

Dylan said nothing for a second and took a swig of beer. "Hmm," he said, his voice more whispered now. "Actually, it was that same night I met you that he thinks I fucked up his car." What was he saying? Did he suspect her? Or was he going to ask her to help prove his innocence? After all, she was Dylan's alibi, she was realizing. She'd seen him drive to the parking lot; he'd picked her up and then left. She was the only person who could prove his innocence. And Dylan knew this, but he didn't ask her to help.

"Let's go" was all he said after that. They'd finished their drinks; it was time to go anyway. The air felt thick with anger and tension. Lindsey didn't understand how both Dylan and Brian were so civil and so contained even though they were right across the room from one another. Maybe if they had stayed longer, they would have lost that composure.

Dylan paid for dinner, quickly, despite Lindsey offering to split it. He insisted and paid in cash, giving a quick handshake to the bartender. "Thanks, man," Dylan said to him as they left.

Lindsey could feel Brian's eyes on them as they walked out. He gave them the kind of stare that felt heavy on her back, like she could still feel his eyes on her even when she was out of his sight. She had to remind herself that Brian really did think that Dylan had keyed his car. Could she really blame him for trashing his car in return? Did it make Brian a bad guy that he had retaliated? She wasn't sure what to think of him anymore.

They walked in silence for a minute. She was glad to be outside now, away from Brian. She worried that she had somehow screwed up the entire night, that she'd been too awkward, too self-conscious. But then Dylan took her hand in his and laced his fingers through hers. The act felt so simple. They kept walking without acknowledging it.

They wandered through Edgartown, past the grand old captains' houses with blooming hydrangeas and plush green lawns, past front porches filled with white wicker furniture. The noises of town were behind them now, and Lindsey could hear the ocean a few blocks away and the gentle ticking of nighttime sprinkler systems going off.

"Still up for going to the beach?" Dylan asked. Lindsey nodded. At the end of the Deckers' street, just a few blocks down, past Joanna's house, the road turned into a little pathway of sand and opened up to a sleepy spot called Fuller Street Beach, where the water was calm, flat, and gray. It was quiet. They were only a quarter mile or so down the beach from the Deckers' house. But everything looked different from this perspective, like they were on another island completely, far away.

They sat on the sand, and Lindsey held her knees into her chest. She knew that if she turned to her left and faced Dylan, he would kiss her, and suddenly she found herself paralyzed. She wanted to kiss him, badly, but she found herself feeling nervous. It all felt overwhelming to her, like if they kissed, there would be no turning back. Turning back from what, she wasn't sure. She just knew that it would change everything.

So she turned. They looked at one another for a few seconds, and then they moved toward one another, slowly, at first just touching their lips together ever so slightly. She could feel the tickle of his facial scruff against her cheek. She could hear his breathing and her own. And then they leaned in.

Chapter 16

GEORGIE

Georgie saw Lindsey go on her date. She was in her room, writing in her journal, when she heard Lindsey go out the front door. She ran to the hallway window that overlooked the street and saw Lindsey walking toward town with a guy. She didn't recognize him. He was cute, in a scruffy kind of way. She tried to stay awake to see what happened when Lindsey got home, but she fell asleep. She was just relieved that the guy wasn't Brian. That's what mattered. If Lindsey was dating someone else, then she wouldn't need to worry so much about Brian being more interested in Lindsey than her.

Her plan with Lindsey at the beach hadn't worked—not yet anyway. Nothing had changed with Catherine or the other girls or with Brian. She just needed another moment, the right one, to show everyone who she was, to get back in with them all. And soon she'd be hanging out with her friends from work regularly—her friends who were already in *college*. She couldn't wait. Things were slowly starting to change.

She'd been working at the Picnic Basket for a few days now. She still enjoyed it, even though most of her time was spent in the office. She'd learned to sync up her breaks with the busiest times in the café so that she could have ample opportunity for run-ins with Brian and chances to help her coworkers when they were really busy. She wanted them to like her.

That morning, she'd been working in a crouched position on her knees for hours. Her body felt cramped, and her armpits were damp; it was hot in the office despite the desk fan she had going. The July heat was nearing.

The office door swung upon. "Hey, Georgie," Emma said, ducking her head inside. "Some guy up front is asking for you?" she said, her voice lifting at the end, like it was a question. She paused. "He's pretty cute."

Georgie burst into a smile. It must be Brian.

"Oh, and hey," Emma said, "don't forget: we're all hanging out tonight after work. You still in?"

"Yeah," Georgie said. "Sure." As if she could forget. Emma smiled and shut the door.

Georgie felt her heart beating. She stood up and looked in the mirror, wiping off some of the grease on her forehead with a napkin and pulling her hair into a messy bun like she'd seen Emma do before. *Be cool,* she told herself.

She left the office and rounded the corner toward the main counter, straightening out her shirt and tugging down the hem of her shorts that kept creeping up her thighs. She saw Brian in front of her. *Holy shit.* She stood there for a moment, waiting to see someone else who made more sense. But it was him; it was really him. He had asked for her.

"Hey, kid," he said, swirling his iced coffee with a straw. "Just wanted to make sure you hadn't quit yet."

Georgie just stood there, wishing that all her coworkers could see what was happening. It might have been the most thrilling moment of her entire life so far. But nobody seemed to care; it was a busy day, and everyone continued on with their work.

"Nope," she muttered, unsure of how to speak and what to do with her face and her hands. "I'm still here."

She thought for a moment that his eyes traveled down her body, just for a second, before returning to her face. It made her feel exposed, like she was naked. "Good. I hadn't seen you in a few days. A guy worries."

Her jaw went slack. She had to search for words to say. "Don't worry," she blurted, "I'm pretty tough."

"Brian!" someone yelled from behind the counter. "Order for Brian!" Brian raised his hand and reached over to grab his sandwich. So he hadn't really been waiting there just for her, Georgie realized. Still, he had asked for her. That was enough.

"All right, then," he said, sandwich in hand. "See you later."

"Yeah, bye," she blurted.

He turned and left, leaving her feeling flush with the hot sensation of pins and needles all over her body.

"Oh my *God*," she whispered out loud, to no one, as soon as he was out the door. She held her hand up to her cheek. It was burning. She could hear her heart and her breathing. She scurried back to the office, where she shut the door and immediately checked her reflection in the mirror. Brian had asked for *her*.

Georgie spent the rest of the day imagining their life together. She thought about what kind of dates Brian would take her on. Maybe they'd go on sunset sails together, or go fishing up island, or go out to dinner at one of the fancy restaurants on Main Street. Maybe they'd hold hands while they walked in town so everyone could see them together, so everyone would know that she wasn't alone, that Brian loved her.

When the café closed at four thirty, she was still working. She'd managed to separate her mind from her body and had ripped through two boxes of paperwork, like a machine. All she could think about was Brian.

"Knock, knock," she heard, and saw Emma and another coworker, Vera, at the office door. "Come on, workaholic. Party time."

The café was closed for the day. Georgie had never worked until closing time. There was a different vibe at this hour. Everyone felt loose, free, more relaxed. Georgie followed Emma and Vera to the back of the café where there was an outdoor patio enclosed by hedges. The rest of the staff were already out there, sitting on teak deck furniture, their feet up, drinking beers. Some of them were smoking cigarettes.

"All I'm saying is, what does it actually mean anymore to be *organic*? It's bullshit, and we're robbing people." Phillip, the guy who wore eyeliner and his hair in a bun, was in a debate with Francesca, whose hair was dyed bright magenta pink.

"No, see, that's where you're wrong. To some people it's important, and they're willing to pay." The debate continued on. Georgie looked around. She was the youngest by far. Everyone there was in college, she guessed. It was exhilarating. She'd never felt cooler in her life.

"So," Emma said to her, "Georgie. How old are you again?"

Georgie's brain reeled. She couldn't lie to her coworkers. Lucy knew the truth, so they probably did too. "Almost fifteen. In just a few weeks."

"Cool," Vera said. "Going into sophomore year?"

"Yup." Georgie nodded.

The three girls sat down around a table. Emma and Vera opened some beers—Blue Moons, Georgie noticed—and looked at one another and then at Georgie, unsure of what to do. There was a pause.

"Want one?" Emma asked. "I mean, just one. It won't kill you. Just don't tell Lucy you got it from us."

"Sure," Georgie said. "And don't worry. I won't." Emma popped the bottle with an opener and handed it to Georgie. She was relieved that Emma had opened it for her; she'd never done it before herself. She took a sip. It tasted citrusy and sharp on her tongue. She didn't like it, but it didn't matter. She'd do anything to stay included in this group, to be part of it.

"So, Georgie," Emma said, taking a swig of beer and leaning in. Her hair was down and flung across one side of her head, framing her face. "Are you friends with that guy Brian?"

Georgie wondered how Emma knew Brian. She hadn't mentioned his name earlier when she had knocked on the office door.

"Yeah," she replied. "We're friends. I've known him a while."

"He's dating that blonde chick," Vera chimed in. "Joanna whatever. Right?"

"Yeah," Emma said before Georgie could say anything. "I think so."

Georgie nodded, pretending like she already knew, but her mind started racing. How could she not have known that he was dating Joanna? She knew Joanna, at least from afar, since their parents were friends. She was really pretty. Georgie felt the hint of a sting behind her eyes, and she pushed it away, taking another sip of her beer.

"Well, we're just friends, so whatever." She remembered now overhearing her parents talking yesterday about Lindsey hanging out with Joanna. So did Lindsey already know Brian? she wondered. Had she known that Georgie was talking about him the other day at the beach? All the possibilities spiraled through her head. She pictured Joanna in her mind—beautiful, confident, *fun*. That's the kind of girl she was: fun. She didn't have the same moodiness that Georgie had. She was light. Georgie looked down at herself, noticing how her stomach folded a little over the waistline of her shorts and how the flesh of her thighs splayed out on the chair. She took another sip.

The rest of the group was talking about Lucy's various romances, a mutual fascination among them all. Lucy seemed to be an enigma to everyone, even the staff who had worked there for several summers.

"Who *isn't* she dating?" Phillip asked, and the group laughed. Lucy, Georgie learned, lived an unconventional life, having never wanted kids or marriage, instead just focusing on her business and a fantastic vacation every winter.

"I think she's got it all figured out," said Francesca. "I mean, her life is *sick*."

"Yeah," Emma said. "True. But I bet, at the end of the day, she's fucking *lonely*." The group hummed in reluctant agreement. Georgie wondered if it was true. Lucy did seem to have an amazing life. But she was alone. Would Georgie end up the same way? Lonely forever?

She lifted her beer bottle to her lips to take another sip. She felt dizzy, and her stomach had bloated out. Her legs felt weak. She wanted to go home. She'd started the afternoon on such a high, but now she felt low, pathetic. She tried to imagine what Brian and Joanna were doing right in that moment. He wasn't thinking about her.

"Okay, guys, I gotta get going," she said, rising from her chair.

"No!" her coworkers cried out.

"Thanks for hanging with us, girl," Emma said. She got up and gave Georgie a hug. Vera hugged her too. They both smelled good. What was it about older girls always smelling good? She made a mental note to buy some perfume or something to keep in her bag at all times.

"Bye, Georgie!" they called after her as she headed out the back entrance.

As Georgie walked home, she had a funny feeling of being sad and happy at the same time. She'd just hung out with college kids. Really, actually hung out with them. They *liked* her. But she was also devastated. Brian was dating Joanna. She felt stupid to think that he had been interested in her. She'd been kidding herself.

At home, Lindsey was having dinner with Berty in the kitchen. Georgie went up to her room without saying hi. Even though she wasn't sure what Lindsey knew about Brian, she nevertheless felt betrayed by her. She went down to get herself dinner only when she knew they were upstairs. Georgie fell asleep fast that night, still feeling woozy from the beer.

Chapter 17

LINDSEY

Once Berty was asleep, Carol didn't care what Lindsey did. As long as she was up on time the next morning, she could do whatever she wanted in the evenings. And if Carol wasn't going out herself at night, she would put Berty to bed herself, and Lindsey could go out even earlier in the evening. So she agreed to have dinner with Dylan the following night too, when Carol was home. Dylan's truck was fixed, he said, and he wanted to pick her up and take her out. She asked him to pull up at the end of the street and said she'd meet him there. She didn't want the Deckers to see her get in his car.

When she met him at the end of the block, she noticed that his car still had some dents and scrapes.

"Well, it's *mostly* fixed," Dylan said to her as she climbed in. "My guy Freddy fixed what he needed to just to get the thing running again, but I can't afford to get it all done just yet." She felt a stab of guilt as she looked at the dented hood, and she imagined Brian bringing a baseball bat down onto it with a roar.

But the car still worked, and Dylan drove her all the way to Menemsha, a small fishing village on the north side of the island. They ordered whole steamed lobsters and corn on the cob from a fish market called Larsen's and ate it on the docks where all the commercial fishermen kept their boats. Dylan brought a six-pack of beer for them to share. When they finished eating, they walked down the dock to the beach to watch the sunset. It was the best sunset Lindsey had ever seen, the kind that flooded the entire atmosphere with gold, like the whole world was melting.

"Didn't I tell you that we've got the best sunsets up island?" he asked. They kissed.

Later, they went back to his place, an apartment above the garage of a house in West Tisbury. "My boss on my last construction job owns the place, and he lets me rent out the apartment up here for a decent price. But I'm saving to build my own place in Chilmark someday." It was a cozy, clean studio apartment.

"I think I've got a bottle of red somewhere," he said. Lindsey took off her sweater and put it on his couch. She had a white tank top on underneath.

"Whatever is fine," she said, looking around. He didn't have a lot of stuff. A few fishing trophies, a stack of fishing magazines on the coffee table, a neat line of shoes by the door—rubber boots, work boots, sneakers. He seemed nervous.

He found a bottle and poured them each a glass. It tasted like vinegar, but Lindsey didn't care. She felt safe there, warm, happy. They started kissing on the couch. It was the first time they'd been able to do that alone, in a totally private place. She let her body soften underneath his touch, and when she fell onto her back, he followed her down, never letting his lips leave her neck. She arched her hips into his. Soon after, they moved to the bed. He peeled off her clothing, and she peeled off his. She wanted him. She was so attracted to him that when his hands moved down the lines of her stomach, over her hip bones, and inside, she thought she might shatter. Her body was a cloud, weightless and floating.

After, they stayed in bed together, under the covers. She rested her head on his arm. She liked the way he always smelled like he'd just been in the ocean. As they stared at the ceiling together, their fingers intertwined, Lindsey remembered what she'd done to Brian's car and what Brian had done to Dylan. It had been easier to forget about it lately, but she had flashes of memory that overcame her and made her want to tell Dylan everything in that moment. But he would hate her. And anyway, she told herself, it all seemed to be over. Dylan said he was back in good standing with his boss, and Joanna said that Brian had seemed to calm down too. Maybe it was all behind them.

She wanted to stay the night, but she couldn't. She had to wake up in the Deckers' house. Even though he lived up island and the Deckers' was about twenty minutes down island, Dylan drove her home. He kissed her goodbye gently.

When she was back in her room, alone, she called Rose. It was late, but she knew that Rose would be up. She went into the bathroom for more privacy, and she still whispered.

"Oh my God, Rose." She sighed. "I really like him."

"I need a visual!" she said. "I'm happy for you. You deserve it."

"Thanks. He's a good guy, I think." Lindsey paused. "And you know, Joanna isn't so bad. We've been hanging out. She's actually pretty nice."

Rose didn't respond for a few seconds. "If you say so," she finally said.

They talked for a few more minutes. Rose was dealing with an arrogant coworker whom she had to partner with on a project, some rich Princeton kid who treated her like she was a joke. "It's fine," she said. "I like being underestimated. Just gives me more ammunition to prove them wrong." Rose was like that; she could turn something negative into something positive. Lindsey wanted to tell Rose what had happened with Brian, with the car, with Georgie, but she couldn't. It wasn't that she was worried about Rose judging her but rather that she'd judge herself if she had to say it all out loud.

Chapter 18

GEORGIE

Georgie had the entire next day off from work. She slept in, waking around nine and coming downstairs to an empty house. She opened the fridge and freezer doors and just stood there for a moment, letting the blast of cold hit her body. It was scorching hot outside, and the heat had permeated the house, making everything feel sticky. They rarely used the air-conditioning at their house, opting instead for open windows and letting in the ocean breeze.

She decided that she'd meet Lindsey and Berty at the beach club that morning, after Berty finished his tennis. She wanted to tell Lindsey that Brian had come to see her at work—to prove to her that maybe he *wasn't* too old for her, that maybe he really *was* interested in her. She'd made up her mind, overnight, that Brian didn't have to be part of some distant fantasy. He was right there, in front of her, pursuing her, and she wasn't crazy.

She was glad that her parents weren't home as she left the house. She wanted to wear her string bikini again, this time underneath her jean shorts and a blue tank top. She threw a towel, some tanning oil, and magazines into her Longchamp bag and headed out, feeling confident. She was different today than she was yesterday. Things had changed.

At the club, there seemed to be no refuge from the scorching sun, even in the shade. Though she tried to arrive after Lindsey and Berty, she somehow got there before them, forcing her to pick a spot on the beach alone. Luckily, she didn't see Catherine or Brian anywhere. After a few minutes, she spotted Lindsey and Berty walking in. Joanna O'Callahan was with them, wearing a tiny bikini and aviator glasses. She and Lindsey were talking, and Berty walked a few paces in front of them. He ran ahead toward Georgie, and Lindsey and Joanna hung back to continue talking for a minute, until they waved goodbye and Lindsey approached Georgie's spot on the beach.

"Sorry," Lindsey said. "The tennis clinic ran over today."

Georgie looked up at her as she pulled off her cover-up, revealing the same one-piece swimsuit that she'd worn the day before. She examined Lindsey's inner thighs, noticing how they didn't touch when she stood up. Georgie already had a burning sensation on her inner thighs from the way they'd rubbed together on the walk to the club.

"It's okay," she said. She wanted to know if Lindsey had always looked that way, but she didn't ask.

They went in the water with Berty, all of them feeling slowed down by the heat. But even a long swim couldn't bring down Georgie's internal temperature. She felt suffocated, impossibly thirsty.

Out of the water, they laid their towels under an umbrella and stretched out. Georgie was contemplating how to tell Lindsey about Brian, but then Lindsey got up.

"I'm going to the bathroom. Are you okay watching Berty for a minute?" Berty was playing with a few other kids on the shore in front of them. It annoyed Georgie that Lindsey would even ask her, like it wasn't really a question of her being okay with it but rather a question of her being *able* to.

"Sure," she said. She didn't really know why, but she felt jealous of Lindsey in that moment.

Several minutes passed and Lindsey hadn't returned. The heat seemed to make time move at half speed, but Georgie still got the sense that it had been longer than normal. She looked down at Berty. There was another nanny now in the water with all of them. He would be fine if she stepped away for a minute. She got up, shaking off some of the sand from her legs, and headed to the snack bar, deciding to get herself an Arnold Palmer and see where Lindsey had gone.

As she waited in line at the snack bar, she craned her head around toward the entrance to the bathrooms, a shady enclave with a wooden bench. She could see the back of Lindsey, off to the side, where Georgie had once sipped warm vodka with Catherine. She was talking to someone, though Georgie couldn't see who. She got to the front of the line and ordered quickly.

When she got her drink, Georgie stepped quietly and quickly toward the bathroom. She was curious now. She hovered around the corner from the restrooms, pretending to be inspecting her drink. She could hear that Lindsey was talking to a guy. Her voice was raised, angry.

"Stay away," she thought she heard Lindsey say, but she couldn't decipher the rest. There was too much noise at the club.

After just a few seconds, Georgie had to give up and return to her towel. She looked too strange just standing there, obviously eavesdropping. So she ran back to her towel, lying on her stomach and facing up toward the bathrooms, hoping to see Lindsey emerge with whomever she was talking to. She propped herself up on her arms and waited.

Soon after, Lindsey emerged. She seemed flustered. Her shoulders looked stiff, and her face was tightened in an angry expression. She began walking back toward the beach and then turned abruptly and ran back into the women's bathroom. And then a second later, to Georgie's disbelief, *Brian* emerged.

Georgie waited, hoping that someone else would follow him— someone else whom Lindsey would have been talking to. There had to be someone else. But no one else followed, and she knew then that Lindsey had been arguing with Brian. Maybe it was about Joanna. But why? How did they even know each other well enough to be having an argument?

She watched Brian march toward the beach and down to the other end, toward a group of people sitting in Adirondack chairs in a circle. He didn't even see Georgie. Or, if he had, he didn't acknowledge her.

Lindsey returned to her towel a few minutes later, acting normal, saying nothing about how long she'd been gone. Georgie felt angry, like Lindsey had lied to her. Maybe Lindsey didn't know that this Brian was *her* Brian, the one she'd told Lindsey about. Maybe Lindsey didn't even know him at all; maybe they'd just bumped into each other outside the bathrooms and had talked about something totally irrelevant. But Georgie knew none of these possibilities were true. Yet it nevertheless felt somewhat comforting to consider them. She sat in silence, waiting for Lindsey to say something, knowing that she wouldn't.

"So," she decided to say, "you know Brian?" Georgie could feel herself growing angry and couldn't wait any longer to find out what they had been talking about. She felt that she had a right to know.

"Barely," Lindsey said without looking up from her book. "I met him briefly at a party the other week." She wasn't giving her much. She had thought that she and Lindsey were friends, but she felt an uncomfortable distance now, like Lindsey was trying to cement the differences between them, to make it clear that they weren't friends at all, that there were secrets Lindsey kept that she'd never tell Georgie.

"You know, he's the same Brian I told you about." Georgie searched Lindsey's face for an explanation.

"I thought so" was all she said. Georgie smoldered. She felt like an idiot.

"Well, what were you guys talking about?" It seemed like Lindsey was keeping something from her, and she didn't like it. She was starting to feel helpless, made fun of, humiliated. Had they been talking about *her*?

"Nothing, Georgie," Lindsey said, looking at her then. "We just ran into each other outside the bathrooms and were chatting. Dumb stuff. He was talking about his boat." Lindsey paused, as if searching for something to say to Georgie to make her feel better. It was obvious that Lindsey was lying. Georgie didn't say anything. She pulled her knees into her chest. She felt betrayed, not only by Brian but by Lindsey.

"Did you know that he was dating your friend? Joanna?"

"They only *just* started dating again," Lindsey said, as though she was defending them. "I can see why you like him, you know," she added. "But I just . . ." She paused again. "I don't think he's the right guy for you."

Georgie had to hold back tears. What did Lindsey know about Brian anyway? What did Lindsey know about *her*, for that matter? Who was *she* to decide who was right or wrong for her?

"Because he's too old for me?" she asked.

"Well, yes," Lindsey responded. "But also . . . I just don't think he's right for you. He doesn't deserve you."

Georgie rolled her eyes.

"Sure. Okay." She returned to her magazine. She was pissed. Maybe Lindsey was just saying this so that *she* could date Brian. Maybe she already *was* dating him. Maybe she was lying to Joanna too.

As though Lindsey knew what she was feeling, she added, "I know you're probably upset. I believe you, you know, that Brian was flirting with you. I'm sure he was. I mean, you're gorgeous; why wouldn't he? But he's too old for you. He shouldn't be doing that."

Georgie knew that she was right, but she still didn't want to hear it. In that moment, she felt connected to Lindsey, but she hated her too. She trusted her, somehow, and even though she didn't know what she and Brian had been talking about, she did have a feeling that Lindsey was on her side. But Georgie was jealous of her. She was jealous of her age, her independence, all of it. Nothing was fair.

Berty emerged from the shoreline then, dripping in wet sand, crying. He'd cut his finger on a shell. It was a small cut that would only require a Band-Aid, but the slice of bright-red blood on his fingertip made Berty feel scared, and he wailed to Lindsey, begging to go home.

"You're all right, sweetie," she cooed, picking him up. Lindsey looked to Georgie as she held Berty in her arms. "We'll see you at home, okay?" She grabbed her things and carried Berty off, leaving Georgie totally alone.

Georgie shut her eyes and rested on her back, submitting to the sun. There had been a distinct shift in their conversation just now, Georgie thought, and it made her sad. Lindsey had lied to her. She knew it. She had lied to her in the way that adults sometimes lied to kids to *protect* them. She had seen the way Lindsey had talked to Brian. There was something about the way Lindsey's muscles had moved and her arms had flailed when they spoke. Something had happened between Lindsey and Brian. They had been fighting about something personal. And fights like that could only happen between people who had something intimate to fight about, something between them: a secret.

With her eyes closed, Georgie let the sounds around her soften. Her body felt stuck to her towel. No clouds passed, and the sun continued to beat down on her. She was tired.

She felt the chill of a lingering shadow, like a piece of ice had just been snaked across her stomach. She opened her eyes, holding her hand up to shield them from the sun. Brian stood in front of her, blocking the sun now, his shadow blanketing her. The sun poked out from behind him in piercing rays.

"Hey, kid," he said. He moved just an inch to the right, shuffling his feet slightly, but it was enough to break his wall of shadow, and the sunlight slapped Georgie in the face, making her squint. She wanted to get up, but the act felt too difficult with him standing so close to her. Everything was slightly out of focus as she looked up at him, and her whole body felt weak, like she was in some kind of dream state.

"Hi," she said. Brian continued walking, past the snack bar and out to the exit. She looked down at her body, worrying that something might be out of place. Why was he doing this to her? She berated herself for not saying anything more than hi. Every time she saw Brian, she felt like he fed her a tiny crumb and left her wanting more. But she didn't know how to get it. She didn't know what to say.

She waited about fifteen minutes, wondering if Brian was going to return, but he didn't. She looked around, wondering if Catherine had emerged. But she didn't see anyone. It was like she was always in the wrong place at the wrong time, missing out on what everyone else was doing in some other place.

She decided to pack up her things and go home. Whatever Lindsey had told her about Brian, she didn't care. Lindsey was wrong. Brian might be too old for her now, and he might have a girlfriend, but there was something between them that was *real*. Her suit was still damp by the time she got home, and as she peeled it off in her room, she thought about the way Brian had hovered above her and looked down, as she lay there exposed, trapped, all flesh and blood, alive and yearning. Maybe that's what sex with him would be like, she thought. She went to her room and shut the door, writing it all down in her journal so she would never forget how good it felt.

Chapter 19

LINDSEY

Lindsey couldn't wait to tell Joanna about her date with Dylan. There was nothing wrong with a summer fling, she told herself as she walked Berty from the tennis clinic to the Chappy ferry. They were going to the beach club for the rest of the day, and Georgie was going to come meet them.

Joanna happened to be standing in the entrance when they arrived, talking on her phone. She waved to Lindsey emphatically and ended her call.

"Hiii," she said. "Hi, Berty!"

"Hello," Berty said. "Come on," he whined to Lindsey.

"So, how was last night?" Joanna asked. Lindsey smiled.

"Honestly . . . it was great. It was really fun. I like him."

"Did you . . . you know?" Joanna winked and did a little shimmy with her shoulders.

"Maybe . . ." They both laughed. Lindsey looked out at the beach and saw Georgie. "Berty, there's your sister—go on and meet her, and I'll be right there, okay?" He ran off.

"Well, I want to hear all about it." Joanna huddled in closer. "And listen, I was with Brian last night. I honestly think this whole car thing is over. You're not going to say anything to Dylan, right? I mean, I think it's all fine now. So let's just forget about it. No one will ever know. Only us."

Lindsey nodded. Joanna was right. It was too late to tell Dylan the truth, and the truth would only ruin things for her, as well as for Joanna. She seemed to be happy with Brian now, and she didn't want to screw that up. In her new happiness with Dylan, Lindsey had decided to just forget about the possibility of Brian being such a bad guy. His text to her had meant nothing, she decided, and Georgie had probably misread his signals. She wanted to like him.

"We'll be down by the dock; come hang with us if you can get away." Joanna gave her a quick wave and then trotted to the other end of the beach.

Lindsey walked toward Georgie and Berty, finally feeling a sense of calm. Maybe everything would be okay. Joanna was happy for her and Dylan, Brian seemed to have moved on from what had happened, and she trusted Joanna to keep everything between them.

Georgie barely looked up when she arrived, like she was annoyed. Lindsey could never tell if Georgie's anger was directed at her or if she was just in a bad mood in general. There always seemed to be something that bothered her. She sympathized, to an extent, but also resented how vain Georgie seemed to be about her own feelings, how dramatic she was. Lindsey would trade lives with her in a second. She didn't have anything to complain about.

"Wanna go for a swim?" Lindsey suggested.

"Sure," Georgie muttered.

"Berty, I need to put some more sunblock on you real quick." Berty obediently stood before her, holding his arms out. Georgie went ahead into the water, not waiting.

"My dad is gone," Berty said, facing away from her as she slathered his back in sunblock.

"You mean he went back to Boston?"

"Uh-huh. He went back home. Mom says she doesn't know when he's coming back."

Lindsey wasn't sure how to respond. She had noticed, on that first night, that Carol and Jonathan were distant, but she didn't realize how bad it was. Even though Carol was so cold, *mean*, even, she felt bad for her, just for a moment.

"Well, I'm sure he will be back soon," she said. She didn't want to make promises when she really didn't know what the situation was.

"Maybe," he said. "I think it will all work out." He pulled his goggles over his head. Sometimes she wondered if Berty was the wisest person in the whole family.

After a swim, she sat with Georgie on the beach while they watched Berty play with his friends in the sand. She didn't really understand why Georgie was alone so much, why she didn't have friends.

"Hey, do you mind watching Berty while I use the bathroom?"

"Sure," Georgie said, seeming annoyed once again. Maybe Lindsey did understand why Georgie didn't have friends after all. Yeah, being a teenager was tough, but come on, she thought to herself as she walked to the bathroom.

As she passed through the shady alcove outside the restrooms, where the cement was cool and damp on her feet, she felt a hand grab her arm. Her instincts made her flip her arm up and away, fast.

"Whoa, easy there." It was Brian, who now stood before her in pastel-blue board shorts, holding his hands up in the air with a grin. She exhaled, relieved that it was just him.

"Hey." She held her hands on her hips. "What's up?" She wondered if he was going to acknowledge his text message to her, hoping that he wouldn't.

"So you're really dating the *townie*, huh?" he asked. She wasn't sure if he was just joking with her. She released an uneasy chuckle.

"Yeah, I mean, we'll see . . ." She lifted her shoulders to her ears in an innocent shrug and leaned her body toward the restroom, expecting the conversation to be over.

"That guy is a piece of shit," he said, staring down at Lindsey. "But I guess you're just a nanny."

She didn't respond. It was like she'd just been slapped. She'd never been spoken to like that, and it felt strange to be under such attack from someone so suddenly, so aggressively. She felt a hint of fear then, as Brian stood before her. Even then, though, she wondered if he was just joking, if he was just saying that to mess with her. She smiled an awkward smile, her jaw feeling tight, her body feeling frozen.

"Georgie, on the other hand . . . ," he continued. *Georgie?* Lindsey stepped back from him. He wasn't joking, she could tell. He was serious.

"Stay away from her," she said, her voice shaking. "Stay away from Georgie. And stay away from Dylan." She turned away from him, but he put his hand on her shoulder, not with force but with a calm sense of authority and control that caused her to stop in her tracks.

"Hey," he whispered. "Lighten up. I'm just joking." She searched his face for some truth—maybe he was joking around, maybe he'd just had too many beers that morning and this was his harmless way of trying to be funny, clever, charming. But nothing on his face conveyed that. She saw only contempt.

She brushed his hand off and walked back toward the beach, forgetting for a second that she really did have to pee, and then pivoted quickly and ran back into the restroom, past Brian, still unsure of whether or not she would be safe in the women's room. A mother and her young daughter came in seconds later. Lindsey sat in a stall, suddenly feeling winded.

She grabbed for some toilet paper and saw that her hands were trembling. She took a few deep breaths. She splashed some cold water on her face at the sink and went back out, looking around. Brian had walked down the beach to where Joanna had gone earlier. She looked closer. Joanna was sitting on his lap, laughing.

Lindsey went back to her spot with Georgie. Berty had returned to their spot as well and was playing with a pile of seashells. She sat down on her towel, saying nothing. A minute or so passed. She could feel Georgie's eyes on her, like Georgie was waiting for an apology or an explanation. She must have seen her talking to Brian. To *her* Brian.

A little while later, Berty cut himself on a shell and started sobbing. The cut was minor, barely a scrape, but he wanted to go home. Lindsey scooped him up, and he nestled into her shoulder.

"I'm gonna stay here for a little while," Georgie said. Lindsey nodded. Georgie was mad at her—that was obvious—but there was nothing Lindsey could do about it. As she left the club with Berty, she looked down the beach and saw Joanna and Brian together in Adirondack chairs, drinking Planter's Punches, laughing. She looked back at Georgie and saw that she was watching them too.

On the walk home, Lindsey felt dizzy. The day had disoriented her. She thought back on her encounter with Brian, the way he'd spoken to her, the words he'd used, what he'd said about Georgie. She considered calling Joanna and telling her everything. That's what she should do, she knew. But what was there to tell, really? That Brian had made a joke, maybe, about Georgie? Or that he'd made a dig at her about being a nanny? She couldn't tell anymore where the lines were, so it was impossible to know when someone had crossed them. Sometimes, she decided, it was better to say nothing than to create drama over what could really be nothing. So she didn't call Joanna.

Later that evening, at home, Berty called for Lindsey to come to his room.

"Quick! Quick!" he screamed.

Lindsey ran upstairs. "Ocean is a butterfly!" Berty yelled. She looked into the glass cage and saw that Berty was, in fact, right. Ocean had come out of the cocoon, which now sat like a discarded, crinkled tissue next to the miniature tree. She was a monarch, bright and orange and bold, powerful.

"The *life spam* of a monarch is two to six weeks," Berty said to her. Lindsey cracked a small smile. "We just need to take care of her."

He reached into the cage and extended one of his little pink fingers down to touch Ocean. He stroked one of her wings, and in a quick, frantic motion, she jerked away, then flew to the other side of the cage, hitting the glass. Berty pulled out his hand. "Oh no," he moaned. The butterfly was now on the ground of the cage, her wings shaking. Berty looked distraught.

"It's okay," Lindsey said, worried that the creature might not recover. "But you can't touch Ocean," she said. "That's the thing about butterflies. If you touch their wings, they won't be able to fly." Berty nodded obediently.

"Let's give her some space. She will be okay." She wasn't sure it was true. The butterfly would probably be dead tomorrow, she thought, and she'd have to explain death to Berty. *Great.* Lindsey went to her room to shower. She thought about calling her mom or Rose to talk through her day. But it was already too much to explain. She thought about calling Dylan, but she knew that he was the last person she could talk to about any of it. She shut her eyes in the shower and just stood there for a minute, feeling homesick for the first time since she'd arrived.

Chapter 20

GEORGIE

The Deckers always did the same thing on the Fourth of July, and this year would be no exception. But for Georgie, this year would be entirely different. Because *she* was different.

Edgartown really went all out for the Fourth. There was a huge parade that marched throughout the whole town. Lots of local businesses and groups made floats that they spent weeks building—everything from a shark's mouth made of recycled beach trash to a giant inflatable rat advertising a rodent-control business. There were veterans who marched in uniform, Scottish bagpipers who played so loudly that everyone had to cover their ears, real fire trucks, and antique cars. There were local sports teams tucked into truck beds, their toned legs dangling off the sides. There was always at least one *Jaws*-themed float. Locals and tourists lined the sidewalks of Main Street, politely elbowing one another to get a prime spot.

The parade went right past the Deckers' house, so viewing it was always something they did together as a family, right on their front lawn. That day, Georgie had to work in the morning. She had wanted to work that day, knowing it was going to be busy. She rushed home after work just as the parade was rounding the corner toward their street. Lindsey was already there with Berty, and even Carol and Jonathan stood with them on the front porch, sipping some cocktails.

The floats and crowds were so loud as they went by the house that no one bothered talking while they watched. It was one of the few times the family actually enjoyed being all together, because they didn't really have to engage with one another. They could just share an experience, watch. Georgie ducked inside the house halfway through. She needed to get changed before the party.

After the parade, every year, the big party was always at the Fitzgeralds' house. It was casual—plastic cups, burgers on the grill, tons of kids running around, splashing in the pool—but *everyone* in Edgartown went. Georgie had been many times before, but she'd had to miss it the past few summers when she was at sleepaway camp. This year, it was like she was going to the party for the first time. She was a teenager now. And she knew Brian. They were friends or something. Everything was different. She needed to look the part.

She'd noticed, outside, that Lindsey was wearing white jean shorts and a white tank top. She looked amazing. Georgie had planned on wearing a floral dress with spaghetti straps, but once she was in her room and tried it on, the outfit looked too juvenile. She hated it. She took out her cutoff jean shorts, the ones she'd been wearing almost every day, and put them on, along with a fitted gray T-shirt and flip-flops. She added a swipe of a pink MAC lip gloss that she'd bought at the mall last year with her own money. It was not an outfit her mother would like. *Too casual, too sloppy,* she'd say, but it was what she wanted to wear. It was the closest she'd get to dressing like Lindsey—effortless and cool. She put her hair down, brushed it out, and swiped on an extra layer of deodorant.

When she came downstairs, her family was just about to walk out the door.

"Gigi," her father called as she ran down the stairs. "Perfect timing," he said. "Let's go."

Her mother looked at her outfit but said nothing, though Georgie could tell from her face that she was annoyed. They were running late; there was no time for Georgie to change. *Perfect,* she thought.

Berty held Lindsey's hand as they all walked the few blocks to the Fitzgeralds' house. Georgie looked over at her mother, who was watching them. She wondered if it bothered her to see how quickly Berty had become attached to Lindsey. Georgie herself had been the same way with her own nanny growing up. It was never her mother whom she cried for; it was the nanny.

The Fitzgeralds' home was an old, historic Edgartown house that had once belonged to a whaling captain. It was white with black shutters, three stories high with a widow's walk on top. In front was a plush green lawn and a sweeping oak tree, enclosed by a white picket fence with a brick pathway leading to the front door. As they approached, Georgie could hear noises from the party—voices, music, jumps in the pool, the slamming of a screen door. She smelled the char of hamburgers and hot dogs on the grill.

The front door was open, and inside the house was a main corridor that went directly to the backyard, where there was a pool, a patio, and a large lawn. Georgie hadn't been in the house in years. As they walked through it to get to the backyard, she darted her eyes around, trying to absorb the presence of Brian. She wondered where his room was and what it smelled like, what color his sheets were, what he looked like when he slept.

Outside, Mr. Fitzgerald was grilling, wearing an apron with red roses on it. Georgie took a big inhale, sucking in her gut and looking around. It wasn't exactly ideal to go to the party with her family and Lindsey. She was the odd person out. Her parents always ditched the kids to go talk with their friends. Berty would inevitably want to run wild, and Lindsey would have to watch him. So Georgie would be left by herself. She was prepared for this, though. Because this year, she would have Brian.

She looked around but didn't see him, not at first. She knew some of the people there, other kids Brian's age. There was the skinny boy she'd seen come into the Picnic Basket with him—Whitney something.

He was holding a beer bottle and talking to a girl Georgie recognized from sailing a few years ago as well. There wasn't really anyone her age there, she noticed. It was all little kids or adults. The last time she was at the party, she would have been one of the little kids: she would have jumped in the pool, eaten ice-cream cake, played tug-of-war. But this year, she was with the adults. She wanted to go to the bathroom to look at herself in the mirror. She could feel the small of her back start to perspire, and she hoped there weren't stains already appearing. As she predicted, Berty tugged on Lindsey's arm and asked to go jump on the trampoline that was set up in the corner of the yard. They ran off, and Georgie was left alone. A woman in a hay-colored tunic with large pearl earrings approached her.

"Well, hello, Miss Georgie," she said. It was Catherine's mother, Mrs. Johnson. "I haven't seen you in ages. How's your summer going?" She leaned in to hug Georgie.

"Hi, Mrs. Johnson." Georgie started to feel like that little kid again, small and powerless. "It's going well, thanks. I've been working at the Picnic Basket." She looked around, wondering now if Catherine was at the party too.

"You know, I wish we could get our Catherine to have the same work ethic as you. But all she wants to do is go to the beach."

"Is she here?" Georgie asked.

"Oh no," Mrs. Johnson said, laughing. "We couldn't drag her here. She went up to Squibnocket with some friends. You know *Catherine*. We can't keep up with her."

"Yeah, I know." Georgie tried to muster a smile. "Well, nice to see you!"

"You too, sweetheart." Mrs. Johnson gave her a wave and walked away. Georgie was humiliated. She didn't belong at this party. There was a reason why there weren't other kids her age—they all had lives, friends, *plans*. They wouldn't be caught *dead* at a party like this with their own parents. She thought about texting Catherine, seeing if she could come meet her. Maybe she could take the bus up island or hitch-hike. But it was too late. And if Catherine had wanted her to come, she would have invited her.

"Hey," she heard behind her. "Glad you made it." *Brian.* She turned around, and there he was. He was sunburned, and it made his blue eyes look electric.

"Hi," she said, wishing that she'd worn a different shirt.

"How's it going?" Brian wore a light-pink polo shirt and khaki shorts. He had bare feet.

"Um, it's good." She pushed her hair back with her fingers like she'd seen Lindsey do before, hoping it looked pretty the way it landed around her face.

"Work still keeping you busy?" Brian looked away from her, like he was searching for someone else. She wanted to grab his attention, keep him locked in her view.

"Yeah, pretty busy." She shifted on her feet and put her hands in her two front pockets.

"How's it going with the new nanny this summer? I mean, Berty's nanny. Lindsey. She seems cool."

Georgie's face dropped. Why was he asking about her? Why did he even care? And did he mean it, that he thought Lindsey was cool? Georgie felt her face redden. She bit her lip before opening her mouth to respond.

"I guess so; it's going okay."

Brian smiled, like he knew the question had bothered her somehow. "Well, that's good." Georgie looked around, wondering if Lindsey could see the two of them talking, wondering where Joanna was.

"Hey, you want a drink?" Brian asked.

"Um, sure." She felt incapable of speaking in full sentences, inca-pable of expressing a confident thought. She didn't even know what her voice sounded like anymore. She was so nervous that she felt she might explode. *So this is what it feels like,* she thought to herself.

"Follow me," he said.

Georgie saw her mother out of the corner of her eye, talking to Brian's mother and pouring herself a glass of wine. Lindsey was watching Berty on the trampoline; it didn't look like she saw them. She could feel her hands rattle with excitement and her heart start to flutter as she walked behind Brian.

They went into the kitchen, a dark space in the back of the house that smelled of lemons and pickles. A housekeeper scurried past them with a tray of sliced tomatoes, lettuce, and onions. Even the most casual party in Edgartown always had an invisible staff behind it. Brian opened the fridge. She felt a hit of the cold air on her skin.

"Let's see," he said. "Vodka lemonade?" Georgie watched him. It was odd being in his house, with him, while he made her a drink. She imagined, for a second, what it would be like to live together. Would he make her a cocktail every night? Would they watch the sunset together?

"Sounds good. Thanks."

Brian grabbed a handful of ice from the freezer with his hands and dumped it into a plastic cup, then added a few inches of vodka and just a splash of lemonade on the top. He stirred it with his finger, which would have grossed Georgie out normally, but it made her excited seeing him do something so impolite, unpolished, something raw.

He handed her the drink, and when she took it from him, their hands touched. He leaned in closer to her. If Lindsey could see her now, Georgie thought.

"Don't tell anyone about this, okay? I remember what it was like to be your age. It's our *secret*," he whispered. He took his own beer bottle and raised it up, clinking her glass. What did he mean, "your age"? She brushed off the comment. It didn't matter. What mattered was that he'd made her a drink—he trusted her with that; he wanted to share a secret with her. Whatever secret Lindsey had with him, now she had her *own*.

Georgie took a sip. It was strong and acidic, but the ice felt good against her tongue. She looked up at Brian, who was staring at her. The voices outside seemed to evaporate, and it felt like she and Brian were the only two people in the world. All she could hear was her own breath and an intense humming between their bodies, pulling them closer. She swallowed, her mouth feeling dry. Was he going to kiss her? The moment felt so different from the moment with Leo at summer camp. Back then, all she could think about were the mechanics of the potential kiss—whose mouth would go where and at what angle, when to stick her tongue out and how far. But now, everything seemed to melt away. She just felt a single force, pulling her closer to him.

There were some murmurs in the hallway just then, followed by the crashing sound of glass breaking. Something had fallen. Georgie and Brian both turned, the moment between them breaking apart.

"*Shit,*" they heard. Georgie recognized the voice. *Dad?* She and Brian walked toward the noise. The door to the bathroom slammed, and someone inside locked it. Outside, in the hallway, Jonathan was on his knees, picking up pieces of a blue-and-white porcelain vase, pulling them from a puddle of water and scattered peony petals.

He looked up, scanning his eyes across both Georgie and Brian.

"Sorry about this, Brian. Hopefully this wasn't a piece from the Qing Dynasty. I've always been a bit of a bull in a china shop."

"Hey, that's okay, Mr. Decker," Brian said, running back into the kitchen to get some paper towels. He returned and got on his knees, helping to clean up.

"What happened?" Georgie asked. She eyed the bathroom, wondering who was in there. Something didn't feel right. She felt like she wasn't being told the truth about something, like everyone else understood what had just happened but she didn't.

"I'm just a klutz, that's all. You know that, Gigi," he said. "Now, where should I put all this, Brian?" Her dad followed Brian back into the kitchen. Georgie stayed in the hallway. There was still a dark spot where the water had hit the wooden floor. She waited for a minute. Brian and her dad had forgotten about her, and she heard their voices travel outside, back to the party. Her moment with Brian was long gone. Her dad had left his cocktail on the hallway table. She picked it up and sniffed. It smelled like gasoline.

She heard the bathroom door unlock then and saw the handle turn slowly. The door opened. It must be her mother, Georgie thought. They probably got into another argument, and she needed a moment alone. That's what usually happened: Carol retreated to the bathroom and just stared in the mirror until something inside her changed and she was able to come out again.

The door opened, but Lindsey appeared. There was a ring of sweat around her forehead, dampening her hairline and creating a glisten over her face. She still looked beautiful, Georgie thought. Lindsey looked at Georgie, and something silent passed between them, a question they both had, a mutual confusion. Had something happened between Lindsey and her dad? What *happened*?

"Hi," Lindsey said, tugging at her tank top and smoothing it out. "What a party, huh?" She paused. "Are you having fun?" Lindsey's energy seemed off somehow. Her voice sounded frantic, shaky, nervous, almost manic. She didn't look like she'd been crying. She looked like someone had flipped her upside down.

"Yeah, I guess," Georgie said.

"See you outside. I've got to get back to Berty." She swiveled her body past Georgie and went outside, jogging back over to the trampoline. Georgie went into the bathroom after her. She took a few wads of toilet paper and dabbed at her armpits and the small of her back. She fanned herself with her hands. She opened the drawers under the sink, curious, but finding only a box of seashell soap, some air freshener, half-used mouthwash, extra toilet paper, and some old potpourri.

She returned to the outdoor patio, her mind wandering to thoughts of what might have just occurred in the hallway. Maybe nothing had happened. Maybe Lindsey had just gone to the bathroom and at the very same time, her father had knocked over a vase. *Maybe.* Except she knew her father, and she sort of knew Lindsey. And something didn't seem right with either one.

Georgie was halfway through her drink. It made her body feel loose and light. She wandered over toward the grill and took a cheeseburger. When she'd added ketchup and lettuce, she went to eat it by the pool. She wondered if anyone suspected that she was drinking alcohol. She didn't care. In fact, she hoped that someone would guess. She wanted to be a little bit rebellious. She dipped her feet in the pool and started to eat.

"Hey, kid," Brian said, coming up next to her. He didn't sit. "You remember Joanna, right? My girlfriend?" Georgie was midbite, and some of the juice from the burger dripped down her chin and fell onto her shorts, staining them. She grabbed at her napkin and brought it to her face. Joanna crouched down, her straight hair falling forward, her tiny butt resting on the tops of her tiny heels.

"Hi, sweetie," she cooed. "You're so grown up this summer!" Georgie swallowed her bite. Joanna straightened back up so that she and Brian were standing above her now.

"Hi," Georgie said, waving her hand up at them. From her perspective, staring upward, Brian and Joanna looked like mannequins, perfect specimens made of long legs and sun-kissed skin and blue eyes and smiles. Joanna put her hands on her hips, punctuating her collarbone.

"Well, I'm going to get myself some rosé," she said. "Babe?" Brian put his hand on her hip and whisked her toward the bar. Georgie looked down at the rest of her cheeseburger. She thought about falling headfirst into the pool and staying there forever, letting herself drown. *Maybe then people would pay attention to me,* she thought, looking around. She noticed that Lindsey had also gone to the bar and was chatting with Brian and Joanna. Once again, she was left alone. She squinted, looking harder, noticing that Brian was watching Lindsey as she poured herself a drink, even though his arm was wrapped around Joanna. She took another sip of her own drink, which was now slightly warm. For several years after that, Georgie's drink of choice would be a vodka lemonade, and it would make her think of moments that almost happened but instead dissolved into a lonely reflection on the surface of a chlorine pool.

Chapter 21

LINDSEY

Lindsey hated that she had to go to the party at Brian's house. But she didn't have a choice. Not only was it her job to go and to watch Berty, but it had also been presented to her as an opportunity. Perhaps *the* opportunity of her entire summer—of her entire future. Jonathan had a lot of connections in the art world that could be useful to Lindsey, but he had mentioned, several times now, that he was most optimistic about getting her a job at the gallery in which the Fitzgeralds had a major stake. This wasn't just a party; it was a job interview.

Carol had told her that it was just a casual barbecue. Joanna had too.

Wear whatever, she had texted her that morning. But Lindsey knew that nothing in Edgartown was that casual, so she put on one of the nicer dresses that she'd brought with her from home: a light-purple dress with a sweetheart neck and a ribbon that tied in back. When she came downstairs before the start of the parade, however, she saw that Carol and Jonathan really were dressed casually for once: faded red shorts and a polo shirt on Jonathan and an elegant but plain shift dress on Carol. Lindsey dashed back upstairs and changed into shorts and a tank top, embarrassed to have put on clothes that were better suited for Sunday church back in Rockville than to a family cookout. She needed to relax, but the idea of meeting Brian's parents, of trying to impress them while reconciling her own confusing feelings toward him, was overwhelming.

Dylan had asked her to join him for a beach bonfire up island with some of his friends later that night, and she ached to go.

"Maybe later, after this party," she had said to him the day before. She told him the truth about where she was going—that it was to the house of his enemy, basically. But she explained why it was important to her.

"You know you don't *need* these people to be successful, right?" It was the first time since they'd met that she felt like he didn't really understand her.

"I know," she had snapped back. "But it's hard—impossible almost—to get the kind of job I want if you don't know people. I need all the help I can get." He'd told her that he got it, that she should do what she needed to do. And even though she did feel that it was important for her to go to the party and see what it could lead to, she also felt like she was betraying Dylan, and maybe betraying herself, somehow.

The parade was a welcome distraction, with its colorful floats, and candy-crazed children, and the tired parents smiling through it all. She sat on the front steps of the house with Berty on her lap. She had to hold him back a few times from running out into the street to collect fallen candy. Carol and Jonathan had both poured themselves drinks. She thought about how Jonathan might introduce her to the Fitzgeralds, what he would say. He barely knew her, she thought to herself. Carol didn't know her either. It didn't matter, though. It wasn't really about her, she knew. It was about a favor between friends. She was just the favor.

When it was time to go to the party, the family walked there together. Georgie walked behind everyone, texting on her phone. She was dressed like she normally dressed for work, Lindsey had noticed, but she'd put on some pink lip gloss that looked a little too bright and ended up making her look even younger than her age, like she was a little girl playing dress-up.

The Fitzgeralds' house was towering and refined, three stories high. It looked like an immaculate, historic dollhouse blown up to size. Jonathan and Carol walked right in the front door, following the sounds of the party out back. Lindsey darted her eyes throughout the home as they passed through. The style inside the house was closer to the Deckers' than the O'Callahans', with oriental rugs, impressionist oil paintings and watercolors, porcelain vases, and floral-patterned furniture. There were more framed photos than there was art. There were photos of Brian sailing, playing lacrosse, playing golf. There were photos of him and other family members wearing navy blazers and salmon-colored khakis standing on white sand beaches or of them smiling atop snow-covered mountains in ski gear. The photos showed a happy family and a happy kid. Brian was an only child, she was realizing. Like her.

The house opened up on the other side to a large backyard, where there was a pool, a giant trampoline, and several tables set up for drinks and food. Someone, presumably Brian's dad, was grilling. There were lots of adults, little kids, and nannies, Lindsey saw. But not many kids Georgie's age.

"Chris," Jonathan called out to the man at the grill, throwing his hands up, "another year, another great party." The men hugged one another. Carol followed, giving the man a kiss on the cheek.

"And where is the fabulous hostess?" Carol asked.

"There she is," the man said, looking over Lindsey's shoulder toward a short, pretty woman with brown hair tied back in a low bun. "Suze!" He waved her over.

Berty was tugging at Lindsey's arm to go to the trampoline.

"Just a second," she said to him, "I think we need to say hi, and then we can go play, okay?" He sulked. Lindsey was standing a few feet away from Carol and Jonathan, who were now talking to the Fitzgeralds. She wasn't sure if she should wait for them to introduce her or not. She felt like she was imposing, standing there, unintroduced. Maybe they'd forgotten about their promise to her.

While they talked, she looked around. She hadn't seen Brian yet. Georgie had gone off on her own, she saw, and was walking around the pool, looking moody. She heard Dylan's words echo through her mind: *you don't need these people.*

Neither Carol nor Jonathan turned around to include her in the conversation, so Lindsey submitted to Berty and went with him to the trampoline. She felt like she was wasting her time. Some of the other nannies lingered around the trampoline as well, watching their designated kid bounce around, bored. She recognized most of them now, from tennis and the beach club, and she nodded and waved. She turned away toward the party, trying to see if she could spot Brian or Joanna. Georgie was still standing alone, looking at the drinks, probably debating whether or not she could get away with taking a beer. She was about to turn back to the trampoline when she saw Brian emerge from the crowds and come up behind Georgie. They chatted, and then Brian led her inside, alone, away from the party. Lindsey felt a kick of energy, a need to protect Georgie from him. Where were they going? She waited for a minute and then made a decision.

"Hey," she said to one of the other nannies, "do you mind watching Berty for a second? He's the one in the green shirt. I just need to go pee."

"Sure," one of them said. It was the unspoken rule to help one another, even if they weren't friends.

"Thanks." Lindsey walked across the lawn and toward the house. Carol was talking to Brian's mom over by the bar. She didn't see Jonathan anywhere. She walked in through the living room door, closest to her. It was a sliding door that was open, so she stepped in. She heard some talking in the kitchen, and she listened. It was Brian and Georgie. It sounded like he was making a drink. She crept closer. She was in the hallway now, just outside the kitchen. And then she felt a hand on her lower back. She turned. It was Jonathan.

"Wh-what," she stammered, unsure of what to say, unsure of what was happening, and suddenly feeling trapped.

"Didn't mean to frighten you," Jonathan said, almost whispering. He moved his hand away but kept it hovered by her side. Lindsey had turned her body to face him so that he had to remove his hand from her back, but now she was close to him, only inches away, and had nowhere else to look, nothing else to breathe except him. He moved closer still.

"I'm just going to the b-bathroom," she stammered, twisting her neck away from him.

"I do want to help you, you know." He lengthened his arm, placing his hand on her shoulder like it was the head of a cobra, twisting itself toward her. She waited for him to elaborate, to explain himself. Maybe he was only trying to give her advice on what to say to the Fitzgeralds. But she felt a wave of goose bumps across her skin and a sickening gripe in her stomach. Something inside her told her to get away from him.

There was a door to her left, probably a bathroom, she thought. She swung it open, causing Jonathan to step backward suddenly, knocking over a vase on a table. Lindsey rushed into the room and slammed the door behind her, locking it. It was a bathroom. She turned the water on and leaned on the sink, waiting for him to leave, waiting for something to happen that would make her feel like this didn't have to be her reality.

She heard voices behind the door. She could tell it was Brian and Georgie. They were helping Jonathan clean up. A few minutes passed, and the voices disappeared. When she opened the door, Georgie was there, as though she was waiting for her. They looked at one another for a moment, but Lindsey just smiled and kept walking past her. She joined Berty back at the trampoline.

She saw Joanna walk into the party a minute later. She could tell Joanna what had happened, at least between her and Jonathan. But she couldn't say anything about why she'd gone in the house in the first place—because Brian had taken Georgie inside. Maybe there was nothing to tell anyway, she told herself. Was she misreading everything? Was *she* the only thing that was off?

Joanna was wearing a flowy Mara Hoffman color-blocked dress that showed off her thin arms and collarbone. Of course, Lindsey thought to herself, Joanna was wearing a gorgeous dress, even though she'd said that the party was casual. Once again, she felt like she'd chosen the wrong way to present herself. She could never get it just right.

"Let's take a break and get something to drink," Lindsey suggested to Berty, who had started to sweat from jumping on the trampoline. He leaped into her arms, and she carried him over toward the bar, where Joanna was pouring herself a drink with Brian.

"Hi," Joanna said in a melodic voice as Lindsey approached. "How are you?" She gave Lindsey an air-kiss, turning her cheek to the side. Joanna seemed out of place now that she was out of the corner of the backyard, with the kids and the other nannies. It occurred to Lindsey, for a second, that Joanna might be embarrassed to be talking to her.

"Hi," Lindsey said back, putting Berty down. "Hey, Brian," she added, unsure of whether or not to hug him. But he decided for her, leaning in to give her a quick hug. "This is a great party," she said when they separated.

"It's fun," Brian responded, wrapping his arm around Joanna's waist. Lindsey noticed how happy Joanna seemed with him, and she almost forgot how different Brian had been with her when they were alone at the club. She almost forgot the terrible things he'd said, the terrible things he'd hinted at.

She poured a glass of lemonade and handed it to Berty, who started slurping it down.

"You can have, like, *one* drink with us, right?" Joanna asked as she surveyed the bar. Lindsey could feel the eyes of the other nannies on her, judging her: *Who do you think you are? What are you doing?*

"You know what? Yes," Lindsey said. She deserved a drink. It was a party. One drink was fine. "Let's do it."

Joanna grabbed a bottle of white wine from an ice bucket and poured her a glass.

"Cheers," she said.

"Cheers," Lindsey repeated. She couldn't tell Joanna about the encounter with Jonathan, not right now—they were surrounded by too many people.

Lindsey felt a tug at her shorts. "I want some lunch," Berty said. "A hot dog!"

"Okay," Lindsey said, picking him up and hoisting him onto her hip. She put her glass of wine down on the bar, abandoning it. "Let's get you that hot dog."

Brian and Joanna gave her a sympathetic smile as she carted Berty off toward the grill. She made him a plate, making herself one, too, and they went to sit by the pool to eat. She was relieved, in a way, that Berty had wanted lunch. She could feel herself getting caught up in Brian and Joanna's world. One more glass of wine and she might have forgotten altogether that she was there to take care of Berty.

She cut up Berty's hot dog in little pieces. She glanced up as she did so, looking around. Carol was sitting under an umbrella on the patio, deep in conversation with a strict-looking woman wearing a gingham headband that seemed better suited for a twelve-year-old than a fifty-year-old. Carol had no idea where her kids were, no idea what they were doing or whom they might be doing it with. She didn't seem to care. Lindsey rubbed the top of Berty's head as he ate.

"Hey, can I sit with you guys?" Brian had come over with her glass of wine. "And I brought you this, if that helps." He handed her the drink.

"Thanks," Lindsey said cautiously. She didn't want him to sit with them. She didn't want to talk to him. But he seemed so different from the person outside the bathroom at the beach club. Maybe he was going to apologize.

She shifted over slightly so that he could sit next to her on the bluestone steps to the pool where she and Berty had staked out a seat. Joanna was talking to Whitney, whom Lindsey hadn't seen yet. Whitney glanced over at them just for a quick moment, but it was long enough for Lindsey to feel somewhat unnerved, like she was in the wrong place.

Lindsey sipped the wine, no longer caring if Carol or Jonathan had a problem with it.

"I owe you an apology, Lindsey," he said, to her surprise. She hadn't actually thought that he'd say sorry. "I was way out of line the other day. I didn't mean it—what I said."

She thought about his words: *I didn't mean it.* She wasn't sure intention really mattered. Intention wasn't the point, after all. The point was that he'd said what he'd said. There was a part of him that must believe it, then, if he'd said it. Was it ever possible to say or do something that at least some part of you didn't believe? But he did seem sorry, she thought, and she wanted to believe him. Her life would be a lot easier if she did.

"It's okay," she said, nodding.

"Good." He nudged her shoulder with his gently. "I'm glad we're good."

"Me too." She felt a sense of relief. It was more comfortable to trust Brian than to not trust him. "So your family throws this party every year?" She turned to face him, changing the topic.

"Yeah, every year. Since forever," he said. "My parents will find any excuse to celebrate, though. They love parties." He paused. "I guess I do too," he added with a laugh.

"Well, it's a beautiful house."

"Thanks," he said. "My parents bought it before I was born. I don't think they've changed a single thing in the house since then. Except for all the photos. I'm sure you saw them on your way in." He rolled his eyes.

"Oh yeah, I sure did." She caught herself off guard by smiling. This version of Brian was nice, welcoming, warm, sincere. "It looks like you had an amazing childhood."

"I did. I'm really lucky." He swigged his beer. "I really am." He exhaled and then pushed on his knees to rise. "Okay, you've got a drink, you had a burger, you're happy. I've got to go finish the rounds or else I'll be in trouble with my mom." He grinned and walked back into the crowds.

Berty was still invested in his pieces of hot dog, but he looked up from his plate.

"I like him," he said.

"Yeah," she said.

When the party was dying down, Lindsey carried Berty over toward the patio, where Carol and Jonathan had started to say goodbye to the Fitzgeralds. Georgie was standing with them. Carol's hand was on Georgie's shoulder, as if to tell her to stay put. Lindsey hovered close by, waiting for a signal to leave. Berty was practically asleep on her, his arms draped around her neck like noodles.

"And this is the incredible, superpowered Lindsey we told you about," she heard Jonathan say, alerting her. Lindsey widened her eyes and stepped forward. "Lindsey, meet Chris and Suze Fitzgerald."

Lindsey extended her free hand, hoisting Berty on her hip with the other. "So nice to meet you both. What a beautiful home." She got her head into performance mode. She wanted to impress them. She knew that it might be her only shot.

"Thank you," Suze said. She had a pretty face, with bright cheeks and small, kind eyes. "And we hear that you're friends with our Brian as well? And Joanna, of course."

"Yes, yes I am," Lindsey heard herself saying. "They've both been great friends to meet this summer." *If Rose could hear me now,* she thought to herself.

"Well, after this summer," Chris chimed in, "we've got to get you in to the gallery for an interview. A meeting, rather. How about that?" Carol and Jonathan were both smiling, too, like the four of them were all doing some good deed, helping her out of destitution.

"That sounds amazing, thank you!" Lindsey gushed with gratitude, though it wasn't entirely genuine. She *was* grateful, but at the same time, she knew what she was capable of, and she knew that she deserved the potential job. "Thank you so much." She kept smiling. Her jaw hurt.

Carol and Jonathan hugged the hosts one last time, and they all walked out the way they'd come in. On the walk home, Jonathan turned toward Lindsey, stating, "Well, that worked out superbly!"

Carol looked at Lindsey as well. "It really did. I'm glad we could help," she said.

They walked the rest of the way home in silence. The sun had just set, and it was becoming dark. The town put on a fireworks show at nine. Georgie had said that they always watched it from their back lawn. It was the best place to watch on the whole island, she had said. Lindsey wanted to go meet Dylan, but she was too tired, too sad, too confused. She texted him when she got home: Long day. Sorry. I can't leave tonight. He wrote back a picture of the sunset from his end of the island. Miss you, he said. She missed him, too, but she felt pulled between where she was and where she wanted to be. She felt an ache in her heart for something simple, something pure, away from herself.

Chapter 22

GEORGIE

Georgie relived the moment in the kitchen with Brian again and again. She was distracted at work all week, moving slower than she usually did, her head in the clouds, daydreaming. She kept waiting for him to come into the café or to see him at the club, but a few days passed, and she didn't see him. She was working in the back office one day and came out for a quick break when Emma breezed by her.

"You just missed your boyfriend, *Briiiiaaan,*" she said with a smile. Georgie deflated. She was always so unlucky. Why hadn't he asked for her this time? she wondered. "He was with that blonde girlfriend of his," Emma added, as though she'd read her mind.

Even Lucy noticed that she wasn't focused at work.

"Whatever's got you down, kid, cheer up," she said later that afternoon. Georgie was embarrassed. She hadn't wanted anyone to feel sorry for her or for it to be so obvious that she was upset. But she was. Her pining for Brian had only expanded. He was all she thought about.

"Thanks," she said to Lucy. "Sorry, I'm fine."

Lucy cocked her head and gave her a look as if to say, *You're not fooling me.* She had a way of doing that with all her employees: knowing them without really knowing them.

"Let me guess," Lucy said. "Boy troubles?"

Georgie considered a response. She felt that she could tell Lucy.

"Yeah." She sighed. "I think I'm in love with this guy, and I'm not sure he loves me." The words poured out of her, and it felt good. She'd finally said it. And when she did, she knew that she meant it. Her feelings for Brian were *real*.

"Oh, sweetie," Lucy said, sitting on the corner of her desk. Georgie was on the floor sifting through another box of papers. "Nothing hurts as bad as love. Trust me, I know. Which is why you should avoid it completely. It's *never* worth it." She patted Georgie on the shoulder and left her alone in the office.

It wasn't the response that Georgie had hoped for, not even close. Sometimes she felt like all the adults in her life discouraged her from pursuing the things that excited her most. Why was everyone so scared of *love*? They were all wrong, she thought.

A little while later, just as she was about to head home for the day, Emma popped into the office.

"Patio time," she said, waving her hands, her fingers splayed. "Come on!"

Georgie walked with her to the back patio, where the staff were all camped out, drinking beers. "Just Dance" by Lady Gaga played through a portable speaker.

She sat next to Emma and Vera at the table. Someone slid her a beer. It was the same dark-brown kind she'd had last time. She still didn't like it, but now she knew what to expect.

"Okay, G." Vera leaned in. Georgie liked it when Vera called her that. "Tell us what's got you so down." Francesca pulled up a chair. They all wanted to listen; they all wanted to help. It felt good.

"Basically, there's this guy," she began. They didn't have to know that it was Brian, she decided. "We have a thing. I mean, nothing has actually happened between us." She paused. "Not yet anyway. But we've *always* had a thing between us."

"Okaaay," Vera said, leaning closer.

"And anyway, he has an on-and-off thing with someone else, but I know he doesn't care about her. But then, also, one of *my* friends sort of seems to have a weird flirtation with him too." She was talking about Lindsey, of course. When she said it out loud like this, she felt a new sense of anger and jealousy toward her. "Basically, I think he just leads them on because he's trying to mess with me, play with me or something. Maybe he thinks I'm not interested anymore."

The girls nodded.

"Sounds to me like he's playing hard to get, making you want him even more," Francesca said. The others agreed.

"Totally," Emma said.

Georgie reveled in the affirmations from her coworkers, finally hearing the responses that she had been craving.

"So what should I do? Should I just go for it? Like, just tell him how I feel?"

"Why not?" Vera asked. "He likes you, you like him, sounds like these other chicks are just pawns. Be up front with him."

Georgie thought about it. Why wouldn't she be up front with him? What would be so wrong about telling Brian how she felt and seeing, once and for all, if he felt the same way? What if, she wondered, all this time, he liked her but just didn't think that *she* liked *him*?

"Thanks, guys," she said, imagining how the conversation might go. She was grateful to her friends from work, her *real* friends.

Someone offered her another beer. She had to pee.

"Sure," she said, taking the beer. "I'll just be right back." She went inside to the bathroom. The next time she saw Brian, she thought, she would tell him everything. Summer felt like it was slipping through her fingers, accelerating, disappearing, but maybe it wasn't too late for this.

She walked through the hallway back toward the patio. The door was propped open, and she could hear her friends chatting outside. She heard her name and stopped, waiting to hear more, listening. They couldn't see her around the corner inside.

"Poor thing," Francesca murmured. "If my mom ever secretly got me hired for a job, I'd be fucking *pissed.*"

"I know," she heard Emma whisper. "I just can't get over how her mom asked Lucy to tell us all to be *nice* to her, like we're her friends. I mean, we would have anyway, but . . ." There was a pause and some other voices chiming in. "It's just so embarrassing."

Georgie froze and felt tears rising up to her eyes. She swallowed them back. She felt ashamed, ridiculous, like she should have known this was all too good to be true. And her *mother*, of all people. How could she do this to her? Georgie waited another minute and then skipped back out to the patio, putting on her best happy face. She took another sip of beer and then told the group she had to get going, that she had some plans with friends. She didn't want anyone to suspect that she'd heard anything. It was too mortifying.

When she stepped outside the café, the tears started rolling down her face. She felt completely alone and lost. She wanted to quit her job. How could she ever go back there knowing that she hadn't really earned the job on her own in the first place? That none of her coworkers cared about her, that they were just following their boss's orders? She stormed into the kitchen of her house, hungry. Lindsey was in there with Berty, getting his dinner ready.

"Hey," she said. It was obvious that Georgie had been crying. She still was. Her face was puffy and red. She was still sniveling.

"What's wrong?" Berty asked. He was molding some Play-Doh on the kitchen counter.

"Let's give Georgie a minute," Lindsey said. "Hey, Berty, will you do me a huge favor and go pick me ten of the biggest pieces of grass you can find on the lawn? I need them for a secret recipe." Berty smiled and leaped into action. Lindsey was pretty amazing at finding creative ways to distract him, Georgie had to hand that to her. He ran outside. They could watch him from the kitchen. Georgie felt grateful to Lindsey in that moment. It was silent for a minute as Georgie roamed the cabinets for a snack, deciding on some pretzels.

"Bad day?" Lindsey asked.

"Bad *summer*," Georgie said. She thought about the people in her life. Her friends at school felt so far away from her, and they were all dealing with their own insecurities; they wouldn't understand what she was going through now. She couldn't tell her mother anything, not anymore, not after what she'd done to her. Her work friends weren't real friends, obviously. Catherine hated her, for whatever reason, and none of the girls in that group wanted to hang out with her. The only person she could even possibly talk to was Lindsey. But she still felt jealous of her. It was a strange pull of two different feelings.

"I've got an idea," Lindsey said. "Your mom is home tonight, so let me get Berty dinner and put him to bed, and then why don't you and I go into town? Get some ice cream or something?" Georgie considered this. The offer felt genuine.

"Okay," she said. "Sounds good." She went upstairs to her room to shower. It had been a long day at work, and she felt sticky in her clothes.

After she showered, she sat on her bed, wrapped in her towel. The sun had just set. She looked out her window at the lighthouse and took out her journal. She skimmed through her last entry from a few days ago: *In the kitchen, I almost thought we were going to kiss. We might have, but then something weird happened in the hallway, and when I went to look, my dad was there and Lindsey had gone into the bathroom really fast. My dad was probably just too drunk. Maybe if my mom was nicer, he wouldn't do stuff like that.* Georgie read it over again. She still agreed with her words, somewhat.

She wrote a new entry: *Mad at mom. Again. Wish she would just let me do things on my own. Feels like I was never meant to be this age. I'm meant to be an adult NOW.* She closed her notebook and got dressed in some jeans and a long-sleeve shirt. She could hear Lindsey reading to Berty in his room. Down the hall, her parents' door was open. She went in. Carol was sitting on her bed, typing on her laptop.

"How was your day, Georgie?" Carol asked without looking up. Georgie couldn't respond. She was too upset with her. Her eyes started to water.

"What happened?" Carol asked, shutting her laptop. Her tone wasn't soft. The question was more inquisitive, like she wanted to know the cause of the problem, not like she actually cared.

"I know what you d-did," Georgie stammered. "How you got me my job and told them to be *nice* to me. How could you *do* that to me?" She was crying now.

"Georgie, you have to understand," Carol said, rising and trying to come closer. Georgie retreated. "Your father was the one who said you had to get a job. Think he was kidding? He *wasn't.* Okay? He thinks it's best to ship you and Berty away to camp, to boarding school. *I'm* the reason you didn't go to boarding school because you didn't want to. And *I'm* the reason you got to stay here this summer. So yes, I called Lucy. She'd done some catering for us before, and I remembered that when you mentioned the Picnic Basket. I asked her for a favor. But I did it for *you.*" Georgie had never been spoken to by her mother like this, so argumentative and impassioned.

"But why did you have to humiliate me by asking them to be nice to me? I'm mortified, Mom!"

"I'm *sorry.*" Carol put her hands on her hips. "I noticed that you seemed lonely. And I just wanted to make sure that you had a good experience there."

Georgie was still seething. "Well, maybe I wouldn't be so lonely if you weren't such a *bitch*!" she screamed at her mother and then turned and ran out the door, clambering downstairs to the kitchen. She knew her mother wouldn't follow her. She'd never said anything like that to her before, ever. She'd never even said that word in front of her mother, about anyone. She sat, waiting for Lindsey, her blood boiling. She wasn't sorry about what she'd just said. But there was a part of her that knew, somehow, that her mother wasn't really capable of closeness, of real love, and that what she had done for Georgie was, in her own way, the nicest thing she'd ever done for her. It made Georgie hurt even more. Lindsey came down the stairs a little while later.

"Ready?" she asked. They headed out, walking in silence for a minute. Georgie appreciated that Lindsey didn't push her to open up. Sometimes it felt better to be with someone but to not talk.

"You know," Lindsey started to say, "I hated being a teenager. I never felt like I had real friends." Georgie turned to look at her as they walked. "And I used to fight with my mom all the time."

Georgie had to admit, just to herself, that it was comforting to hear Lindsey say that. She couldn't imagine a time in Lindsey's life when she didn't have friends or felt uncool or alone. Maybe things would get better for Georgie too. They turned off Main Street and headed down to Dock Street, by the water.

"The best ice-cream shop is this way," Georgie said, leading Lindsey to the Ice Cream and Candy Bazaar on the harbor. It wasn't actually the best ice-cream store—Scoops probably was—but it was Georgie's favorite, because it was where she'd gone when she was a kid. Her dad used to take her there, and he'd always buy her a little something extra—a candy necklace, a rope bracelet, a bag of gummy worms.

Just down the street from the ice-cream store, across a parking lot, the Navigator was blasting live music from a swing band playing inside. It was one of the spots that turned into a bar after dinner hours and catered to an older crowd, the middle-aged people who still liked to party a little too much, Georgie had noticed. She looked over at it, just for a moment, and she saw her father there, walking inside with a

Chapter 23

LINDSEY

"Well, I got a job, maybe," she said to Rose a few days after the party. She'd called her from her bathroom in the morning, something she'd started to do whenever she could. It was the only true alone time she had all day. She had ended up telling Rose more about her life on the island—how she'd started hanging out with Joanna, and how she had thought that Brian was a bad guy but that maybe he wasn't after all, how much she liked Dylan, how the Deckers had secured her an interview at the Fitzgeralds' gallery, and how Jonathan was still creepy.

"Wow," Rose said. Lindsey could hear the buzz of the city on Rose's end of the phone. "I'm glad you got that interview lined up. That's great." She paused. "I just don't want you to feel like that's your only option."

Lindsey was brushing her hair out and getting ready for the day, balancing her phone between her ear and her shoulder.

"Yeah, but it kind of *is* my only option. Don't you remember I applied for literally every job out there last year and nothing happened?" She was annoyed with Rose for not understanding how important this was to her.

"I know; I get it," Rose said. "I just don't want you to lose yourself. Lose who you are." Lindsey rolled her eyes. She wasn't *losing* herself. This didn't have to be so dramatic. This was about her ambition, her career. "And hey," Rose added, "do you still want me to come visit for a weekend before the summer is over? Do you think the family is still cool with that?"

Lindsey paused. She had been hoping that Rose wouldn't remember that she'd encouraged her to come visit back in June. "It'll be so fun," she had said. "I looked into it and there are direct flights from JFK on JetBlue that aren't so bad. Do it!" It had been her idea. Carol had even told her that it would be okay to have a friend visit—*just for a night or two.* But now the idea made Lindsey anxious. She didn't want Rose to judge her. But more than that, she didn't want Rose to interfere with her plans, with her new *life.*

"Oh, uh," she started to say. "Honestly, Rose, I feel like Mrs. Decker would make it weird. I'm just not sure. She's been having me work a lot during the weekends lately. I'm not sure I'd have the time." It was true, anyway, she told herself. She *had* been working throughout most of the weekends, whenever Carol and Jonathan went out, which was often.

"No worries," Rose said. "I get it." There was a moment of silence then, and Lindsey opened her mouth to say something more, but nothing came out.

"Okay, well, I gotta go," Lindsey finally said. "Bye." Rose said goodbye, and they hung up. Lindsey felt the hint of a guilty knot in her gut. It wasn't like her to have those kinds of conversations with Rose—ones where dialogue was strained, difficult, guarded. They were closer than that. But something about the way Rose had warned her not to lose herself had made her want to shut Rose out. She just didn't want to hear it.

She knew that Rose was just looking out for her, but she didn't have time to think about the emotional consequences of accepting this potential job. And it wasn't just any job—it was one that she'd wanted for so long, that she'd been unable to get before. She should be celebrating, not worrying.

She'd been honest with Rose about her friendship with Joanna. Somewhat, anyway. She hadn't told her that she'd seen Joanna almost every day, that she'd gone to her house several times now and had drinks by the pool or gone through Joanna's closet with her, trying on outfits and using her Chanel makeup. Joanna had even suggested that they live together in Boston in the fall, if Lindsey's job worked out. She definitely hadn't told Rose that.

And of course, she didn't tell Rose what she and Joanna had done to Brian's car and how it had backfired on Dylan, of all people. She didn't tell her what Brian had said to her at the beach club. It all seemed so far away now. Things had changed. There was no need for her to ever tell anyone about that.

She'd spent several nights out with Dylan over the last week. He showed her parts of the island she knew she wouldn't see with Joanna or the Deckers. On one of her days off, he took her to a beach called Lucy Vincent, where massive rocks jutted out from the sandy beach, and wide, flat waves rolled into the shore. They stopped along the way for snacks at Alley's General Store. No one at Lucy Vincent was drinking Planter's Punches or wearing seersucker. She couldn't tell who was a nanny or who was just a mom. There was a different vibe up there—more relaxed, more laid-back. Several women were sunbathing topless.

She loved being with Dylan. She loved the way he made her feel beautiful and special. But in their moments of intimacy, or when he held her hand under the sun, or when they ducked under the salty waves together, she remembered what she'd done to him, and how her betrayal continued on in her friendship with Brian, and the potential job ahead of her. She felt like, at some point, she was going to have to choose: Dylan or everything else.

Sometimes she told herself that Dylan was too good for her, that he was too innocent, that his ambitions were too simple. He wanted to stay on the island, start his own construction company, have a family. He wanted to be good. Lindsey didn't want to be good. She wanted to be successful. She wanted to be important. She wasn't sure if she was worthy of love from someone like him. Or maybe that's what she told herself to make it easier to peel herself away from him eventually.

The days of the summer started to blend together. She tried to avoid Jonathan as much as possible and had developed techniques to do so. When Dylan brought her home at night, she went all the way around to the back of the house so that she could prance up the stairs without being seen by anyone awake in the kitchen or Jonathan's study. Whenever she was in the living room or kitchen, if Jonathan was home, she tried to have Berty with her as a buffer. And she always locked her door. Maybe she didn't need to, but it helped her sleep. And she told no one. Because, maybe, as she still thought sometimes, she had misread everything. Maybe he was a decent dad, a decent husband, and he just wanted to help Lindsey get a job. She told herself this often. It allowed her to get through the days and look forward to the future. She had only a few weeks until summer was over anyway. She just had to make it to the end.

Georgie had been busy at work, so Lindsey hadn't talked to her much since the party at the Fitzgeralds'. They both had unanswered questions, she knew, about what had or hadn't gone on in the kitchen with Georgie and Brian and about what had or hadn't happened in the hallway with Jonathan. And Lindsey wasn't ready to confront any of this. What was there to say? Joanna and Brian were happy together. She wanted to put everything that had happened with Georgie behind her, so she was glad that their schedules kept them apart for a little while. And Georgie seemed somewhat happy, too, at least more than she'd been at the start of summer. Maybe she was making friends at work, Lindsey thought. Whenever she came home from a long day, she talked about her coworkers and things that had happened at the café.

Then one day, Georgie came home in tears. Something had happened. Lindsey was making dinner in the kitchen with Berty. Carol was upstairs; Jonathan was out somewhere, probably at that men's-only club on the harbor that she'd heard him mention a few times. Georgie stormed into the house, tearing the kitchen apart. Lindsey wasn't sure what to say to her. Georgie was acting almost as if she was mad at *her*.

She hoped that it didn't have something to do with Brian. But she felt for Georgie. She knew what it was like to feel alone.

"Want to go into town later together, maybe grab an ice-cream cone?" she suggested. She felt like she needed to ask her to do something or offer her some kind of comfort. Georgie didn't really have anyone else, she knew. She secretly hoped that Georgie would say no, that she was fine, that she just was going to her room. That's what she usually did. But Georgie said yes. She wanted to go.

When Berty was brushing his teeth, Lindsey went to Carol's room and knocked gently on the door. She needed to make sure it was okay to go out with Georgie later. Carol was lying on her bed, dressed, over the covers, scrolling through her laptop. She never knew what she was doing, always on her computer, it seemed. Carol looked up. Her face looked tired, sad, thin.

"Hi." Lindsey felt her voice shake slightly. "Sorry to bother you, I just wanted to see if it was okay if Georgie and I walked into town later to get some ice cream. She—" Lindsey paused. "She seems upset. I thought it could cheer her up." Carol lifted her hands from the keyboard and crossed her arms.

"Of course," she said. "Go."

"Thanks." Lindsey started to walk out and close the door.

"I try, you know," Carol said. Lindsey was standing in the doorway, her hand on the knob. She really didn't want to get pulled into some weird conversation with Carol. "I try my best. But it's hard for me." Lindsey nodded. She didn't know what to say. "You grow up, you get married, and you have children. That's what my plan was, always." Lindsey noticed an empty wineglass on Carol's bedside table. She felt sorry for her. "But I'm not sure I ever wanted kids. Isn't that actually a *riot*, when you think about it?" She was laughing now, an unsteady laugh that started to build. Lindsey hadn't heard her laugh once all summer. "I try my best. But she hates me. I know she does. She hates me, and she loves Jonathan."

"That's not true," Lindsey said instinctively, though she wasn't sure she meant it. Georgie did seem to favor her father. Maybe Carol was trying, and what she had to offer just wasn't good enough. She never seemed to show either of her children that they mattered, or that she cared, or that she would love them no matter what. Both Georgie and Berty obviously lacked affection in their lives. But seeing Carol's face now, Lindsey could tell, with full certainty, that Carol wanted her children to know that she did love them. Maybe she just didn't know how to tell them. "I know that Georgie loves you. Very much."

Carol shifted her position on the bed, sitting up straighter, seeming to regret her outpouring of honesty.

"Have a great time. Thank you, Lindsey." She had returned to her normal self, aloof and reserved. Lindsey shut the door. The sadness in the beautiful house hung heavy in the air like smoke.

Georgie didn't want to talk much on the walk into town, and Lindsey knew to tread lightly with her. At the beginning of the summer, Lindsey hadn't felt sorry for Georgie. How could she have? Georgie's life was so easy. She had everything handed to her. But now, as they walked together, Lindsey glanced over at her and felt a throb of sympathy in her heart. She wondered how different Georgie might be if her mother just showed her some affection. If anyone did.

"Your mom loves you," she said. "You're just different people."

"Yeah," Georgie scoffed. "Like, polar opposites. I'm much more like my dad." Lindsey didn't respond.

The ice-cream shop was crowded, and there was a line to the door. It was the after-dinner rush. Lindsey waited in line so that Georgie could go up to the front and look at the flavors. It was one of the only times Lindsey had seen Georgie act like a kid and enjoy herself. As she waited, she felt a hand on her shoulder.

"Hey, stranger." It was Whitney, Brian's moody friend. He was alone.

"Um, hi," Lindsey said, surprised to see him at an ice-cream store. She looked over toward Georgie, who was still up front, her hand pressed against the glass case.

"Where's your boyfriend?" Whitney asked. He had a nasally voice. Everything that came out of his mouth sounded like an accusation.

"I'm just here with Georgie." Lindsey wished she could escape him, but he was standing in line behind her. She looked up ahead. A couple of overwhelmed teenagers were manning the register. It was moving slowly.

"I know what you did," he whispered in her ear. Her shoulders instinctively raised, and she took a step forward, as much as she could without bumping the person in front of her. "I saw you and Joanna in the parking lot that night." Lindsey started to feel sweat forming in her underarms. She thought about grabbing Georgie and telling her they had to go. But she would still have to face this at some point. At least here, surrounded by people in a public place, Whitney probably wouldn't cause a scene.

"I don't know what you're talking about," she said, looking forward.

"Well, I was thinking about telling that boyfriend of yours the truth. Seems like something he'd want to know." There was only one other person in front of her in line now. Georgie was somehow trying samples from one of the teenagers behind the counter. "Maybe I will; maybe I won't. It all depends." *Depends on* what? she thought.

"Do whatever you want," Lindsey snapped. She made it to the front of the line, holding on to Georgie's shoulders, smiling at her. Georgie looked back at Whitney for a second, and there seemed to be a flash of recognition, but she didn't say anything. They ordered their ice cream, and Lindsey paid hastily, telling the teenager behind the counter to keep the change. She didn't say anything to Whitney when they left.

Later, alone in her room, Lindsey texted Dylan. She wanted to make sure everything seemed normal. He told her that he missed her and that he was going to sleep soon. She sighed with relief. Whitney was probably just bluffing, she thought. And anyway, he didn't have proof.

The next day, she saw Joanna at the club. Berty was collecting shells, and Lindsey was watching him from a chair on the beach. Joanna sat on the sand next to her.

"So I saw Whitney last night," Lindsey said. She felt nervous, like Joanna would be mad at her about this, even though it wasn't her fault. None of it was. "He said that he *saw* us," she whispered. "You know, that night. With Brian's car."

Joanna just rolled her eyes.

"It's *fine*," she said. "Whitney is more bark than bite. He doesn't have the balls to stir up that kind of drama. And besides, who would believe that we would do it? That sounds insane!" She had a point, Lindsey knew. It did seem implausible.

"Well, maybe we should beat him to it, just in case. And, you know, tell the truth." She waited a second. Joanna didn't say anything. "I still feel *bad*, Joanna. I know it's been a few weeks, but Dylan shouldn't be blamed for it. What Brian did to him in return, it was awful. People on the island think that Dylan instigated it. And he *lives* here. This is his life we're talking about. We need to clear his name."

Joanna turned to her.

"I'm not clearing *Dylan's* name. And neither are you." She said his name as if even acknowledging him was beneath her. "Just let it go, Lindsey. It's over. Whitney won't say anything—I promise."

Lindsey thought about what might happen if she told Dylan the truth herself. Why should she protect Joanna anyway? But if she did confess, and if everyone found out the truth—the Fitzgeralds, the Deckers, Dylan—then what would she be left with? She wouldn't have anyone. She wouldn't have a job. She wouldn't have a boyfriend. She wouldn't have the future she'd been working toward. She didn't want to go along with Joanna's plan, but she agreed.

"You worry too much, Lindsey," she added. Maybe Joanna was right. She did worry a lot. But it's not like she wanted to be that way. There was just always something to worry about.

Chapter 24

GEORGIE

Georgie avoided her coworkers over the next few weeks. She was ashamed to have thought that they were ever her real friends. They kept inviting her to hang out on the patio at the end of the day, but she always said that she was too busy and just went home. The only friend she had, sort of, was Lindsey. And the only thing she had left to motivate her was Brian.

Her routine became simple: work, home, repeat, sometimes with the occasional trip to the beach club alone or with Lindsey and Berty. Everything she did was fueled by the possibility of seeing Brian. It was like she had blinders on. Lindsey could tell that she was in some kind of funk, because she started being extra nice to her, asking her how she was doing, asking her if she wanted to watch a movie or go for a walk. One night, during a rainstorm, Georgie found an old friendship-bracelet kit in the living room cabinet, underneath the jigsaw puzzles and the Scrabble board. She and Lindsey decided to make matching ones in shades of blue and purple, but Georgie struggled to get the stitching right and gave up halfway through. It was for the best, she thought— Lindsey probably didn't want to wear matching friendship bracelets with *her* anyway. She was just placating her. It was her job, after all.

At work, Georgie started taking note of when Brian would come in for his morning iced coffee or for lunch later in the day, and she would try to make herself useful in the main café during those windows. It didn't always work, and sometimes she had to return to the office without a sighting, another day wasted. But a few times a week, it did work, and she got to see him. It was always a brief encounter, but it was enough to keep her going. He'd ask her how she was doing, how her day was going, if her boss was nice to her. He cared about her.

"Do you have a boyfriend?" he asked her one day. She was sweeping the floors, which someone else had just done only a few minutes prior, but she needed an excuse to be out there. She almost dropped the broom. Should she tell him that she was dating a few guys but no one special? Or should she tell him the truth: that she'd never had a boyfriend, not really, but that she wanted *him* to be her boyfriend, more than anything in the whole world?

"Not really," she said. "I mean, no." She could feel her heartbeat pulsing through her skin, down to her fingertips.

"Well, I'm sure they're knocking down your door." Brian grabbed a straw from the basket on the counter and started to walk away before Georgie could respond. "See ya, kid."

"Bye," she whispered. He'd already left. She gripped the broom tighter. Even though their encounters were always brief, they were *enough*.

But it was the evenings when Georgie felt loneliest. The Picnic Basket gave her a place to go during the day, but at night, she couldn't escape the reality that she really didn't have friends.

She liked it when Lindsey was home for the night. Sometimes Georgie would watch a movie with her and Berty, and after Berty went to sleep, she and Lindsey would stay up and watch *Gossip Girl* or reruns of *Dawson's Creek*. She wished that they'd go out into town together more, like they had when they'd gotten ice cream that one night. That way, maybe she'd run into Brian or even Catherine, and they'd see that Georgie wasn't such a loser. But there were a lot of nights when Lindsey wasn't home. She had a whole life of her own on the island already.

Sometimes she crept into Lindsey's room after she'd gone out for the evening, like she'd done on that very first night. Georgie wasn't looking for anything in particular. She was just looking. Once, she even tried on that white dress with the sunflowers. It hugged her hips but was loose on her chest. She smoothed it out on the hanger when she put it back in the closet, as though she'd never been there. *I wish Lindsey would invite me to hang out with her more,* she wrote in her journal. *She probably goes to parties where Brian is.* It took her a while to fall asleep. There always came a point in the evening when she became overwhelmed with a desperation to do something else, to be somewhere else, to be some*one* else.

The next day, Georgie went to the beach club alone. She had the day off from work. Lindsey did, too, but she'd made her own plans with her friends. So Georgie went by herself to the club, staking out a lonely spot at the end of the beach, hoping no one would see her all alone. She was starting to sunburn but was still hoping that it would turn into a tan. She was envious of how brown Lindsey had become. She went to the bathroom a little while later. When she was washing her hands at the sink, she heard a flush, and Catherine emerged from a stall. She stood next to Georgie, using the sink next to her. Georgie had barely seen her since she had texted her a few weeks ago.

"Hey," Catherine said, looking straight ahead into the mirror and adjusting her string bikini top. "So you've been working at the Picnic Basket this summer, right?"

"Yeah," Georgie said. She wondered how she knew. "You know, I just wanted, like, a real job this summer." She never could tell what Catherine was going to say next.

"Yeah, I think I saw you there the other day. Talking to Brian." Georgie hadn't seen Catherine. She rarely noticed anything else around her when Brian was there. "You should come hang with us again soon. Actually, tonight I think I'm having some girls over for a sleepover. Let me know if you wanna join." Catherine wiggled the bottoms of her bikini and smiled at herself in the mirror. "See ya, Gigi."

Catherine left, and Georgie stared at herself in the mirror. The interaction felt surreal. Catherine had hardly spoken two words to her, aside from a couple of nods here and there when they ran into each other at the beach.

She grinned to herself as she left the bathroom. *Finally,* she thought, *I'll have friends again. Finally, I'll be included in things and can start to have an actual life.* She gathered her belongings to head home. She wanted to get ready for that night.

At home, Carol was in the kitchen.

"I saw Catherine today," Georgie said, entering. "I'm going to her house tonight for a sleepover. So if you could give me a ride, that would be great."

"That's *wonderful,*" Carol chirped, looking up, almost smiling. Georgie was excited about it, too, but it somehow hurt her that her mother was even more enthusiastic. It was like she was happy only when Georgie was in other people's good social graces.

She went up to her room to shower and pack her things. She shaved her legs and blow-dried her hair. It was just a girls' sleepover, but she wanted to look cool. She put on a new off-the-shoulder blouse that she'd bought herself from Rags. She threw her things into her bag and inspected herself in the mirror, content with what she saw.

Catherine lived a few miles away, in Katama, an area just outside of town, near the beach where Georgie knew tourists went during the day and older kids went at night. Catherine's parents had built a sprawling house with a sparkling infinity pool and an accompanying pool house, which seemed to only ever be used by Catherine and her friends. Carol drove Georgie there around seven.

"Bye, sweetie. I'll plan on picking you up tomorrow around ten. Or Lindsey will." Georgie waved goodbye as she slammed the car door shut. She was still angry at her mother, but for the moment, her excitement overshadowed it.

The house was flanked by giant hydrangea bushes bursting with blue flowers. They were all so perfect that they seemed fake. There were lights on both inside and outside the house, but there was a stillness as Georgie walked inside that implied an emptiness. Georgie entered through the front door without knocking; it seemed too formal to ring the bell. The house was quiet. Georgie made her way through the kitchen and living room and out into the backyard, toward the pool. She remembered her way around from past summers when she and Catherine were closer. Everyone was out back.

She saw several girls sitting in the hot tub. There were a few pizza boxes on the table. Taylor Swift crooned from a speaker. Even though Catherine had told her to come at seven, it seemed as though all the other girls had been there for a while.

"Hey, guys," Georgie said, placing her bag down on one of the pool chaises.

"Hey!" Catherine waved. "Come on in!"

Thankfully, Georgie had packed a suit. She went inside the pool house to change, taking a quick look at herself in the mirror and releasing a big exhale before joining the girls in the tub. Georgie moved quickly as she stepped into the hot water, and though she wanted to take her time adjusting to the heat, she plunged herself in so that she wouldn't be exposing her thighs and stomach to all the girls for them to see up close. The heat burned for a few seconds, and then it went away.

They were passing around a bottle of champagne. When it was Georgie's turn to drink, she tipped the bottle a little too hard, and the sugary foam crashed into her mouth, making her dribble some out and down her chin. She hoped no one would notice and that it would just blend in with the bubbles in the hot tub.

One of the girls started talking about a guy she was dating. "He obviously wants to have sex," she said, swigging the champagne with ease when it was her turn. "But I'm just not ready. I mean, I don't know why he can't just be happy with blow jobs for now anyway."

All the girls nodded. *Right. Totally.* Georgie nodded, too, but said nothing.

The only time Georgie had ever done anything with a boy was when she kissed Leo last summer. He had brushed his hand over her breasts with his palm but only for a second. And the only penis she had ever seen before was Berty's.

"I've got an idea," the same girl said, leaning out of the tub and grabbing her phone. "Let's invite the boys over. That's cool, right, Cat?" Georgie didn't know that Catherine was going by *Cat* these days.

"Totally," Catherine said. "My parents won't be home for a while."

Within half an hour, four boys showed up, one of them lugging a case of Coors Light that seemed to weigh as much as he did. Another pulled a small bottle of vodka out of a backpack. "What's up?" they all mumbled as they approached the tub. Georgie recognized most of them from sailing, but she wasn't friends with them. She wasn't sure they knew her name.

The boys took off their shirts to climb in the hot tub. They were all skinny, skinnier than the girls, even, with protruding rib bones and narrow hips. Once they were all in, the tub was so crowded that everyone's thighs were touching side by side. Beers were opened, and the bottle of vodka was passed around. Someone turned up the music. Steam rose from the surface of the water, making everything a little bit foggy and painting them all in a sheen of moisture.

Georgie felt hot. She wanted to sit up out of the tub to cool off, but she was too embarrassed to do it. Everyone else seemed fine. She could feel her face getting red. When the vodka bottle was empty, someone suggested playing spin the bottle. Catherine took the bottle and explained that they'd just spin it on the water.

"Whatever, it'll work," she said.

They each took turns spinning the bottle, though on the water it was more of a toss. Two girls kissed each other—a quick peck—eliciting whoops of elation from the guys. But when the bottle landed on two guys, they spun again, as though that wasn't an option.

"*Gross*, dude," one of them remarked at the notion. It seemed like everyone had kissed someone before it was Georgie's turn. She hoped it would just land on herself; maybe she would get a pass. But when she tossed the bottle, it twisted away from her just slightly and landed with its head pointed toward a boy named Brendan, whose bony face, made even more pronounced by his buzzed hair, was dotted in freckles.

"*Yes!*" Catherine shrieked, though Georgie wasn't sure why.

She and Brendan were sitting across from one another, so they leaned forward, and she braced her quads so as not to tumble onto him completely. Their lips touched. He slipped his tongue into her mouth just slightly. Georgie's eyes shut, and she pictured Brian in her mind. She let Brendan's tongue dart farther into her mouth, and her jaw went somewhat slack. But then, under the water, he grabbed her hand, and she lost her footing, causing her to fall forward, making it look like she was kissing him more intensely. He grabbed her hand and placed it onto his shorts, where she felt a small bulge, like he had stuffed a mouse into his underwear. He moved her hand up and down once, squeezing her fingers in his palm so that it hurt. Her eyes opened, and she no longer imagined Brian. Then Brendan leaned back and pushed her hand away. No one had seen what had happened under the surface of the bubbles, or at least Georgie didn't think so.

The whole encounter had actually lasted a few seconds, but it had felt much longer to Georgie. The rest of the group hollered when Georgie and Brendan parted, and Brendan smirked, fist pounding one of his friends. Georgie wondered if all the other boys and girls had been doing things underwater, too, this entire time, and she hadn't known. She hadn't wanted to touch him there. Her fingers hurt from his squeeze.

Soon after, everyone got out of the tub and wrapped themselves in towels, huddling up on chairs by the pool. Georgie wanted to take a hot shower, to scrub herself clean. She missed home all of a sudden. This had been what she had wanted, she reminded herself. She had wanted to party, to be around cool girls, to kiss boys, to drink alcohol. But now that she was doing it, now that it had happened *to her*, she was scared. She didn't want to be there. She didn't know what she wanted. She just needed to get away.

Georgie waited for a lull in the group conversation to get up and go check her phone in her bag. She only had a text from her mom, telling her to have a great time. Georgie scrolled through her emails and some apps for a minute, pretending to be reading new messages, feeling a lonely emptiness.

"Hey," she said, walking back over to Catherine, who was curled up in a chair, her knees pulled up to her chest. "My boss just texted me. I've got to go in for the early shift tomorrow morning, so I think I'm going to walk home." Georgie was pleased with herself at how easy it was to lie, and not only how plausible it sounded but also how it made her feel needed, like an adult.

"Okay," Catherine said indifferently. "Whatever."

Georgie could feel a separation between them. She wanted to ask Catherine why she was acting that way, what had happened between them, why they were no longer friends, why she had even invited her tonight. But she couldn't. Because even though she had wanted to reconcile their friendship all summer long and had been so lonely, she wasn't sure that being friends with Catherine again was the solution. She didn't feel like herself with her. She didn't want to play spin the bottle. She wished that she wanted to, but she didn't. She was so confused. Why couldn't she just like the same things that everyone else her age did? She'd spent all summer wanting to be part of it all, and now that she finally was, she just wanted to leave.

Georgie threw on some shorts over her suit, which was still damp, and pulled a sweatshirt over her head. The walk home was almost three miles, but she acted like it was no big deal as she waved goodbye to the group and walked out the door. Brendan didn't say anything to her as she brushed past them all and left.

Even though they had been sitting outside all night, once Georgie left Catherine's house, the air felt cleaner and fresher. She felt lighter now that she was gone. She held her palm up to her face and sniffed. It smelled like plastic. Walking alone on that dark road, she felt safer than she had all night.

By the time she approached Main Street, her hair had dried, and she felt tired. She only had a few more blocks until she reached home. She decided that she'd tell her mom the same thing she had told Catherine when she'd left—that she had to work the early shift tomorrow and that she'd just felt like some fresh air, so she had simply decided to walk home. Her mom would be disappointed in her.

Outside the Wharf, a dark, rowdy bar on Main, a group of guys smoked cigarettes. Immediately, Georgie saw that one of them was Brian. She quickly took her phone out and checked her reflection in the camera. She wished that she was still wearing her new top instead of her old sweatshirt. She kept walking but slowed her pace, glancing over at Brian, hoping he'd see her. She was running out of sidewalk and had only a few more steps until the corner, and then her chance would be gone. But then he turned, and they locked eyes. He smiled at her and held up his finger as though to say, *Wait*.

Georgie stood still, and he crossed the street toward her. Everything else in her line of vision stopped. The world was empty for a moment except for Brian and her. He was the only thing in focus.

"Hey," he said once he reached her. They stood just a foot apart. She could smell his cigarette smoke, and she glanced down to his hand that still held it. "Want a drag?"

"Sure," Georgie said. She'd never smoked before. She wasn't even sure what the right way to hold a cigarette was. She took it between her fingers when he passed it to her, trying to steady her hands. She brought the cigarette to her lips and inhaled. It burned against her throat. She tried to stifle a cough but couldn't, and she handed the cigarette back to him and covered her mouth as she released a few rough coughs. Her eyes watered.

Brian didn't say anything as he watched her. He just smiled.

"Thanks," Georgie said. "So what are you up to? I'm on my way home from a party."

"Cool," he said, taking another drag. "I'm just getting some beers with the guys, nothing crazy."

"Cool," Georgie responded, now out of things to say and annoyed that she couldn't go to the bar with him, not that he had invited her.

"Hey, want me to walk you home?" Was he joking? she wondered. Walk her *home*? She shifted her overnight bag on her hip. She wondered if he noticed it and thought it was strange, like she had left a sleepover early.

"Yes," she blurted. "I mean, sure. That'd be great. I mean, if you want." *Shut up,* she told herself. *Just shut up.* He smiled at her and then threw his cigarette on the ground, stubbing it out with his loafer-clad foot.

"Let's go," he said. Georgie was in shock, like she was in some alternate reality, watching her life outside of her own body. She was walking outside, at night, with Brian. This was really happening. He was walking her home. She felt like her whole body was made of snow that was on the verge of melting; it was all too good to be real. She forced herself to keep walking, to act natural, to ignore how much her throat burned from the cigarette and how red she knew her cheeks were and how her mouth wanted to expand into a grin. Maybe tonight, she thought, they could finish what had started between them on the Fourth.

"So, a party?" he asked her as they walked.

"Yeah. At my friend Catherine's. But I have to work early tomorrow, so . . ." She struggled to finish her sentence, unsure of what to say.

"You're always working," he said. "You need to remember to have some fun once in a while." He elbowed her, and it almost threw her off-balance completely. She forced a laugh.

"Yeah, I know," she said too loudly.

They were approaching her house too quickly. She didn't want the walk to end. Every few steps, she could feel the side of Brian brush slightly against her side. It made her feel jolted alive, like being dunked in ice water.

As they approached her house, she saw that all the lights were out except for the one in Lindsey's room. Everyone else was asleep. They stopped outside.

"Well, thanks for walking me home." She found herself talking quickly. She hoped that he didn't think that she wanted him to leave. She just wanted him to reach out and touch her, kiss her.

"Don't mention it," he said. She saw him take his hand from out of his pocket. Everything slowed down as he raised it and brought it forward. *This is it,* she thought. She licked her lips. He moved his hand closer and then rested it on the side of her arm, making her inhale sharply.

"You know," he said, leaning closer, "I've always liked you, Georgie."

She felt the chill of a breeze, and Brian instinctively brushed his hand up and down her arm, warming her. She didn't know what to say or how to even open her mouth to form words. She had to look down at her feet. She was scared of what might happen if she looked up at him, even though she wanted something to happen so badly.

"You too," she whispered. He leaned closer to her. She could smell something sharp, like that gasoline smell of the brown liquor her dad drank sometimes.

Their faces were an inch apart. She shut her eyes, just for a moment, and could feel his face moving closer, the hairs on his chin starting to tickle her nose.

The screen door slammed, and they pulled apart. Georgie looked up. Lindsey was there, standing in front of the house. They all stood in silence for a moment.

"What are you doing?" Lindsey blurted, walking toward them.

"Nothing!" Georgie shouted, angry with her. She had just ruined everything. Had she been spying on them? How long had she been watching? Why had she interrupted them like this? Was she trying to sabotage Georgie's *life*? "Nothing!" she repeated.

Brian had backed away and tucked his hands into his pockets. Georgie noticed that Lindsey was wearing the white dress with the sunflowers. It fit her perfectly. She looked down at herself, in her shorts and sweatshirt, her hair smelling of chlorine, her overnight bag slung over her shoulder. She hated Lindsey in that moment; she hated everything about her, and she knew that she'd never forgive her.

"Georgie, I think you should go to bed." Lindsey lowered her voice to a whisper. "Before your *parents* wake up."

"My parents don't give a shit about m-me," Georgie stammered, a tear escaping from her eye. "And neither do you, obviously." She looked at Brian for a brief second, but tears started pouring down her face, and she had to look away. She ran inside and up to her room, slamming the door behind her. She cried on her bed, muffling her sobs with her pillow, wishing that she could turn back time, wishing that she could change it all.

Chapter 25

LINDSEY

It was the last Saturday in July. Lindsey had less than a week on the island. She had almost made it to the end. That day, Carol told her to take the whole day off.

"Go enjoy yourself, relax," she'd uncharacteristically told Lindsey. Jonathan was home for the weekend, and they were going to take Berty and Georgie to the beach club themselves. Dylan was working a job that day, an elaborate bluestone patio at a house in Chilmark, and they were behind schedule. But she was going to see him that night. He wanted to take her out on her last weekend.

Yes! Joanna had texted when she told her that she had the day free. Let's go to Norton. Norton Point was a beach in Edgartown that four-wheel-drive cars could go onto if they had a beach pass. During the summer, the beach was always packed with cars and people camped out for the day. The waves were smooth and the sand was soft.

Lindsey walked to Joanna's house.

"Up here!" she yelled from her room. A housekeeper was vacuuming the living room floor. Lindsey had never once seen Joanna's parents or brother there. It seemed like Joanna was the only one ever home.

Joanna was naked in her room when Lindsey entered. There was a pile of bikinis on her bed, and she was trying them on.

"Here," Joanna said, pouring Lindsey a glass of rosé from a half-empty bottle. It was just before eleven o'clock.

"Thanks," Lindsey said, accepting the drink. She deserved to have a day where she could just let loose, she told herself, taking a sip. She'd worked hard that summer. Why couldn't she have some fun for one day?

"What do you think about this one?" Joanna asked, trying on a simple black bikini with a tiny flap of fabric covering her butt crack and not much else. She looked amazing, Lindsey thought. And even in a bathing suit as skimpy as that one, Joanna didn't look cheap. Lindsey imagined what she'd look like wearing it: tacky, desperate. "I went a little crazy yesterday shopping up island. I think I bought literally everything at Midnight Farm and Pandora's Box."

"Nice," Lindsey said. "You look incredible."

"Great. Okay, let's finish these drinks, and then we'll go." Joanna threw some things into her bag, and they downed their rosé.

Joanna drove them in her Jeep. They stopped at Espresso Love to grab some lunch, parking in a loading zone right outside. Joanna ordered a few things rapidly—bagel sandwiches and croissants—but Lindsey had a sense that they'd mostly just be drinking that day. They drove to Norton—to the exact same spot that they had gone to on that first night—*Left Fork*. They drove right onto the beach, the way Dylan had first driven off the beach that night. But somehow, that day, it all looked different. Lindsey wasn't sure if she'd changed or if the place had.

It was a hot, sunny, clear day. There was already a long row of cars stretching down the beach. Joanna drove until it opened up and then turned in to a spot so that the car was facing the water. It was the most beautiful beach Lindsey had ever been to—pristine, perfect waves of rich, blue water.

They spread a beach blanket down and arranged their towels. Joanna had thrown a cooler into the car, too, filled with ice, more rosé, beers, and some Smirnoff Ices. It was enough for a whole party. She started to spray tanning oil on herself.

"I think Brian and Whitney are coming," Joanna said, craning her neck around her shoulder and spraying her back.

"Cool," Lindsey said, realizing why Joanna had brought all that alcohol. She suddenly felt herself coming down from her rosé high. She didn't want to see the guys, especially not after her run-in with Whitney at the ice-cream shop, even though Joanna had assured her that everything would be fine.

The girls both rested on their backs, letting the sun beat down on them. As long as she was with Joanna, Lindsey thought to herself, she would be okay. Because with Joanna, she wasn't the only guilty one. They'd done it *together*. If Whitney was going to rat her out, he'd have to rat Joanna out too. And Joanna didn't seem to be worried about it. Not at all.

After only a few minutes, Lindsey felt herself overheating. She was dehydrated.

"I'm going in the water," she said. "Wanna come?"

"Nah," Joanna replied, not moving. "I'm not hot enough yet."

Lindsey stood on the shore for a minute, letting the waves lap at her feet, and then she walked in. The water was cold, refreshing, and it woke her up. She swam farther out and then let herself float, shutting her eyes. When she ducked under, she swam to the bottom and touched the sand with her fingertips. Coming up for air, she heard voices. Bobbing in the water, she could see that Brian and Whitney had arrived. They had spread out their own towels next to Joanna. Lindsey watched as Brian threw himself on top of her, showering her with sand and rubbing his head on her stomach. She yelped and slapped his back playfully. Lindsey sank a little bit down into the water. She wished that she could stay in there forever, wrapped in the cool ocean, safe, away from it all.

She rode a wave in to shore and skipped out of the break, aware of her gait as she walked back toward the group. She could see that Brian was watching her approach. She could feel his eyes on her.

"Hey, guys," she said, wringing out her hair. Whitney just nodded and smirked.

"Hey, Lindsey," Brian said, waving his beer.

She sat down on her towel, hugged in her knees. Joanna was sitting cross-legged, reaching into a bag of chips. Joanna had refilled Lindsey's glass of rosé. She was thirsty, and the wine with ice tasted sweet and cold down her throat. She was dizzy and tired. The sun made her movements feel slow and sticky.

Joanna leaned her body against Brian's, who was leaning on an elbow. He kissed her neck. Lindsey looked over at Whitney, who was staring at them. He didn't say anything, but Lindsey recognized an emotion on his face: jealousy. Was Whitney in love with Joanna? she wondered as she watched him. Maybe that was why he'd been so angry the other night. He had information that could easily split up Joanna and Brian, but he couldn't bring himself to use it. At least not yet. Lindsey shook away the idea. *Stupid idea,* she thought to herself. She was just out of it from the sun and alcohol.

Brian suggested that they all shotgun beers. The sun was at its highest point by then, and everyone's skin was covered in salt from the ocean. He punctured holes in four beer cans and carefully handed them out.

"One, two, three," he shouted. They all popped the cans and chugged, the frothy beer spilling down their chins. Brian finished first, then Whitney. They both slammed their cans on the ground and high-fived one another.

"Fuck!" Joanna yelled after finishing hers. Lindsey followed. She felt wobbly on her legs, like a colt, and sidestepped to catch her balance. They all collapsed back on the blanket, and she started to feel better, more relaxed. Whitney hadn't said anything; Brian was being nice. It all seemed okay.

"So, guys," Brian said, handing out another round of beers to every-one. "A toast is in order." He lifted his beer. "Apparently Lindsey here got a job lined up for this fall." A job? Lindsey's face went blank. She had only lined up a meeting, not a job. "My parents say you're going to work at their gallery. That is, if you want to."

"Yay!" Joanna squealed. Lindsey lifted her beer, though there was something sinister in Brian's toast. It was like he wanted to hold the job over her, to control her, to tell her that she *owed him* something.

"Thanks," she said. "I'd be really lucky to work there."

"No," Brian said. "They'd be lucky to have *you*." He looked her in the eyes.

"Let's go swimming!" Joanna yelled, breaking the silence. They all jumped into the ocean, Lindsey following last. They swam past the break and just let the water sway them. Among the waves, Lindsey noticed, everyone looked so small and light in the water, like they were children.

They packed up their things and left the beach a few hours later. Brian and Whitney went into town for beers. Joanna said she needed to go home and pass out. She talked a big game, but she was a lightweight, Lindsey knew.

By the time Joanna dropped her off at the Deckers' house, Lindsey was fried. She hadn't had a sip of water all day. She needed to hydrate and rest before she was supposed to meet Dylan later that night. She went to the kitchen, downing a glass of water while standing at the sink and then refilling it to drink more. It was cool inside the kitchen. Something about the dark wood gave the bones of the house a perpetual chill. The sliding living room door was slightly open, and a gentle breeze spilled in. Lindsey looked out at the beach and the water. There was a heaviness in the air, like the atmosphere couldn't contain the heat for much longer, and something was going to give.

"Thirsty," she heard. Jonathan was in the kitchen now. She wasn't sure where Carol was, or Georgie. It was that time in the late afternoon when everyone was in between things.

"Yes," she said. Her head started to hurt. "It was hot out today."

"Mm," he murmured. Lindsey took her glass and walked past him to go upstairs. He didn't move, letting her body brush against his to pass. She spilled some of her water on the floor, not caring, and went upstairs. She locked her door and fell onto her bed, her heart racing and head now pounding. She regretted all the things she'd drunk that day. She'd barely had any real food or water. She stripped off her clothes and got in the shower. After, she felt somewhat better, more refreshed, though she was still tired and dehydrated. She had an hour until Dylan was coming to get her, which gave her enough time to pull it together and look amazing. She wanted to have a good time that night with him, to just laugh and enjoy being with him. Everything else had started to feel so heavy.

Dylan picked her up at seven thirty exactly. He pulled up outside in his truck and beeped.

"Wow," he said when Lindsey stepped out the front door and walked up to the street to meet him, where he was leaning against the side of his truck. "You look *hot*." Lindsey tried to act casual.

"Thanks," she said. She could feel herself blushing. She was wearing her favorite dress, which was short and fitted, sleeveless, white with little sunflowers all over it. She was tan, her hair was long and straight, her legs were toned. She felt beautiful.

Dylan drove her to a new restaurant up island called State Road, which had an elegant, modern farmhouse feel to it and was tucked among a blossoming garden of lavender and rosemary plants. Inside, the restaurant smelled of fresh bread and butter.

"This is so nice." Lindsey beamed as they sat down.

"Well, you're leaving soon, and I wanted to do something special." Lindsey could tell that Dylan was proud.

After dinner, he drove them to Lambert's Cove Beach, where they walked a short distance down a path that led them to a quiet beach with velvety sand. They curled up together on a blanket and looked at the stars. Dylan had brought a box of Chilmark Chocolates for them to share. The night air was warm, the stars were bright, the chocolates were the best she'd ever tasted, and Dylan's hands felt electric against her skin.

She couldn't spend the night, she told him. She had another early morning, and she really wanted to get a good night's sleep. The day at the beach had exhausted her. But she hadn't told him that, not really. She only told him that she had gone to the beach with Joanna. She didn't tell him that she'd gotten wasted with Brian, or that she was going to be working at his parents' gallery in the fall, or that she'd probably have to see him in Boston all the time.

When he dropped her off, the house was dark except for the front-door light. Everyone was asleep. Dylan kissed her softly.

"I'm so glad I met you," he said and leaned in to kiss her. Lindsey wanted to respond, but she couldn't speak. Their breakup was inevitable, especially after what Brian had said to her today about the job. Her life was finally coming together, in a way that she'd always wanted it to. And she wasn't sure that Dylan fit into it. So she just kissed him back. They'd see each other in a few days for one last night together.

She tiptoed up the stairs to her room and gently shut the door. She waited a few seconds before turning on the bathroom light and looking at her reflection in the mirror. She stared, feeling, for a moment, outside herself, as though she were looking at someone else. She ran her hand along her jawline, up against her cheekbones, her brows, her hairline. She could see, in her reflection, the person she wanted to be, and she wasn't sure she recognized her old self anymore.

Just as she was about to wash her face and get ready for bed, she heard noises outside. She looked through her window, out onto the street in front of the house. She had to adjust her eyes to the darkness for a few seconds, but then she could see—it was Brian and Georgie, standing there together. Something must have happened at the sleepover. Or maybe Georgie had never even gone to a sleepover. Maybe she'd gone to meet Brian. She looked closer, making sure they didn't see her through her shutters. Brian lifted his hand and placed it on Georgie's arm. That was it. Lindsey turned and ran downstairs.

"What are you doing?" she yelled at Brian as she swung the door open and bolted toward them. Brian's face was next to Georgie's, like he was about to kiss her or like he just had.

"Nothing!" Georgie yelled back, her voice shaky. She ran past Lindsey and into the house, slamming the door behind her, like she was about to burst into tears.

"What the *hell* do you think you're doing?" Lindsey said to Brian once Georgie was inside.

"It's not what it looks like," he said, raising his hands. "Come on, Lindsey. Be reasonable." He paused. His voice was calm. "I saw her alone downtown, walking home. So I walked with her. I didn't want her to be out alone this late at night. I was just saying good night to her now, giving her a hug goodbye. I think she got the wrong idea."

Lindsey suddenly felt stupid, overly dramatic. Maybe she'd screamed at him and at Georgie for no reason. It did look like Georgie had walked home early from the sleepover, and it was totally possible for Brian to have seen her and walked her home. And that was nice of him, actually. Furthermore, she knew that Georgie might have been misreading Brian's signals all summer long. She wanted to believe Georgie, but Lindsey had seen, firsthand, how Brian was devoted to Joanna. So maybe he really was just being nice to Georgie, and she had taken it the wrong way. Now she felt like she owed Brian an apology. She didn't want him to be mad at her; it could ruin everything.

"Sorry," she said. "I'm just . . . I don't know." Her head started to pound then. She was so tired and still dehydrated. She wished that she had just stayed out of it all.

"Hey, it's okay," Brian said. "How about we go for a walk, cool down?"

Lindsey nodded. She wasn't ready to go back inside. Georgie was probably mad at her. She didn't know what to say to her yet. Maybe if she went for a walk with Brian, Georgie would be asleep when she got back, and she wouldn't have to deal with it tonight. So they started walking down to the beach, toward the lighthouse. Back at the Deckers' house, Jonathan's office light switched on.

Chapter 26

GEORGIE

Georgie ran to her bed and cried, holding her head in her hands. She quieted herself, waiting to hear the opening and closing of the front door. She wanted to confront Lindsey when she came upstairs. She needed to ask her *why*. Why had she tried to ruin the only thing that Georgie wanted?

She waited a minute, changing into her nightgown. But she heard nothing. She rose from the bed and was about to leave her room and creep toward the window in the hallway overlooking the street, to see if Lindsey and Brian were still outside, talking. But she happened to look out her window toward the lighthouse. The moon was bright outside, and it reflected on the water like a luminescent oil spill. And then she saw two figures moving down the path to the lighthouse. She squinted to get a closer look. She couldn't see anything other than fuzzy outlines of figures, but she knew in that moment: it was Lindsey and Brian. Where were they going? What were they doing?

Georgie's mind reeled, and she sat still, barely moving, for several minutes, waiting for them to return back up the path, for *something* to happen. But nothing did. She had to find out for herself what they were doing together. Lindsey wasn't meant to be there with Brian, *she* was. Lindsey had ruined her night and then taken her place. Why should she stand by and let it happen?

She flung the covers off her and got up out of bed. She pulled a sweatshirt on over her head; it was just an inch shorter than her nightgown, hovering midway up her thighs, and she crept out of her room. Her hand gripped the smooth wooden banister of the stairs as she descended. She could smell the lilies in the vase on the entryway table as she walked past them and went out the door. She didn't really have a plan, and she wasn't sure what she was going to do when she found Lindsey and Brian or what she would say. But she felt like she was being pulled toward them. She had to go. Her eyes were fixed ahead as she walked, her fingers hanging idly from her hands like frayed rope.

Only when she was halfway down the beach path did Georgie realize she was barefoot. The temperature dropped, jolting her into her reality. The sand felt damp and icy against her feet. She was approaching the lighthouse. It was so dark that she couldn't see the ocean, but she could hear the waves, the crescendo of their crash and the slither of their retreat. The dune grass tickled against her legs, like it was trying to whisper into the pores of her skin.

The lighthouse itself now stood before her, but Lindsey and Brian were still nowhere in sight. *They must be on the other side,* Georgie thought. The lighthouse looked like an oppressive blockade, looming, somehow too big for its surroundings, casting a shadow even darker than the opaque sky. From her window, the lighthouse always seemed miniature, like a figurine in a snow globe. Now it frightened her. The roundness of the structure, a perpetual loop, a path to nowhere, played tricks on Georgie's eyes as she started to creep around it. What was she doing there, after all?

Georgie was shivering now. The noises of the wind and ocean rang through her ears with acute intensity. Everything was too loud. She felt alone and afraid and unsure of how to get back to her house despite being able to see it just up the hill. She yearned to be back in her bed, safe. It had been a mistake to come down here. But her house, and all the other houses up the hill, seemed to be a million miles away now and separated by an impenetrable glass wall.

She climbed the stairs to the stone platform that surrounded the lighthouse so that she could reach out and touch it. She placed her fingertips against it, and for a moment, the wall felt malleable and soft, gentle. But when she pushed her palm flat against it, the lighthouse turned cold and hard. She stood and listened, trying to hear something else besides the roar of the sea.

And then she did. She heard a sound. A voice but not really words. Just a voice. Two voices then, making sounds.

Georgie kept one hand on the lighthouse and began to walk toward the other side, the side where the voices were coming from. She felt like she was walking impossibly slow, her legs heavy and stiff. She tried to tell herself that maybe she hadn't heard anything at all. Maybe she should turn back now and run all the way home, having seen nothing. Or maybe she'd realize, on the other side, that the sounds were just echoes through empty seashells, howling away to no one.

She kept walking until she saw what was on the other side. It was Lindsey. She was lying on her back, her face up toward the sky, her hair blanketed out underneath her like a fan. Georgie's eyes widened. And then she saw Brian. *Her* Brian. On top of Lindsey. She blinked her eyes shut, blistering with the feeling of betrayal, and turned her back away. They didn't see her. It was too dark, and she had only peeked her head toward them for a moment. She opened her eyes, needing to look again. She needed to be sure.

She looked again, her palms gripping the sides of the lighthouse for stability. Except when she focused her eyes, something wasn't right. Her anger subsided to confusion and shock. They were having sex. But most of their clothes were still on, and Lindsey's clothes were half on her body and half off, like they'd been tugged and then ignored. Her bra straps were pulled down so that they dug into the flesh of her arms, constricting her, and only one of her breasts had spilled out and was exposed to the rubbing of Brian's polo shirt. Her underwear was hanging around one of her ankles. She wasn't really moving. Her body was shifting back and forth with the weight of Brian's movements, but she didn't appear to be in control of it. She was making noises, but they were incoherent grunts, not really words or even moans, and Georgie could swear that she could see tears coming from Lindsey's eyes, sticking to her face like the last remnants of a river in a drought. Brian's movements were swift, sharp, and his breaths were heavy and hard. He was in control, and Lindsey wasn't. Lindsey looked like a buoy in the water, helpless against its pounding waves and swells. Her eyes were open and then shut, open and then shut, blinking out tears. Georgie couldn't even tell if she was fully awake, except that one of her hands was gripping Brian's shoulder, digging tiny indentations into him with her fingertips, as though all her muscle and might were channeled into those five fingers, and it was all the power she had. But then her hand slipped off and fell slack into the sand. It made no difference to Brian anyway, who kept on moving like a train, forward and forward, over and over.

Georgie had a choice. She could yell out and try to stop Brian. Or she could turn and run. She opened her mouth.

"Stop," Georgie whispered. "Stop. Stop. Stop. Stop!" But they didn't hear her against the drumming of the sea and the swirling of the wind. She opened her mouth again to scream, but fear overcame her, and she took the other choice. She turned and ran, leaving behind the cold sand, the tickling reeds, the crashing of the ocean, and she didn't stop running until she was back in her bedroom, under the covers, wrapped up in the warmth of her blankets, in the safety of her family's house. She couldn't stop shivering. She tried to close her eyes and go to sleep. But she heard a whisper. *Stop, stop, stop.* Was it her own voice she was hearing? Had Georgie imagined it all? Georgie shut her eyes, realizing now that *Lindsey* had been the one saying those words, ever so slightly, until they were pushed out from behind her lips by her beating heart, clawing and crawling out of her throat, desperate to be heard. And all Georgie had done was run away.

Chapter 27

LINDSEY

With just her thin cardigan over her dress, Lindsey immediately shivered when she and Brian started walking down the path toward the lighthouse. The silence of the neighborhood made her aware of how alone they were. She was always alarmed by how quiet Edgartown was at night, unlike her hometown, where the echo of the nearby highway was constant. She looked back up at the row of perfect houses overlooking the water. It looked like an abandoned movie set full of thin flaps of wood painted to look like a neighborhood, ready to collapse at any minute, leaving a cloud of dust.

"I was smoking outside the Wharf when I saw Georgie," Brian said, his hands in his pockets. "It was late. She seemed upset."

"Well, thank you," Lindsey said, peering over at him with a quick smile.

When they reached the beach, the wind seemed to pick up.

"This way," Brian said, pointing to the other side of the lighthouse. "Where the wind is blocked."

"It's cold; let's go back," Lindsey suggested. She had been okay going for a walk with him, but she didn't like the idea of staying here with him now. It felt wrong. She was still tipsy from all the drinking she'd done that day and that evening, and she was tired; she felt weak.

"Trust me," he said, and he took her hand. They walked to the other side of the lighthouse, and he was right: the wind was blocked on the other side, and it instantly felt warmer. They sat down on the sand, leaning against the base of the lighthouse. Lindsey looked back up the hill toward the Deckers' street. It seemed to be shrinking before her, moving farther and farther away.

Lindsey wasn't sure what to do with her legs because of her short dress. She bent them in half and wrapped her arms around her knees. It was too dark for Brian to see anything if the wind kicked up her hem.

"Want some?" he asked, taking out a miniature bottle of Fireball. "I always have a nip or two in my pocket."

"I'm good," Lindsey said. She didn't want to drag this out. They were sitting too close together now. This wasn't what she had agreed to, and he knew it.

"Suit yourself," he said, taking a swig.

"Fine, I'll have a sip." She didn't know why, but she wanted to prove him wrong or keep up with him; she wasn't sure which. The alcohol tasted like hot cinnamon, and it burned her throat.

"Listen, Lindsey," Brian said, turning his body toward hers, "I'm glad we're both here."

No, no, Lindsey thought. *Back off.* She knew what was going to happen if he got any closer. She didn't want this, none of it. She'd come around about Brian, for the most part, and she'd decided that he wasn't so bad. She was probably going to work for his parents. She was probably going to live with his girlfriend. She *had* to accept him. But that didn't mean that she *liked* him. Not for her. She loved Dylan. She didn't want to be with Brian.

He leaned closer. "I just feel like you and I got off on the wrong foot." She could smell the Fireball and cigarettes on his breath.

"I have to go," she said, starting to rise. He grabbed her arm and pulled her down.

"Hey, wait," he said. He put his hand on her shoulder, pressing her down. "Come here." And then his mouth was on hers, hot and wet and unwanted. She tried to shut her mouth and push him, but he kept prying his tongue between her lips.

"Come on, Brian," she said, pulling her head back. "We can't."

He pulled back, raising his hands. He reached in his pocket for another nip. "Sorry." He turned to her. "I'm really sorry, Lindsey." She believed him for a second. Maybe he just got caught up in the moment. Maybe she gave him the wrong idea. "I just thought, you know, you really want that job, right?"

Lindsey stared at him in disbelief. She had been right about him. But was he actually doing this—threatening her? Dangling the job in front of her like a carrot? She didn't think that he would go that far, even Brian. *No,* she told herself. *Run away.* She'd never let anyone control her like that, she thought.

"Not that badly," she said. "No." And she started to get up.

Brian grabbed her by the legs then, throwing her balance off, and she fell. He dropped the nip, and it spilled down her dress, soaking her.

"Get *off* me!" Lindsey screamed. But Brian had put his chest onto hers now, his entire weight, and she could feel his hand snake downward and in between her legs. "What the fuck are you doing? Stop! Stop!" Was he serious? Was this really happening to her? She felt her blood course through her body like an electric volt, and she kicked up with her knees. He only pressed down harder. He nestled his head into her neck and started kissing her—big, flat, broad kisses, like he was covering her in paint, whiting her out, erasing her. "Brian, *stop!*" Her eyes raced around for anyone else to help her, but no one was there, and it was dark.

She felt her cardigan slip off her frame, and then a dress strap was pulled down. And then the other one. It was like Brian had four hands instead of two. He was everywhere at once. She kept trying to fight him off. And then she suddenly felt so tired, so depleted, like her body was shutting down to survive. She was hot, sweating, cramped, her skin prickly. She kept telling him to stop, but he kept going.

"Stop!" she said one last time. And then she decided not to speak anymore. She couldn't. She stopped moving. It had already started, she thought. It would be over soon. It would all be over soon. *Stop,* she heard again in her mind, or maybe she heard it ringing through the night air. *Stop, stop, stop.* She wasn't sure anymore if she was screaming or if she was imagining it. It didn't matter. The only relief was the wind against the parts of her body that weren't covered by Brian. And so she let the wind wash over her. She felt the sand against her neck and focused on that. It felt good. It was cold and slightly damp. She wanted to melt into it, all the way down to where it was coldest and darkest, where she could make a cocoon and go to sleep forever.

After some time—she wasn't sure how much time—she felt Brian's hands on her shoulders. She was now sitting up, leaning against the lighthouse. He must have propped her there. She had become limp, like a rag doll. She was covered in sweat and shivering. She blinked her eyes and saw flecks of light. She looked down at her dress and saw the alcohol stain. She smelled.

Lindsey heard the sounds of Brian standing up. She heard a zipper and sand being brushed off. She felt her hands being grabbed by Brian, and then he pulled. Her arms shot forward from their sockets, her entire weight falling forward instead of up.

"Come on," she heard Brian say. His voice was rough. "Let's go."

They started walking. She was in shock. It had all taken only a few minutes, but it had happened. She'd had sex with Brian. Her eyes started to water. What had she done? What had he done to her? Could she have escaped? Could she have fought harder?

The lights of Edgartown up the hill seemed to be miles away. But they made it. Outside the Deckers' house, Brian leaned in and kissed her on the cheek, resting his hand on her arm. Why was he acting like they'd just gone on a *date*? Why was he acting like nothing bad had happened?

"Good night, Lindsey," he whispered. Something inside her stomach flipped, and she brought her hand up to her mouth. She felt like she was going to be sick. She turned and ran inside, shutting the door behind her too loudly.

She sat at the base of the stairs, holding her head in her hands. *Call the police,* she told herself. *Call the police. Call anyone. I've been raped. Get help.* She took out her phone and hovered her finger over the number nine.

"Lindsey?" she heard and put down her phone. Jonathan was standing in the doorway to his office. She braced herself. She knew how she looked. Her hair was tangled, she smelled of booze, her feet were covered in sand. "Are you all right?"

She thought about the question and how to answer. Did he actually care? She got the sense that he was less concerned about her well-being and more curious about what she'd done to get herself in that kind of state. What would happen, she wondered, if she told him what Brian had done to her? Would he believe her? Would he tell her to just sleep it off? Would he call the cops? Would he call the Fitzgeralds and wake them up?

"Sorry," she found herself whispering. "Sorry to disturb you. I'm just going to go up to bed. Sorry." She began to walk upstairs. She was apologizing for being raped, she realized, like it was all her own fault. And maybe it had been, she thought. She was the one stupid enough to have gone for the walk with Brian in the first place. Jonathan watched her go but said nothing else. Maybe she had misread him as well. But there was no point in trying to tell him—or tell anyone—what had happened. Who would believe her? What was there to say? And what good would it do her? She passed by Georgie's door at the top of the stairs and considered, for a moment, opening it. But she just went to her room instead and shut the door, alone at last.

Chapter 28

GEORGIE

Georgie stayed awake, clutching her comforter, waiting to hear Lindsey come home. She finally heard her come up the stairs. Her footsteps sounded uneven, labored. After Lindsey shut the door to her room, Georgie got out of bed and walked there. She pressed her ear against Lindsey's door. She thought she heard Lindsey fall onto the bed with a groan. She waited a few minutes, listening. She opened Lindsey's door and peered inside. Lindsey was still in her clothes, on the bed, asleep. She was breathing deeply. Georgie could see her stomach rising and falling. She was okay, at least in an immediate sense—she was home, she was sleeping, she was safe.

Georgie went back to her own room. She turned on her light and took out her journal. *Something bad happened tonight . . . It was all my fault . . .* She felt a sense of panic as she walked through what she'd seen, what Brian had done to Lindsey. What if Lindsey hadn't come outside? What would have happened between *her* and Brian? Would he have done what he did to Lindsey to her? Was it meant to be her instead? Would he have hurt her too? She felt nauseous, like she'd eaten something sour. It was guilt that she felt. Lindsey had only tried to help her, she knew, and it was *her* fault that Lindsey had gotten hurt. She knew this. But there was something else that lingered inside her, too, something confusing and frightening: a remaining sense of jealousy.

How was it that she still envied Lindsey despite what she'd seen? How was it that she still wished that she'd finished her moment with Brian and gotten to experience the rest of it?

She woke early, around seven, not really sure if she had slept at all the night before. She opened her eyes gradually, unsure whether parts of last night had been a dream. She saw her sweatshirt strewn across the end of her bed, and she remembered what she'd seen and what had happened. Her lips felt dry.

Turned out, she actually did have to go into work early that morning. Lucy had texted her early that morning asking her to come in. Her lie to Catherine the night before seemed so far away. She was glad to have work. She needed a distraction. She needed time to think, to process what she'd seen or what she thought she'd seen. Georgie took a quick shower and got dressed. Before she left the house, she peered down the hall toward Lindsey's room. Her door was still closed.

It was unusually cold that morning. It must have dropped twenty degrees since the day before. She walked quickly to keep warm. Georgie looked at the ocean as she walked. There was a layer of mist rising from the surface. She'd seen it before, on a cold ferry ride to the island once. "Sea smoke," her dad had explained to her. "It's when the air is colder than the water. When the air and the surface of the water meet, it creates this kind of smoke that rises from the sea."

She was pretty sure that it was too warm for the ocean mist she saw to actually be the sea smoke her dad told her about, but as she walked to work, just for a few minutes, she pretended that it was. She liked that there was a hidden little space between the sea and sky, where all kinds of things blossomed and swirled and existed, even though it was a space that didn't really exist at all. It was a small, invisible world, tucked safely in between two others.

When she arrived at the Picnic Basket, Lucy seemed somewhat hysterical. "New inventory," she huffed, leading Georgie to the back hallway, which was crammed with cardboard boxes filled with new items. "I completely forgot about it. Don't know why I ordered more when summer is basically over." Lucy's brow was matted with sweat, and her cheeks were red. "But it's going to be fine," she told Georgie, as though Georgie was the one who needed consoling. "Just gotta unpack it all and record the inventory. You got this!" She gave Georgie a pat on the shoulder.

Georgie was mad at Lucy. Not really, but that's where she was directing her anger. She felt betrayed by the revelation that Lucy had hired her only because her mom had asked her to. She wondered if every word of validation that Lucy had given her had been a lie. Was she even doing work that mattered? Did Lucy even want her there? Everyone around her was hiding something from her, she thought.

Georgie looked at the boxes. There were at least two dozen; she could hardly wedge herself a pathway through the hallway. But she knew she would get through it all today. And she was grateful to have the task. She wanted to be thrown into work.

She got an orange juice and then started slicing open the boxes with a pair of scissors and gently sifting through them. She sorted through bubble-wrapped candles, serving platters, woven baskets, quilts, glass bowls, and expensive sparklers, wondering who was going to buy them all and where they'd end up.

Each time the front door to the café opened, Georgie peered her head out the office door and down the hallway to see who was coming in. She hoped that it wasn't Catherine, or Brendan, or Lindsey, and especially not Brian. She decided that if any of them did come in, she would hide behind the boxes until they were gone. What would she say to any of them? How would she explain any of it? How did she know if it was even her place to speak up? She never seemed to get that right. Maybe the best thing to do was to just say nothing, she thought.

She felt her phone vibrate in her pocket. It was a text from Catherine: Sooo . . . Brendan likes you! Georgie didn't reply. She put her phone back in her pocket. She felt another wave of guilt for even thinking about anything other than what she'd seen at the lighthouse. But things had happened to her before that, too, and she hadn't processed any of it. She hadn't liked what Brendan had done last night in the hot tub. She didn't like him. And yet she felt a pressure, an obligation, to please him somehow, to pretend that she was interested, to simply avoid angering him. She wished that she had an ability not to care, to just ignore it all, but she didn't.

Georgie continued unpacking the boxes. It was easier to think about what had happened at Catherine's house than it was to think about what she had seen at the lighthouse. Because she *knew* what she'd seen, but she wasn't ready to acknowledge it. She didn't know how. She didn't know so many things. The only thing she was certain of was that it might have been her instead.

As she continued her work, the sounds from last night kept ringing through her ears: the wind, the waves, and Lindsey's own voice, yelling for help.

She took out her phone and called home. She needed to check in, to make sure Lindsey was okay. Her mother answered.

"What's up, Georgie?" She sounded busy, bothered. It was unusual for Georgie to call home when she was at work.

"Um, nothing," she said, searching for an excuse. She didn't want to raise an alarm with her mother. "I just wanted to see what everyone was doing today."

"Lindsey is about to take your brother to the beach club."

"Oh, good. So she's there?"

"Who's where? What do you mean?"

"Lindsey, she's there?"

"Why wouldn't she be?" Carol asked. Georgie heard noises in the background. It sounded like her mom was in the kitchen. "She's right here. Do you need to talk to her?"

"No, no. No," Georgie said quickly. "I have to go. See you later."

Georgie hung up, somewhat relieved. It didn't sound like her mother could sense that anything was wrong. Lindsey was up and going about her day like normal. Maybe, Georgie thought, nothing *was* wrong. She wondered, for a moment, if she was absolutely sure of what she'd seen. She *was*. Or she had been. But what confused her was the complete and utter *normalcy* of today. How was it possible for Lindsey to have an ordinary day if what happened last night had really happened? If something bad had happened to her, wouldn't she have told someone? Would she be *doing* something about it?

Georgie decided that she would go meet Lindsey and Berty at the beach club when she was done with work, and maybe she'd tell Lindsey what had happened, how she'd followed her. She thought through the scenario. She wasn't sure how she would be able to explain to Lindsey why she had followed her in the first place. The potential confrontation made Georgie feel sick, scared, nervous. The easier thing to do was to do nothing. *Maybe Lindsey should handle this how she wants to,* Georgie thought, *and I should just stay out of it.*

By late morning, the Picnic Basket had become crowded with the early lunch rush of beachgoers picking up sandwiches and snacks for the day. Georgie was now stacking rolls of linen place mats and napkins on one of the shelves, trying to re-create the pyramid that Lucy had shown her when she first started. She was standing on a small stepladder in order to reach the top shelf and had locked herself into a dulling rhythm of work that allowed her to avoid thinking about last night.

But she was jolted out of this state when she saw Brian walk through the door and go to the cashier. She heard him order an iced coffee. She froze. And for a second, she forgot about what he'd done last night, and just for a moment, he was the same Brian he'd always been to her, and she found herself smiling. And then she remembered and looked away, ashamed and confused.

She watched him out of the corner of her eye. He paid, got his coffee, and went to the milk-and-sugar station. He seemed calm, like his usual self, she noticed. He wasn't in a hurry. Nothing seemed to be wrong. He poured cream into his coffee just like he always did. His polo shirt was wrinkled, and his pastel-colored swim trunks hung on his hips with an air of casual nonchalance, like he had just thrown everything on and walked out the door that morning, ready for another beautiful day in the sun. He seemed completely unbothered by everything around him.

Just as he turned toward the exit, Brian spotted her, his eyes darting around the room as though he had wanted to see her before he left. They locked eyes, and he paused. *Please keep moving,* she thought. *Just go.* She couldn't talk to him; she wasn't capable of it. But he turned and walked toward her. She felt her whole body stiffen and her face grow hot.

"Hey" was all he said. He stood beside her. On the ladder, Georgie's stomach was level with his face so that her denim shorts–clad buttocks and her bare thighs were just inches from his chest and shoulders. She hadn't shaved her legs in two days, and in the midst of her panic upon seeing him, she also hoped that he wouldn't notice the blanket of stubble along her limbs. How could she be thinking about that right *now?*

"Hey," she responded, trying not to look at him. Georgie felt anger toward him start to boil up. She hated him for what he'd done to Lindsey. But she also felt betrayed by him personally. He had led her on, only to pursue Lindsey instead and then do something terrible to her. And what made her feel the lowest was realizing that she cared, that she still had feelings for him despite it all. That she was almost *jealous* of Lindsey somehow. She was sick, she thought; she was terrible. She felt the backs of her eyes begin to throb and grow heavy with tears. She needed to get away from him, but she was trapped on the ladder. She wanted to jump off, run away, slam a door in his face. Or maybe she wanted him to reach out to her, to draw her in close, and to hold her. She didn't know which one she wanted. She hated him, but she somehow still loved him. How was it possible to want opposite things at once? she wondered. She felt as if she were going to burst into flames or scream at the top of her lungs if she looked at him.

"Worker bee, always working," Brian said. Georgie wondered if he could tell that she was bothered. She kept her eyes focused on the stack of place mats, now just pretending to adjust them. She didn't want him to see her face. She didn't respond. What was there to say?

She felt something warm on the back of her thigh and then quickly realized that it was Brian's hand. His palm was flat against the top of her thigh, almost where her shorts began. She felt hot and scared. She didn't know what to do, how to move, how to react. No boy had ever touched her like that, so gently, with such tender attention. It made her knees weak. She had to remind herself to breathe.

"Just making sure you don't fall," he said before removing his hand and turning to leave. "See you later." After he left, she could still feel an imprint on her leg, like he had left a stamp on her skin.

Georgie looked around to see if anyone had witnessed the encounter. She could feel a heavy weight in her throat. Something had to give; she had to cry or vomit or scream or something to release everything she was feeling. She wished that she had said something to him. She wanted to push him, punch him, or kick him. She wanted to yell in his face that she hated him. But she also wanted to kiss him, smell his neck, run her hands through his hair. If she could turn back time, just for a minute, she would have done something else other than just stand there. How could he not have said anything else, like nothing had happened? How could he chat normally, like he hadn't turned her entire world upside down the night before?

By the time her shift ended, Georgie didn't want to go to the beach club, but she knew she had to. She felt anxiety about the potential of seeing Lindsey. But she was also desperate to see her. Georgie looked at the ocean as she walked to the club. It was hot outside now, and the sun was bright and clear. The sea smoke on the water had disappeared. She wondered where the invisible world had gone.

Chapter 29

LINDSEY

When Lindsey woke up, her whole body ached. She was severely hungover. She felt weak and dried out. Her head throbbed. Her skin felt like paper, and her bones felt like they were made of shattered glass. She had slept in her clothes, something she never did, and this confused her when she first woke up. She looked down at her dress, wrinkled and damp with her own sweat, stained with alcohol. She touched her forehead. It was warm and clammy. The blinds on her windows were open, and the sunlight coming through felt like needles stabbing her face.

She peeled her dress over her head and let it drop to the floor. She hugged her arms in to her stomach, which felt hollow and concave, like she hadn't had food or water in days. She gently moved her legs over to the side of the bed. Everything hurt. She suddenly realized how incredibly thirsty she was, which propelled her to the bathroom, where she poured water from the tap into her hand and drank it while hovering over the sink.

She drank until she was breathless, then sat on the floor for a few minutes with her head between her knees. She got up to pee. She slipped off her underwear and pushed them aside on the floor with her foot. Her urine was bright yellow. As she wiped, she felt an acute soreness, like she had just been punched in a ripe bruise. She started to cry, quietly at first, and then the tears escalated into muscular sobs that came from her gut, uncontrollable and wild. She grabbed a towel and held it over her mouth. She didn't want anyone to hear her. She kept crying, remembering what had happened to her last night, remembering how she had fought until she couldn't anymore.

She heard her phone's alarm go off. It was early, not even seven thirty yet. She walked to her bed and shut off the alarm. She was supposed to get Berty up and ready for the day. They were going to the beach club. What she had done nearly every day that summer now seemed impossible, exhausting, inhumane. She only had a few more days of this, and then she would be going home. She just had to make it until then.

She selected the keypad on her phone and hovered her finger over the number nine. That was still her instinct. *Call the police.* She had thought about it last night, but she couldn't do it. She had been too tired, too upset. She could do it now. All she'd have to do was dial three numbers, and someone could help her. She pressed nine. She pressed one. She waited a second, and then she cleared the screen. She couldn't do it.

She thought about calling her mom. She became overwhelmed by a deep longing to be a child again, to be held by her mother, to be told that she would be okay. She wished that she could smell her mother's skin, feel the sink of the old sofa in their family living room, taste the food her mother made for dinner. She thought about calling Rose, telling her everything that had happened, asking for her advice. She would know what to do.

But she imagined what would actually happen if she called her mom or Rose. They would call the police. They would probably call Jonathan and Carol. And the thought of getting the police involved right now—the thought of *anyone* getting involved right now—felt, somehow, too overwhelming. Maybe if Lindsey's mom were actually there, physically with her, it would be easier. But Lindsey would have to go to the police by herself. She'd have to explain it all to the Deckers, what had happened, why she couldn't take Berty to the beach that day. And she'd have to explain to Jonathan that she hadn't just been out partying, that she'd been raped.

Maybe she could tell Carol, she thought just for a moment. Carol was a mother, a wife, a woman, after all. Maybe she would believe her. But then Lindsey remembered how Carol had treated her when they'd first met, how Carol had looked at her with judgment, how she'd told her that she couldn't have guests in her room and how she'd said it with raised eyebrows. Carol wouldn't believe her, she decided. Or worse, Carol would blame her.

And then, she realized, she should call Joanna. She pulled up her contact and thought about what she would say: *I caught your boyfriend kissing a fourteen-year-old last night, and when I broke it up, he raped me.* How would she even explain any of it to Joanna? Was she absolutely sure that she'd seen Georgie and Brian kissing—or almost kissing? She rubbed her eyes. She'd been drunk, exhausted, but she knew what she'd seen. But how did that explain why she agreed to go on the walk with Brian, why she agreed to sit on the beach with him, why she agreed to have a drink with him, why she let him kiss her? It didn't explain any of it. None of it made sense.

There was no one she could tell. No one here would believe her; no one here would understand. Things like this didn't happen to women like Carol or to girls like Georgie or Joanna. Those types of girls were too smart, too well behaved. Guys didn't even try to pull anything with them because those were the types of girls they wanted to marry, not the ones they wanted to fuck. For Lindsey to acknowledge what happened to her would also be to acknowledge the fundamental, absolute difference between them, she thought. *It's why this happened to* me, Lindsey told herself, holding her head in her hands.

And coming forward now, she thought, would derail the entire reason she was on the Vineyard in the first place: to get a job. She had come this far. And if she told them what happened, and the police got involved, and Brian's family hired a lawyer, and if the crime wasn't just swept under the rug but instead was brought to light and fought and dragged on, well, then, even if she got justice, she wouldn't have anything else. She could obviously forget the job at the Fitzgeralds' gallery, and she could surely forget any other potential help from the Deckers. They would never see her the same way. They would take Brian's side. It would be too *complicated* for them not to. Even if she was the victim, she had a feeling that they wouldn't want to be associated with her. She would be the girl who went through this *horrible ordeal*. It would be messy, awkward, uncomfortable to acknowledge. The Deckers could never know. No one could.

She hesitated before getting into the shower, knowing that if she were to ever actually want to press charges, she shouldn't wash herself but that she should instead go to the hospital and get a rape kit done. But how could she? When? She was supposed to be downstairs by now, acting cheery and normal and spreading almond butter on a banana for Berty. Before she got in the shower, she stood before the mirror naked. She was bruised along her shoulder and collarbone and on her hips and inner thighs. She pulled her hair over her neck, making sure it was long enough to disguise it. She made the decision to step into the shower. She let the water fall over her. Her body felt like it belonged to someone else.

Out of the shower, Lindsey heard her phone buzz. She had several messages from Dylan: Last night was so fun. Are you sure you have to leave so soon? She'd forgotten entirely that she'd seen Dylan last night, before she saw Brian. She had been a different person then. She didn't reply.

She was supposed to see Dylan the next night. They'd made plans to have one last evening together before she had to go back to Maryland.

She put some moisturizer on her face and tied her wet hair back in a bun. All her joints felt rusty and creaky. She put on a bathing suit and her cover-up but noticed in the mirror that her collarbone was dotted with plummy bruises, so she undid her bun and let her hair fall around her neck to hide her injuries. She started to feel tired just thinking about Berty's energy and having to run after him all day. She gathered her things in her bag and walked, one foot in front of the other. There was no choice except to just keep going.

The kitchen seemed brighter and louder than usual, and Lindsey narrowed her eyes as she entered. Carol was there, spooning oatmeal into a bowl for Berty. She already had on her tennis whites.

"Good morning, Lindsey," Carol said with a quick, closed-mouth smile, sliding her a cup of coffee. Lindsey had emerged nearly half an hour later than usual, and it was clear that Carol was annoyed at having to pick up the slack and feed Berty. Something about the way Carol gave her a cup of coffee, something she'd never done once, all summer, indicated to Lindsey that Carol was already judging her for oversleeping and assuming that she'd had a late, overindulgent night. Lindsey felt ashamed without having said a word yet.

"Just thought you could use some extra caffeine this morning," Carol added before Lindsey could respond. "It's always so busy at the beach club this time of summer."

"Thank you," Lindsey said, though it came out in a crackly whisper. Berty was sitting at the island, and he started prodding his oatmeal, kicking his legs under his stool.

Carol left to go play tennis. Lindsey didn't say anything to Berty. She took tiny sips of her coffee and watched him eat his breakfast. When he was done, she cleaned up his dishes and went upstairs with him to get him dressed. The coffee had helped her headache, just slightly, but she still worried about making it through the rest of the day. It seemed impossible.

"Ocean doesn't like me anymore," Berty whined to Lindsey while she tugged his rash guard over his skinny frame. "She never wants to play."

"That's not true," Lindsey said, feigning interest. She just wanted to get out of the house, get some fresh air, and then collapse on the beach forever.

"She just sits there," he said. "She doesn't want to play."

Lindsey peered into the cage and saw that Ocean was on the ground, among the pebbles, not moving. Her wings were open. Something didn't look right.

"She's probably just sleeping," she lied to Berty. "Let's let her rest. She will be okay. Let's just leave her alone, and we'll check on her later, okay?" Lindsey swallowed hard, feeling a wave of sadness, and stepped aside to take a breath.

"Okay," Berty said. He had his swim goggles on his forehead. He seemed skeptical of Lindsey's explanation.

The club was crowded that day, as Carol had predicted. She and Berty picked a spot close to the water, and for the first time all summer, Lindsey asked one of the teenage staff members there to pitch an umbrella for her. She needed shade that day. Berty ran into the water immediately. Lindsey slumped down into an Adirondack chair that she'd dragged under the umbrella and watched him. Just across the harbor was the lighthouse. There it was, that narrow spit of sand that whipped out into the water, and the lighthouse itself, with its hopeful white exterior. Only hours earlier, the lighthouse had been a monster of shadows, a tower filled with screams, an endless sinkhole that had swallowed her and then spat her out in a million pieces. It looked harmless now, far away, small, like she could crush it in her fingers.

She had a flash of memory as she looked out. The sand between her legs, in her hair. The feeling of fingers digging into her skin, bearing down, the feeling of warm breath against her neck, the way her body tightened and then released because it was easier to release. Behind her sunglasses, Lindsey cried, wiping away her hot tears with the edge of her towel.

It hadn't even occurred to her until then that she might actually *see* Brian that day at the club. She felt afraid. She tried to imagine what she'd do if she saw him. She'd swim out into the sea, as far as she could, she decided. Maybe she wouldn't come back. And what if she saw

Joanna? It was obvious that she'd been crying. Her face was probably red and splotchy. She'd just make something up about not wanting summer to end. It didn't matter.

Her phone buzzed with another text from Dylan. She'd forgotten about his earlier message and still hadn't replied. It was too much work. He asked her now if she was okay. His kindness stabbed her, causing more tears to spill out and down her cheeks. She wrote back: Everything's good, just a busy morning. See you tomorrow! She shoved her phone back into her bag, trying to distance herself from the exchange. She couldn't handle his care for her; his compassion only caused her more pain. His affection felt like a hangnail that she needed to snip off. It ached. The nicer he was to her, the more duplicitous she felt. She had, in a way, betrayed Dylan last night, she thought to herself. After all, what *had* she been thinking in agreeing to walk with Brian? What did she *think* was going to happen? She could never tell Dylan about it. Never. Because, she knew, once his rage simmered and the initial shock wore off, she'd know that he would wonder the same thing: *Why were you there in the first place?* Maybe she had been starting to fall in love with Dylan yesterday. Now, she wanted to forget about him altogether. He was a reminder of what had happened and the secrets she now needed to keep.

Lindsey walked into the water and sank under the surface, letting herself be submerged for a few seconds. The sound of the underwater world soothed her with its echoes and vibrations. She rose, breaking through the surface, and the sounds of her world flooded back in. She returned to her chair and wrapped herself in her towel, hugging herself, waiting for the time to pass.

As she stared out at the water, she saw Brian emerging from underneath the dock. Had he been in the water when she was there? How had she not seen him? She hugged her knees in tighter and started to make a slight humming noise. Could she run? Could she get away in time? She wanted to get up and sprint as fast as she could, but she felt glued to her towel. She couldn't move. *Don't look at me. Don't look at me,* she thought. She wasn't sure where to cast her eyes. She didn't want to let him out of her sight, but she didn't want to look at him either. There were so many people around, and there was nowhere to hide. This was Brian's place, not hers. She couldn't hide here. And when he finally saw her, he began to walk right toward her.

She felt her breathing pick up, and she looked around, trying to find someone who could come to her rescue. But she couldn't speak. He was like a shark, cutting through the water, rushing toward her as a dark, unstoppable force. Her eyes widened. Flecks of water spun off his body as he walked. He stopped a few feet in front of her. She wasn't sure she was breathing.

"Hey," Brian said. "Last night was fun." He smiled and brushed his hair back from his eyes. She felt like he'd just punched her in the gut, knocked the wind out of her. She couldn't find her breath.

"I . . . ," she started to say. She didn't know what she wanted to say. Her mind was running faster than her body, everything mixed-up and confused. "You . . ."

"Don't worry," he said. "Our secret." He turned and walked away, down to the other end of the beach. Lindsey watched him go. She saw him bend over and kiss someone on the cheek, a girl sitting in an Adirondack chair. Joanna. Lindsey squinted, watching the two of them talk. Joanna then looked back at Lindsey and waved, as if to say, *Come join us!* Lindsey raised her hand back and pointed at Berty, grateful that she had an excuse not to come sit with them. She couldn't face Joanna. She needed time to figure out what she was going to tell her and how.

Tears started falling down her cheeks. She picked up Berty's towel and buried her face in it. She didn't want anyone to see what was happening to her, but at the same time, she wished that someone would reach out, help her, see if she was okay, tell her what to do. She felt tricked, like Brian had pushed her off a cliff and watched her plummet, laughing.

Was Brian friendly toward her because he genuinely didn't think anything wrong had happened just a few hours earlier? Did he not remember? Was he pretending? He was so confident, so calm, so *happy* that, for a moment, Lindsey wondered if *she* was confused. Was it possible that she had gotten drunk and forgotten what had really happened? Had she somehow given Brian the idea last night that she was okay with what he had done to her? She looked around at all the other people on the beach. She wasn't even on the same planet they were. Nothing seemed real. It was like she was watching a movie instead of living her life.

Lindsey drifted through lunch with Berty, letting him order fries and ice cream and a Chipwich. She didn't care if Carol found out and got mad. She inhaled a large Diet Coke and ate half a grilled cheese. She still felt weak and exhausted.

She returned to her Adirondack chair after lunch, needing to curl back up in the comfort of her towel and the shade. Berty begged her to come swimming with him, but she couldn't. He sulked into the water alone. Georgie showed up then. She put her things down without saying anything. She was probably mad, Lindsey realized. She'd ruined Georgie's night with Brian. Whatever was about to happen between them, or whatever *had* happened, Lindsey had destroyed it. And Georgie didn't know what had happened to her at the lighthouse. She couldn't blame her for being mad at her.

"Georgie," Lindsey said. "Last night . . ." She paused, trying to find the words. "I'm sorry that I interrupted you and Brian. I just didn't want to see you get hurt." She looked straight ahead. She wasn't sure what would happen if she looked directly at Georgie.

"I know," Georgie said. "I know. It's okay." It was a strange response from Georgie, who was normally so defensive and almost combative. "Want one?" Georgie asked, reaching behind her and pulling a cold can of seltzer out of her bag. There was an unusual sense of concern coming from Georgie. Maybe she had realized that Lindsey had only been trying to help.

"Thanks," Lindsey said. She ran the cold can over her cheeks. It felt nice.

The two girls sat there in silence for a while, watching Berty. Normally, Lindsey would try to fill silences with Georgie, asking her about work or boys, but today she couldn't bring herself to.

"Are you okay?" Georgie asked after a minute. Did Georgie know something? Could she tell that something had happened?

"Oh yeah," she said, trying to brush it off, forcing a smile. "I'm just sad that I have to leave this place in a few days."

Georgie nodded slowly, staring at Lindsey and then turning her eyes toward the water.

"I know what you mean," she said. "I never want to leave."

They sat for a while longer, until the sun cast a rich, golden afternoon light on everything and Berty's fingers were wrinkled from the ocean water. When it was time to go, Georgie helped Lindsey pack everything up, and they all walked home together. Though Lindsey felt somewhat better than she had that morning, the walk was still difficult. Her body still felt bruised.

At the house, Berty raced upstairs to check on Ocean. He called out for Lindsey, and she came to his room, slowly this time, trying to think about what she'd say. She didn't care. She had a feeling that the butterfly was going to be dead, and she wasn't sure how she'd explain this to Berty. Her brain felt like it had been drowned. They peered into the cage, and Lindsey braced herself. Ocean was moving, only slightly, her wings fluttering with obvious exertion, a desperate, small flutter, like the last rotations of a rusty propeller.

"This is because I touched her, isn't it?" Berty looked up at Lindsey with wet eyes. "I touched her, and now she's going to die."

Lindsey thought about how to respond. Normally, she would sugar-coat her answer, taking any blame away from him. But today she didn't see how she could. Berty had been careless with this creature, and now she might die because of it.

"Probably," she answered. Berty began to cry. It was the first time she had spoken to Berty like that—cold and indifferent. "Let's just take her outside," Lindsey said, regretting her words. She couldn't look at Berty. "She will be fine. She's stronger than you think," she said, not sure she meant it.

She carried the cage downstairs, Berty whimpering behind her. They went out to the backyard, all the way down the lawn to the edge of the sea. There was no wind that afternoon. The air was still, and the sun was high.

"Okay," Berty said. "You take the top off."

They both crouched down next to the cage. Lindsey took the top off slowly. Nothing happened. Ocean's wings fluttered just as before, and she remained in her spot on the pebbles. A few seconds passed. Lindsey was not scrambling to find the words to say to Berty. His face was covered in tears.

But then the butterfly flapped her wings in smooth, strong, milky strokes and rose from the inside of the cage, hovering above it for a moment, then rising higher and higher until she flew off over the water.

Berty shrieked and jumped up and down, waving his arms, yelling goodbye. "You were right!" Berty screamed. "She was strong enough."

Lindsey's eyes watered. She could no longer see the butterfly; it was gone.

On their way back inside, Jonathan emerged from the living room and waited on the patio, watching them ascend the lawn.

"Lindsey," he said. He was holding a glass tumbler with ice and a clear drink. Lindsey worried she was in trouble. She remembered how she must have looked last night when she came back from the beach, how she'd looked like a wasted mess. He'd probably said something to Carol. *This is it,* she thought. *My summer has gone down the drain.*

"I just talked to Chris Fitzgerald," he said. Her body tightened. Had Brian beaten her to the punch and somehow spun what had happened and pinned it on her? "I wanted to make sure, now that summer is almost over, that this job was secure for you. They're really excited to have you come in. They're only calling it an interview for formality's sake. But really, the job is yours." He lifted his glass to toast her.

This had been what she'd wanted. She'd gotten her dream job. This was the first step in creating the life for herself that she'd always hoped to have. Now she felt that she had to choose: the job, the life, the dream—or the truth. She couldn't have both. The thought of doing anything to dismantle everything she had worked for seemed impossible, ridiculous, unfair. She wished, for a second, that Jonathan hadn't followed through on his offer to help, that he had let her down and never made any calls. But now, there would be no looking back.

"Thank you" was all she could muster. "Thank you so much. I really do appreciate your help."

"It's the least we can do," he said. "You've been such an invaluable member of the family this summer. The kids really love you. We all do." She felt dirty, uncomfortable standing there with him.

"Well, they're great kids," she said half-heartedly. She tried to motion herself toward the inside of the house, to get inside.

"And Chris mentioned that you and Joanna might be roommates this fall. How terrific." This surprised Lindsey. Why were all the parents talking about her, Joanna, Brian, their lives? She hated how well they all knew one another, how closely connected everyone was. It was like she couldn't have anything from them without giving up everything else that was her own. Lindsey just nodded and pushed her face into a smile, unable to speak.

"There you are," she heard Carol say from the doorway. Carol stepped outside holding a large Nikon camera. "Lindsey, we need to get a few photos with you and the kids. I just realized we don't have any photos with you from the whole summer."

"Okay." She nodded. Something about the suggestion made her want to burst into tears. It seemed odd for Carol to suggest taking pictures. She never showed an interest in anything sentimental like that. She wasn't the type of mother to make her kids pose for pictures or to document the happy times. She was rarely even around for those times.

"Come on," Carol said, pointing toward the water. "Let's go down the lawn a bit." She paraded Georgie and Berty out onto the grass.

"Lindsey, you go right in the center," she directed. "Now, everyone turn to the right a little bit."

Lindsey smiled, doing as Carol told her to do. Only after the photographs were taken did she realize that her bruised collarbone was exposed in the photo. She hoped that Carol wouldn't say anything about it.

Afterward, Lindsey went into the kitchen for some water. Georgie entered a few seconds later, searching for Diet Coke in the fridge and finding one in back. She cracked it open and gulped. They sat together on the island stools. There was a tension between them, like Georgie was holding back from saying something or like she was mad about something. She seemed suspicious of Lindsey somehow. Lindsey wondered whether she'd done something to upset Georgie in the fog of that morning when she was only partially human.

They sipped their drinks in silence for a few minutes. Sitting without talking felt good. Just before Lindsey was about to get up and go to her room to shower, Georgie opened her mouth as though to say something, and she leaned her body in toward Lindsey.

"Hey," she said, her legs dangling from the stool, her hips twisting back and forth, fidgeting to fill the space. She seemed nervous now. "Are you really okay? You seem . . ." She paused. "I don't know. *Off.*"

Lindsey felt an acute curtness in the way Georgie described her as being *off.* Was it possible, she wondered, that Georgie had seen something, or maybe seen her come home, disheveled and hurt? Or maybe

Georgie had seen nothing. Maybe she was just acting weird for no reason.

"I'm really okay," Lindsey finally replied. "I promise," she said. "I'm fine." Georgie didn't respond. Whether or not she knew anything about what had happened to Lindsey last night, she was still the only person all day to ask Lindsey if she was okay.

"I'm going to go shower," Lindsey said.

"Okay," Georgie said.

Up in her room, Lindsey sat on the bed and took out her phone. She thought again about calling Rose, her mother, Dylan. Telling one of them what had happened. Asking for help. She just couldn't do it. Was it possible, she wondered, to just put this behind her and live her life? What if that's what she wanted to do? Why did she have to humiliate herself and ruin her chances of success? She didn't have to, she decided. It was her choice. If she wanted to stay silent, she could.

She looked at her clothes from last night, which were still in a heap on the floor. She wasn't sure why, but she picked them up and threw them in a plastic shopping bag, tying it up tightly. She stuffed it into her suitcase.

Chapter 30

GEORGIE

Georgie went to the beach club straight after work. She'd packed her suit in her bag that morning. When she got there, it was obvious from Lindsey's tear-stained face that she wasn't okay. Georgie didn't know how much she should reveal, if anything. She decided she'd wait and see if Lindsey said anything to her.

Except Lindsey didn't want to talk. Georgie noticed Brian and Joanna down the beach. Lindsey never looked over there, instead remaining fixed on the water ahead, sitting in silence, until finally she told Berty that it was time to go home. Georgie went with them.

She had expected the day to offer answers, clarity, conversation about what she'd seen last night. In a way, she'd expected to be proven wrong. She wanted someone to tell her that she hadn't actually seen what she saw, that it never happened, and that she and Brian could pick up right where they'd left off in front of the house. But the day was filled only with silence, and Georgie was reminded of what her mother had always told her: *There are certain things that are simply not yours to discuss.* Perhaps this was one of those things, she thought. Maybe she should let it be unspoken.

That night, everyone went to bed early. The house was quiet. Jonathan had left that afternoon to go back to Boston. Carol had let Lindsey order pizza for everyone, something they almost never got to do. Georgie and Berty and Lindsey ate it together in the living room while they watched *Beauty and the Beast*. When Jonathan wasn't home, everyone knew that Berty could watch his favorite Disney movies.

The next day at work, there wasn't much for Georgie to do. She puttered around the main area, cleaning and organizing the display shelves. It was the first time she felt like she didn't need to be there, like she didn't have a real role or purpose there. She'd pulled away from Emma and the other staff after the night she'd heard them talking about her. It was too embarrassing for her to spend time with them. It made her feel like a kid.

She left for the day without saying goodbye to anyone. But when she stepped outside, Lucy was there on the front patio, replanting the window boxes, filling them with chrysanthemums in anticipation of the fall season.

"Georgie," she said, wiping her gloves on her jeans and standing, "great work today."

"Really? Do you mean that?" Georgie wasn't sure what came over her suddenly, but she felt the urge to snap, to yell. She'd contained herself for two days, and now she wanted to scream. She didn't care anymore what anyone thought, at least not in that moment. She'd been through too much, and she didn't have the energy to hide her feelings anymore. She was angry with Lucy for lying to her, for telling her that she did a great job when she didn't mean it. She'd gone behind her back with her mother, of all people. "I know that you only hired me because of my mom."

"Oh, honey," Lucy said, moving closer to Georgie. "I hired you because I knew that you'd be a great part of the team. Yes, your mom called me. But she didn't make me do anything. She was just calling to recommend you. She told me that she believed in you, that she was proud of you, and that she could promise me that you'd work harder than anyone else all summer. And she was right." Georgie felt even worse than before. She'd been so mad at her mother all this time. Maybe her mother had only tried to help. "Your mom was just looking out for you, you know. You'll probably do the same thing one day for someone you love more than anything in the world."

"Okay," Georgie whispered. "I'm sorry. I'm really sorry." She was sorry about everything.

"Don't mention it." Lucy smiled. "And hey, I happen to know that someone has a birthday in a few days. Fifteen, right?" Georgie remembered that the entire staff had to write their birthdays on the calendar in the kitchen. Lucy was big on celebrations.

"Yeah," she said. "But it's no big deal."

"Well, if you want the day off, you know you can take it."

"N-no," stammered Georgie. That was the last thing she wanted. "I want to work. I'll be here."

"See, that's the girl I hired." Lucy winked and returned to her window boxes.

At home, Carol was sitting at the island, typing something on her laptop. Georgie sat down next to her. The house was quiet. She had the urge, briefly, to run to her mother and hug her, to tell her everything.

"Mom," she said, "I'm sorry I got so mad at you for calling Lucy."

Carol looked at her. "It's okay, Georgie." They sat there together for a few minutes without saying anything. "I made a reservation at the yacht club for your birthday dinner. Anyone you want to invite?"

Georgie thought about it. Her birthday was in three days. Lindsey would be gone by then. There was no one she wanted there. Catherine had been texting her, but now Georgie was the one who didn't want to hang out. She didn't even want to celebrate. She'd waited all summer to turn fifteen, to be older. And now all she wanted to do was turn back time.

"No, just us," she said.

Chapter 31

LINDSEY

It was Lindsey's last night on the island. She had made it. She was supposed to see Dylan later. He had planned something special. But she was going to meet Joanna at her house for a drink first. She needed to tell her the truth. She realized that this wasn't just about her—it was about her friend.

There's something I need to tell you, she'd texted Joanna.

Joanna might not believe her, but it didn't matter. She had to know. She had to know what Brian had been doing to Georgie and what he'd done to her. And if Joanna hated her as a result, fine. She would accept those consequences. Joanna had to know the truth in order to be safe.

As she knocked on the door, it opened. Brian stood before her.

"Hey, Linds!" she heard Joanna call out from the kitchen.

"Hey," Brian said. He opened the door and stepped aside for her. It was all too normal, too relaxed. She felt like she'd stepped into an alternate universe where Saturday night had never happened. She could feel her conviction to tell Joanna start to slip away.

Joanna emerged from the kitchen with the usual glasses of rosé.

"So, great news," she said, handing Lindsey a glass. "Brian and I were just talking about it." They all started to walk toward the patio. When they got there, Joanna held out her glass in a toast. "My parents bought me an apartment in Boston. A two-bedroom right in the South End. Super cute, gym, rooftop pool. We can figure out whatever rent is fair, maybe a thousand a month?" Joanna inched closer. She was so excited. "So, what do you say, roomie?" Lindsey could hardly find an apartment in Rockville for a thousand bucks a month, let alone a beautiful one in the heart of Boston. She glanced over at Brian, who was grinning. She tried to decipher his face, looking for a clue as to what he was thinking. Joanna waited for her response.

"Yes," she said without hesitation. "Yes! This is amazing. Are you sure, Joanna?"

"Of course. It's the perfect plan. We're going to have so much fun." She sat down at the patio table. "All right, Brian," she said. "Lindsey and I have to talk. There's something she needs to *tell* me," Joanna said in a joking voice. Lindsey remembered how she'd texted Joanna.

"Oh, really?" Brian chimed in, moving closer to the table. "I hope it's nothing too serious. Would be a shame to ruin such an epic summer." Lindsey felt a lump in her throat. Was that a threat? Joanna swatted her hand at him playfully.

"We need our girl time. Go!" She jumped up to give him a quick kiss. "Love you. Alchemy? Eight?"

"You bet," he said with a wink. He turned to leave.

"So what's up? Your text kind of freaked me out, to be honest," Joanna said.

Lindsey opened her mouth to begin. She looked at Joanna—how light she was, how happy, how hopeful about the future she was. How would she begin to explain what had happened and be the one to ruin everything for her friend?

"I th-think," she stuttered. "Um, I'm going to end things with Dylan." It was true—she was going to end things with him, even though she didn't really want to. She just hadn't planned on telling Joanna that, at least not now. But it was all she could say.

"Honestly, I think that's the right call. I know it sucks. But we're going to be in Boston, living our lives. Why be tied down with a long-distance thing, right?"

Lindsey nodded. "You're right. Exactly. I knew you'd understand."

"But hey—enjoy your last night together. Why not?" Joanna grinned at her. "And then," she added, "when we're settled in Boston, Brian can set you up with so many eligible friends. He'll find you a great guy like *that*." She snapped her fingers.

She left Joanna's house a little while later, feeling depressed and defeated. She'd been a coward. If she was really a good friend, she would have told Joanna. But she'd just buried herself even deeper in a lie, and now there was no going back. All she could do now, she told herself, was stay close to Joanna to protect her, to wait for the right time to tell her the truth, when she was ready.

She walked into town and up Main Street, toward Atria, where Dylan had suggested they go to dinner. He had told her to go downstairs, to the cellar part of the restaurant that served what he promised were the best burgers on the island. She arrived first, a few minutes early, and a beautiful hostess brought her to a table in a cozy nook in back by an old brick fireplace. Lindsey ordered them both beers. As she waited, she made up her mind: she had to end it. Not because she wanted to, and not because she didn't care about him. Not even because she couldn't see a future with him. She could. It was because she felt like she could never tell him the truth. She couldn't bear the thought of telling him and knowing that he would look at her differently after that forever. It would change everything. And she couldn't be with him and not tell him the truth. She couldn't lie to him. Her only option was to end it.

She hadn't anticipated how difficult it would be to actually see him. But when he walked in, her body felt like it snapped in two, and she had to stop herself from crying. She felt an urge to run to him, to wrap herself in his arms. He looked at her with so much kindness and tenderness that it made her feel broken.

"Hi," he said, leaning down to embrace her. She smelled his neck and closed her eyes. She felt safe. And for a moment, she forgot everything that had happened. She let herself enjoy the possibility of being in love, of being with Dylan. But when they pulled apart, she remembered.

They looked over the menu, and Dylan rambled on about his three favorite burgers there. "It really depends on what mood you're in," he said. Lindsey wasn't in the mood for anything. She couldn't focus on the menu. All she could focus on was what she knew was coming between them. "I'll have the McRipoff," Dylan said when the waitress came by. "Medium, please." Lindsey asked for the same, mustering a smile in the process.

He'd gone to so much trouble to orchestrate a romantic last evening for them, Lindsey knew. And on any other night, it would be perfect. But not tonight. Tonight, when he put his hand on her knee, she recoiled. Tonight, his touch made her angry. He was making this so much harder than it had to be.

"So," he said, leaning toward her, "I think I can manage to get Fridays off this fall, or at least half days. I could come up to the city on weekends."

Lindsey looked down at her hands, bundled in her lap.

"Dylan," she said. And he knew. "I don't know," she whispered. She felt like a coward, a liar. "I'm not sure it will work." She couldn't look at him.

"You're wrong," he said. "I know it can. Boston to the Vineyard is nothing. We can see each other all the time." She felt her eyes well up with fiery tears, and she breathed to hold them back. If he reached out his hand to touch her right now, she thought, she would crumble.

"It's not just the distance," she said. "I just can't. We can't."

"But I don't get it. Things are so good between us. I . . ."

"No," she said. "You don't want to be with me. Trust me."

The waitress brought out their food—bountiful plates of french fries and hot burgers with gleaming buns. The dishes remained untouched for several moments while Lindsey finished her thought. She knew what she had to tell him. She had to tell him what she'd done on that very first night. How it had all been her fault. How she'd lied to him all summer. Then, he would hate her. And it would be over. It was the only solution to all this. The only way to extricate herself.

"I lied to you," she said. "I'm the one who fucked up Brian's car. It was Joanna and me. And I knew that he thought it was you, and that he was going to do something to get you back, and I didn't say anything. Okay? I lied to you this whole time. I lied to you because I cared more about *them*, about being accepted, than I cared about you. So go ahead, hate me. You don't want to be with me."

Dylan took a bite of his burger and shoveled in a couple of fries. He didn't say anything. She looked at his face but couldn't tell what he was thinking. She had expected him to blow up, to storm off, to break up with *her*.

"I forgive you," he said.

"Well, I don't forgive myself," she said. She cut into her burger, going through with the motions of dinner. She shouldn't have told him so early into the meal. She hadn't timed it right, and now they both ate their food in uncomfortable, heavy silence.

"I can't do this," she finally said, pushing away her plate. His quick forgiveness of her only made her want to pull further away from him. "I'm sorry, Dylan. I really am. I'm so sorry."

"You don't have to do this," he said, looking at her, almost as if he understood. "We can figure this out. If there's something else bothering you, just *tell me*." He knew her. He could tell there was something else she was keeping from him. And she wanted to tell him. She wanted to tell him so badly. But his face was so sweet, so innocent, so good. She couldn't tell him. She knew that she never would.

"I just can't. I'm sorry." There was nothing left for her to say. She took out some cash from her purse and put it on the table, feeling terrible for leaving him behind like that, alone in a beautiful restaurant, on a night that he had wanted to go an entirely different way. But it was the only thing she could do. "Goodbye," she said, starting to cry and turning to leave, running up the stairs and out the doors onto Main Street once again.

She wished that she could take it all back and turn around and run into his arms, leaving everything else behind. But she couldn't do it. She had to let go. She cried on her walk home, and she gave herself a few minutes to calm down before she went inside the Deckers' house. Thankfully, she didn't see anyone when she went up the stairs to her room and shut the door behind her.

She was leaving the next morning and needed to pack. She laid out her clothes for tomorrow and threw the rest in her suitcase, not caring about what was clean or dirty. She'd sort it all out at home. She just needed to get there. She saw the plastic bag with her clothes from Saturday night, wedged in the corner of her bag like a hidden explosive. She left it there, covering it up with clothes and zipping her suitcase.

The next morning, Carol gave her a ride to the ferry. Berty and Georgie came along. She stepped out of the car in Vineyard Haven and heaved her duffel bag and rolling suitcase out of the trunk.

Berty was crying. "No!" he yelled. He tugged at the hem of her shorts. Carol picked him up, but he only screamed more for Lindsey. She felt terrible. But she needed to escape.

She gave Carol an uncomfortable hug. "Thank you for everything, Lindsey. I'm sure we'll see you in Boston." Lindsey nodded.

Georgie hugged her last. "I'm sorry I'll miss your birthday," Lindsey said. "But I actually have something for you." She'd almost forgotten that a week ago, she had finished the friendship bracelets that they'd started to make earlier that summer but never did. It felt silly—disingenuous, even—to give the bracelet to her now, but she'd spent the time making them, so she figured she would. She pulled the bracelets out of her bag. "One for you, one for me," she said. Georgie smiled just a little.

"I'm sorry," she said then, hugging Lindsey close. What did she mean by that? "I'm sorry," she said again.

It was time to get on the ferry. Lindsey took her bags and walked up the ramp. She turned and saw them all get back into their car and drive off. *Another day at the beach for them,* she thought. Life would just go on.

She sat on the outside deck of the ferry, just as she'd done on her trip there. The island looked so different to her now than it had just a few months ago. She missed Dylan, and for a moment, she imagined leaping off the boat, swimming to shore, and running to find him. She wished that everything that had happened could just stay there on the island forever, that it didn't have to follow her wherever she went. In Woods Hole, she boarded the bus, and then an airplane, and finally she was back home in her parents' house in Rockville. The journey home had felt so much longer than the initial trip there. It was as if now, everything was so much harder than it was before.

Chapter 32

GEORGIE

It was Georgie's birthday. Jonathan had come home that morning. The family was having dinner at the yacht club that night.

"Be ready to leave at six fifteen, Georgie," Carol called to her as she left for the Picnic Basket that morning.

At work, the staff lit a candle on a cupcake and sang to her in the kitchen. It made her want to cry, and she almost did, but she held back her tears. The last few days of summer, turning fifteen, Lindsey leaving, her feelings toward Brian—everything had become too much. She felt nostalgic for something she couldn't identify. But most of all, she felt guilt. She had let Lindsey, her friend, leave, and she hadn't helped her. She hadn't even tried to stop it when it happened. She wasn't worthy of her friendship. She wasn't worthy of anyone's friendship. She was ashamed.

After work, she went home to change for dinner. She wasn't looking forward to it. She would have to dress up in one of her preppy floral shift dresses and comb her hair with a clean side part the way her mother used to do for her. What kind of lame fifteen-year-old would celebrate their birthday with their parents and younger sibling at a stuffy old club? It was the last thing she wanted to do tonight. But she had no other options. She had no other friends. If Lindsey were here, she thought, they'd go out for ice cream together later, or maybe to that popular place on the water that everyone called the Shanty. But since Lindsey was gone, Georgie reverted back to being alone. She'd waited so long to be a year older, and now it just felt like a letdown.

Georgie took a long shower. She chose a dress with a hydrangea pattern on it, one that her mom had picked out for her from Nell as a birthday present. She slipped into her old Jack Rogers sandals. For most of the summer, Georgie had resisted dressing up in this kind of outfit, the kind that made it obvious that she was a rich summer kid. She wanted to blend in with the locals and hardworking college kids in her jean cutoff shorts, messy hair, and funky bracelets. She looked at herself in the mirror now: clean, shiny, feminine, iron-pressed, nothing out of place. She wasn't sure which version of herself was really *her*.

She stayed in her room until it was time to go, staring out the window and looking down at the lighthouse beach. It all looked so far away now. The sand looked white against the water, which was a deep cornflower blue under the late-afternoon sun. There were people scattered along the beach. Georgie wondered how she'd feel if she went down there right now and stood at the spot where she'd seen Brian and Lindsey. Would she feel anything at all? Would the beach look the same as it always had to her, or would it look different somehow? She wondered if she'd ever go back to that beach again in her entire life. She took out her journal. *Lindsey left,* she wrote. *I didn't say anything, and now I feel like I never will. It's too late. She didn't want my help. Maybe she didn't want anyone to know.*

The club was just a few blocks away, down North Water Street and then over to Dock Street. The air was still warm, and the family walked together. It was actually nice, she thought, being all together, something they rarely did. Georgie couldn't even remember the last time they had done it. She felt a wistful pang in her stomach, a longing for the present moment to last.

Berty did most of the talking at dinner, wanting to tell everyone about his newly expanded seashell collection. Georgie felt detached.

She was thinking about Lindsey. She tried to imagine what she was doing right now. She looked at her friendship bracelet and wondered if Lindsey was wearing hers too.

Dinner at the club was always social; everyone knew everyone, and half the entire evening was spent waving to other families and listening to parents chat while their kids waited impatiently. All the grown-ups loved to hear about how Georgie had a *job* that summer. She was an anomaly among the kids at the yacht club. She wasn't sure why, but it seemed to amuse many of her parents' friends that she had *chosen* to work.

Just before dessert, Georgie went to the restroom, which was a small, cramped space with wooden walls. The musty smell and something about the narrow stalls always gave her the wobbly feeling of being out at sea. Outside the bathroom was a darkly lit vestibule where the sailing-race results were posted, along with some photos. Georgie stopped to look, curious as to who was winning this year's 420 series. She squinted to make out some of the faces in the photos; she knew a few, but only from her old days of sailing as a kid.

"You could be up there if you wanted to be," she heard from behind her. She turned and saw Brian. He was wearing a navy-blue blazer, khaki pants, and a pink tie with tiny green palm trees on it. For a moment, Georgie couldn't believe that this was the same person she'd seen at the lighthouse with Lindsey, the same guy who had touched her leg just a few days before. She wondered, for a moment, if Brian knew that she had seen him that night. She searched his face for an answer. He leaned his elbow on the wall, encasing her inside his frame.

"Well, I don't want to be," she responded after a moment, looking at him directly. "I don't want to be up there." She wasn't sure if she was talking about sailing anymore.

Georgie crossed her arms, unsure of what would come next, and suddenly felt hyperaware of her body, her smell, her close proximity to Brian in such a public yet hidden place. Brian put his hands in his pockets. Georgie could feel their dynamic shifting somehow, like her rejection of sailing was a rejection of him. When, in reality, all she wanted, despite everything, was to have him want her. She crossed her arms tighter and looked off to the side. Her eyes felt hot and ready to burst into tears.

"Why so sour, kid?" She felt like he was stabbing her heart. He moved closer, like a chess piece winding its way toward a victory.

"I guess I just thought . . . ," Georgie started to say. She struggled to find the right words. "Can you just *tell me* . . . why are you doing this to me?" She hadn't planned on asking him that. She wasn't even sure what she meant.

Brian smiled. "Because you like it," he said. "And because I *can*."

Georgie didn't respond. She turned away from him and walked back to the safety of her family's table, not looking behind her even once. She regretted it immediately, thinking of all the smart things she could have said to him, all the ways she could have let him hear it, all the moves she could have made. But somehow, walking away was the only thing she was capable of doing. Out of the corner of her eye, she saw Brian return to his table as well. It was strange, seeing Brian with his own parents, just like her.

After dinner, at home, when everyone had gone to sleep, Georgie was still awake in bed. She cradled her phone in her hands, debating again whether or not she should reach out to Lindsey. But Lindsey hadn't even texted her to wish her a happy birthday, which hurt Georgie's feelings. Maybe they weren't real friends after all. Maybe Lindsey was just their nanny for the summer, nothing more. Georgie felt uncertain of everything and everyone. She wasn't sure she would be able to trust anyone again.

She put her phone facedown on her bedside table and shut her eyes, trying to sleep. Her body still hummed with everything that had happened that day. She was a year older now. A lot had happened to her in the past few months. In just a few days, she would be back in high school. She'd saved a few hundred dollars of her own from her job, and now she could buy anything she wanted with it. She felt proud of herself, for the most part. Or at least, she *had* felt proud of herself until the other night. Now she felt like everything she thought she knew had been wiped away and replaced with a puzzle that she couldn't figure out.

Georgie knew that she needed to make a decision about what she was going to do, or not do, about what she'd seen at the lighthouse. But now that some time had passed and Lindsey was gone, there was a new sense of distance from it that allowed Georgie to wriggle free from its weight. She told herself again and again that if Lindsey had wanted to do something about what happened—if she had wanted to ask someone for help—she would have. Perhaps this was a secret that was just not meant to be shared. It was a secret that belonged to someone else, she told herself, one that she was never meant to have.

So Georgie buried it, like a relic never meant to be found. She buried the whole night, deep down in the depths of herself, stuffing it into a rumbling, cavernous place of shame and regret that sometimes bubbled up when she was in a deep slumber, waking her with a tickling echo of those tiny words: *Stop, stop, stop, stop!*

Chapter 33

Georgie

2019

On the Tuesday before Thanksgiving, Charles Street in Boston was filled with people scrambling to prepare for the holiday. Georgie walked along the narrow brick sidewalk toward her apartment, twisting herself sideways to cut through the crowds. The storefronts were aglow in autumnal hues, and though Beacon Hill was beautiful, the distinct energy it radiated during the holidays was one that Georgie found exhausting and stressful. **Get Your Bird Before It's Too Late!** one market urged customers with a bright-red sign out front. **Half Off Holiday Decor!** another one beckoned. For a holiday that was meant to be about gratitude, it always seemed, to Georgie, to be mostly about rapid and inflated consumption.

Tomorrow, Georgie was driving down to the Vineyard with her mother and Berty. They hadn't been back to the island for Thanksgiving in years, not since Carol and Jonathan first split up. Jonathan had moved out of the family's town house about five years ago and into an apartment in the Four Seasons.

"It's temporary," Carol had said at first. "We just need a few months apart." But then he didn't come back. During the last few holidays, Georgie and Berty had shuffled between their dad's apartment and the town house, which Carol ultimately got to keep. The holidays were never fun; they were exhausting. Everyone was upset, but no one ever said so, not explicitly. That wasn't their way. Instead, everyone just drank a lot and muttered passive-aggressive comments under their breath.

This year, Carol said that she was going to the Vineyard for Thanksgiving—she got to keep that house too. Georgie and Berty agreed to go with her. Thus far, their parents hadn't really made them choose sides. Jonathan lived right across Boston Common, so it was easy for the kids to go back and forth, even though they didn't like it. But put in the position of having to choose, both Georgie and Berty chose their mother.

It hadn't been like that at first. Georgie had resented her mother for their separation, telling her that she had driven her dad away by being so cold. By then, Georgie was a freshman in college.

"Your dad has been cheating on me for almost our entire marriage. I'm sorry to tell you like this, but you should know the truth," Carol had told her. Georgie *had* known, but she hadn't wanted to admit it to herself. She'd seen her parents fight for years as a kid, and she'd noticed her dad's indiscretions—his late nights, his travel, the way he was never affectionate with Carol. She just hadn't wanted to see it. Her dad loved her and believed in her, and she loved him back. It broke her heart when she finally admitted to herself that he'd been a shitty husband and, really, a shitty, absent father.

"I let you down, Gigi," her father had said to her when she'd met him for dinner at the Somerset Club after the divorce was finalized. He'd asked to see her, one-on-one. "I let you down and I let your mother down." He seemed remorseful, she thought, as he talked through the meal. But only because he seemed lonely now and missed his old life, his family. Never once did he say that he was sorry. It was the delicate difference between remorse and penitence. Her father wished that things were different now, but he still couldn't take responsibility for what he'd done.

Throughout all this, Georgie and Carol didn't become *close* as a result, but they became closer than they had been before. Georgie understood her mother more and felt protective of her. They didn't totally know how to communicate with one another, still, but once Carol told her about her marriage, Georgie felt like she saw a different side to her mother: a real one.

She'd hoped that Carol wouldn't want to go to the Vineyard for Thanksgiving, but she'd just finished redecorating the house—now it was filled with sharp edges; glass tables; white sofas; and clean, geometric rugs—and she really wanted Georgie and Berty there with her. But Georgie was scared to go. She didn't like to be there, not anymore. Not since that summer. She'd tried to tell her mom that she was busy grading papers and that she'd need to be close to campus, but her mother wouldn't hear it. She was going.

Walking into her apartment now, Ocean ran to her, as he always did. He was a small mutt and looked sort of like the miniature cousin of a yellow Lab. Georgie had found him at the pound last year when she started graduate school. She'd always loved dogs, but the real reason she wanted to get one was that the dog was the perfect excuse to hide from the world. Having Ocean meant that Georgie always had an anchor pulling her back home, into the safety of her bubble, away from everyone. She always had an easy out to avoid sleeping over at a guy's house. She could leave parties early. Traveling was usually out of the question, even a weekend trip. She could even leave a dinner before dessert if she wanted to. Not that she was getting many of these kinds of invitations lately, but just in case, she always had an excuse.

She'd named the dog after Berty's pet butterfly. When she'd told Berty about it last year, he'd responded, as a cranky teenager, "Okay . . . that's weird." Georgie didn't take it to heart; she knew that it was just the hormonal demon that lived inside all teenagers talking. Berty, a star lacrosse player who, as a freshman, was already starting on Milton's varsity team, had become exactly the kind of guy who wouldn't have given

Georgie the time of day in high school. He was preppy, athletic, slightly arrogant, wickedly smart, handsome, and hypermasculine. Whenever he was home for a weekend, Carol was always telling him to please put his phone away. It was constantly chiming.

"*Girls,*" he'd once said to Georgie when his phone dinged five times in a row. "What can I do?" Sometimes Georgie looked at her brother—with his sharp jawline that echoed his father's, his strong shoulders, his cocky attitude—and she couldn't believe that she was related to him. Of course, Berty didn't want to acknowledge anything that recalled his more tender years, when Disney princesses excited him more than real-life girls.

After washing her face and changing into a robe, Georgie started packing. She knew the whole weekend would be casual. Carol wouldn't want to socialize, not anymore. She'd streamlined her life since the divorce and had focused more on herself. She was even *cooking* their Thanksgiving dinner this year, a true first.

"Too bad there's no Domino's on the island," Berty had said when Carol told them this.

Georgie finished packing quickly. There was nothing to do on the island this time of year but drink, eat, read, sleep, and drink some more. And remember.

She was grateful to be packing warm clothes instead of beachwear. At least the off-season on the Vineyard was quiet, she thought, and she didn't have to worry about running into long-lost summer friends she didn't want to see, like Catherine, who Georgie knew from her Instagram posts was *still* going to the beach club every weekend in the summer, except now she could drink legally and had upgraded her illicit warm vodka to chilled glasses of rosé at the Covington and mezcal margaritas at the Port Hunter.

"I saw all your old friends today at the beach club," Carol used to tell her sometimes during the summer, urging her to come down for a weekend. "I'm sure they'd love to see you." It seemed to really disappoint Carol that Georgie hadn't maintained those friendships, if she could ever even call them that. It disappointed her so much, in fact, that she seemed to be totally in denial that Georgie hadn't spoken to any of those girls in years. But that had changed when Carol divorced Jonathan. Once she took the pressure off herself to be a certain person and to live a certain way, she took that pressure off Georgie too.

Georgie didn't go back to the Vineyard for a whole summer after that first year when she turned fifteen. She couldn't. She went to different arts camps, got internships in Boston, stayed at home, traveled. She went to the island for weekends here and there, mostly in the off-season, but she could never bring herself to spend an entire summer there again.

The last time Georgie had been on the island during the summer was during her junior year of college, when she had a few weeks off from an internship in New York. She went by the Picnic Basket her first morning there, only to discover that it had a new owner and now sold mass-produced beach towels and inflatable flamingos, nothing like the beautiful handcrafted pottery and candles that Georgie used to stack on the shelves. Lucy had moved to Napa.

"I guess she threw in the towel," the new manager had told Georgie. It made Georgie sad to think that she might never see Lucy again, and their separation came without warning. She wondered if something had happened to make Lucy leave the island suddenly. Maybe she had snapped. The island did that to some people. But Georgie would never know. She told herself that Lucy was probably living a happy, bohemian life in wine country, surrounded by rolling vineyards, and that made it all somewhat okay.

She still went into the Picnic Basket whenever she was on island, though, almost as though she hoped that it would transform back into the way it was each time she opened its doors. The staff was still predominantly young women, and even though the girls behind the counter were now younger than she was, they always seemed older, more confident, possessing some secret that she'd never know, and to her, they'd forever be frozen in time as those beautiful girls.

Even though the off-season was more forgiving, with its peaceful, bare-branched streets and cool morning chill, Georgie still didn't want to go. Being back on the island catapulted her into a memory tunnel that she had tried so hard to crawl her way out of. It took her back to that night at the lighthouse—as if she needed a reminder. For the past decade, it had been all she'd thought about.

She'd put on a good front for a while. High school at Milton was miserable for her. She'd gotten through it by throwing herself into school activities—the newspaper, the debate team, and photography class. She was a loner. A nerd. She wanted to be; any attention made her nervous, overwhelmed. But college was different for her. Her father wanted her to go to Bowdoin, but she didn't even apply. She knew that if she got in, she'd have to go.

"It's not for me, Dad," she'd told him. He hadn't argued with her as much as she thought he would. He seemed to have abandoned his investment in her and thrown his chips into Berty's future instead. She was fine with that.

Instead, she went to Wesleyan. There, she found people she actually liked for the first time in her life—people who were interested in more than just her last name or her bank account. People who had fascinating backgrounds and cared about the world and politics. At Wesleyan, Georgie could be whoever she wanted to be. And if she could be someone else, then she didn't have to bear the full burden of the memory of that night. She learned that she felt comfortable in the world of academia, so she stayed there, continuing on to Harvard to earn her PhD in sociology, with a secondary field in women, gender, and sexuality studies. At Harvard, Georgie was buffered by other nebbish intellectuals who didn't probe her about her personal life. She could hide behind her computer and her books. She could forget.

But the truth was, she never forgot that night. She thought about it every single day. She thought about it whenever someone touched her or whenever she heard someone say *Shhh* or whenever she smelled the ocean. And it came to her in her dreams too. Night after night, she revisited the lighthouse and retraced her steps to it. But some form of self-preservation allowed the dream to end just before she reached the other side. She always woke up before being confronted with the terror of what she'd really seen. So she started most of her days from this place, this place of guilt and uncertainty but also absolute certainty, a festering and painful mix of emotions. She felt rotten inside from the moment she got out of bed. And she wondered, always, what might have happened if she'd gone down to the beach with Brian instead of Lindsey. What if it had been *her* instead? Was it supposed to have been her? Every day, she told herself that it was her fault. And every day, she thought about reaching out to Lindsey. But she never could.

It was only a few weeks ago that all that had changed for her. She was working late one night in the Lamont Library when one of the other teacher's assistants sidled up to her.

"Come on, Georgie, let's go," he said. His name was Bart. He was gay and had a thick New York accent. "We're all going to Daedalus. You need a break. Come *on*." Daedalus was a bar that all the grad students would frequent after long days, but Georgie rarely joined.

"I can't," she pleaded. "Too much work."

"One drink." Bart had always been nice to Georgie and had once loaned her his laptop when hers crashed right before a lecture.

"Fine. One drink," she said, grabbing her things.

Daedalus was crowded that night, packed with undergrads and grad students wrestling their way to the bar. Georgie and Bart found some friends from the Sociology Department, and Bart got everyone a round of drinks. One round turned into four, and Georgie wobbled to the bathroom a little while later. There was a long line, but Georgie knew that there was a handicapped bathroom downstairs that most people didn't know about, so she made her way there.

Just as she shut the door to the restroom, a hand pushed the door open, and a man stepped inside.

"What the hell," Georgie said. "Get out!" She didn't know him. He looked older; maybe he was a graduate student, but she didn't know. She tried to move past him so that she could leave, but he blocked her. It didn't occur to her that this stranger was trying to do anything more than use the bathroom before her, until he reached out his hand and pawed at her chest.

"Hey," he whispered, "come on . . ." He grabbed her wrist with one hand and leaned in toward her, but then he lost his balance and slipped on the floor. "Fuck," he moaned. Georgie escaped out the door and got straight into a cab, going home. She never saw him again, and she never told anyone what happened—or what might have happened.

But since then, she felt unable to hold inside the secret she'd been carrying about Lindsey. She'd thought that she could live her whole life without telling anyone and that she'd be fine. After that night in the bathroom, though, she couldn't wait. Now that she had almost experienced something similar herself, she could no longer contain it. It was like a seal had been broken, and now her thoughts were consumed by that memory. What if she hadn't gone downstairs to the bathroom? she wondered. Would she have continued to ignore the memory of that night, or would it have found its way back to her some other way? After that, the dream returned to her in a different way. This time, she rounded the bend of the lighthouse and saw, once again, what she'd been hiding from for so long. She saw herself there, witnessing it all, doing nothing, and whispering into the wind: *Stop, stop, stop!*

The recollection frightened her and made her sick with guilt. There was no denying what she had seen. And there was no denying the fact that she'd done nothing and told no one. She'd abandoned Lindsey. It was possible, she knew, that she was still the only other person on the planet, besides Brian, who knew what had happened that night. Lindsey might not have ever told anyone. This realization terrified and isolated Georgie. And sometimes, she thought that maybe she should just continue to stay silent. She liked being shut off from the world; she liked being inward, like a snail curling itself into its shell, tighter and tighter, blocking off all light and air. She wanted to keep her life locked in. If she stayed within her routine, if she stayed at home with Ocean, if she didn't talk to anyone about what she'd seen, she could be safe. No one could blame her. Maybe she could convince herself that nothing had even happened. But she knew that she was guilty of silence, and what kind of a person did that make her?

She had tried to live normally, whatever that meant. But she wasn't very good at it. She lived her life like a ghost, wandering Beacon Hill with Ocean, passing by bubbly college graduates who were going to bars and parties. She went on a few dates here and there. Mostly setups by other grad students, and only after she tired of protesting. The last date she'd gone on was with an engineering grad student from MIT named James. He took her out for Korean barbecue. He was well mannered and well groomed, eager to hear about Georgie's life and eager to share about his own. At one point during dinner, through the smoke of the grill, Georgie looked at him and even thought he was handsome. She forgot about Lindsey for a few minutes and felt the rush of what it might be like to be someone without worries, someone who could let go and experience joy with another person. They went back to his apartment, a clean space that smelled like Febreze. They kissed on his black leather sofa, but Georgie quickly got up to leave when his hand brushed her breast over her sweater, muttering something about needing to get back to her dog. James texted her the next day, but she didn't respond. She never heard from him after that.

"But you're so *pretty*," a well-meaning female classmate said to her after Georgie politely refused another setup, as if her looks made her obligated to shop herself out to the male population, she thought. What did her looks have to do with anything? The next day, she wore the baggiest sweater she owned, a brown turtleneck that was really more of a woolen kaftan than a sweater.

And now Georgie wasn't sure that she would be able to return to the island with all these unhinged feelings. How could she sleep in her old bedroom and look out at the lighthouse without being reminded of all the time that had gone by since that summer with Lindsey and all the things that Georgie *hadn't* done to help her?

It didn't help knowing that her mom would interrogate her about her personal life throughout the next few days. As she threw her toiletries in a travel case, Georgie mentally prepared herself for the usual inquisition: was she dating anyone, what was she going to do after grad school, how was her apartment, and so on. She saw her mother about once every month but usually just for a quick meal. She rarely saw her father now. He had a young girlfriend and spent a lot of time in Antigua. She was mostly sad for Berty, who still idolized him. She worried about when he'd finally see their father for who he was—or if he ever would at all.

One day last year, Georgie decided she should see a therapist. She'd avoided the idea for a while, but the potential of a consistent sleeping-pill prescription finally convinced her to get a reference from a colleague and make an appointment. The therapist was a pixie of a woman in her sixties who wore monochromatic outfits. Some days it was all red; other days it was all mauve. Georgie would talk to her while rubbing a glossy stone that the therapist said helped ease stress.

It took Georgie three sessions to tell the therapist what had happened that night at the lighthouse. The therapist nodded and jotted down some notes, saying nothing. Georgie believed in therapy, in general, but she was skeptical about it working for her. When she finished telling the therapist about that night, she waited for a response, some kind of solution. Nearly half a minute went by.

Georgie wanted to yell, *So? Now do you get why I'm so fucked up?* But she didn't. The therapist didn't say anything.

"I guess I should reach out to Lindsey," Georgie finally found herself saying, "and see if she wants my help. It's been a long time, but I suppose it's not too late."

Georgie couldn't believe it when she said this. It was as if the words came out of her without her mind processing them. She'd never actually intended to *do* anything about what happened with Lindsey, at least not at that point. She had figured that her window of opportunity had closed long ago, when she had first witnessed it all. She'd waited too long. And she had been raised, she realized over a few more sessions with the therapist, to believe that if it wasn't your business, then you should stay out of it. This was so deeply ingrained in her that going to the police or telling her parents about it wasn't ever *really* a possibility that Georgie felt existed. Eventually, Georgie also admitted to herself that, at the time, she was further dissuaded from telling anyone about what had happened because she was actually heartbroken upon seeing Lindsey with Brian. In retrospect, this truth was what caused her to feel the most shame.

Even though it had been ten years, Georgie knew how to reach Lindsey. In fact, she knew a lot about her. She'd seen her only once since that summer, briefly, when her parents invited Lindsey over for dinner back in the city. It was only a few months since that summer had ended, and Georgie didn't know what to say to her. It was strange, she remembered thinking, seeing Lindsey off the island, living like a grown-up, working in Boston. She felt distant from her. And seeing how well Lindsey was doing—how happy she was, how successful she was becoming, confused Georgie. Lindsey didn't appear to her to be some-one who had been through a traumatic event. She could smile, laugh, make conversation, hug. She didn't fit the description that Georgie had in her mind of what a victim should look or act like.

Social media had allowed Georgie to keep track of Lindsey. Georgie often looked Lindsey up on Facebook and Instagram, scrolling through photos of her and her friends. Lindsey's life seemed incredibly joyful. It looked like she went out a lot. Her hair was glossy and straight. She was thin but toned, like she did a lot of workout classes. She lived in Boston, too, but Georgie had never run into her, not even from afar. Georgie wasn't all that surprised by that, though, since Georgie never went to the bars or trendy restaurants in the South End that she saw Lindsey go to.

From some of Lindsey's photos, Georgie could see that Lindsey was still friends with both Joanna and Brian. It was strange to Georgie, and made her feel conflicted, that Lindsey had stayed close with them. But she remembered that Lindsey had gotten the job at Brian's parents' gallery, and she had gone to live with Joanna. She wondered, often, if Lindsey had felt like she'd had to stay silent in order to get those things. Georgie had barely seen Joanna or Brian since that summer, and now that her parents were split up, they didn't see much of their families either. Everyone seemed to have grown apart—except for Lindsey, Joanna, and Brian.

Georgie had looked up Brian on Facebook too. He was still dating Joanna, after all this time. Their life in Boston was nothing like hers— lots of fund-raisers, parties, weddings. Lindsey was in a lot of their photos. They all seemed to have a great life together. Looking at pictures of them was like looking at pictures of strangers. She didn't know them. Brian wasn't the person she had once been in love with.

All these circumstances, and the pictures of Lindsey's happy life, gave Georgie doubt about her plan to reach out to her. So she waited. She told her therapist, week after week, that she was going to do it. *I'm just not ready,* she'd say. *Soon.* She waited as though she thought it all might just go away, somehow, or that she'd wake up one morning and realize that she'd been wrong this whole time. It wasn't until that night in the bathroom of the bar that Georgie really knew that morning wouldn't ever come, and she decided that it wasn't about whether or not she was *ready*. It was about doing the right thing. She gave herself a few more weeks to think about what she would say, and then she knew it was time.

Even in the final moments before reaching out, Georgie felt waves of doubt creep in. Maybe Lindsey really had put the whole thing behind her and didn't want to deal with it. Maybe, if she was still friendly with

Brian, just *maybe* Georgie hadn't actually seen what she thought she saw. But no matter how many times Georgie's mind went in that circle, it always returned to the same, unwavering truth. She knew what she had seen, and nothing would change that. But still, was it Georgie's place, after all these years, to force Lindsey to uncover all this if she didn't want to? Maybe not. But until she did, she couldn't really live her own life. She needed to tell Lindsey. She had to.

Chapter 34

Lindsey

2019

Lindsey sucked in her stomach as she zipped up the skirt, being careful not to snag her skin in the teeth of the zipper. The skirt cost just about a week of Lindsey's salary and was a size two. It was a buttery brown leather and a cut that few women could pull off: high waist, tight, and just skimming the top of the knees. She turned a few times and looked at herself in the mirror, carefully examining the curve between the top of her thighs and her stomach and the arch of her backside. She took off the skirt, grabbing her black pants almost simultaneously so that she didn't have to stare at herself in the mirror with just her lace underwear on. The lighting at Neiman's was relatively kind, but nevertheless, it wasn't what she needed to see on her lunch break. She decided against the skirt. *Too showy,* she thought.

And she was never going to buy it anyway, at least not in the store. If she liked the skirt, she'd find a slightly used version of it online for half the price, or a similar one at Zara. No one would know the difference. Lindsey had developed various tricks for looking the part without paying the price—one she couldn't afford, even though she had an incredible career. Although, once in a while, Lindsey would actually buy something at Neiman's, mostly so that the salespeople would remember her and respect her. It was always a statement piece that she saved up for. Something they'd take note of her buying: a leather-piped Burberry trench coat, a pair of black YSL heels, and once, a real splurge, a Chanel clutch as a Christmas present to herself.

Shopping wasn't always so enjoyable for her. She used to hate trying on clothes. No matter what she wore, Lindsey felt like she somehow cheapened the look with the voluptuousness of her figure. That was, until six years ago, when she got a breast reduction and lost fifteen pounds during the recovery process, which she kept off. She knew that she had never been overweight before, but she was tired of feeling like her body prevented her from being seen the way she wanted to be seen. She was tired of being viewed as so overtly *sexual*. It was like her body didn't match who she wanted to be or who she was. So she decided to take matters into her own hands. She spent more than a year setting aside money for the surgery, opting out of dinners and ordering seltzers at bars instead of expensive cocktails. She never even told her parents about it. She just did it. Within two months of the operation, Lindsey was up and running again and had never felt better. She went from a double-D cup down to a small C. Finally, she could exist without feeling the constant weight of men's eyes on her chest. She could go jogging without wearing two sports bras and without the pull of her breasts reminding her of her own limitations, labels, burdens.

Lindsey often preferred to go for a walk or to go shopping during her lunch break instead of actually going to get food. The sight of other young women clutching plastic salad-bar boxes or falafel pitas depressed her. Even if she wanted to, she would never whip out a tuna melt at work, the way one of her interns once did. Lindsey's face had curled into a scowl of disgust at the sight and had more or less stayed that way in the presence of the intern until the end of that summer.

She'd been at the gallery for ten years now. The Fitzgeralds were still part owners of it. The gallery director had hired Lindsey right off the bat, when she first came in for a meeting. They hired her as an intern but made a special exception for her by paying her.

"We don't normally pay our interns," she was told by Hilga, the director, a sharp-boned woman in her sixties with jet-black hair, "but this is a *special* case."

So much had changed since that day, at least on the surface. She and Joanna had moved in together just a few weeks after that summer had ended. The time in between being on the Vineyard and moving to Boston had been a blur for Lindsey—a strange, uprooted period of time at her parents' house when she spent most of her days torturing herself with memories from that night and debating whether or not she should tell someone about it. The question for her wasn't just about right and wrong. She wished that it was—she wished that it was that simple. But it wasn't. If she told anyone what had happened, she would be derailing all her plans, her entire future. But if she didn't tell anyone, then she was betraying Joanna. She was betraying other women, potentially. And most of all, she knew, she was betraying herself.

She decided that she'd go to Boston and just give herself time. She didn't have to say anything just yet, she told herself. Maybe Brian and Joanna would break up, she hoped. Maybe Brian would just conveniently disappear.

But once she took the job at the gallery, she again started to feel like she was lying to herself. Was she ever really going to tell Joanna? Was she going to tell anyone? By taking the job, she was indebting herself even further to Brian and his family. And by living with Joanna, she was indebting herself to her too. It only made it more impossible for her to speak up.

Being busy helped. She consoled herself by occupying her time with work and by trying to improve herself, push herself, get *better* at everything. She didn't make much money, but she made just enough to get by, as long as she was careful not to spend anything frivolously. She always took public transportation, she tried to make her own food at home, and if she went out to dinner or for drinks, she was careful to just order a cocktail or two and an appetizer only. She did whatever the gallery needed: coffee runs, office organizing, even the occasional cleaning. After paying her dues for two years, they promoted her to assistant gallery manager, a position they concocted as an excuse to pay her slightly more without losing her. She knew how hard she had worked, but she couldn't fully enjoy that first promotion because the thought that she didn't deserve it still loomed heavy over her. Was she only there because of the Fitzgeralds? Had Brian said something to his parents to make them think that they had to keep her around?

Still, just a few years later, she was promoted again, this time to assistant director. That position gave her a huge salary boost, the kind that allowed her to order entrées and buy new shoes once in a while without feeling guilty. There was only one person above her at the gallery now—Hilga, whom Lindsey admired. Hilga let Lindsey run the gallery when she was gone for weeks at a time on vacation. She encouraged Lindsey to run with her own ideas, pursuing new talent and curating new events and shows. Lindsey had much more freedom and autonomy than most assistant directors. She was sure that when Hilga retired, she would become the gallery's director. She had done it. She had found success. By then, she was confident that she'd earned the promotions all on her own. She'd made the gallery more money than ever before, garnered incredible press and publicity for it, lured in some of the hottest global artists to showcase their work there. And yet, no matter how many times she validated herself in her mind, it was undeniable that she wouldn't have been there in the first place had it not been for the Deckers and the Fitzgeralds. And she hated that. But she loved the job, she loved the work, and she was good at it.

The gallery specialized in postmodern art. It was nestled on the second floor of a Newbury Street brownstone, in between a Diane von Furstenberg boutique and the Met Back Bay, a stylish restaurant with a

how she coped. And that's how she managed to have Brian come back into her life.

The first night that Brian came over to pick Joanna up for dinner, Lindsey had opened the door, not knowing that he was coming. It was like seeing a ghost at first. She balled up her fist and thought about winding it up and clocking him in the face, and then kicking him in between the legs, and then elbowing him in the neck, maybe slamming her foot into his stomach over and over again once he was on the floor. But she just stood in the doorway and stared at him, incapable of moving. They looked at one another in silence for a few seconds. Lindsey could feel a prickly flame of anger building up beneath her skin, like he had lit her on fire. And then Brian reached out, opened his arms, and wrapped them around Lindsey in a hug. Her breath shortened into fleeting gasps. His arms were long and seemed to wrap around her torso several times, like a boa constrictor. She wanted to scream but couldn't. Always, she couldn't.

"Hey," he said, leaning back and placing his hands on her shoulders, "it's great to see you!" He burst into the apartment and plopped himself onto their couch, spreading himself out. He was out of place in their apartment, which now seemed like a dollhouse with him in it, like he could shatter everything with the slightest movement.

Lindsey didn't say anything. She'd prepared herself for the possibility of seeing Brian again at some point. She'd tried to, anyway. But nothing she had rehearsed or practiced could have actually informed how she'd feel in that moment. She watched Brian sitting on the couch, scrolling through his phone, waiting for Joanna to finish getting ready. He was disgusting, she thought. His hair looked greasy. She had to turn away.

"Give me five!" Joanna shouted from the bathroom.

As Lindsey watched him, her anger and disgust seemed to evolve into a strange sensation of numbness. Her initial rage and fury and repulsion had been replaced by a void. She suddenly felt *nothing*. Her body and mind removed themselves from the past, like some act of self-preservation.

Later that night, when it was late and Lindsey had gotten into bed, she got a text from Joanna: Sleeping at Brian's tonight. Xx

Months went by, and Joanna and Brian stayed together as a couple. Joanna was happy with him, it seemed. He made her laugh and took her on amazing dates and listened to her when she had bad days at work and needed to vent or cry. Lindsey couldn't deny that he seemed to treat Joanna well. It seemed like he had *changed*. His arrogance had wilted. He was polite, soft-spoken, humble. Eventually, it became comfortable to Lindsey having Brian around—it became normal. And he was always around. He lived only a few blocks away, in an apartment his parents owned, which he described as their "pied-à-terre away from Wellesley."

Rose had only been kidding about never visiting. She took the Amtrak from New York one weekend in April, when everything was starting to bloom and Boston was fragrant with tulips and daffodils. Lindsey had a great weekend for them planned—a visit to the new Institute of Contemporary Art, pizza in the North End, and, thanks to a generous client at the gallery, orchestra seats to *Wicked*. She felt the need to fill their time throughout the weekend. She wanted to avoid excessive interactions between Rose and Joanna. She already felt somewhat guilty having a guest in their apartment, as though it was really Joanna's apartment, not hers.

"Wow," Rose said when she first arrived, looking the place over. "This is *seriously* nice." Lindsey knew that Joanna wouldn't be home when Rose first got there; she was at Brian's. As Rose put her bags down, Lindsey noticed that she was smiling, laughing, almost.

"What?" she asked.

"Nothing," Rose said, zipping open her practical rolling suitcase. "It's just weird, I guess. I still can't believe you live with *Joanna O'Callahan*."

Lindsey understood what Rose meant, but she was annoyed. This was her life now, she thought; this was who she was now. Who was Rose to judge that? Who was Rose to judge *her*? She shrugged it off, and they went out to dinner.

When the weekend was over, she brought Rose to South Station to catch her Amtrak back to the city. They hugged, and Lindsey felt a distance between them that wasn't there before.

"Rose," she said. She opened her mouth to tell her something. She wanted to tell her, as they stood together in the filthy train terminal crowded with people, what had happened to her and what Brian had done. Rose would know what to do. "Text me when you're back" was all she could say. Lindsey walked home, enjoying her anonymity and wondering what Rose had thought about the weekend and what Rose had really thought about her. She didn't come to visit again.

She let a few more months go by, hoping that Joanna and Brian would break up. She waited for some inexplicable moment when she would suddenly feel liberated to tell Joanna the truth. But the moment never came, and Joanna and Brian never broke up. Lindsey continued to see Brian frequently. Sometimes he even spent the night with Joanna at their apartment. On those nights, Lindsey rarely slept, instead crying silently in her pillow, wishing away her reality and how far she'd let everything go.

Sometimes she even joined Joanna and Brian for evenings out. Brian always had tables or tickets to charity events.

"Come on, our table will be boring without you," Joanna would say to her whenever there was a gala that Lindsey couldn't afford. Joanna never said it directly, but she seemed to know that Lindsey couldn't afford it. "Brian's covering our tickets anyway. So you have no excuse!" And it was true; Brian often footed the bill, and always with a smile.

"Don't mention it," he'd say with a wink. "I hear you're working hard at the gallery." He asked about or mentioned her job only occasionally, but it was always just enough for her to know that he was still holding it above her head, that he had all the power. She hated herself for going along with it.

One night, the three of them were at a dive bar on Charles Street, swigging Bud Lights and eating peanuts, when Joanna got up to use the restroom. Brian turned to Lindsey. They had somehow avoided actually being alone together most of the time over the years. She didn't like being in a cramped booth with him.

"Darts?" he asked. The question startled her, and suddenly, violently, like a rogue strike of lightning, she wasn't in the bar. She was on the beach that night, under the lighthouse, and the tremendous roar of the ocean engulfed her, drowned her. She grabbed her things and ran out, telling Joanna later that she'd felt a bad stomach bug come on. She realized, that night, that she didn't feel *nothing* after all. She felt the opposite, in fact. She felt everything. She felt more anger and hurt than she knew was possible. She had just buried it away, deep inside her, in order to cope with seeing him at all. But she was livid, furious, resentful. All the time.

Another night, they'd been at a black-tie party benefit on the top floor of the Prudential Center—a fund-raiser to help the theater programs in the Boston public schools. Joanna was wearing a strapless dress that showed off her collarbone and shoulders. It was a beautiful, clear night, and from every angle, there was a spectacular view of the city and the sparkling sky behind it.

Lindsey was talking to a former Bowdoin classmate whom she'd run into, a real estate developer who was talking to her about the housing boom in Boston. She was interested—one day, she hoped to buy her own place in town. She glanced over at Brian and Joanna, who were standing by the bar, waiting for another round. Brian lifted his hand from the small of Joanna's back and moved it up her spine, onto her shoulder blades. Her hair was up in a bun, off her face and neck. His hand continued inching up until it was resting on her shoulders. Lindsey thought she could see his fingers pushing into her skin as he wrapped his hand more around the curvature of her neck. And then she felt his hands on her own collarbone, pushing down into her. She dropped her glass of white wine, letting it fall and crash onto the floor, causing the real estate developer to bound backward and people to turn and look. Brian and Joanna turned to look, as well, and saw her staring at them. They gave her a look back like she was crazy. Her heart was pounding against her body. And then she returned to reality, embarrassed, flustered.

And now, ten years since that summer, Joanna and Brian were still together. Joanna had a suspicion that Brian had even bought a ring from Firestone and Parson, one with a giant ruby surrounded by diamonds on a gold band. Their engagement was imminent. Lindsey had let too much time pass. She had come to terms with the fact that she would simply never tell anyone what had happened. In a way, she started to deny that it had ever happened. Denial allowed her to live her life. It allowed her to focus on what was important to her.

What was important to her was creating a future for herself that she actually wanted. She'd always been ambitious, but her dreams only expanded when she settled in Boston, and they continued to expand beyond her career and into who she wanted to be and how she wanted to live. She wanted to pay off all her debt. She wanted to help her parents with the second mortgage that they had put on their house years ago when Lindsey went to Bowdoin. And she wanted things for herself too—nice things. So she worked hard, and she pushed everything else aside.

And at thirty-two, Lindsey was one of Boston's youngest stars in the art world. A more handsome salary came with her title, but it still wasn't nearly enough to get her the life she really wanted. For now, it was enough to rent a sleek but small apartment in Back Bay, and enough to buy nice things at Neiman's once in a while. But even with years of saving, she'd never have enough money to cross over into that other world of debt-free college tuition and second homes. She'd never be able to buy her apartment, let alone a town house. She had graduated college during the recession, and ten years later, it still weighed on her. The kind of wealth to which she aspired could only be gotten through deep investments, birth, or marriage.

It was important to Lindsey that she look like she *might* have that kind of wealth, or look like maybe she *could* have it someday. Lindsey's whole job was to rub shoulders with artists and buyers—a sophisticated, educated, wealthy crowd of people whom she had to put at ease. She had to pretend to be one of them. She blended in well, almost exclusively wearing all black with an occasional brown or gray. Most of her outfits were form-fitting and flattering. She wore expensive high heels and thick-framed glasses. She had subtle eyelash extensions touched up every two weeks. Her hair, professionally highlighted with buttery flecks of gold, was blown straight several times a week before work. Hardly anyone ever saw her hair in its natural, wavy state. Sometimes Lindsey even forgot what she looked like without all the help. She didn't want to remember. And even though she knew she could be putting all this money into her savings, she considered it an investment in her career. If she didn't *look* like someone who belonged, she'd never *be* someone who belonged.

Unlike Joanna, who would always look like she belonged, even without trying, Lindsey had to put in a tremendous amount of effort and kept herself on a tight schedule: blowouts on Monday and Friday mornings; in the office by eight every day; out around seven; then social events, work dinners, or dates two or three times a week. On weekends, she went for long runs or to a spin class and often to some party or charity event on Saturday night. But her life wasn't mundane just because it was routine. Lindsey took full advantage of what Boston had to offer. She was a junior board member of Dress for Success Boston, a group that helped disadvantaged women prepare for job interviews by donating appropriate outfits and teaching them professional communication skills. Her life was rich. Some might even say it appeared to be perfect.

She dated too. A few months ago, she had broken up with a real estate developer named Dennis. They'd dated for nearly a year after meeting at a seaside wedding in Marion. He was a few years older and not particularly handsome, but he was incredibly stable and raked in more than a million dollars a year. He had once whisked her away for the weekend to a seaside resort in Miami, where they stayed in a suite with a private plunge pool and had their own personal concierge on call. She'd never experienced anything so indulgent. But Dennis was too agreeable. Too passive. This was what bothered Lindsey in the end. He always agreed to whatever she wanted or suggested. She finally exploded at him one night.

"Don't you have an opinion about *anything*? I feel like I don't even know who you are!" The fight had erupted when Dennis had simply asked her where she wanted to go to dinner that night. But the question had set her off. She was so tired of making all the decisions. He was so docile—subservient, even. She apologized for her outburst but told him that they had to go their separate ways. He didn't even put up a fight. *Typical,* Lindsey had thought as he left her apartment with his head down, sullen.

Joanna had set her up on a few dates with different guys over the years. One of them took her out for sushi on a Friday. He was a funny and handsome guy named Ed whom Joanna knew through a tennis clinic she'd started attending. An urban planner, Ed was brilliant, and they talked for hours over baked crab hand rolls about smart city technology and the impact of big tech on public transportation. After dinner, they wandered together to a nearby bar, where they sat next to each other on barstools, their knees touching—reminding her, just for a moment, of her first date with Dylan. The bar was crowded and dark, and they had to inch their faces together to have a conversation. Just after ordering a second round of drinks, Ed leaned in and kissed her. It was nice, and Lindsey leaned into it, letting herself relax, separating her lips. But when she closed her eyes, she smelled that familiar scene of gasoline—that burning, sharp smell from years ago—and she pushed him away, shooting upright, throwing down a twenty-dollar bill and running out the door.

Despite nights like these, Lindsey continued to go on dates here and there. It was easiest if she went out with men she didn't completely respect—the ones she knew she'd never truly fall for, the guys she could just have fun with. And there was no shortage of them in Boston: bankers, lawyers, real estate developers. Guys who wore ties every day and worked out at Equinox in the morning and used loud voices if they had a witty joke to tell but who couldn't change a flat tire if their lives depended on it. Sex with these guys was always the same. It was always about them, never about their partner. *Does that feel good?* they'd ask, probing away, and she'd lie to them. *Yes, yes,* she'd say. But they didn't really care how it felt to her. It was about their own validation. Sex like this—routine, detached, choreographed—was what Lindsey was capable of. The idea of intimate, thoughtful, passionate sex, with eye contact and gentle touches, was frightening to her. She wasn't sure she'd ever have that again, or whether she even wanted it.

Dylan was the last person she had been comfortable with, sexually, and she often missed him, knowing that it wasn't really *him* she missed but rather who she used to be when they were together. She sometimes wondered where he was, what he was doing in that moment, how he'd react if she told him what had happened. He had called her a few times when the summer first ended, seeing if she wanted to come visit the island or if he could come see her in Boston. He had wanted to try. It was tempting at first, because by the end of that summer, she thought that she might have really been in love with him. But her desire to just move on was more powerful. And after that night at the lighthouse, something else had shifted within her. She developed an ability to shut off certain emotions, including her feelings for Dylan. She replied to his first few messages and said that it wasn't a good time for a visit. And then she stopped replying completely, and he stopped reaching out. She had a new life, and he wasn't part of it.

She never understood how Dylan didn't hate her after what she'd told him about Brian's car. The consequences for Dylan weren't just that his car got damaged. His reputation was tarnished after that. People thought that he had started the whole thing. She hoped that he had told people the truth after she had left that summer. But it probably wouldn't have mattered. Maybe no one would have believed him, just as Joanna had said. And it didn't really seem like Dylan to try to rectify something that he knew to be untrue in the first place. He never had a need to prove anything to anyone, unlike Lindsey, who oftentimes felt propelled entirely by that.

She'd come a long way since she was with Dylan. She'd built an amazing life for herself. But at night, when she was in bed, listening to the sounds of the city outside—the lonely wail of an ambulance, the dissolving laughter of friends walking home, the sad trickling of water from a gutter—her body would stiffen, and her mind would flood with memory. She'd remember everything then, as though she were right back there and could feel Brian's hands on her body, pushing her down into the sand, plundering into her, erasing her. She'd shut her eyes and try to will away the memory. She tried to make the Vineyard out to be a fictional place in her mind. A place where she had never even been. That entire summer, not just that one night at the lighthouse, was like a cloud in the sky; one moment it was right there in front of her, moving ever so slightly, and then suddenly it was gone, and a new cloud was there instead. In Lindsey's mind, that summer grew smaller and smaller as time went on, until it was no longer there at all.

Chapter 35

Georgie

It was cold outside during the ferry ride over, but the Deckers braved the weather and stood up on the top level of the steamship after they drove on board. The forecast had called for snow that day, but there was only a sporadic fall of whispery flakes that drifted through the sky like dust. The water below was an icy shade of blue, frothing around the hull of the boat like boiling water. Without greenery, the island, as they approached, looked like a gray bramble of shingles, naked trees, and rocks, a moody etching come to life. But it was still beautiful. Perhaps even more so than during the summer.

The house smelled of wood polish and bleach, and the countertops glistened. Carol had gotten the house cleaned the day before. They carried their bags in, Berty doing most of the unloading from the car.

"Just let me do it," he said, elbowing Georgie out of the way as he grabbed five grocery bags at once and carried them into the house like they weighed nothing.

Georgie often thought about how Berty treated girls his age, the ones he dated and the ones he hooked up with. She wondered if he'd already had sex, and while she didn't like to think about it, she decided that he most definitely had. He was popular, good-looking, and had no shortage of confidence. It was hard for her to imagine Berty—whom she knew to be sweet, kind, and gentle and who had grown up around women—ever being cruel to girls. But she also knew that Berty had his own identity outside his role as her little brother and that he was like his father in many ways. He might be that guy who never calls when he says he will. He might be the guy who tells his friends what a girl looks like naked after he sleeps with her.

After unpacking, Berty dumped out a thousand-piece puzzle on the living room table. "Whaddaya say, sis?" Once in a while, a glimmer of her silly little brother reemerged.

Georgie dove into the puzzle, but Berty lost interest after a few minutes and became glued to his phone.

"We could walk into town, Georgie," Carol suggested, joining them in the living room after putting away the groceries. Georgie still wasn't used to the way her mother wanted to do things *with* her now. "I think Slate's still open. They have some dresses in the window that would look beautiful on you."

"Maybe," she said. It was almost like their roles had reversed when it came to fashion. Georgie now wanted to hide herself, whereas Carol had become more relaxed, more accepting.

They decided to stay home and get an early start on dinner. Georgie helped Carol cook—a simple salad, roasted vegetables, and some Cape Pogue Bay scallops they'd picked up at Edgartown Seafood on the way in, followed by chocolate chip cookies from Rosewater Market & Takeaway. It was the kind of meal that Georgie never could have imagined Carol fixing for everyone ten years ago. Afterward, they all went to bed early. Georgie was tired even though she'd spent most of the day sitting. Later that night, in bed, she cracked open her window an inch, letting the cold air whip inside and ice her face. She looked down at the beach, and at the lighthouse. She had somewhat expected the lighthouse to have disappeared, evaporated, drifted out to sea since her last visit. But there it was, with its bright white walls and dark black edging screaming out from the shore, its pointed head piercing the sky.

She kept the window open, letting the night air punish her with its polar grip, and shut her eyes, eventually falling asleep.

Carol started cooking early on Thanksgiving morning. She didn't like to cook, and she wasn't particularly good at it, but she had insisted on doing it this time. Georgie kept watch from the kitchen island, even though she wasn't much help either.

There was something sad about the meal this year, as much as there was something triumphant. It was their first Thanksgiving back on the island, but without Jonathan. Georgie didn't miss him. She was glad he wasn't there. But she missed being young enough to ignore everything that was wrong. She missed the time when she had thought her father's love for her was enough. Even though she was an adult now, it didn't feel good to have to be so strong all the time for her mother.

"Really, Georgina, you're driving me crazy just sitting there watching me," Carol said to her. "Go do something. I don't need help." Berty had gone to the yacht club gym to work out. Georgie decided to go for a walk. She hadn't slept well, and she needed to stretch her legs anyway.

She zipped up her puffer jacket and left the house, not sure yet where she was going. The street was empty, but there was life inside the houses and food being cooked. Smoke poured out of chimneys, and the air smelled like burning firewood and late fall. Georgie walked away from the house, and just a minute later, she found herself descending the pebbly pathway to the lighthouse.

There was no one down on the beach. It was windy there, and the shore smelled like the inside of a seashell, slightly rotted and crusted in salt. It was low tide. Georgie walked past the lighthouse itself and sat on the shore, just above the high-water line, which was marked with a thin line of dried seaweed. The sand was coarse and slightly damp in her hands.

It was remarkable, she thought, how the beach hadn't changed at all since her childhood. She was sure there must have been some erosion that had shrunken the shoreline somewhat, but nothing she noticed.

On that beach, she felt like a child again, small and cold, in the shadow of the towering lighthouse and under the spray of the sea. There were other places in Georgie's life that had grown smaller as she grew up. She had gone back to her elementary school a few years ago, for a reunion, and was struck by how the school, the fields, and the classrooms lacked the spatial vastness that she had wondered at as a child. She had outgrown it all. But the lighthouse and the beach still engulfed her. No matter how much time passed, she always saw it the way she had seen it when she was a child. It never grew smaller. It loomed over her like a giant made of stone.

Georgie took out her phone. Away from her family, alone at the very place where her entire life had once shifted, she decided that it was time to reach out to Lindsey. She'd found an email for her on her Facebook page and hoped that it was still active. She wondered whether she should be up front in the email about why she was reaching out. She started writing: I know what happened to you. I know because I saw it. She deleted it. What was the right way to explain it all, after ten years? How would she even begin? There was so much to say that Georgie felt incapable of saying anything at all.

Still, she wrote.

> Dear Lindsey, I know this email might seem out of the blue. I hope you're doing well. I'm with my family here on the Vineyard for Thanksgiving right now, and we all think of you fondly even after all these years. I wanted to reach out to you to see if we could get together sometime soon and talk. There's something I need to tell you. Please let me know if we can meet up. Love, Georgie.

She read it over twice and then hit "Send" before she could stop herself. She tucked her phone back into her pocket and then swiveled her head and looked back at the lighthouse behind her. The sun bounced off the structure, making it look slick and wet, almost like it might melt into a puddle of wax if she touched it. Georgie's eyes fell on the spot where she had seen Lindsey and Brian. It was now just a blank patch of sand like any other spot on the beach, nestled next to the base of the lighthouse. She wondered what else might have happened in that exact spot. Maybe happy things had happened there, to other people. Or maybe there had been other crimes that happened there, without any witnesses but the roaring sea and the howling wind.

Back at the house, Georgie thawed out her cold body in the living room by the fire. She joined Berty in a game of gin rummy, and they decided to open some red wine even though it was still early. It was vacation, after all. Berty lost three rounds before throwing his cards down on the table in a huff.

"The problem is that you can't shuffle for *shit*," he yelled.

"Robert," Carol called from the kitchen, "please go change out of your gym clothes into something suitable for dinner. We'll be eating in half an hour." Berty rolled his eyes and went upstairs. Georgie hung back in the kitchen, watching her mother. Carol moved quickly around the stove, but her movements were smooth, even, always controlled, never frazzled. She had a red apron on over a cream-colored turtleneck.

"Mom, are you sure you don't need any help?"

"Actually, yes," Carol said. "Can you please put the napkins in the napkin rings with the seashells on them? And then put them on the table?" Carol always wanted the table to be set in a certain way, even when it was just the three of them.

The task took Georgie only a minute, and once she finished, she returned to the kitchen and just stood there, continuing to watch her mother cook.

"Mom," she finally said, "I need to tell you something."

She paused, nervous. Carol looked up from the cutting board on which she was dicing onions.

"What is it, Georgie?" Carol put down the knife. *"Tell me."*

"Do you remember the nanny we had that one summer, Lindsey?" Carol continued chopping.

"Of course," she said. "What about her?"

Georgie traced her finger along an orange in a bowl on the counter, feeling its bumpy, spongy skin. "Did you notice something *off* about her right before she left? Like something had happened to her?"

Carol craned her head backward toward Georgie but remained in her position toward the stove, spoon in hand, hovering it over the simmering pot of gravy.

"Yes, actually," she said and didn't say anything else. Georgie let the silence hang for a few seconds. Georgie had assumed that her mother would say no. She'd thought, for all these years, that no one knew what had happened to Lindsey except for her.

"What do you mean?"

"Well, I remember thinking that morning that she wasn't herself. She was upset about something, or she seemed to be, anyway. I think I assumed it was just issues with that boy she'd been seeing. Never mind."

Georgie knew that her mother wasn't telling her something. It wasn't like her to start expressing a thought and not finish it. And it certainly wasn't like her to notice someone else's feelings, their emotions. She must have known something, Georgie thought. She felt angry then. She had lived with this secret all alone for ten years. If her mother had known something and never done anything, she wasn't sure she could forgive her. But the same could be said for herself, by Lindsey.

"Well, why didn't you do anything about it? And what do you *mean*?" Georgie's voice was getting louder.

Carol kept her head down, as though she was unable to look Georgie in the eye.

"I don't *know*. And I don't know why I didn't do anything," Carol said, her voice curt. "It wasn't my business." Georgie couldn't tell if her mother was annoyed at her or at herself. Maybe both. "I noticed something off about her during her last few days with us, yes," Carol added, now looking up, her face in distress, a look Georgie had rarely seen. "She had bruises all over her, I remember. Something had obviously *happened* to her." She paused. "But it was none of my business. So I didn't ask."

Georgie couldn't believe what she was hearing. While her mother couldn't have known the extent of what had actually happened, not exactly, anyway, she had just revealed to her that she knew *something* had happened to Lindsey that night. How could it be that her own mother hadn't helped someone who clearly needed help? Why was her mother so conditioned to believe that the right thing to do was to do nothing?

"Well," Georgie responded, "something *did* happen." She paused. "I know because I saw it. I know because it should have been me."

Carol didn't say anything. Georgie could see thoughts racing behind her mother's eyes.

"What do you mean, you saw it? What do you mean, it should have been you? *What, Georgie?*"

"I was with Brian that night. Brian Fitzgerald. I mean, he walked me home. We, he . . ." Georgie struggled. She was ten years older than she had been on that night, but describing it all out loud made her feel young, immature, naive. "We were standing outside, and he leaned in to kiss me. Lindsey must have seen it and came out to break it up. She was trying to help."

Carol nodded. She knew the story wasn't over.

"I was so mad. I ran up to my room. But then I saw them—the two of them—walking down to the beach together. So I followed them. And I saw . . ." She looked outside. She could see the lighthouse there, exactly the same as it had always been. "Brian raped her, Mom. I saw Brian rape Lindsey." She took a deep breath. "And it's all my fault. All of it. None of it would have happened if it wasn't for me. She was just trying to help. It might have been *me* in that position, but instead it was Lindsey. And I didn't do anything about it." Georgie was crying now.

She hadn't even noticed that tears were streaming down her face uncontrollably. "I never told anyone, not really anyway, just my therapist, and I'm horrible. It's all my fault." Her words came out in breathless spurts.

And then she was in Carol's arms, and Carol was crying too.

"Brian *Fitzgerald*?" Carol asked, as though she had only just heard Georgie say his name and she couldn't believe it. "Oh my God," she said. "Oh my God." Carol stepped back and started pacing. "You know that Lindsey went to work at the Fitzgeralds' gallery, right? She's still working there. Oh my God." Carol brought her hand to her forehead, like she was suddenly realizing a million things at once and was trying to contain them.

"I know," Georgie said. "I know. And they're all still friends. Joanna O'Callahan is still dating him. That's part of why I never said anything to anyone. But I want to now. I think I have to."

Carol didn't say anything for a while. She shook her head and looked down. Georgie wondered what she was thinking.

"I have some photos," Carol finally said, dabbing under her eyes with her sweater sleeve. "I have photos that I took just before she left. They show the bruises. I remember it so well now. I don't know why, but I remember that I *had* to get a photo of her that day."

They went upstairs to where Carol kept old family photo albums and boxes of memorabilia. Thankfully, Carol had labeled everything by year, so they found the envelope from the photo developer easily. And there it was, a snapshot of time: Lindsey, Georgie, and Berty outside on the lawn the day after. They were all turned to one side, in an awkward-looking position, but in a way that very clearly showed Lindsey's neck, collarbone, and the tops of her shoulders. And just as Carol remembered, they were swollen, red, and starting to bruise a deep-purple color.

"You know, I wrote it all down in my journal too," Georgie said. "I've never shown anyone, obviously." They went to Georgie's room together, and she dug out her journal from a box in the back of her closet, where she'd hidden it long ago. It was all there—everything she'd seen. She'd written down what Lindsey and Brian had been wearing, what their body movements were, how she'd heard Lindsey yell *Stop* over and over, how she'd tried to yell it out too.

Carol squeezed Georgie's hand when she finished reading. "It's not too late. This is the right thing to do."

"But, Mom," Georgie said, "is it possible—" She paused. "Is it possible that I was wrong? That I wasn't sure about what I saw? I mean, I thought I was in *love* with Brian that summer, you know. And now, I mean, I've kept it *secret* for so long that I don't even know anymore . . . what's real. I don't even know who I am."

"That's the thing about secrets, Georgie," she said. "When you try so hard to hide a secret from everyone, you just end up hiding yourself from the world." Georgie wondered if her mother was talking about herself now. "You *know* what you saw, Georgie. I believe you. And . . ." She paused. "I think I knew it too."

Georgie looked up at her mother, confused.

"I didn't *know*. But I guess I recognized myself in her that morning. In Lindsey." Carol looked out the window. "It was a long time ago. I've never spoken about it. But the way Lindsey was that morning, I . . ." She looked back at Georgie. "I just should have known. Part of me did know. I was that girl once."

Georgie looked in her mother's eyes and saw something she had never seen before, a vulnerability, a world of secrets that her mother had kept about herself, and a strength. She wondered what other things had happened to her mother that she had never known about, people she had loved, bad things that might have happened to her, bad things she did to other people. "It's not your fault, Mom," Georgie said. "You couldn't have known." Georgie was certain that her mother would never disclose any more details to her about whatever had happened to her. But she didn't need to. She understood now. Maybe, throughout all this time, Carol's somewhat puritanical reign over her daughter's femininity had been some buckled effort to protect her, as though the wearing of a halter top might guarantee a sexual assault.

The women wiped their eyes and returned to the kitchen to finish the cooking. Georgie's cell phone buzzed with an email response from Lindsey. She read it with Carol:

> Georgie, It's so nice to hear from you. It's been FOREVER! I'd love to see you. Are you in Boston too? So crazy we haven't run into each other yet. I can't believe you're all grown up . . . seems like yesterday you were a budding teenager. How about next week, Tuesday or Wednesday night, for drinks? Xx, Linds

Georgie hadn't expected Lindsey to respond in such a light, casual tone. She must have some idea why Georgie was reaching out. Or maybe she didn't. Georgie felt another pang of guilt and a wave of doubt. Maybe she had expected Lindsey to have become a depressed person incapable of using exclamation points in lighthearted email exchanges. Her jovial tone threw Georgie off. She looked at her mother for an answer.

"This is good," Carol said. "You need to explain everything in person."

Georgie nodded. It was better that Lindsey didn't suspect why Georgie was really reaching out. She might not be receptive to meeting her if she knew. She might be too angry with her. After all, Georgie could have helped her that night. But she never did.

"Do you want me to come with you when you meet her?" Carol asked.

"No," Georgie said. "Thank you. I need to tell her this myself."

"Okay," Carol said. She looked at Georgie. Her face, for a moment, lost its hardness. Her eyes were wet. "I'm proud of you, Georgie."

Chapter 36

Lindsey

Lindsey went home to Rockville twice a year, for Thanksgiving and for Christmas. A few years ago, she had tried to tell her mother that it didn't make sense for her to make the same trip twice and only a few weeks apart. She wanted to skip Thanksgiving so that she could stay in Boston and work. But her parents wouldn't allow it.

"Thanksgiving is about family," her mom would say over the phone. "You're my little girl. You're coming home and that's that."

When Lindsey protested further, her dad would chime in. "Do you need help with the flights?" he would ask. "We can help you out. I think we've got some miles." Sometimes Lindsey wished her parents would stop being so nice to her. It made it difficult to shut them out when she needed to. And it made it impossible to think about ever telling them something that might break their hearts. Despite her desire to stay in the city, Lindsey always did go home for the holiday. It was really the only time she let anyone else take care of her.

But Thanksgiving truly was a busy week at the gallery, so she always chose not to fly home until Thanksgiving morning. Thanksgiving marked that time of year when people started to think about what to buy their loved ones for the holidays. Buying art took time for many clients, Lindsey had learned, and oftentimes she'd start the process with a client in November and they wouldn't pull the trigger until just before

Christmas. Last year, she sold a large mixed-media piece for $65,000 to a young tech start-up CEO who wanted to "get into collecting." It took him two months to make the decision. He'd come into the gallery almost once a week and just stare silently and then leave. The first few times, Lindsey chatted with him, but after that, she let him have his sessions in silence. She'd known that she'd done her work and that if he was going to buy the piece, she just had to give him his space and let him come to the decision on his own. A lot of male buyers were like that, she'd observed; you had to make them think that they were deciding it all on their own, without your influence. Once they felt empowered to make the purchase, the tables turned, and suddenly it was as though the man could teach Lindsey about the piece he was buying from her and impress her with his knowledge. She saw this cycle happen every time.

The flight home wasn't so bad, just an hour and a half into Baltimore. The drive from the airport to their home was nearly an hour, but Lindsey's dad always was there to pick her up. It was sweet of him, Lindsey thought, but they also shared the truthful joke that it was better to be out driving in Thanksgiving traffic than it was to be in the house with Lindsey's mom when she was on a cooking tear. Lindsey could tell that her dad relished the excuse to get out of the house, even if her flight was delayed and he had to wait in the car parking lot with the engine running for heat, reading that morning's paper and drinking a cup of coffee gone cold.

This year, as usual, her dad was there, pulled up to the curb just at the right moment when Lindsey walked outside, rolling her black suitcase behind her. She hopped in and gave him a kiss on the cheek.

"Good to have you back," he said, patting her on the shoulder with the broad palm of his warm hand, and then they set off for home. They talked for a while about her job and a big sale she had just pulled off. She asked him about his recent knee surgery. Her dad never probed her about her personal life. He wasn't a big talker. But he was kind and gentle. Sometimes, Lindsey thought that she might have written off men entirely if it wasn't for her dad proving to her that decent, honest men did exist.

After a few minutes of catching up, they rode in silence the rest of the way home. Lindsey gazed out the window at the billboards and at some of the decrepit, old buildings of Baltimore, until they winded their way outside the city and the hum of the highway lulled her to sleep. She woke up from a soft nudge from her dad when they pulled into their driveway.

Their house smelled like Thanksgiving, warm and buttery, when she walked in. It was always the same, and it always made Lindsey feel safe. She hugged her mom, who was scuttling around the kitchen at a high speed, seemingly stirring and chopping five things at once. Lindsey offered to help, but her mom waved her away, as Lindsey knew she would. She went to her room to settle in. Her parents hadn't changed anything about her room even though Lindsey was home for only a handful of days a year. Sometimes this deeply endeared her parents to Lindsey, and she felt overcome with emotion and nostalgia upon seeing her old trophies and worn-out paperback books. Other times, it annoyed her, and she felt like her parents were holding on to the memory of who Lindsey used to be, not who she was. Every year, Lindsey would spend a morning or afternoon combing through her things and filling trash bags with clothing and items for Goodwill, but she never committed enough time to finish it all. She swung her suitcase onto her bed and opened it up, pulling out a pair of jeans and a loose, chunky turtleneck sweater. It was chilly, and she wanted to find a specific pair of old fuzzy red socks to wear. She searched in her top dresser drawer, digging toward the back. Her fingers brushed against something cold and soft, a plastic bag. And there it was: her clothing from that night at the lighthouse, still stuffed into the same dingy plastic bag. Throughout all these years, Lindsey had held on to it. She had never known what to do with it. The bag seemed too dangerous, somehow, to simply discard like trash. It scared her, this limp bag of dirty clothing from ten years ago, as though if she opened the bag, she might be sucked back into that very night and be forced to relive it all, over and over again. She found the socks and shoved the bag back into the depths of the drawer and then slammed it shut.

Back in the kitchen, her mom was making two different kinds of stuffing. "My famous stuffing and an experiment," she told Lindsey when she asked what was on the menu this year. The excess of food at her parents' house had started to disgust Lindsey over the years, and then it angered her. It was all so unnecessary, she thought, especially since it was just the three of them every year. Lindsey always felt like her mom wanted to impress someone with all the cooking, and Lindsey was never sure who, until Thanksgiving a few years ago when Lindsey had refused to touch half the things on the table because she thought they had too much butter and fat in them.

"All this is for you, you know," her father had said to her when her mother had left the room for a few minutes, silent, upset. He rarely got involved in the occasional, brief fights she ever had with her mother. He was quiet that way. Lindsey had nodded, realizing, for the first time, that he was right. Her mother had known all along that Lindsey wanted more for herself. And all this time, she was just trying to give her that, in her own way. When her mother returned to the table, Lindsey piled her plate high and ate it all.

Now Lindsey sat at the kitchen table, leafing through catalogs and magazines while her mom finished up the cooking. They didn't talk; her mother hummed. That's what she always did while she cooked.

"Okay, I'm going to go freshen up," Lindsey's mom said, looking around the kitchen, nodding to herself that everything was under control. "I need you to baste the turkey every twenty minutes." Lindsey nodded. They'd been through this routine before.

Lindsey started reading a *Vanity Fair* that she'd bought at Logan. She turned on an egg timer in front of her for twenty minutes. It ticked away gently. The house was quiet now. Her father was in his office doing some work. It was that time when everything was basically done, and all that was left to do was wait. In that moment, Lindsey was glad to be home. She felt calm.

Her phone chimed. She didn't look for a few minutes; whatever it was could wait. She was engrossed in an interview with Kim Kardashian, scanning the article to see if Kim talked about her diet. She finished the article and took out her phone. She was surprised to see an email from Georgie Decker. She hadn't seen Georgie in years.

She read the email twice and then put her phone down and thought in silence, staring at the wall. For just a quick second, she had to remind herself who Georgie was. She'd blocked out most of the Decker family in her mind, not thinking of them. The email was like hearing from a dead person. There was something distinctly unnerving about the email, she thought. Georgie wanted to see her not to catch up but to tell her something specific. Lindsey felt her stomach muscles tighten, and she got a swirling, sinking feeling in her gut. So much time had passed without Lindsey having to really think about Georgie or the Decker family, and now she was being forced to. The egg timer rang, rattling her and waking her from her trance. She basted the turkey.

Lindsey had seen Georgie just once since that summer, and it was only a few months after the summer had ended. When she had first moved to Boston, Carol had invited Lindsey over for dinner. Berty had screamed when she first arrived, shrieking down the stairs and running to her, wrapping his arms around her. Georgie had come down the stairs after, slowly, and hugged her without the same enthusiasm. Teenage attitude, Lindsey had thought, even though they had become close by the end of that summer.

Jonathan hadn't been there that night, though Lindsey didn't ask where he was. She felt awkward as a guest of Carol's, being served dinner, and not the other way around. Carol asked her about work, life at the gallery, whether she was still friends with Joanna and Brian. But it didn't really seem like Carol wanted her there. The invitation felt like a formality, and Lindsey wished she hadn't come. It was as if Carol had wanted to do something charitable by having her over for dinner, but she only wanted to feel good about it afterward, not actually do it.

Georgie had barely said a word at dinner, and Lindsey ran out of things to say after the first ten minutes. After that, Berty talked about school. Lindsey was out of the house within an hour and a half. When she left, she had the feeling that she wouldn't see the family again, at least not formally. It was like the dinner was a silent agreement: *you helped with our kids for a summer, we helped you get a job, we can have this dinner, and now we'll go our separate ways.* And that was fine with Lindsey, who didn't like revisiting her role as a nanny anyway, even if it was only for ninety minutes. That was ninety minutes of her life that she wouldn't get back. Lindsey never went to their house again or saw the kids. They got new nannies and they grew up. She never even saw Carol or Jonathan pop into the gallery.

In the year that followed that summer, Lindsey pushed them all away in her mind. They were all too entrenched in that night at the lighthouse. If she had stayed in closer touch with the family, she wouldn't have been able to escape the grasp of the memory of that night. The wall that the family put up was a welcome one for her. She wanted the separation.

But now, staring at the email from Georgie, Lindsey was thrown back to that summer, wondering what this reunion could be about. She remembered Georgie's obsession with Brian. Georgie had been angry with Lindsey, she remembered, when she thought that Lindsey and Brian had something going on. *If she only knew,* Lindsey thought. Was it possible, Lindsey wondered, that something had actually happened between Georgie and Brian? Or maybe Georgie wanted to apologize for something. There was a slight hint of an apologetic tone in the email, Lindsey thought. And that summer, Georgie had been on that jagged, bittersweet cusp of faux adulthood that bred blinding insecurity and often fueled cruelty. But what could Georgie possibly be apologizing for? Maybe something had happened to someone in the family, and Georgie needed to tell her about it in person. Lindsey didn't know.

After reading the email a few times, Lindsey decided to reply. She wanted to make the note sound particularly chipper and carefree. She didn't even ask what the matter was about. *Keep it short and light,* she thought, *because chances are,* she told herself, *Georgie really does just want to catch up.* Maybe Lindsey had read the email too literally.

Lindsey suggested that they meet for drinks. If she was going to go through with the whole awkward encounter, the very least she could do for herself was to be somewhere that had alcohol. The idea of getting coffee with Georgie during the light of day somehow seemed harsher and more pronounced. She wanted to go somewhere dark where she wouldn't be slapped with the actual uncomfortable and strange fact that she was meeting the girl she used to nanny, who was now an adult and had something to tell her.

She put away her phone after she replied. Georgie and Lindsey had been close, that was true, but so much time had passed that they were basically strangers now. Lindsey thought back to her last few days on the island. Georgie had been particularly kind to her in the days after the night at Lighthouse Beach, she remembered, almost as if she knew that Lindsey needed help. But in the years since then, so much had changed, so much had happened, and now that morning was a lifetime ago, and it didn't matter. Whatever Georgie had to say, it wasn't going to change anything in Lindsey's life.

Chapter 37

GEORGIE

They made a plan to meet on Tuesday night at a wine bar on Charles Street. Georgie was relieved when Lindsey suggested a place. Georgie would have had no idea where to go and would have spent hours combing Best of Boston lists to find the right spot. Something trendy but not too trendy, somewhere they could have a table but not be pressured to order a whole meal. Georgie hadn't been to the place Lindsey suggested. It was one of those spots with an inconspicuous sign above the door outside, so subtle that one could easily miss it, as if it didn't need to advertise.

After work, Georgie went home briefly to take Ocean for a quick walk. She thought about changing her clothes, putting on something that felt dressier, hipper. She looked in her closet and realized she didn't own anything anymore that even fit that description. As their meeting time approached, Georgie started to feel fourteen again, insecure and unsure of herself.

Beacon Hill was beautiful during that time of year. All the brick buildings were covered in tasteful Christmas decorations: lush evergreens draped over windows, fat wreaths hung on every door, frosted windows and twinkling lights tucked among the hedges. The whole neighborhood was illuminated and glowing.

Georgie arrived a few minutes early. Her cheeks were red and cold from the walk, and when she stepped inside, she felt her body begin to thaw. She chose a high-top table toward the back of the place. She hung her purse on a hook underneath the table, and she kept her coat on for now, still cold. She and Lindsey hadn't seen each other in so long, and Georgie looked different now than she had then. Even though she'd seen pictures of Lindsey online, Georgie wondered what Lindsey would look like in person and if Georgie would still think she was beautiful, perfect.

The bar was narrow and dark, with crimson walls and candles on each table. A waitress arrived with a glass of water. "Two glasses, please," Georgie said to her, feeling awkward and out of place, aware of her solitude. The waitress returned with another water and a menu. "We have a special Super Tuscan tonight that's really delicious," she said, deadpan. "Do you know what you'd like to drink?"

Georgie scanned the menu. She didn't know much about wine. She could distinguish really bad wine from really good wine, but that was basically it. They all kind of tasted the same to her. "I'll just have a glass of cab, please." The waitress nodded and swiveled away.

The other patrons all seemed to be on dates. It was the kind of venue where you could cuddle up next to the person you were with and whisper something about what you wanted to do to them later; at least that's what Georgie imagined some of them might be saying to one another.

After about fifteen minutes and half her cab, she saw Lindsey walk in. She was wearing a black trench coat and knee-high boots, her hair blown straight and smooth around her face. She looked older, more serious, glamorous. Georgie straightened her posture, suddenly incredibly nervous. She'd rehearsed this so many times in her head, but now her mind went blank. She had to remind herself how to say hello, how to hug, how to nod in conversation.

Lindsey spotted her, too, and waved, walking toward her while simultaneously taking off her coat. She wore a tight gray cashmere sweater and a black skirt. Georgie immediately noticed how thin Lindsey was. It threw her off, seeing how much she'd changed. Her face had hardened, her jawline was pronounced, her gait was severe, and her entire build was more rail-like. She had lost the softness that Georgie had seen in her years before. But she was still beautiful, and she still had a glow to her, though now more subdued. Her eyes still twinkled and darted around the room the way Georgie had remembered.

"Wow," Lindsey said as she leaned in and hugged her. Lindsey smelled like orange blossom, not vanilla. "This is surreal. Look at you!" Lindsey put her hands onto Georgie's shoulders and stood back, smiling. "I can't believe this. You look great!"

"Thanks," Georgie said. "You do too. I can't believe it's been ten years." Georgie's words came out in a robotic tone, her voice almost shaking.

"Jesus, I guess so," Lindsey said. She put her coat and purse down on another chair and then sat across from Georgie. "What are you drinking?" she asked, grabbing Georgie's glass and taking a sniff.

"Oh, I just got a glass of cab," Georgie responded. Lindsey seemed like someone who actually knew about wine. Georgie felt slightly intimidated and childlike around Lindsey's energy.

"Can't go wrong here," Lindsey said, looking around, her chin raised and her back straight. The waitress returned. Lindsey greeted her; they seemed to know one another. It was clear that Lindsey was a regular. She ordered a glass of something Italian, "And," she added as the waitress was leaving, "some of those yummy nuts."

When the waitress left, Georgie felt a sense of panic. She suddenly regretted asking Lindsey to meet her. Lindsey seemed so utterly confident. She didn't necessarily seem happy, but she seemed *together*. Her life seemed to be in *order*. Georgie knew all this before, but now, seeing Lindsey in front of her, she wondered whether telling her the truth was actually the kind thing to do. Her mouth felt dry, and she sipped her water.

Lindsey leaned forward, putting her elbows on the table. She wore a rose-gold watch on one hand. Her manicured fingernails were painted red. Georgie pulled her own sleeves over her dry, scraggly hands. The waitress returned with a bowl of nuts. Lindsey grabbed a few and popped them into her mouth.

"So," she said in between bites, "what have you been up to? You're in grad school now, right? God, this is so wild."

Maybe, Georgie thought, she could still back out of this. She could avoid the whole thing and just pretend that she wanted to catch up.

"Yeah, grad school. It's good but, you know, a lot of work. I don't go out much."

"That's okay," Lindsey said. "You're doing something you love. That's awesome."

Already, Lindsey was comforting her, just like she had done ten years ago. Georgie felt simultaneously at ease with this familiar dynamic and also stifled by it. She needed to remind herself of why she was here and how much time had passed since that summer. She had grown up. They both had. Lindsey needed *her* help now, not the other way around.

They chatted for a little while longer. Georgie asked her about the gallery and her apartment. Lindsey didn't ask Georgie about dating, which she appreciated, and Georgie didn't ask her about it either.

By the time they were each finishing their second glass of wine, Georgie knew she couldn't delay it much longer. She had to tell Lindsey why she had reached out. She found it strange that Lindsey hadn't just asked her already. It was almost as if Lindsey were pushing Georgie to do it on her own, like she could tell that Georgie didn't want to.

"So," Georgie said, looking down at her hands, which were knotted up together in her lap, sweaty. She couldn't look at Lindsey. "I asked to see you for a reason. Something happened that summer, when you lived with us." She paused. "I saw something."

Lindsey gave her a blank stare. She put down her wineglass. "Okay," she said. She seemed impatient and annoyed, like she had already decided on a rebuttal to whatever Georgie was going to say. "What did you see?"

Georgie felt another wave of doubt creep over her. Not only about what she'd seen but about the process she was about to start. She was potentially about to unravel Lindsey's entire life.

"I want to say, first, that I am so sorry." Her voice started to crack, and she felt tears well up. "I am so sorry that I never said anything for all this time. It was terrible of me. But I couldn't hold it in any longer." She took a big breath in and exhaled slowly. A tear escaped from her eye. "It was that night . . . that night with Brian, when you saw us outside and stopped him. I . . . I want to thank you. I don't know what would have happened if you hadn't . . . because . . ." She had to pause. "Because I saw what he did to you after that. I followed you. I saw what Brian did to you."

Lindsey didn't respond at first. Georgie wiped her eyes with her napkin and looked up. Lindsey was leaning back in her chair slightly, looking around the room, as though she were concerned that someone might hear them. Georgie stared at Lindsey, trying to identify how she was feeling. But Lindsey's face gave away nothing.

"What are you talking about?" Lindsey finally asked. "What did you see?"

Georgie hadn't prepared herself for this. She'd prepared herself for the possibility of Lindsey telling her that she didn't want to confront it, that she didn't want to deal with it, that she had moved on. But Lindsey was acting like she was insane, like she had no idea what she was talking about. Was she certain, after all this time, of what she had seen?

"It was just before you left, at the end of the summer," Georgie continued, now looking Lindsey in the eyes. She didn't want to say it all in detail, but she needed to. She couldn't hold it back anymore. "I snuck out and went down to the beach that night, for some reason; I don't know why. I followed you. I was angry. I was jealous. I wanted to be with Brian so badly, and you stopped it. I don't know what I expected to see, but I saw what happened, Lindsey. I saw Brian Fitzgerald *rape you*." She put her hand out to touch Lindsey's, resting it on top of hers.

"I'm so sorry, Lindsey," she continued. "And I'm sorry to be telling you this now, so suddenly. I know that it's been a long time, and I should have said something sooner. I'm so sorry. But I had to tell you now."

Lindsey didn't say anything. She took another drink of her wine. And then she looked at Georgie. Her face conveyed nothing but a slight irritation.

"Georgie," Lindsey said, holding her glass and gently circling its contents, "I'm not sure you know what you saw. You were a *kid*."

In that moment, Georgie did feel like a kid. A kid who knew nothing about the world, about life, about love, relationships, trust, friendship, pain. Nothing had changed, she thought to herself: *I'm exactly who I was then, making the same mistakes.*

"I'm sorry," Georgie said immediately. She had anticipated that Lindsey might not want to talk about it or that she might even be in denial about it in some way. But she hadn't expected Lindsey to be so cold to her in response. Now, she wasn't sure where to go from here.

"I'm sorry," Georgie whispered. "I thought I was sure of what I saw, and I'd been keeping it to myself all these years. And I wanted to make sure you knew that you weren't alone. You're not alone. And it's not too late to do something about it, if that's what you want." She hadn't planned on saying any of that, but the words came out of her from a deep, warm place inside her, near her heart.

"I should get going," Lindsey said. She took the last sip of her wine and then fished in her wallet for some cash. She placed it on the table and then started to put her coat on. Georgie just sat there, out of words to say. "I'm not mad at you," Lindsey said then, looking at Georgie. Lindsey's face had softened. "In fact," she said, "I'm sorry too. It must have been hard for you to carry this around for so long. Whatever you think this was, anyway."

Lindsey slung her purse over her shoulder and walked around the edge of the table so that she was standing by Georgie's chair. They were face-to-face.

"But I'm *okay*," Lindsey assured her, putting a hand on her shoulder. "And anyway," she said, tying her coat belt around her tiny waist, "even if you saw what you saw, there's nothing to be done now. Sometimes it really *is* too late." Georgie sensed a tone of indecision in Lindsey's voice. Did she just admit to something? Lindsey gave her a hug, and then she left, walking out of the bar and off into the city.

Georgie cried silently when she was gone, wiping the tears away with the sleeves of her sweater. The waitress returned and gave Georgie a sympathetic look. Georgie ordered another glass of wine. "On the house," the waitress said when she returned with it.

Georgie sat there for a while, sipping her wine. She felt dizzy. She was hungry, and the wine had gone to her head. She wasn't used to drinking three glasses on an empty stomach. Her meeting with Lindsey had left her even more confused. Lindsey hadn't totally denied it. At first, she had, but then she seemed to indicate that maybe Georgie was right. It just seemed like Lindsey didn't want to *deal* with it, which Georgie understood. It was exactly what Georgie was afraid of—that she would come in and derail Lindsey's life just to get something off her own chest. She felt selfish.

Georgie finished her wine, zipped up her coat, and left. It was cold. The city seemed different now somehow, unfamiliar. The air smelled like old snow, stale and icy. She walked home. The walk felt like the same one she had taken years earlier, from the lighthouse that night. She felt lost, alone, unsure of everything before her, and now, everything behind her.

Chapter 38

LINDSEY

After Lindsey received the email from Georgie, she found herself thinking about that summer on the Vineyard more than she ever had before. She didn't want to, and she tried not to, but the memories kept resurfacing in her internal vision. What if, she wondered, she had never taken the job at the Deckers'? How would her life have turned out? She would have moved home to Rockville, probably, and maybe she would have just stayed there. She would have met some local guy, married, and had kids before she was thirty. She would have had an unremarkable life, she thought.

And maybe her life would have been different in other ways, too, not just in terms of circumstances. She had been raised to be sensible, straightforward, honest. And she had lived her life that way until that summer. But her relationships with Joanna, Brian, Dylan, and Georgie had made her realize that life was gray, shrouded in confusing layers of complications, questions, doubt, history. Things weren't always so simple, and sometimes the truth wasn't what served her the most. That summer, she learned to lie. She lied to Dylan. She lied to Georgie. She lied to Joanna. She lied to Rose. She lied to herself. Or maybe it was just that she withheld the truth about some things. Either way, keeping secrets, holding them close, guarding them like a flame she needed to keep burning, had grown to be her natural condition. She didn't even know anymore how it might feel to live a life free from secrets. This was her life now.

The secret followed her everywhere and influenced her entire being. Anyone who met her, anyone who thought they *knew* her, didn't really know her at all. In many ways, she was who she was because of that night at the lighthouse. It changed how she reacted to the touch of a person's hand on her arm, to the way she heard the wind, to the way she didn't like to hold eye contact for too long, to the possibility of trusting anyone, ever. She was lying to *everyone*, in a way, because the person she presented to the world wasn't really who she was. An entire side of her was hollow. She just kept it hidden. In anticipation of seeing Georgie, this feeling of guilt burned inside her, itching at the back of her throat and squeezing her windpipe until she felt like she was choking. Why was it, she thought, that being a victim of a crime could morph into feeling like the perpetrator of a crime just because she hadn't wanted to tell anyone about it?

She asked herself if she would have done things differently if she could turn back time. The answer was always the same. She wished that she had felt like she *could* have done things differently, but really, she probably wouldn't have. Wanting to do things differently wasn't the same as actually having the ability to do things differently, she knew. It was so easy, in retrospect, to say that she would have called the police, asked for help, pressed charges. But on that late-summer morning, when her body ached in pain and she felt lost and lonely and confused, calling the police never really felt like an option she was capable of facing. She had been in shock. She had been traumatized. The notion of telling Carol and Jonathan that she needed the day off so that she could go tell a bunch of male policemen that she'd been raped was never something she was going to do. She didn't want to go to the hospital and shiver in a paper gown while a doctor swabbed the inside of her vagina. She didn't want to explain to Joanna or Dylan or anyone else what had happened and have to answer questions about why she had been on that beach in the first place. She didn't want to have to recount that night again and again to lawyers. She didn't want to tell her parents. It would kill them.

She felt guilty because of this, too, of her decision not to come forward. As though her trauma was everyone else's trauma, as though she was responsible for anything bad that might happen to anyone else. And this was compounded by time. The world was different in 2019 than it had been in 2009. There was a different discourse now about sexual assault. Women were coming forward all the time about sexual assault and harassment. It was an empowering time for women, she thought. Except, for her, the movement was just a reminder that she was one of the women choosing to stay silent. She thought about what would happen if now, a decade later, she came forward. She seemed immune to that wave of feminine strength and solidarity around her. Even now, the only thing she felt, thinking about that night, was shame. Acknowledging the crime would only worsen that. She'd worked hard to diminish her sexuality, to lessen her curves. She didn't want to put herself back on display. It would only beckon more questions that would hammer away at the shell around her that she'd built. *Girls like her,* people might say. *Her dress was pretty short. Why did she go meet him in the first place? She was a nanny. She asked for it.*

She'd worked too hard to be respected. She didn't want to be looked at as a *problem*. Even if she did come forward with what happened, and even if she found a way to *prove* that Brian had raped her, she didn't want to forever walk around with a cloud above her, one that would always spark just the slightest eyebrow raise from other people who were doubting or judging her silently.

It was pointless to ponder all the *what ifs*, Lindsey thought, because there wouldn't be a way to prove that Brian had raped her anyway. It really was too late. And it was probably too late back then too. His word against hers. And his would have won. It probably still would.

Maybe Georgie had reached out to Lindsey about something that had nothing to do with any of this, but Lindsey still couldn't shake the feeling that it did. She couldn't separate Georgie from Brian, from the lighthouse, from everything inside her. She dreaded having to see her. And then the day came.

Lindsey went to the bar straight from work. She wondered if she'd even recognize Georgie. She didn't know what she looked like as an adult. She was curious to see what Georgie's style was and how she presented herself to the world now. The last time they'd seen each other, Georgie had just been a kid. Lindsey had been, too, in a way.

But when Lindsey entered the bar, she recognized Georgie right away. Georgie looked older, but she somehow looked exactly the same. Her face was still warm and soft and kind, a face that gave everything away with just the smallest bite of her lip. Lindsey looked at her for a few seconds before Georgie saw her. What had changed was Georgie's style. She seemed to be hiding in her clothes now, hunched forward, letting her sweater swallow her, disguising whatever was underneath.

Lindsey smiled at Georgie and was momentarily brought back to their very first meeting, when they'd met in the Deckers' kitchen. She remembered how Georgie had sought out answers and advice from her on life, as though Lindsey knew anything at all. The thought amused Lindsey now, imagining herself at twenty-two and considered wise by anyone. How little she had actually known then.

They chatted for a while, eventually ordering another glass of wine. Lindsey couldn't focus on their conversation, though, not really. She overcompensated by gesticulating and asking too many questions. But all she wanted to know was why Georgie had asked to meet her. She needed to know whatever the secret was that Georgie was keeping from her.

"I saw Brian Fitzgerald rape you," she finally heard Georgie say. The words hit her like a sudden sheet of hail, hard and angry, whipping her skin. So that was the big secret. Something that Lindsey had been living with alone this whole time. She suddenly became incensed with the reality that Georgie had asked her here simply to assuage her own guilt.

"Georgie," Lindsey said, purposely using a condescending voice and tilting her chin down, "I'm not sure you know what you saw. You were a *kid*." She wasn't about to open up to Georgie, not after so many years. She had worked too hard to put everything behind her. She had to get out of there.

"It's not too late," Georgie exclaimed as Lindsey turned to leave.

Georgie didn't get it. She never had, Lindsey thought to herself as she walked out. If she had actually cared about Lindsey, she would have said something to her about this ten years ago, when it had happened. Instead, she had been selfish. Georgie got to have the ability to love, to feel joy, to experience pleasure over all these years, while Lindsey had been consumed by anger, bitterness, hatred for the people around her. Maybe Georgie was trying to do the right thing now, but it didn't matter. It was too late. It had *always* been too late, Lindsey thought.

She hailed a cab and jumped in. In the warmth of the back seat, Lindsey exhaled, her breath heaving and full of regret and yearning—for what, she wasn't sure.

Before she had left, she had muttered to Georgie that she was sorry for what *she* had been through, that she was sorry that *she* had been carrying around this secret for so long. By doing so, she'd accidentally confirmed to Georgie that she had, in fact, seen something that night. The words had slipped out of her, and she hadn't meant to say them. But it didn't matter, Lindsey thought. Nothing mattered. Let Georgie know the truth; what difference would it make? Nothing would be different anyway.

Except, Lindsey realized suddenly, like a flash of lightning, Georgie was a witness. She had *seen* it. She felt a spark of hope inside her gut, an unfamiliar feeling. *No,* she thought, *forget about it.* Except that she couldn't. Georgie wasn't just any witness. She was a witness from *Brian's* world. For the first time since that night, Lindsey felt a foreign feeling of security, confidence, empowerment. She felt validated. Someone had *seen* what had happened to her. Someone else knew the truth. She wasn't lying; she wasn't alone. And maybe Georgie was right. Maybe it wasn't too late.

She hopped out of the cab a block away from her apartment. She had started crying, and she wiped away tears as she walked underneath the glow of the streetlamps.

She took out her phone and dialed a number. It rang a few times, and then someone answered.

"Mom?" Lindsey said, her voice shaking. "I need to tell you something. I need your help." Lindsey stood outside on her stoop and told her mom everything. She hadn't thought it was possible to ever say the words out loud, but she finally did. She didn't care who heard. She let it all go, finally, her voice quaking and her emotions rushing out of her like a swarm of bees.

When she got inside her apartment, she took off her clothes and tossed them on the floor. She looked at herself in the mirror, and for the first time in ten years, she really saw herself, and she cried. She cried for the time in between then and now. She cried for Georgie. She cried for Dylan. She cried for her mother and her father. But mostly, she cried for herself, for the pain that she'd kept hidden all these years, and for never giving herself the time to heal or the chance to seek justice. She cried all the tears that she should have cried a long time ago but was never able to.

Her mom arrived the next morning. Lindsey told the gallery director that she needed some time off from work. She wasn't sure what she was going to do, not exactly, but she was going to do something. Maybe Georgie was right. Maybe it wasn't too late.

Chapter 39

GEORGIE

A week passed, and Georgie still hadn't heard from Lindsey. "Give it time," Carol consoled her over the phone. "I think she'll reach back out." Ever since Georgie had told her mother about that night, a quiet bond had formed between them that hadn't existed before. Georgie always knew that her mother cared about her, but it was the first time in her life that she actually saw Carol as her *mother*.

She was right. A few days later, Georgie received a call from Lindsey. She let it go to voice mail. She was scared. Since Lindsey had left their first encounter angry and upset, Georgie wasn't sure if Lindsey was calling to berate her, to blame her for a decade of pain, for leaving her alone when she needed someone else the most. She wouldn't blame her if she did. But Lindsey's tone on the voice mail surprised Georgie. Lindsey sounded calm—friendly, even. Georgie called her back.

"I lied to you," Lindsey said. "You were right about what you saw. I just didn't want to admit it. Not in that moment. I couldn't. So I'm sorry. But I'm glad you reached out to me about this. I'm ready to talk about it now."

Lindsey asked if they could get together to talk about that night, to go over everything that Georgie remembered. Georgie agreed, but when she hung up the phone, she felt terrified and unprepared. It was one thing to admit to witnessing the event itself and speaking about it in broad terms without description, without peeling back the surface layer. It was another to admit to remembering the textural details, the way the sight of it made her feel, the reason she was compelled to follow Lindsey in the first place. Those were the things she'd been hiding behind for the last ten years. Georgie had kept herself hidden from the world in order to hide those secrets, and now it was time for her to let them go.

They met for lunch later that Saturday at a tapas restaurant off Newbury Street. "It's quiet but not *too* quiet," Lindsey said when they sat down at a table. Lindsey had picked the place. Georgie arrived earlier than she did again. Even though Lindsey didn't seem to be angry with her when they'd spoken on the phone, Georgie didn't want to risk upsetting her again by being late.

Georgie scanned the menu, but all the words looked blurry to her. She didn't care what they ordered; she was too distracted by the conversation they were about to have. Her stomach already felt like it was full of rocks, grinding against one another and weighing her down. She was waiting for Lindsey to say the inevitable: *Walk me through that night.*

After they had ordered a few things to share, Lindsey put her hand out and laid it on top of Georgie's. Lindsey's hand was small, Georgie noticed, birdlike with its delicate and intricate system of bones and graceful, manicured fingers, but it felt strong pressed against her own. Lindsey kept it there and looked Georgie in the eyes.

"I'm sure this is going to be uncomfortable," she said. "For both of us. But I need to know what you saw that night. I need to know everything. I need to know the truth. Anything you can remember."

Georgie had thought that Lindsey wanted to know as a kind of way for her to heal. But when she took out a notepad and a pen, she realized that she was actually gathering information, facts.

"I'm hiring a lawyer," Lindsey said, "to see if there's a chance of, I guess, justice." Georgie saw the trial in her mind: going on the stand, admitting to what she'd seen that night, admitting to how she'd kept it a secret for all that time. She wondered, selfishly, if it meant that she could be punished.

She reached into her bag and took out her journal. "I thought a lot about what to do with this," she said, handing it to Lindsey. "But you need to have it." She'd found the journal over Thanksgiving and had painfully read through it. It documented everything—her feelings about Brian, her jealousy of Lindsey, how mad she was at her that night for ruining her chance, and her devastation upon seeing Brian rape Lindsey that night at the lighthouse.

She opened it up to a dog-eared page. It was the night of the rape. They read the entry together. It was all there—every detail that Georgie saw, the way she felt about Brian, how confused she was. It was all there.

"I want you to know," Georgie said, "that I was going to call the police, or tell my mom, or ask you about it. But the next day, everything just seemed so normal. I thought that maybe I was confused. Or that you didn't want anyone to know. I'm so sorry, Lindsey; I'm so sorry." She couldn't say it enough times. She would give anything to go back in time and change it all, to *act* on it instead of letting it pass by.

"Georgie. It's not your fault." Lindsey looked at her. "I mean it, Georgie. It's not your fault."

Georgie nodded. But she wasn't ready to agree with Lindsey, not yet. She might not ever forgive herself, she knew. After lunch, she gave Lindsey her journal to keep, knowing that the reveal of whatever secrets were in there didn't matter anymore, except the ones that might be able to help her.

"I hope," Lindsey said as they were putting on their coats, "that you find a way to let this go." Georgie wasn't sure what Lindsey meant. Let it go? They had just revisited it; that night was more alive in Georgie's mind than ever. "I just mean, I hope that you can live your life without feeling guilty about this, without feeling like any of this was because of you, and without feeling like this is going to happen to you."

It was as though Lindsey could tell that Georgie had been living underwater for the past ten years, disguising herself, burying herself, trying to erase herself so as not to get hurt. Years had gone by, and Georgie had never even acknowledged how that night had shaped her, made her fearful of touch, intimacy, connection. She thought of that night in the bathroom at Daedalus. How lucky she had been to escape. How unlucky Lindsey had been.

They said goodbye, and Georgie began her walk home. The sun was bright and high in the sky, and it glinted off the dirty banks of snow piled up on the edges of the street. She passed by a newsstand, caught a glimpse of the glossy women's and teen magazines, and was reminded of one of her journal entries from that summer: *Create your own destiny instead of living out your fate.* She smiled at the thought. Because she had strayed so far from the destiny she had wanted and intended to create for herself. Everything she had planned, everything she had wanted to be, had been left behind in that journal. Except now, she could start again. Just as she had said to Lindsey, it wasn't too late.

Chapter 40

LINDSEY

The crossroads that Lindsey had found herself at ten years ago—when she felt like she had to choose between telling the truth and living the life she had always wanted—had drawn her back into its clutches. She was there again, except this time, she chose differently. This time, she chose herself.

She learned quickly that if she wanted any kind of justice, she'd have to take matters into her own hands. That meant that her best shot was hiring a lawyer and bringing a civil case against Brian. After extensive research, she realized that a criminal case involving the state would probably go nowhere, and she wouldn't have any control over the process. The downside, of course, to choosing a civil suit was that it was wildly expensive and Brian would probably never face jail time. He'd most likely just pay her a fee and move on with his life. If she was lucky, he'd be branded as a sex offender by the state, but there was no promise of that happening. She didn't want his money—it wasn't about that for her. And anyway, a life-changing sum of money in her eyes would be a drop in the bucket for Brian and his family. What she really wanted out of all of this was for Brian to be exposed to the world as who he really was: a monster.

She decided that she would quit her job as soon as she hired a lawyer. She wanted to quit before she really knew whether there was a real possibility of bringing her case to trial. There was no way she could stay at the gallery while accusing the owner's son of rape. But there was also no way that she could stay there anymore at all, regardless of whether or not she came forward about Brian. She had changed.

She scheduled a meeting with Hilga on a Monday morning after the gallery's staff meeting.

"It's time for me to move on," she told her. She'd rehearsed what she was going to say—that she needed a change, that she'd never worked anywhere else and wanted to try something new—but until then, she hadn't believed it. They were just words that she had rehearsed. But now, sitting across from her boss, she knew that she was actually right. It was time for her to finally prove to herself that she didn't need to be there. She could go somewhere else.

"But we can't lose you," Hilga said. "Did something happen?" Lindsey often wondered, despite Hilga's aloofness and frequent absences from the gallery, how much Hilga had endured herself in rising through the ranks of the male-dominated art world. She hadn't planned on telling her the truth about Brian. But looking at her boss in that moment, she saw an ally, an older woman who, she thought, must have experienced similar situations before in her life. Maybe she would understand.

"Actually, yes. And you might hear more about it in the future. It might become public. Something happened about ten years ago." Lindsey realized, as she sat there, that this was the first time she was telling someone what had happened besides her parents. "Brian Fitzgerald . . ." She paused. "He raped me." She took a breath and looked at Hilga, who brought her own hand to her mouth, her eyes blooming wide. "I'm only just now confronting it, dealing with it. But I'm going to take him to court. It's still within the statute of limitations."

Hilga released a loud breath. "Lindsey," she said, "I'm so sorry. Oh my God, all this time that you worked here." Lindsey thought about the moments, over the years, when Brian's parents would come into the gallery. It wasn't often—they were only partial owners, and they weren't too involved in the day-to-day operations. But every time they came in, they greeted Lindsey like she was an old friend of their son's, a friend of the family's. Lindsey saw Hilga's face reel with memories, and then her face shifted. "Are you sure?" she asked. "I mean," she added quickly, "are you sure you want to do that?"

"Yes," Lindsey said. "I wasn't sure I wanted to for a long time. But I'm tired of keeping it a secret. And I don't want him to hurt someone else."

Hilga nodded. "I always thought that Brian was a nice young man," she said, shaking her head. Lindsey sensed Hilga's skepticism. "I can't believe he'd do something like that." And then Lindsey felt it—it was undeniable. Hilga *didn't* believe her. She didn't want to believe her. She could feel Hilga's discomfort, sitting there across from her, listening to her story, as though Lindsey's words were infecting her with a disease.

But it didn't matter to Lindsey. Her boss didn't have to believe her. She knew what was true. And in a way, she was glad that she'd seen that side of Hilga. Because now she knew that she'd never want to work for someone like that.

That was Lindsey's last day at the gallery. She didn't reach out to the Fitzgeralds. They would find out whenever and however they found out.

Through some clients of her father's, her parents helped her find a lawyer in Boston, a gum-snapping woman named Maura Levinson. She sounded like a character from a crime show, Lindsey thought. She had frizzy black hair and a large, circular mole below her left nostril. The first thing she asked Lindsey when they met was whether or not Lindsey would be willing to testify.

"You know," she told Lindsey with sympathetic but firm eyes, "only a third of rape cases are even reported in the first place. Women don't want to come forward." Lindsey understood why. She was scared to take the stand, scared to talk about what had happened to her. But she knew that she had to. She wanted to go all in.

Lindsey had gotten a call from the Harvard Art Museums the day after she'd left the gallery. They needed a new receptionist and part-time docent. Someone had given them Lindsey's name. *Georgie,* she thought. She had told Georgie that she was going to quit the gallery. Since Georgie was at Harvard for grad school, she must have asked someone there about job opportunities for her. The position was several big steps down from her job at the gallery but at a much more prestigious and large-scale operation. A world-famous museum made the gallery seem like a quaint mom-and-pop shop. So Lindsey took the job, which was mostly administrative. She sat at the front desk, directing guests toward different parts of the gallery, and she trained with the museum docents so that she could give tours a few times a week as a docent herself. She wasn't making nearly as much money as she had been before, but she was grateful to be in a place that allowed her to be herself and not walk around trapped in her own secrets.

Her parents had to help her pay for the lawyer. It ended up costing them their house, so they sold it and moved to Somerville, just outside Boston, to a small one-bedroom apartment. They justified the move by assuring Lindsey that they wanted to downsize anyway. They wanted to be closer to their daughter, they said. Her mom took a leave of absence from work, and her father managed to service his clients remotely. Lindsey begged them not to, telling them that she'd find a public defender or maybe even someone who would do the case pro bono. But they wouldn't hear it. They insisted on hiring the best lawyer they could find, whatever it cost. And Maura was it.

Maura said that the biggest shot they had in winning the case was Georgie. "She's the linchpin, that girl," Maura said. "Do you know how rare it is to have an actual *witness*?" Georgie's journal was also something that Maura said would help them. She got it authenticated by a specialist who could testify that the ink and paper were at least ten years old. Maura had gone to meet with Georgie herself, and she reported back to Lindsey that Georgie had agreed to testify, to do whatever she could to help.

When Lindsey told Maura that she still had the clothes from that night, she assumed that Maura would consider it a big win. The clothes had remained, for all those years, wrapped up in that same plastic bag. Maura said that it would help, but it wouldn't really prove anything. "He's going to say that you had consensual sex," she warned Lindsey. "That's all that this proves, really."

Lindsey had thought that their case would be stronger, easier to prove. They had evidence and a witness. But she was wrong. Because none of that mattered. All that mattered was that Lindsey had chosen, since that night, to remain friends with Brian. Not just acquaintances but *friends*. She'd worked at his family's gallery.

"You shouldn't have quit the gallery like that," Maura scolded her. "We should have handled it together."

It all made Lindsey want to take it back, to stay silent, to forget the whole thing. What if she went through with all this and lost? She'd given up her job; her parents had given up their home, and for what? she thought.

Only once she met with her lawyer and the reality of her situation started to sink in did she reach out to Joanna to tell her. Her lawyer had told her that anyone in her life that summer, and in Brian's, would be needed as potential corroboration to prove a motive. But that's not why she needed to tell Joanna. She needed to tell her because, finally, the time had come when she was ready to do so.

They met at a coffee shop on a Saturday morning. Joanna came in wearing workout clothes, fresh from a SoulCycle class, still sweating and rosy-cheeked. They hadn't seen each other in a few weeks—a long time for the two of them, who normally hung out every other day. It was clear that she had no idea what Lindsey was going to tell her.

"Joanna, something happened a long time ago that I never told you about. Something between Brian and me."

"What? What are you talking about?" Joanna's eyes widened with a look of bewilderment.

"It was a long time ago. That first summer on the Vineyard. Right before I left. Brian raped me." Joanna looked away, her face frozen. It was easier to tell Joanna than Lindsey had anticipated. She was ready. "He had walked Georgie home, and I saw them outside. It looked like he was about to kiss her or something. I broke it up, but then he asked me to go for a walk to the lighthouse with him." She thought about what to say next, deciding that Joanna didn't need to hear all the exact details, not now. "Look, I know this sounds insane. I know it sounds out of the blue. It's been ten years, and I never said anything. But what happened that night . . . He raped me, Joanna. And then he acted like nothing ever happened."

Joanna kept her face turned away from Lindsey. Her eyes were fixed, staring out into the street.

"Oh my God," she whispered. "Oh my God." She stared into her coffee. Her facial expression shifted from one of sympathy to one of shock, like she had just realized something or remembered something. "Oh my God," she repeated, looking up. "I just can't . . . I don't know . . ." Her words came out like unformed sounds, and she gasped for air, reaching for her glass of water and gulping some down.

"I need to get this straight," she said, and for a moment, Lindsey's worst fear came true: that Joanna wasn't going to believe her, that she was going to take Brian's side after all this time. "Brian raped you?"

"Yes. Yes." Lindsey paused. "You don't have to respond, Jo. I know this is a lot to take in all of a sudden."

Joanna nodded but remained silent. Lindsey wondered again if she was going to believe her or if she was going to take Brian's side. After all, this was the guy Joanna wanted to *marry*. Joanna was quick to make up her mind about things, though, so maybe she didn't need time to process this. She was a quick decision maker. Except that once her mind was made up, she usually kept it that way. Lindsey braced herself, expecting Joanna to tell her she couldn't talk about it, that it couldn't be true. She somewhat expected their friendship to end then and there.

"I have to go," Joanna said. She gathered her things and looked at Lindsey with what appeared to be tear-filled eyes. She was right, Lindsey thought: Joanna didn't believe her. Though she had somewhat prepared herself for that outcome, it nevertheless stung. A hollow pit of loneliness formed in her stomach, and she sat alone for a while after that. She wondered what Joanna was going to do now. Would she stand by Brian's side? Would she tell any of their mutual friends that Lindsey was a liar, that she was making up a crazy story? Or, perhaps even worse, did she believe Lindsey and would she hate her forever for withholding the truth?

Later that evening, Joanna called her. "I'm sorry," she said. "I was just so caught off guard. I just didn't know what to say."

"It's okay," Lindsey said, expecting Joanna to start to extricate herself from their friendship. It was probably too complicated for her, she thought, and she wouldn't blame Joanna if she wanted nothing to do with her after this.

"The truth is," Joanna continued, "I remember that night. Brian came over. He told me that you guys kissed but that it was a drunken accident and didn't mean anything. He played it off like . . . like it was nothing. He said you were both so drunk, you could barely walk. I never said anything to you because, I guess, I didn't want to embarrass you. I just didn't think . . . I never could have thought . . ." Lindsey could hear Joanna inhale and exhale loudly.

"I know," Lindsey said. She was surprised by Joanna's recollection, and she felt sorry for her. She tried to imagine what it felt like to be in Joanna's position, to know that the person you were going to spend your life with was the exact opposite of who you thought they were.

"I *believe* you, Lindsey," Joanna added. "And you have to believe me that I didn't *know*. I mean, I know that Brian has a dark side, but this . . . I just . . ." Joanna paused. "I'm so sorry." Lindsey wondered if perhaps this had been a confirmation of what Joanna had quietly suspected of Brian's true character, a confirmation she had never wanted to face. "I was so blind. I guess I still am."

"Joanna, I'm sorry," Lindsey found herself saying in response, though she wasn't sure why. She was the victim, not Joanna, and yet she *was* sorry. Lindsey had done nothing for a decade while she watched a woman stay in a relationship with a rapist. She was ashamed of that. She wouldn't blame Joanna if she wanted nothing to do with her. "I should have told you back then."

"No," Joanna said. "Stop. *I'm* sorry. I'm so sorry, Lindsey. I'm sorry that this happened to you. And I'm sorry that you couldn't tell me. And I'm sorry that all this time . . ." She choked back some tears. "All this time, he was around, and you never *said* anything."

"Has he ever . . . has he ever hurt you too?" Lindsey asked.

"No," Joanna said swiftly. "I promise, never. But I wonder, sometimes, about other women. He's come home late before . . ." She exhaled. "And there've been a few times when he hasn't come home until the next day. Oh God."

Joanna decided that she would move out that night and go stay with her parents. She wasn't going to tell Brian why, she promised Lindsey. She didn't want to interfere with the case. She only wanted to help. Lindsey could tell, from the expression on Joanna's face, that she meant it: she was leaving Brian for good.

"One thing, though," she said to Lindsey before they hung up. "You should know that Brian . . . he plays dirty. I'm telling you, Lindsey. He's not going to make this easy. Are you sure you want to go through with this? I mean, really?"

Lindsey knew that Joanna was right. She knew that Brian would do everything in his power to prevent her from bringing him down, to prevent her from bringing out the truth. But she'd known that all along. He'd been playing her all along. Except now, she was ready to face it.

Chapter 41

GEORGIE

Somehow, Georgie hadn't seen Brian since that summer. Or, really, she hadn't interacted with him. She'd seen him on Instagram and Facebook. She'd even seen him in person, from afar, on the Vineyard, when she'd been there. But she had managed to avoid actually being with him, talking to him, for ten years.

The trial was starting soon. Georgie was a big part of it. She was Lindsey's entire case, basically. But no one was sure if it was going to go Lindsey's way. So far, all they had was circumstantial, Lindsey's lawyer said. "We need *more*," she'd tell them. Georgie was under strict instructions not to have any contact with Brian, not that she would. He had become an unanswered question to her, a ghost from her past.

Except that Brian had emailed her suddenly. She thought, at first, that someone was pranking her. The case had been a splashy local news story, so maybe it was someone messing with her. But something else told her that it was real. He needed her help, and he thought that he could get it.

Georgie, he wrote her in an email. It was easy to get her email address, since it was an official Harvard.edu one, and the formula was always the same.

> Congrats on Harvard. I always knew you were
> smart. It's been a while, I know, but I need to talk
> to you. Can we meet in person? It's important. I'd
> like to discuss it with you so you can get my side
> of the story.

She stared at the email for a while, considering her options. She knew that she should just forward it to the lawyer, not reply. She went to sleep that night without doing anything. But she couldn't sleep, again. She got up in the middle of the night feeling restless, unsure. She opened the email on her phone and hit "Reply":

> We can meet. When and where?

When she woke the next morning, she wasn't sure if she'd actually written the email or if it had been a dream. But Brian had already replied:

> After work tonight? Why don't you just come to my
> place so we can talk privately.

He gave her his address and told her to come anytime after six. Turned out, Brian lived a few blocks away from Georgie all this time, just over on Arlington Street. She wondered if he had ever seen her before and not said anything.

She knew that she shouldn't go. She knew that it wasn't fair to Lindsey, that it could interfere with her entire trial, that it was a total violation of everything Georgie had told her she would do. And she knew that it might not be safe. And yet, she wanted to go. Brian was asking her to be there, to listen, to hear him. Though every sensible part of her told her not to, she went.

The doorman buzzed her in. In the elevator on the ride up, she looked at herself in the mirrored wall. She was wearing her usual clothes—a loose sweater, corduroy pants, and a long wool coat. But in her reflection, she was wearing the Picnic Basket T-shirt, her cutoff shorts. Her face was sunburned, and she had some pimples on her jawline. Her hair was in a loose ponytail. Her blonde eyelashes were smudged with mascara that she'd poorly applied. She was just a kid again. And Brian was Brian.

"Hey," Brian said when the elevator door opened. He had one of those apartments that took up the whole floor, where the elevator opened right up into the foyer. She stood in the elevator for a few seconds, not moving. The doors started to close, until Brian bolted his hand out to stop them. "Thanks for coming."

He led her inside, toward a living room that looked out over Boston. It was dark now, and the lights of the city looked small and fleeting from ten stories up.

"Drink?" he asked, pouring her a glass of red wine even though she hadn't said yes.

"Sure" was all she could say. Brian looked different, older. His hair was thinner, his cheekbones more pronounced. But he still had the same walk, the same movements, the same air about him that could make you feel special or invisible, depending on the day.

He sat on the living room sofa, and she sat in a chair opposite him. He had his right leg crossed over his left so that his ankle was resting on the opposite knee.

"So, how's life?"

Georgie cradled the wineglass in her hand. *It was a mistake to come here,* she thought to herself. Even now, years later, she wasn't sure she was strong enough to weather Brian's manipulation. She thought about how she wanted to respond, how she wanted to appear to him. Why did she care what he thought?

"Good," she said. "Life is great. I'm really busy."

"That's great," he said. "You always did work so hard; I remember that. Always wanted to be busy." He sipped his wine. "I guess not much has changed, then." He smiled at her. She remembered the way he'd smiled at her at the Picnic Basket on that first afternoon when he spoke to her, the way she'd felt electrified by it, twisted from the inside out. Looking at him now, she didn't feel that. She saw someone who wanted something, who needed something, but that thing wasn't her. He was using her now, just as he had been using her then.

"I guess not," she responded. But he was wrong. Everything had changed. Brian kept talking about himself—his health-care start-up, his recent trip to Dubai, his parents' Fourth of July party last summer. He was acting as though he were innocent, like the whole trial was just a nuisance for him. Georgie nodded as he talked. She was going to ride this out. She knew he'd get to the point he needed to make eventually.

"So, Georgie, thanks for coming," he finally said. "I'm sure Lindsey has told you that ridiculous thing that she's telling people. And I've heard, from some sources, that you're helping her? That you claim to have been there that night. Seen us, you know, *together*."

Georgie didn't say anything. She wanted him to wonder. She'd done enough of that herself for years. It was his turn to be nervous.

"But, Georgie," he continued, "you know that it's not true. Didn't I walk *you* home that night, after all? You're the one I wanted to be with, not her. After all this time, I still remember." Georgie looked at him. He was staring into her eyes, as though pleading with her.

"But I saw what happened," she said, looking down.

"Georgie, come on. If you saw, then you know that Lindsey was into it. Maybe she changed her mind halfway through, or whatever, but I knew that she wanted it."

"I heard her say no. I heard her tell you to stop."

"Okay, maybe she said no. She told me to stop, sure. But she didn't mean it. A guy knows when he's with a girl. She was into it."

"So you admit it, then?" It was almost as though he was proud of it.

Brian's facial expression changed. He was annoyed, angry, his fuse burning out. "I mean, we had sex, okay? She was only saying no so that she didn't feel like a slut, sleeping with her friend's boyfriend." He took a breath, calming himself, realizing the aggression of his eruption. "Georgie," he whispered, "I was pretending she was *you*. I guess I couldn't help myself." He put down his wineglass. "Can't we figure this out together? You and me?"

Georgie felt her throat tighten up. "I shouldn't be here," she said, rising from her chair. "I need to go." She put her glass down and grabbed her coat.

"Wait," he said, standing. He reached out and touched her arm. She looked down at his hand. She'd imagined, so many times, this moment, when he would touch her, and their faces would be inches away, when he'd *need* her, not the other way around. He leaned in closer. She could feel his breath on her skin. And then his lips were on hers, just for a moment. She was kissing him. She was kissing Brian Fitzgerald. The moment that had so abruptly been taken from her a decade ago was back, and suddenly she was in it, after all this time. She was finally in it.

And then she stepped back, and before she realized what she was doing, she had swung her knee backward and then slammed it up toward him and into his crotch with all her weight. He went down like a collapsed building, crumpling.

"What the *fuck*!" he shrieked. But Georgie was gone. She was running out of the apartment and into the elevator, exhaling only when the doors closed and it started to descend.

She raced back home and called Lindsey, telling her what she had done: she had recorded it all on her phone.

Chapter 42

LINDSEY

Maura was all about knowing the facts and statistics. Lindsey's mother hated it.

"It's so depressing," she said. "I don't want to know about how many women lose their rape cases." But Lindsey disagreed. She wanted all the facts. She wanted to know what they were up against.

"Did you know that ninety-nine percent of rape perpetrators in the United States walk free?" Maura asked. "*Ninety-nine percent.* Can you *believe* that?" She paused. "Disgusting." She shook her head. Lindsey often wondered if Maura was a survivor of an assault herself. But she never asked her. "You're one of the exceptions," Maura once said to her. "You've got an actual fighting chance."

And she did feel that she had a fighting chance. The evidence they had gathered felt strong. Joanna offered to help in any way she could, recounting the story of how Brian had come over that night and told her that he'd kissed Lindsey. When she eventually took the stand, she told the jury that Lindsey would never have slept with him. "She just wouldn't have done that," Joanna said. "She's not that kind of person." It was the first time Lindsey had seen Joanna recognize her for who she really was. After all this, maybe they really did know one another, Lindsey thought.

Even Whitney, Brian's snobby, skinny sidekick that summer, ended up helping the case. Maura said that an apparent lack of motive on Brian's part was going to be a big obstacle for them to get past. And it was Joanna's idea to ask Whitney for help there too. Whitney remembered his conversations with Brian that summer, in the weeks leading up to that night.

"He had a real thing for Lindsey," he said when he took the stand. "And he hated her boyfriend. He really had it out for both of them. He wanted to get back at the boyfriend because he thought the guy wrecked his car. And he wanted to teach Lindsey a lesson for rejecting him, I guess. No one rejected *Brian*." Whitney had no problem throwing Brian under the bus. He and Brian hadn't been friends in years. Whitney was now living in Manhattan with his husband. Turned out, he'd had a massive crush on Brian throughout all those years. "I was jealous of *you*," he explained to Lindsey when she had first called to ask for his help. "I was in love with Brian, and he was into you. I'm so sorry, Lindsey." He remembered how he had threatened her that night at the ice-cream shop. "I'm a different person now," he said. Though he never said it out loud, Lindsey got the sense that Whitney felt somewhat responsible for what had happened to her too. After all, he had seen Lindsey and Dylan drive off in Dylan's truck that very first night at Left Fork, and perhaps he had been the one to plant the idea in Brian's head that Dylan had trashed Brian's car. It didn't matter now, either way.

Even Carol ended up contributing something. She had insisted on taking photos of Lindsey and the kids the morning after that night, and she still had them. The first time Lindsey saw the photos, she felt like she was looking at someone else entirely. It all seemed so far away. But there she was, standing on the Deckers' lawn, smiling, her arms around Berty and Georgie. And when she looked a little bit closer, she could see her collarbone and neck, bruised. She could also see a sadness in her face, a darkness behind her eyes.

"I just wanted to take some photos of you and the kids," Carol had said when she came to drop off the photos with Lindsey. "No reason. I just wanted to take a picture." She struggled to look Lindsey in the eyes, as though she was having difficulty maintaining her stony facade. Lindsey tried to imagine how Georgie's conversation with Carol had gone when she told her what she had seen. She seemed remorseful, though Lindsey knew she would never admit it. Maybe Carol would be more aware of her own children after this, she thought. Maybe she'd start to pay attention to the things around her instead of just herself.

But even with all this evidence, Lindsey's lawyer was right: the fact that Lindsey had maintained a *friendship* with her perpetrator veiled the entire case in a cloud of doubt. The case had been going on for a few weeks now, and Brian's lawyer was slamming the jury with skepticism. He pushed hard against Georgie's credibility, saying that she was just a child at the time and that her memory couldn't be trusted. He also questioned why she, not just Lindsey, waited so long to tell anyone about it.

"Not just one but *two* women decided to stay mum about this alleged crime for ten years?" Brian's lawyer asked the jury. "Makes me ask, why *now*, all of a sudden?" Lindsey wasn't quite sure what Georgie would have to say to address this. Maura had advised Georgie to straddle the tricky line of explaining that she had been scared and traumatized and that's why she never came forward, but that she was certain of what she saw. There was a difference between fear and confusion, Georgie explained to the jury. Lindsey knew that part of the reason Georgie had stayed silent was because she had been in love with Brian, and she couldn't hide that—it was evident in the journal, facts that Brian's lawyer also used against her credibility. But Lindsey also knew that Georgie was ashamed of this, so she didn't probe Georgie on it. Georgie already felt bad enough, Lindsey knew.

"Would someone who had been raped by someone else have *dinner* with that assailant on multiple occasions? Go on group *vacations* with that person? Spend time in that person's *home*? I don't think so. Doesn't sound right to me," Brian's lawyer said to the jury.

And Lindsey often wondered if he was right. She knew what it looked like to other people. It was suspicious enough that she'd never reported the crime, that she'd never even told anyone about it, but it was even more suspicious that she had watched her friend date Brian and that she'd lived her life with him as a close friend herself. She wasn't sure how she would explain it to the jury.

She and her lawyer practiced for hours. When she finally took the stand, she said exactly what they had rehearsed. "I kept him close on purpose," Lindsey said. "And I know how that sounds. But it made me feel safer knowing where my assailant was, what he was doing, where he might be. I could protect myself if I could avoid surprise. I felt powerless, and when you feel powerless, you feel hopeless. I just didn't think coming forward was an option. I didn't think anyone would believe me. I didn't think anyone would care. I was on my own. If I could keep track of Brian myself, if I could be in control of when and how I would see him, that made me feel safer."

It was the truth.

"So basically," her lawyer said in response to this, "you were trying to survive?"

Lindsey paused. She hadn't been prepped for that question. It hadn't occurred to Lindsey that that's what she might have been doing for all these years: surviving.

"Yes," she said, realizing, for the first time, that her lawyer was exactly right. "I was trying to survive."

Brian's lawyer also tried to use Dylan to speak against Lindsey, hoping to capitalize on the fact that Lindsey had broken up with him in a somewhat callous, sudden manner at the end of that summer. But Dylan refused. He told Lindsey and her lawyer that he'd do whatever he could to help her. Lindsey's first phone call with him, to explain the situation, was one of the more difficult ones she'd ever had in her life.

She hadn't spoken to Dylan in ten years, and their lives had changed so much. He was married now, had three kids, and was running his own construction company on the island. He was doing well. He had the life that he'd always talked about having. He choked up on the call, and she thought she could hear him trying to muffle the sound of his crying.

"How could I not have known?" he asked repeatedly. "I mean, I saw you after that night. I just thought you were sad to leave."

"It's okay," Lindsey had told him. "It's not your fault." Lindsey's lawyer didn't end up needing Dylan to testify, but Lindsey appreciated that Dylan offered. She felt that, after all this time, he was still someone she could call on for help if she needed it. And she was glad that he knew. Because even though it had been ten years, she had never explained to him why she was able to turn on him so suddenly, to leave and never look back. Now he would know.

After a few weeks, Lindsey felt like she might break. She wanted to be left alone. She wanted it all to be over. Sometimes, she regretted having come forward at all. Life was easier before, in hiding, she often felt. She was tired of hearing people telling her that she was brave, that she was strong. Hearing words of support and encouragement from people somehow hurt more than anything else.

Rose reached out to her. "I'm so sorry, Lindsey. I should have been there for you," she cried over the phone. "You're so courageous," she told her when she showed up on her doorstep a few days later with a suitcase, ready to stay and help. But Lindsey felt incapable and undeserving of these words. She didn't want old friends or even strangers to tell her how they admired her or how she'd inspired them to come forward with their own experiences of sexual assault. Those were the things that made Lindsey want to crumble. But she reconciled with Rose—after all, she was the one who had abandoned Rose, not the other way around. Rose would never say it, but she'd been right all along. And yet she was still there for Lindsey, after all that time.

Maura had warned her that it would be painful to have to recount her trauma again and again. And it was painful. She didn't want to relive it, what it had felt like to wake up covered in bruises, with sand and other things dried up between her legs, her head pounding, her skin dry and thirsty. But she recounted it so many times that she became somewhat numb to it. People would listen, shake their heads, cover their mouths, mutter "I'm sorry" throughout her story. And then they'd usually say, "The way you've carried on with your life is nothing short of remarkable. Look how far you've come." And Lindsey would smile and say thank you. But she hated that part. Because she didn't think she had come far at all. She felt exactly the same now as she did then. Ten years had passed her by, and she felt like she hadn't actually grown or changed. She had been on a pathway, moving forward, evolving, and then that night at the lighthouse happened, and she was stunted. She had kept living, but she hadn't actually moved forward. Everything she had accomplished and worked for—in her career, in her personal life, in her health—didn't matter. It was all a joke now, she often thought. She had been robbed of feeling any kind of triumph or satisfaction in what she did. But throughout the trial, she felt obligated to act strong, to act like she'd persevered despite her assault, to act brave, proud.

Lindsey thought that the hardest part about taking the stand would be trying to justify her choices over the last decade. But the hardest part was having to recount the graphic details in the presence of her parents. She could see them, sitting in back, trying to look stoic and supportive. She refused to look at them directly. Even at almost thirty-five years old, she felt mortified to have to admit to her parents that she had ever even *had* sex. She felt as though she was letting them down, revealing to them that she wasn't perfect, that she wasn't even close. It was a deeply painful kind of humiliation to vividly describe what it felt like that night when Brian entered her, how her vagina had felt sore the next day, how her dress had his semen on it. She didn't feel as much shame telling the jury, a group of strangers, all of this. But to have her own *father* listen to these details made Lindsey want to dissolve into nothingness.

But all of that changed when Georgie told Lindsey what she had done. She'd called her, breathless, panting. "I did it," she said, over and over again. "I did it." And she had. She'd somehow gotten as close to a confession as they'd ever get from Brian, all recorded on her phone.

Maura screamed with joy. "We *got* him! We got that motherfucker!" She had hugged Georgie when she brought her in to hear the recording. "Well, not yet; let's think about this. We need to use this the right way. This isn't exactly kosher . . ."

Lindsey listened to the recording several times with Maura and Georgie. Maura scolded Georgie for meeting Brian in the first place but ultimately thanked her for getting such a helpful piece of evidence. As Lindsey listened, she watched Georgie's face. She knew, without asking, that even though Georgie had gotten a good result from going to see Brian, perhaps the recording had only been part of her plan. She knew that there was still that fourteen-year-old girl inside Georgie who was in love with Brian, and this was how she was finally letting go. It was Georgie's way of moving on and of saying that she was sorry.

Maura used the recording in the perfect way. When Brian took the stand, he didn't deny having sex with Lindsey that night, but he said that it was consensual. "We shared a nice evening together" was what he had said when he went on the stand, wearing a navy suit and a light-pink tie. "We made love. I never would have hurt Lindsey, or any woman, like that. Ever." Lindsey's face coiled up in anger and repulsion whenever he spoke. She wanted to scream out at him: *Liar!* She wanted to run up to him and squeeze his neck with her hands until his veins popped out of his skin and he begged with his eyes for air. She wanted to ruin his life just as he had ruined hers. But she sat and listened, holding her hands tight in her lap, waiting for his turn to be over, hoping that no one would believe him.

"So when you told Georgie Decker, just a few days ago, that Lindsey 'said no,' you meant that it was consensual?" The case was pretty much over after that. There was no denying what Brian had admitted to Georgie.

And still, the trial went on for a seemingly unimaginable amount of time. The press got involved until the very end, splashing weekly updates across the *Boston Globe*, the *New York Times*, even the *New York Post*: **Son of Boston Philanthropists Accused of Rape; Martha's Vineyard Nanny Accuses Summer Resident of Sexual Assault; Fitzgerald Case a Classic He Said / She Said.** Lindsey tried not to read the stories at first, but eventually she had to. It was surreal, seeing her name in a newspaper article, reading descriptions of the alleged incident, hearing quotes from people who wanted to get involved, give their opinion, argue against her.

As the trial was coming to an end, everyone around Lindsey told her that even if she didn't win, she was still a hero. "Whatever happens," they told her, "you're an inspiration." Lindsey hated hearing this. She didn't think it was true. If she didn't win the trial, she didn't know what she would do with the rest of her life. The thought of appealing the case, if they lost, seemed insurmountable and unfathomable. She and her parents were out of money and, more important, out of emotional steam. This was it. Lindsey knew now that so many women never got any glimmer of justice after surviving a sexual assault. And she wanted that justice. Not just for herself but for those other women who she knew could never get it.

Lindsey couldn't sleep the night before the jury delivered their final verdict. She tossed and turned for hours, finally getting up and going to her closet. She pulled down an old shoebox from the top shelf and brought it to her bed. It was filled with old photos from college, high school, and earlier years. She looked at herself in the photos, holding each one close to her face. She was smiling in most of them. She saw a girl who didn't know things, a girl who had no clue of what was to come, a girl who wanted things for herself in life, a girl who thought that people were good and kind, a girl who was happy. Lindsey wanted to believe that that girl hadn't been blotted out, that she was still there somehow, somewhere.

The next morning, a woman on the jury stood to deliver the verdict. Everything seemed to slow down. Lindsey could hear her own breathing, in and out, slow and steady, and she let herself fall into a daze so that whatever happened next, she wouldn't feel it.

She looked around as the woman spoke. She looked at her parents, who were holding hands and staring at the jury with eager eyes. Lindsey was grateful to them.

She saw Georgie, whose head was raised, staring at her through teary eyes. They held their gazes on one another for a moment. Neither one of them smiled, but there was something in their faces that conveyed a sense of comfort, of remorse, but also of hope. She wondered, just for a moment, what both their lives might have been like had she never gone down to the lighthouse that night. She wondered if the younger versions of themselves, at just twenty-two and fourteen, would be proud of who they'd become today. And then the corners of Lindsey's mouth did turn up, just slightly, as she looked at Georgie and decided that yes, they would be proud.

She turned her gaze away from Georgie and toward the jury, but something in the back of the room caught her eye. She thought she saw someone else standing there, behind the rows of seats. It was the girl in the photos. The girl with a suntan and long hair, wearing a white dress with flowers on it. She was alive; she was vibrant; she was full of breath and muscle and tears and laughter. Lindsey wanted to reach out to her, to tell her never to let go of herself.

"Guilty," Lindsey heard. The girl disappeared. Lindsey turned and looked at the jury. "Guilty," she heard again. She saw everyone around her exhale and hug. *Guilty.* Lindsey had done it. She wasn't wrong. She wasn't crazy. She had won. It had taken her years to get here, but she had done it. She stood still for a few moments, frozen, in disbelief. Somehow, she had made it here. Somehow, she had survived. And now, finally, she could move on.

When she stepped outside the courthouse, the world was the same as it had been before, except now Lindsey felt things come into focus that hadn't been there before. She saw people and colors and puddles and windows and lights and clouds. She felt the sun on her skin. She heard the buzz of the city, the opening and closing of doors, the rush of air among bodies on their way to meetings, to restaurants, to whatever it was they were doing to live. And now she was right there with them. There was so much life around her, and she was part of it. It was all still there. *She* was still there. She closed her eyes and listened closer. She waited to hear the familiar rush of ocean waves, the terrible crashing of water and wind and shore, but this time, instead, she heard her own words from years ago echo back into her mind: *She's stronger than you think.*

Acknowledgments

Thank you to my parents, Vivian and Lionel; and my sisters, Becca and Laura, for your unwavering support. Thank you to my superhuman agents, Cait Hoyt, Michelle Weiner, and Ali Trustman, for being by my side throughout this entire process and without whom none of this would be possible. Thank you to my brilliant editor, Alicia Clancy, for having faith in me and for seeing the potential of this story—and for making it infinitely better. Thank you to the entire Lake Union team for your support and relentless hard work, including Stacy Abrams, Laura Barrett, Rosanna Brockley, Kathleen Carter, Dennelle Catlett, Gabe Dumpit, Spencer Fuller, Jill Kramer, Danielle Marshall, Philip Pascuzzo, Nicole Pomeroy, Emma Reh, and Christina Troup. Thank you to the friends who read my book during its most clunky stages and gave me thoughtful notes or simple words of encouragement, both of which I needed: Caroline Vik, Sarah Wick, Isabelle Esposito, Molly Valle, Miriam Ritchie, Kim Januszewski, Kiran Pendri, and Charlie Melvoin. Thank you to everyone at Rosewater Market & Takeaway and at the Edgartown Public Library for providing me and the island community with two beautiful places to write all year long. Thank you to Casey Elliston for being there for me. Thank you to Ben Bruker for giving me the confidence I needed to accomplish this. Thank you to Emily Graff for holding my hand through so much of this journey. Thank you to many of my former colleagues, particularly Greg Silverman, Courtenay

Valenti, Jesse Ehrman, Susan Wenzel, and (especially) Patrick Cadigan. Thank you to Laurie Frankel for your compassion. Thank you to my friends who really encouraged me to take the leap, including Jonathan Blankfein, Sofia Warner, Fahad Missmar, Bree Taylor, Kate Harris, Chris Baker, Chris Bruno, and Wendy Shattuck. Thank you to all of my amazing island friends, especially my girl gang, for supporting me. Thank you to everyone at Evolve, and an impossibly huge thank-you to all my riders. Thank you to Tim Carey, Bill Bussey, and Dick Baker at Nobles for not only teaching me how to write but also for letting me believe that I could.

Book Club Questions

1. How are Georgie and Lindsey similar? How are they different?
2. Which character do you relate to most? Why?
3. Why do you think Georgie has such a hard time speaking up about what she saw that night at the lighthouse?
4. What role does ambition play in Lindsey's story?
5. In what ways do Georgie and Lindsey try to protect themselves in the present-day scenes?
6. How would you describe the environment in which the story is set, and what role does that environment play in the decisions that both Georgie and Lindsey make?
7. Carol reveals something toward the end of the book that shows a side of her to Georgie that she had previously hidden. How do you think that reveal has impacted the kind of mother she has been to Georgie?
8. Would you describe the story as plot driven or character based, and why?
9. What are the most prominent themes of the book that spoke to you?
10. How did the oscillation between the two main characters affect your read?

About the Author

Photo © 2019 Chandler Cook

Julia Spiro was born and raised in Boston, Massachusetts. After graduating from Harvard College, she lived in Los Angeles and worked in the film industry for nearly a decade. She now lives year-round on Martha's Vineyard. *Someone Else's Secret* is her first novel.